NOWHERE TO HIDE

A MEG SAWYER MYSTERY

BOOK ONE

NOWHERE TO HIDE

A MEG SAWYER MYSTERY
BOOK ONE

ANGELA DODSON

CONTENTS

CHAPTER ONE

LOST AND FOUND

The rain pattered against the windows of the beach house, a steady rhythm that might have been soothing under different circumstances. Meg Sawyer sat cross-legged on the oversized couch, a half-empty glass of cabernet balanced on the armrest beside her. The lamp cast a warm glow over the living room, but failed to dispel the shadows that seemed to have taken up permanent residence in the corners of her mind.

She adjusted the fleece blanket around her shoulders and shifted her laptop to a more comfortable position. This was day three of what her friend Claire had enthusiastically dubbed "Meg's Coastal Healing Retreat." So far, the healing part remained elusive.

"Some retreat," Meg muttered to herself, taking another sip of wine. "Just me, this enormous house, and absolutely nowhere to hide from my thoughts."

Outside, the wind picked up, driving the rain harder against the glass. The sound transported her back to that night six months ago, when she'd sat in her car outside their—no, *his*—house, rain hammering the roof while she worked up the courage to retrieve the last of her belongings. Daniel hadn't even been home. He was probably with *her*.

Meg shook her head, as if the physical movement could dislodge the unwelcome memory. At thirty-six, she hadn't expected to be starting over, certainly not after twelve years of marriage. But here she was, house-sitting for her best friend in Seacliff, three hours from her apartment in the city and her job as an insurance claims investigator, trying to remember who she was before she became Mrs. Daniel Harrington.

The divorce had left her questioning everything—her judgment most of all. How had she missed the signs? How had she failed to see that Daniel had been leading a double life for the past two years?

"Focus on something else," she whispered, the mantra her therapist had suggested whenever the spiral began. She took a deep breath and clicked open her laptop's browser.

Her photography website stared back at her, unchanged from six months ago. Before everything fell apart, photography had been more than a hobby—it had been her escape, her way of seeing beauty in the world. The last photo she'd posted was of Daniel at his law firm's Christmas party, smiling at the camera with what she now recognized as guilt in his eyes.

Meg closed the browser tab with more force than necessary and opened Google Maps instead. If she was going to reignite her passion for photography, she needed new landscapes, new perspectives. Seacliff and its surroundings seemed as good a place as any to start.

She zoomed in on the coastal town, familiarizing herself with its layout. Claire had left a handwritten guide to local points of interest, but Meg found herself drawn to the less traveled areas beyond the tourist spots. She followed the coastline north, where the map showed dense forests and more rugged terrain.

"That might be worth exploring," she murmured, noting a hiking trail that wound along dramatic cliffs. She continued her virtual exploration, zooming in and out, occasionally dropping the little yellow streetview figure to get a better look.

An hour later, her wine glass empty and the rain still falling, Meg had mapped out a tentative itinerary for the next few days. She was about to close her laptop when something caught her eye—a remote area about two hours north of Seacliff, where the forest gave way to a series of small clearings.

Curiosity piqued, she zoomed in further. The satellite image showed what appeared to be a cabin nestled in one of the clearings, accessible only by a narrow dirt road. Something about the isolation of the place resonated with her. Perhaps she could capture that sense of solitude in her photography.

She zoomed in even further, and that's when she saw it—large, crude letters on the roof of the cabin that seemed to spell out "HELP ME."

Meg blinked, certain she was mistaken. She adjusted her screen brightness and leaned closer. The letters were unmistakable, though they appeared to have been made hastily, perhaps with paint or some other material visible from above.

"What the hell?" she whispered, her pulse quickening.

She refreshed the page, expecting the image to remain the same. Instead, when the map reloaded, the roof of the cabin appeared normal—no message, no distress signal, nothing out of the ordinary.

Meg frowned and refreshed again. Still nothing. She tried to revert to the previous image but couldn't seem to navigate back to it.

"That's... weird," she said to the empty room, a chill running down her spine despite the warmth of the blanket. She stared at the screen for a few more moments, then slowly closed the laptop.

"You're overtired and you've had too much wine," she told herself firmly. "And you listen to way too many true crime podcasts."

She gathered her empty glass and headed to the kitchen, trying to dismiss the image from her mind. Claire's beach house was beautiful but isolated, and Meg's imagination had always been overactive. It was probably a glitch in the satellite imagery, or perhaps just a strange configuration of shadows on the roof.

By the time she'd rinsed her glass and brushed her teeth, she'd almost convinced herself she'd imagined the whole thing. She climbed into the guest bed, listening to the storm that had intensified outside. The rain lashed against the windows, and somewhere in the distance, thunder rumbled.

"Goodnight, crazy brain," she murmured, switching off the bedside lamp and settling into the unfamiliar bed.

Sleep came eventually, but it was fitful and filled with fragmented dreams. She was running through a forest, searching for something, the distant sound of someone calling for help driving her forward. But no matter how fast she ran, the voice remained out of reach.

She woke with a start at 3:07 AM, the glowing digits of the bedside clock casting an eerie blue light across the room. The storm had passed, leaving behind an unnatural stillness. Meg lay motionless, her heart pounding, the dream—and the image from Google Maps—still vivid in her mind.

"Help me," she whispered into the darkness, hearing the echo of the unseen voice from her dream.

She sat up, suddenly wide awake. The rational part of her brain insisted that what she'd seen was nothing—a glitch, a misinterpretation, a product of too much wine and an overactive imagination. But another part, the part that had made her an excellent claims investigator, nagged at her.

What if it wasn't a glitch? What if someone had actually written those words as a desperate plea for help?

Meg switched on the lamp and reached for her laptop, which she'd left on the nightstand. She reopened Google Maps and navigated back to the remote cabin. The roof appeared normal, just as it had after she'd refreshed the page earlier.

But Google Maps had a feature she hadn't thought to use before—historical imagery. She could look at satellite images from different points in time. With newfound determination, she clicked through the options until she found it—a timestamp from just three weeks ago.

And there it was again: "HELP ME" in large, unmistakable letters on the cabin roof.

Meg's breath caught in her throat. This wasn't a glitch or her imagination. Someone had written those words, someone who needed help, and then—judging by the more recent imagery—the message had been removed.

"Holy shit," she breathed, staring at the screen.

She took a screenshot, capturing the image with the timestamp clearly visible, then continued to explore the historical imagery. The message first appeared about a month ago and was gone in the most recent update.

Meg's mind raced through the possibilities. Maybe it was a prank, kids messing around in an abandoned cabin. Or perhaps it was something innocent—a film project, an art installation. But she couldn't shake the feeling that it was exactly what it appeared to be: a genuine cry for help.

She should call the police, she decided. It was the responsible thing to do. But what would she say? That she was browsing Google Maps in the middle of the night and found a distress signal that was no longer there? They'd think she was crazy or, worse, wasting police resources.

She needed more information before making that call.

Meg opened a new browser tab and searched for information about the area. It fell just outside the jurisdiction of Seacliff, in a county called Pine Ridge. She found the website for the Pine Ridge Sheriff's Department and clicked through to their recent news releases, scanning for any mentions of missing persons or investigations involving remote cabins.

Nothing stood out.

She returned to Google Maps and studied the cabin more closely, noting its location relative to nearby landmarks. The dirt road leading to it connected to a larger forest service road, which eventually joined Highway 18 about fifteen miles inland from the coast.

Meg chewed her bottom lip, a habit from childhood that resurfaced whenever she was deep in thought. She could drive out there herself, just to take a look. It wasn't that far, maybe two hours each way. She could bring her camera, make it seem like she was just out photographing the scenery if anyone asked.

"This is insane," she said aloud, even as she found herself plotting the route. "Completely insane."

But the image of those desperate letters wouldn't leave her mind. If someone had needed help badly enough to write it on their roof, hoping to be seen from above, what had happened to them? And why was the message gone now?

Meg glanced at the clock: 3:42 AM. Too early to set out, but too late to go back to sleep. She climbed out of bed and headed to the kitchen to make coffee. As the rich aroma filled the beach house, she leaned against the counter, looking out at the dark ocean beyond the large windows.

The rain had stopped, and the clouds had cleared enough to reveal a sprinkling of stars and a waning moon that cast a silver path across the water. In a few hours, the sun would rise, and she would set out on what was probably a wild goose chase.

But she couldn't ignore it. That wasn't who she was.

By 6:30 AM, Meg had showered, dressed in jeans, a flannel shirt, and hiking boots, and packed a small backpack with essentials—her camera, water, energy bars, a first aid kit, and a power bank for her phone. She left a note for Claire, who had mentioned she might stop by later that day:

Gone exploring with my camera. Back this evening. Don't worry! –Meg

She felt a twinge of guilt about the deception by omission, but telling Claire the truth would only result in her friend trying to talk her out of it—or worse, insisting on coming along. Claire was many wonderful things, but subtle wasn't one of them.

Meg loaded her equipment into her Subaru Outback and pulled up the directions on her phone. The GPS estimated the drive would take just under two hours. She took a deep breath, gripped the steering wheel, and backed out of the driveway.

The early morning light painted the coastal landscape in soft pastels as she drove north on Highway 1. The road wound along the cliffs, offering breathtaking views of the Pacific Ocean on her left. Under different circumstances, she would have stopped multiple times to capture the scenery with her camera.

But today, her mind was fixated on a different destination.

After about an hour, she turned inland on Highway 18, leaving the coast behind. The landscape changed gradually, the seaside vegetation giving way to denser forests of pine and redwood. Traffic thinned the further she drove from the coast, until she was often the only car on the road for miles at a stretch.

The GPS directed her to turn onto Forest Service Road 42, a well-maintained gravel road that cut through the heart of the Pine Ridge National Forest. Sunlight filtered through the canopy of trees, creating a dappled pattern on the road ahead.

"What exactly are you hoping to find out here, Meg?" she asked herself, voicing the question that had been lurking in the back of her mind since she set out. She had no answer, only the persistent feeling that she needed to see for herself.

Twenty minutes later, she reached the turnoff indicated on her map—a narrow dirt track that branched off from the main forest service road. A weathered sign marked it as "Deer Creek Trail." There was no gate or barrier, just a rutted path disappearing into the trees.

Meg hesitated, eyeing the rough track dubiously. Her Subaru could handle moderate off-roading, but she wasn't sure about this. She pulled over to the side of the forest service road and checked Google Maps again.

According to the satellite imagery, the cabin was about three miles down this track. She could drive it slowly, or she could park here and hike in. The latter seemed safer—less chance of getting her car stuck, and quieter if she wanted to approach undetected.

Undetected. The word made her pause. What exactly was she planning to do? Stake out a remote cabin based on a message that might have been removed weeks ago?

"This is how horror movies start," she muttered, but she was already pulling her backpack from the passenger seat and checking that her phone was fully charged.

She locked the car, pocketed the keys, and set off down the dirt track. The morning was warming up, but the dense forest provided ample shade. Birds called from the trees, and occasionally something small rustled in the underbrush beside the path.

Meg maintained a steady pace, stopping occasionally to check her position on the map and to listen. The forest was alive with natural sounds, but there was no evidence of human presence—no distant voices, no machinery, no signs of recent passage along the trail.

After about forty-five minutes of hiking, the trees began to thin, and she could see patches of open sky ahead. According to her map, she was approaching the clearing where the cabin should be located.

Meg slowed her pace, moving more cautiously now. She left the main track and circled through the trees, wanting to get a view of the cabin before potentially announcing her presence.

The forest opened up to reveal a small meadow, maybe two acres in size, ringed by tall pines. In the center stood the cabin she'd seen on the satellite imagery—a substantial structure built of dark wood with a sloped metal roof. A small porch wrapped around the front, and a stone chimney rose from one end. A weathered pickup truck was parked beside the building.

Meg crouched behind a fallen log at the edge of the clearing, observing. The place looked well-maintained, not abandoned as she'd half-expected. Smoke curled from the chimney, suggesting occupancy.

She raised her camera and zoomed in, capturing several images of the cabin and its surroundings. From her position, she couldn't see the roof clearly, but the rest of the property appeared normal, if isolated.

There was a small garden plot to one side of the cabin, with what looked like vegetables growing in neat rows. A stack of firewood was piled against the side of the structure, and various tools hung on the exterior wall.

It looked, for all intents and purposes, like a typical remote cabin—the kind of place someone might build to get away from it all. Nothing sinister, nothing to suggest distress or danger.

Yet someone had written "HELP ME" on that roof.

As Meg considered her next move, the front door of the cabin swung open. She quickly lowered her camera and shrank back behind the log.

A man stepped onto the porch—tall, broad-shouldered, with a beard that reached the middle of his chest. He wore faded jeans and a flannel shirt with the sleeves rolled up, revealing forearms corded with muscle. He appeared to be in his early forties, with dark hair streaked with gray at the temples.

He stood motionless for a moment, seeming to survey the clearing, then descended the steps and walked toward the garden. He carried a watering can in one hand and what looked like gardening tools in the other.

Meg raised her camera again, focusing on his face. There was nothing particularly threatening about his appearance, but something in his demeanor—a tension, a wariness—made her uneasy.

He worked methodically in the garden for about fifteen minutes, tending to the plants with practiced efficiency. Occasionally, he would straighten and scan the tree line, as if sensing he was being watched.

Meg kept perfectly still during these moments, hardly daring to breathe.

When he finished in the garden, he returned to the cabin, disappearing inside. Meg waited, expecting him to emerge again, but minutes passed with no sign of movement.

She checked the time: nearly 10:30 AM. She'd been observing for almost an hour, and while the situation seemed odd—who chose to live this far from civilization?—she hadn't seen anything that explained the desperate message she'd found.

Maybe she needed to get closer, perhaps circle around to see the roof properly. Or maybe she should just leave, report what she'd found to the local sheriff, and let them handle it.

Before she could decide, a sound from behind made her freeze—the unmistakable crack of a twig under foot.

"Don't move," came a woman's voice, low and steady. "And don't turn around."

Meg's heart hammered against her ribs. She hadn't heard anyone approach.

"I'm not armed," Meg said quickly, raising her hands slightly. "I'm just—"

"Trespassing," the woman finished for her. "And spying. Neither of which explains why you're here."

"I'm a photographer," Meg said, gesturing slightly with her camera. "I was just looking for interesting landscapes."

"Three miles down a private road, hiding behind a log, photographing someone's home?" The disbelief in the woman's voice was palpable. "Try again."

Meg swallowed hard. "Look, I know how this seems, but—"

"Stand up. Slowly. Keep your hands where I can see them."

Meg complied, rising carefully to her feet, still facing away from the voice.

"Now turn around. Equally slowly."

Meg turned to find herself facing a woman roughly her own age, with short-cropped blonde hair and sharp green eyes that seemed to catalog everything about Meg in a single glance. She wore hiking boots, cargo pants, and a olive-green jacket. In her right hand, held casually but confidently, was a hunting knife.

"Who are you?" the woman demanded. "And don't bother with the photographer story again."

Meg took a deep breath. The truth seemed like her only option, however bizarre it might sound.

"My name is Meg Sawyer. I'm staying in Seacliff, house-sitting for a friend. Last night, I was browsing Google Maps, looking for places to photograph, and I saw something strange on the satellite imagery of this cabin."

The woman's expression didn't change, but something flickered in her eyes. "What did you see?"

"Words," Meg said. "On the roof. 'Help me.' When I refreshed the page, they were gone. But when I checked the historical imagery, I could see that they'd been there, recently, and then removed."

The woman studied her for a long moment, her face carefully blank. "And you decided to drive out here and investigate yourself instead of calling the authorities because...?"

"Because it sounded crazy," Meg admitted. "And because... I don't know. I'm an insurance investigator. I guess I wanted to see for myself before involving anyone else."

The woman's posture shifted subtly, some of the tension leaving her shoulders. She lowered the knife, though she didn't put it away.

"An insurance investigator," she repeated, as if testing the words. "With a hobby in photography and, apparently, amateur detective work."

"Something like that," Meg said, allowing herself to relax marginally. "Look, I know I shouldn't be here. I'll leave, forget I ever saw anything."

The woman shook her head slowly. "It's too late for that, Ms. Sawyer. You've stepped into something... complicated."

A chill ran down Meg's spine. "What do you mean?"

Instead of answering, the woman glanced toward the cabin. "He'll be coming out again soon. He keeps to a schedule." She looked back at Meg, decision forming in her eyes. "We need to move. Now."

"We?" Meg echoed, confused.

"Unless you'd prefer to explain to him why you're spying on his property," the woman said with a hint of dark humor. "In which case, I wish you luck."

She gestured with the knife toward the trees, away from the direction of the main trail. "This way. Quickly and quietly."

Meg hesitated only briefly before following. Whatever was happening here, this woman seemed to know more about it than she did, and Meg's instincts—the same ones that had led her here in the first place— told her to trust her. For now.

They moved swiftly through the forest, the woman leading with the confidence of someone intimately familiar with the terrain. Meg followed as best she could, grateful for her hiking boots as they navigated over fallen logs and through dense underbrush.

After about twenty minutes of steady progress, they emerged onto another, narrower trail that Meg hadn't noticed on her map.

"Where are we going?" Meg asked, keeping her voice low.

"Somewhere we can talk," the woman replied without slowing her pace. "Somewhere safe."

They walked for another ten minutes before the trail widened slightly and curved around a massive boulder. On the other side was a small clearing, in the center of which stood what appeared to be an old hunting blind—a small, elevated structure typically used by hunters to conceal themselves while waiting for game.

The woman approached a ladder leaning against the side and gestured for Meg to climb.

"After you."

Meg eyed the rickety-looking structure doubtfully. "Is it safe?"

The woman's mouth quirked in what might have been amusement. "Safer than where we just left."

Meg couldn't argue with that logic. She slung her camera over her shoulder and climbed the ladder, pushing open the trap door at the top to reveal a small, sparse interior—maybe eight feet square, with narrow windows on all four sides. A camping cot occupied one wall, a small propane stove another. Various supplies were neatly organized in plastic bins.

The woman followed her up, closing the trap door behind them.

"Welcome to my temporary residence," she said dryly. "It's not the Ritz, but it serves its purpose."

Meg looked around, trying to make sense of what she was seeing. "You live here? While watching that man at the cabin?"

"Not exactly," the woman said. She moved to one of the windows and peered out, then turned back to Meg. "I haven't properly introduced myself. My name is Alex. Alex Reeves."

"Nice to meet you, Alex," Meg said automatically, the social nicety feeling absurd under the circumstances. "Are you going to tell me what's going on?"

Alex studied her for a moment, as if deciding how much to share. Finally, she nodded and gestured to the cot. "Have a seat. It's a long story."

Meg sat, and Alex took a position by the window, maintaining a clear view of the approach to the hunting blind.

"Three months ago," Alex began, her voice carefully measured, "my sister disappeared. Her name is—was—Emily. We were close, talked almost every day. Then, suddenly, nothing. No calls, no texts, no social media activity. She missed our weekly Sunday dinner. When I went to her apartment, her neighbor said she'd left with a man a few days earlier, said she was going on a spontaneous vacation."

"But you didn't believe that," Meg guessed.

"Emily wasn't the spontaneous type. And she would have told me. She was also..." Alex hesitated. "She was in recovery. Two years sober after a battle with prescription painkillers that nearly killed her. She wouldn't have just taken off."

"Did you go to the police?" Meg asked.

Alex laughed, a sharp, humorless sound. "Of course. They took a report, but made it clear that a thirty-four-year-old woman choosing to go away with a man wasn't high on their priority list. 'People have a right to disappear if they want to,' they said."

"But you kept looking," Meg said. It wasn't a question.

"I hired a private investigator," Alex confirmed. "He managed to track her phone activity to this general area before it went dark completely. And he found security footage of her at a gas station about thirty miles from here, with a man matching the description her neighbor gave."

"The man at the cabin," Meg said, the pieces starting to fall into place.

Alex nodded. "His name is Nathan Blackwood. On paper, he's a freelance graphic designer who works remotely and keeps to himself. No criminal record, no red flags. But my investigator discovered that three other women have gone missing after being seen with him over the past five years. Different cities, different backgrounds, but the same pattern."

Meg felt a chill creep up her spine. "And no bodies have been found?"

"None," Alex confirmed grimly. "The PI reported his findings to the police departments handling each disappearance, but without physical evidence, they couldn't get a warrant to search Blackwood's property."

"So you took matters into your own hands," Meg concluded.

"I've been watching the cabin for three weeks," Alex said. "Looking for any sign of Emily, any evidence I could take to the police. Two weeks ago, I managed to get close enough to see the roof. That's when I saw the message."

"'Help me,'" Meg whispered.

"Written in what looked like red paint," Alex confirmed. "I took photos, went straight to the sheriff in Pine Ridge. But by the time they sent a deputy out to check—claiming they needed to follow procedure—the message was gone, the roof had been repainted, and Blackwood acted like he had no idea what they were talking about."

"They didn't search the property?"

"They did a cursory walkthrough of the main rooms," Alex said bitterly. "Blackwood was cooperative, invited them in for coffee. Said he lived alone, enjoyed his privacy. The deputy reported nothing suspicious, suggested I was mistaken or that it was a prank by local teens."

"But you know what you saw," Meg said.

"Just like you did," Alex pointed out. "Except you have proof. Your screenshot with the timestamp."

Meg nodded slowly, comprehension dawning. "Evidence they can't dismiss. But it's still not enough for a warrant, is it?"

"Probably not," Alex admitted. "But it's something. It corroborates what I reported, proves I wasn't imagining things."

"So, what's your plan?" Meg asked.

Alex's expression hardened. "I'm going into that cabin. Tonight, when he leaves for his weekly supply run to town. He always goes on Thursdays, stays gone for about three hours."

"You can't just break in," Meg protested. "That's illegal, and dangerous. If he comes back early--"

"I don't have a choice," Alex cut her off. "My sister has been missing for three months. If she's still alive, still being held somewhere on that property, everyday matters. And if she's not..." She swallowed hard. "Then I need to know that too."

The raw pain in Alex's voice silenced Meg's objections. If it were her sister, or Claire, or anyone she loved, wouldn't she do the same?

"What if I go with you?" Meg heard herself say.

Alex looked surprised. "Why would you do that? You don't know me or Emily. You could just take your evidence to the sheriff and wash your hands of this whole situation."

"Because I saw that message too," Meg said simply. "And because two pairs of eyes are better than one. I'm also pretty good at finding things people try to hide—it's part of my job."

Alex studied her for a long moment, then nodded. "Alright. But we do this my way. I've been watching his routine for weeks, I know the property. And if I tell you to run, you run. No questions, no hesitation."

"Agreed," Meg said, though part of her was already wondering at the wisdom of what she'd just committed to. Breaking and entering, potential confrontation with a man who might be a serial abductor or worse—this wasn't exactly what she'd had in mind when she set out that morning.

Yet a deeper part of her recognized that this moment of decision had been set in motion the instant she'd spotted those desperate words on a satellite image. Perhaps even earlier, when her life had fallen apart and left her adrift, searching for something—purpose, meaning, a way to make sense of a world that had betrayed her expectations.

"We have about eight hours before he leaves for town," Alex said, all business now. "Get some rest if you can. Tonight's going to be... challenging."

Meg nodded, suddenly aware of how exhausted she was after her sleepless night and morning hike. "Wake me when it's time."

As she stretched out on the narrow cot, the reality of what she'd agreed to began to sink in. She was about to become involved in something dangerous, possibly illegal, with a woman she'd just met, based on a message she'd seen on Google Maps.

If Daniel could see her now, he'd think she'd lost her mind.

Maybe she had. Or maybe, for the first time in months, she was thinking more clearly than ever.

Either way, there was no turning back now. When darkness fell, they would enter Nathan Blackwood's cabin, searching for evidence of Emily Reeves and the other missing women. Whatever they found—or didn't find—would change everything.

As sleep claimed her, Meg's last conscious thought was that she had nowhere to hide anymore. Not from her failed marriage, not from her uncertain future, and certainly not from whatever awaited her in that cabin tonight.

And strangely, the thought didn't frighten her as much as it should have.

CHAPTER TWO

SECOND GUESSING

Meg woke with a start, disoriented by the unfamiliar surroundings. The hunting blind's wooden walls seemed to close in around her, and for a moment, she couldn't remember how she'd gotten there. Then it all came rushing back—the message on the satellite image, the cabin in the clearing, the woman with the hunting knife.

Alex. Emily. Blackwood.

She sat up on the narrow cot, wincing at the stiffness in her neck. Sunlight filtered through the small windows, casting a honeyed glow over the spartan interior. Alex sat by the north-facing window, a pair of binoculars raised to her eyes, her posture alert but relaxed—the vigilance of someone accustomed to long waits.

"What time is it?" Meg asked, her voice rough with sleep.

Alex lowered the binoculars and glanced at her watch. "Just after two. You needed the rest."

Meg stretched, trying to work out the kinks in her back. "You should have woken me sooner. We have planning to do."

A hint of a smile touched Alex's lips. "I've had three weeks to plan this, Ms. Sawyer. I'm fairly confident in my approach."

"Meg," she corrected automatically. "And I'm sure your plan is solid, but now there are two of us, which changes things. Plus, I'm guessing you weren't planning on acquiring a partner today."

Alex considered this, then nodded. "Fair point." She moved away from the window and settled on a plastic storage container opposite the cot. "Let's talk strategy, then."

The afternoon sun warmed the small space as they discussed their plan for entering Blackwood's cabin. Alex had mapped out his routine with meticulous precision—the product of weeks of patient observation.

"Thursday nights are predictable," she explained, unfolding a hand-drawn map of the property on the floor between them. "He leaves at 8:15, drives into Pine Ridge for supplies. He follows the same route—" She traced a line with her finger. "—and returns approximately three hours later."

"He never deviates?" Meg asked.

"Not in the three Thursdays I've observed. He's... methodical." There was something in the way Alex said the word that sent a chill down Meg's spine.

"Tell me about your sister," Meg said suddenly.

Alex looked up, surprise flickering across her face. "Why?"

"Because if we're going to break into a potentially dangerous man's cabin looking for her, I should know who we're looking for. And because—" Meg hesitated. "Because I want to understand why you're risking so much for her."

Alex was quiet for a long moment, her green eyes searching Meg's face as if looking for the true intention behind the question. Whatever she saw there seemed to satisfy her, because she nodded and reached for her backpack.

From an inner pocket, she withdrew a phone and thumbed through its gallery before passing it to Meg. The screen displayed a photo of two women, arms around each other's shoulders, standing on what looked like a hiking trail with a waterfall visible in the background. Meg recognized Alex immediately, her blonde hair longer in the photo but her stance the same—confident, protective. Beside her stood a woman with the same striking green eyes but with long chestnut hair and a smile that didn't quite reach those eyes—cautious, as if happiness were a fragile thing she was afraid to fully embrace.

"That's Emily," Alex said softly. "My little sister. That was taken about a year ago, on her birthday. I took her hiking in Olympic National Park. It was her first birthday since getting sober."

Meg studied the photo, noting the family resemblance—the same high cheekbones, the same determined set to their jaws. But where Alex's face showed strength and resilience, Emily's reflected a harder journey, the kind that left invisible scars.

"She's beautiful," Meg said truthfully. She swiped to the next photo—the sisters at what appeared to be a holiday gathering, Emily looking more relaxed, her smile more genuine.

"She is," Alex agreed. "She's also brilliant. Has a master's in environmental science. Was working on a project to restore wetlands along the coast before..." She trailed off, swallowing hard.

"How did the addiction start?" Meg asked gently, handing the phone back.

Alex tucked the phone away, her movements careful, deliberate. "Car accident, four years ago. Drunk driver hit her head-on. She survived, but with a shattered pelvis and two broken legs. The pain was... significant."

"Prescribed opioids," Meg guessed.

Alex nodded grimly. "For months. By the time her doctors tried to taper her off, she was dependent. When they finally cut her prescription, she turned to less reputable sources." She ran a hand through her short hair, a gesture of frustration that seemed habitual. "I didn't realize how bad it had gotten until I found her unconscious in her apartment. Overdose. If I'd been an hour later..."

She didn't finish the sentence. She didn't need to.

"But she got help," Meg prompted.

"Eventually, yes. After I literally dragged her to rehab." A small, sad smile tugged at Alex's lips. "She hated me for it at first. Refused to speak to me for the first month. But she did the work. Got clean. Stayed that way for two years, until she disappeared."

"And you think this Blackwood somehow targeted her because of her history with addiction?"

"I think he preys on vulnerability," Alex said, her voice hardening. "The PI found a pattern—all four missing women had some form of trauma or struggle in their past. One was recently divorced after an abusive relationship. Another had lost her child to cancer. Emily had her addiction history. The fourth had been in treatment for severe depression."

"Women who might not be missed immediately," Meg observed. "Or whose disappearances might be attributed to their personal struggles."

"Exactly." Alex's eyes flashed with anger. "He chooses his victims carefully."

"How did Emily meet him?"

"Online, as far as I can tell. Her neighbor said she'd mentioned a new friend who 'understood what she'd been through.' Said he had his own history with pain and recovery." Alex's lip curled in disgust. "Classic predator tactic—create a false connection, build trust, then exploit it."

Meg nodded, her mind circling back to her own failed marriage. Hadn't Daniel done something similar? Created a false sense of security, of shared dreams and values, only to betray that trust in the most fundamental way? The scale was different, of course, but the mechanism felt uncomfortably familiar.

"What's our best way in?" she asked, refocusing on the task at hand.

Alex seemed to appreciate the shift back to practicalities. "There's a window at the rear of the cabin, partially obscured by a stand of cedars. It's the bathroom window, frosted glass but not reinforced. I've been carrying this—" She reached into her pack and withdrew a small glass cutter. "—since I first saw the message on the roof."

"Once we're inside, what exactly are we looking for?"

"Anything that connects Blackwood to Emily or the other missing women. Phone numbers, photos, personal belongings. Even better would be some indication of where he might be keeping them. If they're still..." Alex's voice caught, and she cleared her throat. "If they're still alive."

Meg felt a heaviness settle in her chest. They were both avoiding saying the obvious—that after months of captivity, the chances of finding Emily or the others alive were diminishing by the day. But hope was a powerful motivator, and Meg wouldn't be the one to extinguish it.

"We should be methodical," she said instead. "Start in the main living areas, then move to more private spaces—bedroom, office, any locked rooms. I'll document everything with my camera."

Alex nodded. "We'll have about three hours, assuming he stays true to his routine. Should be enough time to search the cabin thoroughly."

While Alex dozed, taking her turn to rest before their night's work, Meg retrieved her laptop from her backpack and opened Google Maps again. She studied the satellite imagery of Blackwood's property more carefully now, knowing what to look for. She zoomed in and out, adjusting the angle, examining the surroundings of the cabin with a more critical eye.

That's when she noticed it—a structure she'd missed before, partially hidden by the tree line behind the main cabin. It was small, perhaps a shed or outbuilding, but its roof was a different material than the cabin's, which was why it hadn't immediately caught her attention. From above, it blended with the surrounding forest, visible only at certain angles and with the right lighting.

Meg's pulse quickened. She checked the historical imagery again, looking at the images from before and after the "HELP ME" message appeared. In the earliest images, the structure was barely perceptible. In the most recent images, after the message had been removed, there appeared to be a faint path leading from the main cabin to the smaller building—a path that hadn't been there before.

"Alex," she said, keeping her voice low but urgent. "Alex, wake up."

Alex was instantly alert, a trait Meg suspected came from military training or similar experience. "What is it?"

Meg turned the laptop toward her. "There's another structure on the property. Here—" She pointed to the screen. "Behind the main cabin, partially concealed by trees. And look—this path connecting it wasn't visible in the earlier imagery."

Alex studied the screen intently, her expression sharpening. "I never saw this. Not from my observation points." She looked up at Meg, a new intensity in her eyes. "If he's holding them somewhere on the property..."

"It could be there," Meg finished for her. "An outbuilding, far enough from the main cabin that no one would hear anything, but close enough to monitor."

A muscle jumped in Alex's jaw as she stared at the image. "We need to check it. Tonight."

"Agreed. But we should still start with the main cabin—look for keys, entry codes, anything that might help us access that building. If it's where he's keeping them, it's bound to be secured somehow."

They spent the remaining hours of daylight refining their plan, checking and rechecking their equipment, and watching the cabin through Alex's binoculars. Blackwood emerged occasionally—to tend his garden, chop wood, perform maintenance tasks—but never ventured toward the area where the satellite imagery showed the second structure.

As dusk settled over the forest, painting the trees in deepening shades of purple and blue, Meg felt a familiar tension building in her chest—the same feeling she experienced before conducting an insurance fraud investigation that might turn confrontational. Part apprehension, part exhilaration, part grim determination.

"It's almost time," Alex said, checking her watch. The digital display read 7:45 PM.

They gathered their essentials—Meg's camera, Alex's glass cutter, flashlights with red filters to minimize visibility from outside, gloves to avoid leaving fingerprints. Meg tucked her phone into an inner pocket, ensuring it was fully charged but silenced.

"One last thing," Alex said, reaching into her pack. She withdrew a hunting knife—not the one she'd threatened Meg with earlier, but a smaller, more practical model—and offered it to her. "Just in case."

Meg hesitated, then accepted the knife, securing it in her belt beneath her jacket. "Just in case," she echoed.

They descended from the hunting blind into the gathering darkness, moving through the forest with practiced quiet. Alex led the way, her knowledge of the terrain guiding them along a circuitous route that kept them well away from the main trail.

They reached the edge of the clearing just as the cabin's exterior lights flickered on—likely on a timer, Meg thought. From their position behind a dense stand of cedars, they had a clear view of the front porch and the pickup truck parked alongside the cabin.

At precisely 8:12 PM, the cabin door opened, and Nathan Blackwood emerged. He wore a dark jacket now, his beard neatly trimmed, looking for all the world like a regular guy heading into town for supplies. He locked the door behind him, tested the handle once, then walked to his truck with the unhurried confidence of a man on a predictable schedule.

The engine rumbled to life, headlights cutting through the darkness as the truck backed up, turned, and headed down the dirt track. Meg and Alex remained motionless until the sound of the engine faded completely and the red taillights disappeared among the trees.

"Now," Alex whispered, rising from their concealment.

They crossed the clearing swiftly, keeping to the shadows as much as possible. When they reached the cabin, they circled around to the rear, where a small window was set at eye level in the wooden wall.

Alex produced the glass cutter and worked quickly, scoring a circle in the frosted glass large enough for a hand to fit through. She then applied a suction cup to the center of the circle and pulled gently. The glass came away with a faint pop, leaving a clean hole.

"Good thing he doesn't believe in alarm systems," Meg murmured as Alex reached through the opening to unlock the window from inside.

"One of the benefits of extreme isolation, I suppose," Alex replied, pushing the window open. "He probably thinks the remote location is security enough."

Meg went through first, being smaller, then helped Alex navigate the narrow opening. They found themselves in a simple bathroom—clean, functional, with a shower stall, toilet, and pedestal sink. The medicine cabinet above the sink was closed, a potential treasure trove of information they would explore shortly.

They moved into the main living area, clicking on their red-filtered flashlights. The cabin's interior was exactly as methodical as Blackwood himself seemed to be—everything in its place, surfaces clean, possessions minimal. A leather couch and armchair formed a sitting area before a stone fireplace. Bookshelves lined one wall, filled with volumes arranged by height. A dining table with four chairs stood near a kitchen area equipped with modern appliances that seemed out of place in the rustic setting.

"Four chairs," Meg whispered, indicating the dining set. "For a man who supposedly lives alone."

Alex nodded grimly. "Let's start searching. Kitchen cabinets, drawers, anywhere that might hold documents or keys."

They worked in tandem, moving through the cabin with careful efficiency. Meg began with the kitchen, noting the contents of the refrigerator—foods that seemed varied for one person's preferences, including items like almond milk and gluten-free bread alongside more traditional staples. The cabinets yielded nothing of interest, nor did the drawers, though Meg noted that one contained an assortment of vitamins and supplements labeled with different initials.

Alex, meanwhile, had moved to a small desk in the corner of the main room, methodically going through its contents. "Bills, property taxes, internet service agreement," she reported quietly. "All in Blackwood's name. Nothing connecting him to Emily or anyone else."

Meg turned her attention to the bookshelves, scanning titles that ranged from wilderness survival guides to technical manuals on carpentry and electrical systems. One section held medical texts—anatomy, pharmacology, first aid. She pulled out a book on emergency medical procedures, leafing through pages marked with Post-it notes.

"He's got quite the interest in medical knowledge for a graphic designer," she observed, replacing the book carefully.

A framed diploma on the wall caught her attention—Nathan Blackwood, Bachelor of Science in Biology, University of Washington, dated fifteen years earlier. Beside it hung a certificate in Wilderness First Response.

"Alex," she called softly. "Did your investigator say what Blackwood did before becoming a 'freelance graphic designer'?"

Alex joined her, examining the framed credentials. "No. Just that he'd been in this area for about five years, and before that, he moved around a lot. Seattle, Portland, Boise. Never staying in one place for more than a year or two."

"He has medical training," Meg said, pointing to the certificates. "And those books—pharmacology, emergency procedures. Advanced stuff."

A shadow crossed Alex's face. "That... might explain some things. If he's keeping women captive..."

She didn't finish the thought, but Meg understood. Medical knowledge would be useful for someone keeping people restrained, sedated, or worse.

They continued their search, moving down a short hallway that led to what appeared to be the cabin's only bedroom. Like the rest of the house, it was meticulously organized—a queen-sized bed with military corners on the bedspread, a dresser with nothing on its surface, a closet with the door closed.

Alex headed for the dresser while Meg opened the closet door. Inside hung men's clothing—flannel shirts, jeans, a few more formal options— all in a single size. The floor of the closet held several pairs of boots and shoes, and on the shelf above the clothing rod sat a few sealed plastic bins labeled "Winter" and "Summer."

Nothing unusual, except...

Meg ran her fingers along the back wall of the closet, feeling a slight difference in the texture of the wood paneling. She pressed gently, and a section of the wall gave way slightly.

"Alex," she whispered urgently. "There's something here."

Alex was at her side instantly. Together, they applied pressure to the panel, which slid aside to reveal a small hidden compartment. Inside sat a metal lockbox.

"Bingo," Alex breathed, carefully removing the box and carrying it to the bed.

It was locked, of course, but the lock was a simple one. Alex produced a set of small tools from her pocket—more evidence of her preparedness—and had it open within minutes.

Inside, carefully arranged, were four driver's licenses, each belonging to a different woman. Emily Reeves's face stared up at them from one of them, her green eyes and cautious smile identical to the photo Alex had shown earlier.

Beside the licenses lay personal items—a silver necklace with a pendant shaped like a mountain range, a pair of sapphire earrings, a delicate gold ring with a small diamond, and a bracelet woven from colorful threads.

Alex picked up the silver necklace with trembling fingers. "I gave this to Emily," she said, her voice barely audible. "For her thirtieth birthday. She never took it off. Never."

Meg placed a steadying hand on Alex's shoulder, feeling the tension beneath her palm. "This is evidence, Alex. Concrete evidence connecting Blackwood to Emily and the others."

"But where are they?" Alex's voice cracked slightly. "These are trophies. He's keeping their personal items as... as souvenirs. But where are the women themselves?"

Before Meg could respond, a sound from outside froze them both—the distant rumble of an engine, growing louder.

"Headlights," Alex hissed, moving to the window. "He's back. Early."

Meg's heart hammered against her ribs. "How? It's barely been an hour."

"I don't know. Maybe he forgot something." Alex was already moving, returning the necklace to the lockbox. "We need to hide. Now."

Meg quickly snapped photos of the driver's licenses and items in the box with her camera, then helped Alex replace the lockbox in its hiding place. They slid the panel closed just as the sound of tires on gravel reached them—Blackwood pulling up to the cabin.

"Under the bed," Alex decided, already dropping to the floor. "Quick."

Meg followed, rolling beneath the bed frame seconds before they heard the front door open. From their hiding place, they could see a slice of the hallway, illuminated now as lights came on throughout the cabin.

Footsteps moved through the main room—heavy, measured steps that spoke of a man who never rushed, never wavered from his path. Meg held her breath as those steps approached the bedroom, passed the door without pausing, and continued down the hall.

A door opened and closed—another room they hadn't yet explored.

"There's more to this cabin than we've seen," Meg whispered, her lips close to Alex's ear. "Another room at the end of the hall."

"Probably leads to the basement," Alex replied just as quietly. "Most of these old cabins have them. Root cellars originally, but they can be expanded."

Meg thought of the satellite image, the second structure behind the cabin. "Or it could be how he accesses the outbuilding we saw. Maybe there's a tunnel, or at least a direct path."

They lay in silence, listening to the muffled sounds of movement from the other room. Minutes ticked by, agonizingly slow.

"We can't stay here," Alex finally whispered. "If he decides to go to bed early…"

"We need to find a way out, or at least a better hiding place until he leaves again," Meg agreed.

The sound of a door opening reached them, followed by footsteps returning to the main room. A new sound joined the footsteps—water running. The shower.

"Now's our chance," Alex said, already sliding from beneath the bed. "He'll be occupied for at least a few minutes."

They crept down the hallway, past the bathroom where the sound of running water provided cover for their movements, and back into the main living area. Meg paused at the door they hadn't yet investigated— the one Blackwood had entered earlier. It was closed now, and locked when she tested the handle.

"We need to come back," she whispered to Alex, who nodded in agreement.

They moved toward the front door, their original entry point now too risky with Blackwood in the bathroom nearby. Alex reached the door first, testing it—still locked, with a deadbolt that required a key from the inside as well as outside.

"Key?" Meg mouthed silently.

Alex shook her head, pointing to the kitchen—the keys must be there, but retrieving them would take precious time they didn't have.

The water shut off abruptly, plunging the cabin into near silence. Both women froze, eyes locked in mutual alarm.

A decision crystallized in Meg's mind. She reached into her pocket and withdrew her phone, quickly opening the notes app and typing a message she showed to Alex:

The evidence. We need to take it. Now.

Alex hesitated only briefly before nodding. They turned back toward the bedroom, moving as silently as possible. Meg's foot caught the edge of a small table, jostling a lamp that teetered precariously. She lunged to catch it, but too late—the lamp crashed to the floor, the sound deafening in the quiet cabin.

"Who's there?" Blackwood's voice called from the bathroom, deep and somehow unsurprised, as if he'd been expecting intruders all along.

"Go," Alex mouthed, pushing Meg toward the bedroom.

They raced down the hall, reaching the bedroom seconds before they heard the bathroom door open. Alex went straight to the closet, sliding open the hidden panel and grabbing the lockbox while Meg positioned herself near the door, the hunting knife now in her hand.

Footsteps approached—unhurried, deliberate, confident. Meg tightened her grip on the knife, her pulse pounding in her ears.

Alex appeared at her side, lockbox tucked under one arm, her other hand holding a heavy metal flashlight—a makeshift weapon. She nodded once to Meg, a silent communication that needed no translation: *Ready?*

Meg nodded back. They would have one chance at this. One moment to slip past Blackwood and reach the front door.

The bedroom door swung open, revealing Nathan Blackwood in the doorway. He wore only a towel wrapped around his waist, his hair wet from the shower, his beard glistening with droplets of water. But it was his eyes that captured Meg's attention—dark, calm, and utterly devoid of surprise or alarm at finding two strangers in his bedroom.

For a suspended moment, they all stood frozen in a tableau of confrontation.

Then Blackwood smiled—a small, knowing curve of his lips that sent ice through Meg's veins.

"You shouldn't have come here," he said, his voice as calm as if he were discussing the weather. "Now I'll have to deal with both of you."

He lunged forward, faster than a man his size should move, reaching for Alex with hands that seemed to know exactly where to grab, where to hurt.

Alex swung the flashlight, connecting with his shoulder but missing his head. The blow hardly slowed him as he caught her arm, twisting it at an angle that made her gasp with pain. The lockbox tumbled from her grasp, spilling its contents across the floor.

Meg reacted instinctively, swinging her camera bag in a wide arc that connected solidly with the side of Blackwood's head. He staggered, momentarily dazed, his grip on Alex loosening just enough for her to wrench free.

"Run!" Alex shouted, scooping up Emily's necklace and as many of the other items as she could grab in one swift movement.

They bolted past Blackwood, who was already recovering, a hand pressed to his temple where blood welled from a cut left by the corner of Meg's camera bag. His eyes, when they met Meg's, held a promise that made her blood run cold.

"I'll find you," he said simply. "I always do."

Meg didn't wait to hear more. She raced after Alex, who had already reached the front door and was fumbling with the locks. Behind them, Blackwood moved with the same unhurried confidence, seeming almost entertained by their panic.

"There's nowhere to hide, you know," he called after them, his voice pleasant, reasonable. "Not out here."

The deadbolt finally gave way under Alex's desperate manipulation, and they burst through the door into the night air. Without hesitation, they sprinted across the clearing toward the forest, the very darkness that had concealed their approach now offering a shield for their escape.

Behind them, the cabin door remained open, light spilling across the porch. Blackwood stood in the doorway, watching their retreat without making any move to pursue them immediately. That, somehow, was more terrifying than if he had given chase—the confidence that he didn't need to rush, that he would find them regardless.

They ran through the forest, branches whipping at their faces, roots threatening to trip them with every step. Unlike their careful, silent approach, their retreat was fueled by pure adrenaline, heedless of the noise they made crashing through the underbrush.

"Not toward the hunting blind," Alex gasped as they reached a fork in the path. "He'll check there first. This way—" She veered right, onto a trail that Meg didn't recognize.

They ran until their lungs burned and their legs trembled, putting as much distance between themselves and the cabin as possible. Finally, when Meg thought she couldn't take another step, Alex slowed, leaning against a massive pine to catch her breath.

"We need to get to your car," she said between gulps of air. "He'll be coming after us as soon as he gets dressed. Probably knows these woods better than I do."

Meg nodded, unable to speak yet. Her camera bag had grown heavier with each step, the strap digging into her shoulder. She lowered it carefully to check that her equipment hadn't been damaged in the chaos.

"Did you get anything?" Alex asked, gesturing to the camera. "Photos of the licenses? The items?"

"Yes," Meg confirmed, relieved to find her camera intact. "Everything in the lockbox, plus the room it was hidden in."

Alex uncurled her fist, revealing Emily's necklace and two of the driver's licenses—Emily's and another woman's. "It's not everything, but it's enough. Proof that he had their personal items, that he's connected to their disappearances."

"We need to get to the police," Meg said, straightening with renewed purpose. "The sheriff in Pine Ridge—"

"Won't do anything," Alex cut her off bitterly. "Not without more evidence. Two women breaking into a man's remote home, stealing his property? He'll claim these were gifts, or that we planted them. We need more."

"The outbuilding," Meg realized. "We never got to check it."

"And we can't now." Alex's expression hardened. "Not tonight. He'll be watching for us. But we have this—" She held up the items clutched in her hand. "And your photos. It's a start."

A distant sound made them both stiffen—the unmistakable roar of an engine starting up.

"He's coming," Alex said grimly. "We need to move. Now."

They set off again, Alex guiding them on a circuitous route that avoided the main trail while still heading in the general direction of where Meg had parked her car. The forest was dark, the canopy blocking even the faint light of stars and a quarter moon, but Alex moved with the confidence of someone who had memorized every turn, every landmark.

After what seemed like hours but was probably closer to forty-five minutes, they emerged onto Forest Service Road 42—the gravel road where Meg had left her Subaru. The car sat exactly where she'd parked it, a dark silhouette against the lighter surface of the road.

"Thank god," Meg breathed, pulling her keys from her pocket with shaking hands. "Let's go."

They hurried to the vehicle, the relative openness of the road making them feel exposed after the dense cover of the forest. Meg unlocked the car with trembling fingers, and they climbed in, both breathing sighs of relief as the doors closed with solid thunks.

The engine started on the first try, and Meg swung the car around, heading back toward Highway 18. Her hands were still shaking on the steering wheel, adrenaline coursing through her system in waves that left her feeling alternately superhuman and utterly drained.

"We made it," Alex said, her voice tight with emotions Meg couldn't quite identify—relief, yes, but also disappointment, frustration, and a lingering fear.

"We got out," Meg corrected gently. "But we still don't know where Emily is. Or the others."

"No," Alex agreed, staring out the window at the dark forests slipping past. "But we have proof now. Proof that Blackwood is connected to their disappearances. That's more than we had this morning."

Meg was about to respond when a glint of light in her rearview mirror caught her attention—headlights, distant but advancing rapidly.

"We've got company," she said, pressing down on the accelerator. The Subaru responded with a surge of power, eating up the gravel road at a speed that sent stones pinging against the undercarriage.

"It's him," Alex confirmed, twisting in her seat to look behind them. "He's found us faster than I expected."

The headlights grew larger in the mirror, gaining ground despite Meg's increased speed. The truck had the advantage on the rough road, its higher clearance allowing it to navigate the ruts and potholes that forced Meg to slow the Subaru.

"Highway 18 is about four miles ahead," Meg said, gripping the wheel tightly as they bounced over a particularly rough section. "If we can reach it—"

"He'll still follow," Alex cut in. "But at least there might be other traffic. Witnesses."

The headlights loomed closer, close enough now that the bright beams illuminated the interior of Meg's car. A horn blared behind them—long, angry bursts that made both women jump.

"He's trying to run us off the road," Meg realized, her mouth dry with fear. "Hold on."

She pressed the accelerator to the floor, the Subaru's engine whining in protest as it reached the upper limits of its capabilities. The speedometer crept past sixty, dangerously fast for the unpaved road, but the headlights behind them began to recede slightly.

"It's working," Alex said, hope creeping into her voice. "Keep going."

Meg navigated a sharp curve, the car's tires sliding slightly before finding purchase again. The forest was a dark blur on either side, the narrow beam of her headlights barely illuminating the road ahead in time for her to react.

A mile passed, then another. The junction with Highway 18 was close now, maybe a mile away. The headlights behind them had fallen back further but remained persistently in pursuit.

"We're going to make it," Alex said, her knuckles white where she gripped the dashboard. "Just a little further."

The words had barely left her mouth when the road before them changed—a sharp drop where recent rains had washed out a section, leaving a miniature ravine cutting across their path. Meg saw it too late to stop completely. She slammed on the brakes, the car skidding on the loose gravel, but momentum carried them forward and into the washed-out section.

The Subaru bottomed out with a sickening crunch, then lurched forward as the wheels found purchase on the other side. The engine sputtered but kept running as they cleared the obstacle.

"You okay?" Meg asked, glancing at Alex, who nodded tightly.

Behind them, the pursuing truck had slowed, approaching the washout with more caution. It gave them precious seconds to increase their lead.

The gravel road merged with Highway 18 just ahead, the smooth asphalt a welcome sight after the punishing forest service road. Meg turned onto it without slowing, tires squealing in protest as she accelerated toward Seacliff.

In the rearview mirror, she watched as Blackwood's truck navigated the junction, still in pursuit but now falling further behind as the Subaru found its rhythm on the paved highway.

"We're going to lose him," Meg said, relief flooding through her as the distance between them grew. "The Subaru's faster on the highway."

Alex kept her eyes on the road behind them, shoulders tense, until the headlights dwindled to distant pinpoints and finally disappeared around a curve. Only then did she exhale slowly, some of the rigid tension leaving her body.

"We should go straight to the police," Meg said, keeping her speed steady but legal now. "The Pine Ridge Sheriff's Department—"

"Will be closed for the night," Alex finished for her. "Small department, minimal staffing. There might be a deputy on patrol, but the office itself closes at 6 PM. I checked, multiple times, when I was trying to get them to investigate the message on the roof."

Meg frowned, considering their options. "My friend Claire knows the deputy in Seacliff. We could go there, ask him to contact the Pine Ridge sheriff."

"And say what?" Alex's voice held an edge of frustration. "That we broke into a man's cabin, stole his property, and now claim it's evidence of kidnapping? Without proof that the women are being held there, we're the criminals in this situation."

"We have the licenses," Meg reminded her, reaching into her camera bag and checking that the memory card was secure. "And my photos. That's more than we had before."

Alex studied the two driver's licenses she still clutched in her hand, her thumb tracing over Emily's face—her green eyes haunted, her smile hesitant.

"Let me think," Alex said, rubbing her temple where a headache was clearly forming. "We can't just walk into a police station with stolen property. We need to approach this carefully."

Meg nodded, understanding the delicate position they were in. Despite having found evidence linking Blackwood to missing women, their methods of obtaining it had been less than legal. If they didn't present it properly, they risked being dismissed or even arrested themselves.

The highway stretched before them, a ribbon of black cutting through the darker mass of forest on either side. Meg's thoughts raced almost as fast as the car, trying to formulate a plan that wouldn't immediately backfire.

"What about the PI you hired?" she asked suddenly. "Could he help create a buffer between us and law enforcement? Present the evidence in a way that doesn't immediately incriminate us?"

Alex considered this. "Maybe. He's got contacts in several departments, some credibility. But he's based in Seattle, and I'd rather not wait until morning to get this to someone who can act on it."

They lapsed into tense silence, each wrestling with the impossible situation. The adrenaline that had carried them through their escape was beginning to ebb, leaving exhaustion and doubt in its wake. Meg's hands had stopped trembling, but a bone-deep weariness was settling in, making her blink hard to keep her focus on the road.

"Take the next exit," Alex said suddenly. "There's a 24-hour diner about two miles south. We need to regroup, get some coffee, figure out our next steps."

The diner—Roadside Jo's according to the neon sign—was just as Alex had described, a small roadside establishment with windows that spilled warm yellow light onto the nearly empty parking lot. A semi-truck and two pickup trucks were the only other vehicles present at this late hour.

Meg parked at the far end of the lot, positioning the car so they could see anyone approaching. They took a moment to compose themselves before entering—smoothing disheveled hair, brushing forest debris from their clothes, trying to look like normal late-night travelers rather than women who had just fled for their lives.

The bell above the door jingled as they entered, drawing a brief glance from the lone waitress behind the counter—a woman in her fifties with faded red hair pulled back in a messy bun. She offered a tired smile and gestured to the empty restaurant.

"Sit anywhere, ladies. I'll be right with you."

They chose a booth in the corner that offered a clear view of both the parking lot and the door. Meg slid onto the cracked vinyl seat with a wince, her muscles protesting after the night's exertions. Alex took the seat opposite, positioning herself to watch the entrance.

The waitress approached, depositing two laminated menus and a pot of coffee. "You two look like you could use this," she said, filling their cups without waiting for confirmation. Her name tag read "Darlene."

"Thanks," Meg said, wrapping her hands around the mug, grateful for its warmth. "You're a lifesaver."

Darlene chuckled. "Just doing my job. Take your time with the menus. Kitchen's open all night."

When she'd moved away, Alex leaned forward, her voice low. "We need a plan. Blackwood knows what we look like now, and he knows we have evidence connecting him to Emily and the others. He's not going to just let that go."

Meg nodded, taking a sip of the surprisingly good coffee. "And we still don't know where the women are being kept. If they're in that outbuilding we spotted…"

"Then they're still in danger," Alex finished, her face tight with renewed urgency. "And now Blackwood knows someone's onto him. He might move them, or worse."

The weight of this realization settled heavily between them. The evidence they'd obtained might ultimately mean nothing if Blackwood decided to eliminate the living proof of his crimes.

Meg pulled out her phone, checking the signal—full bars, thankfully—and opened her contact list. "I'm going to call Claire. She can meet us at the sheriff's substation in Seacliff, maybe smooth things over with the deputy there."

Alex nodded reluctantly. "Fine. But be careful what you say on the phone. If Blackwood has connections, he might have ways of monitoring calls."

The warning sent a chill down Meg's spine, but she dialed anyway. After four rings, Claire answered, her voice thick with sleep.

"Meg? It's after midnight. What's wrong?"

"Claire, I need your help," Meg said, keeping her voice steady. "Are you home?"

"Yes, why?"

"I need you to meet me at the sheriff's substation in Seacliff. It's urgent. I'll explain everything when I see you."

A pause, then Claire's voice came back, fully awake now. "Are you in trouble? Are you safe?"

"I'm safe right now," Meg assured her. "But I've stumbled onto something… complicated. I need your legal expertise, and your connection to Deputy Reid."

"Ellis Reid?" Claire sounded surprised. "Meg, what have you gotten yourself into?"

"I'll explain everything, I promise. Can you be there in thirty minutes?"

A rustling sound came through the phone—Claire already getting out of bed. "I'll be there in twenty. And Meg? Be careful."

"I will. Thank you."

She ended the call and looked up to find Alex watching her with an unreadable expression. "Claire's meeting us at the substation. She knows Deputy Reid personally, which might help our case."

Alex nodded, but her eyes remained wary. "You trust her completely?"

The question caught Meg off guard. "Of course. She's been my best friend for years."

"And you've told her about me? About Emily?"

"No," Meg admitted. "I haven't had the chance. Why?"

Alex's gaze flicked toward the window, scanning the parking lot before returning to Meg. "Because once we involve more people, the risk increases. Not just for us, but for Emily and the others if they're still alive. If Blackwood has connections, influential friends, we need to be careful who we trust."

There was something in her tone that made Meg uneasy—a paranoia that seemed excessive even given their circumstances. But then again, Alex had been living with this investigation for weeks, had seen how local authorities dismissed her concerns about the message on Blackwood's roof.

"Claire's solid," Meg assured her. "And Deputy Reid seems competent. Between the four of us, we should be able to figure out how to proceed legally while still keeping pressure on Blackwood."

Alex didn't look entirely convinced, but she nodded again. "Let's eat something quickly and go. I don't want to stay in one place too long."

They ordered sandwiches to go, Meg suddenly aware of the hollow emptiness in her stomach. The events of the day—from discovering the hidden outbuilding on the satellite image to their narrow escape from Blackwood's cabin—had driven all thoughts of food from her mind until now.

As they waited for their order, Meg studied Alex more carefully. The woman's face was drawn with exhaustion and worry, dark circles underlining her striking green eyes. Those eyes constantly moved, scanning windows, doors, the other patrons, never still for more than a moment. Her right hand remained close to her jacket pocket where Meg knew she kept her hunting knife.

"How long have you been doing this?" Meg asked quietly. "Living in that hunting blind, watching Blackwood?"

Alex's gaze shifted back to Meg, something like surprise flickering across her features. "Three weeks, like I said."

"And before that? What do you do, when you're not tracking missing persons?"

A ghost of a smile touched Alex's lips. "You mean what's my day job? I was—am—a photojournalist. Spent most of the last decade in conflict zones—Syria, Ukraine, South Sudan. Came back to the States about a year ago to help Emily after her accident."

This explained a lot—her tactical awareness, her comfort with surveillance, her methodical approach to gathering evidence. She'd been documenting much darker stories than missing women long before her sister disappeared.

"That must have been difficult," Meg said. "Transitioning from war zones to... this."

Alex's expression hardened. "You'd be surprised how similar they are. Different scenery, same human capacity for cruelty." She looked down at Emily's driver's license, which she'd kept close rather than returning it to her pocket. "I've seen mass graves less disturbing than the thought of what might have happened to my sister."

Before Meg could respond, Darlene returned with their sandwiches packaged in styrofoam containers, along with two cups of coffee to go. "You ladies be safe out there," she said, her motherly tone a stark contrast to the darkness of the conversation she'd interrupted.

They paid and left, the bell jingling again as the door closed behind them. The night air had cooled significantly, carrying the scent of pine and distant rain. Meg scanned the parking lot before heading to her car, Alex's paranoia apparently contagious.

As they pulled back onto the highway, heading toward Seacliff, Meg found herself watching the rearview mirror more carefully than before. Every set of headlights triggered a momentary spike of anxiety, every vehicle that maintained the same distance for too long became a potential threat.

"You feel it now, don't you?" Alex said softly, noticing Meg's vigilance. "The weight of being hunted."

Meg nodded, her mouth suddenly dry despite the coffee. "Is this how you've felt since Emily disappeared?"

"Every moment." Alex turned to look out the passenger window, her profile sharp against the darkness. "It changes you, living like this. Makes you see dangers everywhere, question everyone's motives. I sometimes wonder if I'll ever feel normal again, even if we find Emily alive."

The raw honesty in her voice struck a chord in Meg. For all her investigative experience with insurance fraud cases, she'd never been on this side of the equation—the one being pursued rather than the pursuer. It was unsettling how quickly her perspective had shifted, how easily fear had become her companion.

The lights of Seacliff appeared in the distance, a small cluster of illumination against the vast darkness of the coastal night. Somewhere in that town was the sheriff's substation where Claire would be waiting. Somewhere was Deputy Reid, whom they hoped would take their evidence seriously despite how they'd obtained it.

And somewhere out there was Nathan Blackwood, methodically planning his next move, his unsettling calm more frightening than any rage could have been.

Meg tightened her grip on the steering wheel, pushing the Subaru just a bit faster toward the promise of safety and help. But deep down, a voice she couldn't quite silence whispered that they'd crossed a line tonight—stepped into something darker and more dangerous than either of them had anticipated.

And there was no going back.

CHAPTER THREE
OLD HABITS

The fluorescent lights of the Seacliff Sheriff's substation flickered with a temperamental buzz, casting a sickly green pallor across the worn linoleum floor. Meg Sawyer felt the weight of the previous night pressing against her temples—a cocktail of adrenaline, fear, and unresolved questions that refused to be silenced.

Deputy Ellis Reid's office was a testament to decades of law enforcement. Faded photographs of past investigations lined the walls, their edges curling slightly, like memories struggling to maintain their shape. A vintage filing cabinet stood in the corner, its metal surface scratched and dented, holding stories of countless investigations that had passed through these walls.

"Start from the beginning," Reid said, his voice carrying the patient tone of a man who had heard a thousand different versions of the truth.

Meg took a deep breath. Her hands, still bearing slight scratches from their escape the previous night, traced the edge of the incident report. "It wasn't supposed to be anything more than a routine investigation," she began.

Alex sat beside her, silent but tense. Her fingers, usually steady from years of photojournalism, trembled almost imperceptibly when she reached for a cup of coffee. The styrofoam cup wavered, a physical manifestation of her internal turmoil.

The driver's licenses they'd discovered lay spread across Reid's desk like a macabre puzzle. Each one represented a life interrupted, a story left unfinished. Valerie Cortez's photo seemed to stare back at them—a young woman with dark eyes and a smile that now existed only in a past tense.

"Valerie went missing from Pine County last summer," Reid murmured, more to himself than to them. His thumb traced the edge of her license. "No body was ever found. No solid leads."

Claire stood by the window, her attorney's mind visibly processing the legal implications of everything she'd just heard. Her normally confident posture was rigid with concern, the shadows under her eyes testament to being awakened in the middle of the night. She'd arrived at the substation before them, her relationship with Reid evident in the easy way they communicated without words.

"So, you broke into this man's cabin," she said, turning from the window, "because you saw a message on his roof through Google Maps. A message that disappeared when you refreshed the page." Her tone wasn't accusatory, simply clarifying the facts with a prosecutor's precision.

"Yes," Meg confirmed, meeting her friend's gaze directly. "I know how it sounds, Claire."

"It sounds like a potential civil rights violation," Claire said bluntly. "Unlawful entry, theft of personal property—"

"Property that proves he's connected to at least four missing women," Alex cut in, her voice tight with restrained frustration. "One of whom is my sister."

Claire raised a placating hand. "I understand. I'm not saying you were wrong to investigate. I'm saying we need to be very careful about how we proceed from here if we want any of this evidence to be admissible."

Reid leaned back in his chair, the ancient springs protesting beneath his weight. Unlike Claire, his expression held less concern about legal technicalities and more about the darker implications of what they'd found.

"The four chairs at the dining table," he said thoughtfully. "The varied food in the refrigerator. The medical training." He tapped a pencil against his desktop, a rhythmic counterpoint to the humming fluorescents. "He's keeping them somewhere."

"There's an outbuilding," Meg said, pulling up the satellite imagery on her phone and passing it to Reid. "Here, partially hidden by trees. We never got to check it before Blackwood returned early."

Reid studied the image, his weathered face growing more serious. "This is enough for me to request assistance from the Pine Ridge Sheriff's Department. They have jurisdiction over that area." He glanced at the wall clock—3:47 AM. "Sheriff Hanover will be in her office by six. I'll call her directly."

"And until then?" Alex asked, the edge in her voice betraying her impatience.

"Until then," Claire interjected before Reid could answer, "you two need to give formal statements. Everything you saw, everything you found, in exhaustive detail." She held up a hand as Alex began to protest. "I know it seems like a waste of time when Emily might be in danger, but trust me—if we don't do this properly, Blackwood walks. Period."

The logic was impeccable, but it did nothing to ease the restless anxiety Meg felt. Every minute spent in this office was a minute Blackwood could use to cover his tracks, to move Emily and the others, to vanish completely.

"I agree with Claire," Deputy Reid said, opening a drawer and extracting official statement forms. "But I'll add this—we need to move quickly. If Blackwood is as methodical as you described, he's already making contingency plans. Men like him always do."

The next two hours passed in a blur of detailed statements, careful documentation of the evidence, and the gradual formulation of a plan. Reid contacted the night duty officer at Pine Ridge, informing them of a potential development in multiple missing persons cases. Claire helped ensure their statements were thorough while protecting them from self-incrimination as much as possible.

By the time the first gray light of dawn filtered through the blinds, they had created a comprehensive case file that even the most skeptical sheriff would have to take seriously.

"I've just heard from Hanover," Reid announced, returning from a call taken in the hallway. "She's coming directly here rather than going to her office. Should arrive in about forty minutes."

"That's a good sign," Claire observed. "She's taking this seriously."

"Abigail Hanover takes everything seriously," Reid replied, a hint of respect in his voice. "Twenty-seven years with the department, the last twelve as sheriff. She doesn't play politics and she doesn't ignore evidence, even when it comes through... unconventional channels."

Meg found herself studying Deputy Reid more carefully. Early fifties, she guessed, with the weathered face of someone who spent significant time outdoors. His movements were deliberate, economical, like a man who had learned to conserve energy for when it truly mattered. Despite the late hour and the unusual circumstances, his uniform remained crisp, his bearing professional.

"You've worked with her before?" she asked.

"Trained under her," Reid corrected. "Before she made sheriff. Best investigator I've ever known." A small smile touched his lips. "Also the most stubborn. Once she sinks her teeth into a case, she doesn't let go until it's solved."

This was encouraging news, but Meg couldn't shake the feeling that they were moving too slowly. Somewhere out there, Emily Reeves and possibly three other women were being held against their will by a man who now knew his security had been compromised.

Alex seemed to share her impatience. She'd been growing increasingly restless, checking her watch, pacing when not giving her statement, her eyes repeatedly drawn to the driver's licenses on Reid's desk—particularly Emily's.

"I need some air," she announced suddenly, standing with an abruptness that drew everyone's attention. "Just five minutes."

Claire exchanged a glance with Reid, who nodded. "Of course," Claire said. "We could all use a break. I'll come with you."

"I'd rather be alone," Alex replied, already moving toward the door.

"Not a good idea," Reid said firmly, rising from his chair. "Blackwood knows what you look like, knows you have evidence against him. Until we have him in custody, neither of you should be alone."

Alex looked like she wanted to argue but seemed to realize the sense in Reid's caution. She nodded reluctantly. "Fine. But just outside the door. I need to think."

Claire followed her out, leaving Meg alone with Reid. The deputy began organizing the statements and evidence photos, creating order from the chaos of their night's adventure.

"You believe us," Meg observed. It wasn't a question.

Reid looked up, his expression serious. "I've been in law enforcement for twenty-three years, Ms. Sawyer. I've learned to trust my instincts. And right now, they're telling me you and Ms. Reeves stumbled onto something very dark."

"Call me Meg," she said automatically. "And thank you. For taking this seriously."

Reid nodded, returning to his organization. "Insurance claims investigator, you said?"

"For fifteen years. Specialized in suspected fraud cases."

"That explains it," he said, almost to himself.

"Explains what?"

Reid gestured to the detailed timeline she'd created as part of her statement. "Your approach. Methodical, evidence-focused, connections clearly drawn. Most civilians who bring in evidence are scattered, emotional. You presented like a professional."

Meg felt a small flush of pride at the compliment. "Old habits. You spend enough years investigating people trying to commit insurance fraud, you develop a certain approach."

"It's a good approach," Reid said simply. "Might have saved several women's lives, including Ms. Reeves' sister."

The door opened before Meg could respond, Claire returning with a slightly calmer Alex. They'd brought coffee—real coffee from the diner across the street, not the ancient sludge from the substation's break room.

"Sheriff Hanover just called," Claire announced, distributing the cups. "She's ten minutes out and bringing a full team. They're taking this very seriously."

Alex's posture relaxed slightly at this news. She sipped her coffee in silence, her eyes distant, obviously wrestling with thoughts she wasn't ready to share.

Precisely seven minutes later, the relative quiet of the substation was broken by the arrival of several vehicles. Through the blinds, Meg could see three sheriff's department SUVs and what appeared to be a crime scene van pulling into the parking lot.

"That's Hanover," Reid confirmed, straightening his already impeccable uniform. "And she's brought the cavalry."

The sheriff's department personnel filed into the substation with practiced efficiency—deputies, forensic techs, and finally Sheriff Abigail Hanover herself. She swept into Reid's office with the force of a controlled storm, her silver-streaked black hair pulled into a bun so tight it seemed to defy gravity. When she moved, it was with a deliberate precision that suggested years of navigating both bureaucratic and criminal landscapes.

"Deputy Reid," she greeted with a nod. Her sharp eyes quickly assessed the room and its occupants. "These are our witnesses?"

"Yes, Sheriff. Meg Sawyer, Alex Reeves, and Claire Winters." Reid indicated each woman in turn. "Ms. Sawyer discovered the initial evidence through satellite imagery. Ms. Reeves is the sister of one of the potential victims. Ms. Winters is a prosecutor with the district attorney's office who's been assisting them."

Hanover acknowledged each with a brief nod before turning her attention to the evidence spread across Reid's desk. She examined the driver's licenses without touching them, her expression revealing nothing of her thoughts.

"I've reviewed your initial report, Deputy," she said finally. "And I'm authorizing a full investigation. We'll need search warrants for Blackwood's property, including the outbuilding identified in the satellite imagery." She turned to Claire. "Ms. Winters, I understand you have concerns about how the evidence was obtained."

Claire straightened, slipping easily into her professional persona. "Yes, Sheriff. The initial entry to Blackwood's cabin was unauthorized, which could create admissibility issues."

"Noted," Hanover replied, seemingly untroubled. "Fortunately, we have enough here to establish probable cause independent of the entry itself. The missing persons cases, the satellite imagery showing the message and its subsequent removal, the connection between Blackwood and the locations where the women were last seen." She turned back to Reid. "I want a full briefing in the conference room in fifteen minutes. Bring everything you have."

As Reid gathered the materials, Hanover's attention shifted to Meg and Alex. Her gaze was penetrating, assessing, but not unkind. "You two have taken a significant risk bringing this forward. I appreciate your courage, but I need to be very clear about what happens next." Her voice took on a firmer edge. "This is now an official investigation. We'll follow procedure, gather evidence legally, and build a case that will stand up in court. That means you step back and let us do our jobs. Understood?"

Alex bristled visibly at being sidelined, but Meg placed a restraining hand on her arm. "We understand, Sheriff. But please—time could be critical. If Emily and the others are still alive..."

"I'm well aware of the urgency, Ms. Sawyer," Hanover interrupted, though not unkindly. "Which is why I've already dispatched deputies to establish surveillance on Blackwood's property while we secure the warrants. He won't be moving anyone without us knowing."

This was clearly not open for negotiation. Hanover turned back to Reid, the two of them discussing tactical approaches and resource allocation with the shorthand of colleagues who had worked together for years.

Meg guided Alex to the small seating area by the wall, out of earshot of the increasingly technical conversation. Claire joined them, her expression conveying both sympathy and caution.

"What now?" Alex asked, her voice low with frustration. "We just wait while they go through their procedures? Emily could be—"

"In the best possible hands," Claire finished firmly. "Sheriff Hanover's reputation is legendary in law enforcement circles. If anyone can find Emily and the others, it's her department."

Meg nodded in agreement, though she understood Alex's frustration. After weeks of investigating alone, being asked to step aside would feel like abandonment. "Claire's right. And we haven't been sidelined completely—they'll need our statements, our knowledge of Blackwood's routines, your insights about Emily."

Alex didn't look convinced, but she nodded reluctantly. "I just can't stop thinking about what might be happening to her right now. While we sit here drinking coffee and filling out forms."

The phone call to Sheriff Abigail Hanover transformed their informal interview into something more official. Her voice, crisp and authoritative, cut through the substation's ambient noise like a scalpel.

"Bring them in," she had instructed Reid. "And secure those evidence bags. I want forensics to go through everything."

The Pine Ridge Sheriff's Department was a study in controlled chaos. Modern computer systems sat alongside decades-old filing cabinets. Digital crime scene photos were pinned next to hand-drawn maps marking jurisdictional boundaries.

"County lines are complicated," she explained, spreading a large map across her desk. Her finger traced the borderlines where Blackwood's cabin sat—a geographical no-man's-land where jurisdictions blurred and legal authority became a complex negotiation.

Meg's investigative instincts were firing on all cylinders. She studied the map, noting how the property seemed strategically positioned. Not by accident, but by design.

The missing persons board caught her attention. Dozens of faces stared back—some recent, some years old. Amanda Chen's photo stood out. The driver's license they'd found matched the woman in the picture—young, hopeful, now just another name without a resolution.

"What do you know about Axion Enterprises?" Meg asked, her voice cutting through the room's tension.

Hanover's eyes narrowed. A microscopic shift in her expression suggested Meg had just touched something significant.

Alex's phone buzzed. The message was short, clinical, terrifying.

"You took something that belongs to me. Return it, and she lives."

The attached photo of Emily—holding a newspaper with today's date—transformed their investigation from an abstract inquiry to a desperate, time-sensitive rescue mission.

Outside the department's windows, a black SUV with tinted windows sat perfectly still. When Meg pointed it out, the vehicle pulled away with a smoothness that suggested professional surveillance.

"We need protection," Hanover declared. It wasn't a suggestion.

THE MOTEL THEY WERE TAKEN TO SEEMED FROZEN IN A 1970S TIME warp. Faded floral wallpaper peeled at the corners, and the carpet bore the kind of stains that told stories better left untold. Deputy Reid positioned himself outside—a human shield against whatever darkness was pursuing them.

Meg's laptop became her weapon. She dove into digital archives, tracing Axion Enterprises' property acquisitions. A pattern emerged—remote locations, strategically purchased over the past five years. Wilderness areas. Places where people could easily disappear.

As midnight approached, exhaustion battled with her investigative drive. Her fingers hovered over the keyboard, tracing connections that were just beginning to take shape.

A sound. Slight. Imperceptible to most.

But Meg Sawyer was not most people.

Her door—which she knew she had locked—stood slightly ajar.

Moving with instinctive caution, Meg set her laptop aside and reached for the bedside lamp, switching it off to leave the room in darkness except for the blue glow of her computer screen. She eased herself off the bed, bare feet silent on the threadbare carpet as she moved to the wall beside the door.

Her heart hammered in her chest, but her mind remained oddly clear—the same focused calm that had served her well during confrontations with insurance fraudsters caught in their lies. Except those people hadn't been kidnapping women and possibly worse.

With her back pressed against the wall, she strained her ears for any sound from the hallway. Nothing. Not even the ambient noises of the motel—distant television sets, ice machines, other guests—reached her. The silence felt manufactured, deliberate.

Meg glanced at her phone on the nightstand, calculating the risk of trying to reach it. Reid was stationed outside, presumably just down the hall. One call would bring help. But crossing the room meant leaving the relative safety of her position by the door, exposing herself to whoever might be watching through that narrow opening.

The decision was made for her when a shadow shifted in the doorway—a subtle darkening of the already dim light from the hallway. Someone was there.

Meg held her breath, muscles tensed for either fight or flight. The door swung inward slowly, silently, revealing a silhouette that was immediately, unmistakably familiar.

"Alex?" Meg whispered, relief washing through her like a physical force.

Alex Reeves stepped into the room and closed the door behind her with a soft click. She was dressed exactly as she had been earlier—practical hiking pants, weathered jacket—but something in her demeanor had changed. The constant tension that had radiated from her since they met had intensified, transformed into a coiled energy that filled the small room.

"We need to talk," Alex said, her voice barely audible. "Not here. Meet me at the vending machines in five minutes. Come alone."

Before Meg could respond, Alex slipped back into the hallway like a ghost, leaving Meg staring at the closed door, mind racing with questions. How had Alex unlocked her door? Why the secrecy when they were supposedly safe under Sheriff Hanover's protection? And most pressingly—should she trust her?

The last question gave Meg pause. She barely knew Alex Reeves. Their entire relationship consisted of less than twenty-four hours of high-stress, life-threatening circumstances. Yet she'd followed her into Blackwood's cabin, trusted her to lead them to safety through unfamiliar forest, and handed over evidence to law enforcement largely on her word.

Trust had never come easily to Meg, not even before Daniel's betrayal had shattered what remained of her faith in people. Her work as an insurance investigator had shown her how easily people could lie, how convincingly they could play victims while perpetrating fraud. Alex's story could be verified, certainly—Emily Reeves was genuinely missing—but the rest?

Meg moved to the window and peeked through the blinds at the nearly empty parking lot. Deputy Reid's cruiser was visible, parked in a spot with clear sightlines to the motel's entrances. No sign of the black SUV that had been following them earlier, but that didn't mean it wasn't out there somewhere, beyond the radius of the motel's sickly yellow security lights.

Five minutes, Alex had said. Four remained now. Meg weighed her options quickly. Ignoring the request meant potentially missing crucial information about Emily or Blackwood. Meeting Alex alone meant leaving the relative safety of her room. Calling Reid meant violating Alex's trust, potentially for no reason.

With a resigned sigh, Meg pulled on her shoes, grabbed her room key and phone, and moved to the door. She'd compromise—she'd meet Alex, but she'd text Reid first, a simple message that wouldn't raise immediate alarms but would leave a breadcrumb if something went wrong: "Getting snack from vending machine. Back in 10."

The motel corridor was dimly lit and eerily quiet as Meg made her way toward the ice and vending area at the far end. The place had clearly seen better days—the carpet pattern faded into obscurity, water stains marking the ceiling tiles, the occasional loose baseboard revealing glimpses of the wall behind. It reminded her unpleasantly of motels she'd stayed in during her early days as an investigator, when budgets were tight and accommodations were an afterthought.

The vending area was tucked into an alcove near the rear entrance—a pair of humming machines offering overpriced sodas and stale snacks, a perpetually empty ice maker, and a single plastic chair with a cigarette burn on the seat. Alex was already there, her back to the wall, eyes constantly sweeping the corridor.

"You came," she said as Meg approached. Not a question, not quite relief, something else in her tone that Meg couldn't immediately identify.

"You said it was important," Meg replied simply, positioning herself where she could see both the corridor and the emergency exit. "What's going on, Alex?"

Alex reached into her jacket pocket, an action that momentarily sent Meg's pulse racing before she produced a folded piece of paper. "I got another message. After the one at the sheriff's department."

She handed the paper to Meg, who unfolded it carefully. It was a printed photograph of Emily, holding a newspaper dated that morning. She appeared unharmed but frightened, her eyes wide with an emotion that made Meg's stomach twist with empathy. Below the image was a typed message:

"The authorities can't help her. Only you can. Come alone to the coordinates below at 3 AM. Tell no one. No police. No witnesses. Bring what you took. She lives or dies by your choice."

Meg looked up from the paper, meeting Alex's gaze. "When did you get this?"

"It was slipped under my door an hour ago," Alex replied, her voice tight with controlled fear. "I didn't see who delivered it."

"Have you shown this to Reid or Hanover?"

Alex shook her head emphatically. "Didn't you read it? 'No police.' Whoever has Emily is watching us, watching this place. If I involve them, Emily dies."

Meg glanced back at the paper, reading the geographic coordinates listed at the bottom. "This could be a trap, Alex. Blackwood luring you away from protection."

"Of course it's a trap," Alex said, a bitter edge to her voice. "But what choice do I have? That's my sister. If there's even a fraction of a chance she's really there, that I could save her..." She trailed off, the rest of the sentence hanging unspoken between them.

Meg understood the impulse all too well. Despite her professional training, despite everything logical telling her this was exactly the wrong move, she couldn't dismiss Alex's position. If it were Claire in that photo, wouldn't she consider exactly the same reckless course?

"What's your plan?" Meg asked finally.

"I need your help," Alex admitted. "I've stolen a maintenance worker's uniform from the supply closet—it'll get me past Reid without raising immediate alarms. But I need a distraction to create enough time for me to get clear of the motel."

"And then what? The coordinates are where? How will you even get there?"

"There's a truck in the parking lot with keys left in the ignition—careless, but lucky for me. The coordinates are about twenty miles north, in a clearing near the forest service road we were on earlier. I can be there in thirty minutes."

"And walk straight into Blackwood's hands," Meg pointed out. "Alex, think about this. Even if Emily is really there, what's your plan for getting both of you out? He'll have backup, weapons, the advantage of choosing the location."

A flash of something—desperation, perhaps—crossed Alex's face. "I don't have a plan, okay? I just know I can't sit here doing nothing while my sister is in danger. While the clock runs out." She drew a shaky breath. "I understand if you don't want to help. You've already risked enough. But I'm going, with or without a distraction."

Meg considered their options. The safest course was clear—alert Reid and Hanover, let professionals handle the situation with proper resources and backup. But professionals meant procedures, warrants, time that Emily might not have.

"Let me come with you," Meg said, surprising herself with the offer.

Alex blinked, clearly not expecting this response. "What?"

"Two of us have a better chance than one. I can drive while you navigate. We can approach more carefully, assess the situation before committing. And if it is a trap, at least you'll have someone watching your back."

"Why would you do that?" Alex asked, genuine confusion in her voice. "You barely know me. You barely know Emily."

It was a fair question, one Meg had been asking herself since she first decided to drive to Blackwood's cabin. Why was she so invested in this case, in these strangers' lives? Was it just the investigator in her, unable to leave a mystery unsolved? Or something more personal—her own sense of being lost, of needing to find purpose after her life had collapsed around her?

"Because it's the right thing to do," she said finally, settling on the simplest truth. "And because I've seen enough evidence to believe Emily is in real danger. If there's a chance to help her, I want to take it."

Alex studied her for a long moment, green eyes searching Meg's face for any sign of hesitation or deception. Whatever she was looking for, she seemed to find it, because she nodded once, decisively.

"Okay. But we need to move fast. It's already past one, and we need time to approach carefully."

"I need five minutes," Meg said. "Wait for me by the rear exit. I'll create a distraction that should pull Reid away from his post long enough for us to slip out."

Alex nodded again and moved toward the exit, pausing briefly to look back at Meg. "Thank you," she said softly, the simple words carrying the weight of everything they both knew they were risking.

As Meg watched her disappear through the emergency door, a quiet voice in the back of her mind whispered a warning. She was about to violate Sheriff Hanover's direct instructions, potentially compromising an active investigation and placing herself in grave danger. All for a woman she barely knew and a missing person she'd never met.

It wasn't rational. It wasn't safe. Daniel would have called it reckless, impulsive, emotional.

Maybe that's exactly why she had to do it.

Back in her room, Meg moved with efficient purpose, gathering essentials—her phone, camera, the hunting knife Alex had given her earlier. She pulled a dark jacket over her t-shirt and changed into jeans and hiking boots. Whatever awaited them at those coordinates, she wanted to be prepared.

She paused before leaving, deciding to leave one final breadcrumb. On the motel notepad, she scrawled a brief message:

"Following lead on Emily. Coordinates below. If not back by dawn, send help."

She copied the coordinates from the photo, then tucked the note under her laptop where it wouldn't be immediately visible but would be found if someone searched the room. It was a risk—if Blackwood did have someone watching the motel, her absence might be noticed before Reid found the note. But it was a calculated risk, a final safety net if everything went wrong.

The distraction was simple but effective—a call to the front desk from the room phone, a manufactured report of suspicious activity in the parking lot, specifically near Reid's cruiser. Primitive but reliable psychology—a law enforcement officer would always check a potential threat to their vehicle.

As predicted, within minutes of placing the call, Meg watched through the blinds as Reid emerged from the motel lobby and moved briskly toward the parking lot, hand resting near his holstered weapon as he scanned for the imaginary threat.

Meg slipped out of her room and moved swiftly down the corridor in the opposite direction, toward the rear exit where Alex waited. They exchanged a silent nod as they pushed through the door into the cool night air, then moved quickly along the back of the building toward the service area where employee vehicles were parked.

The stolen truck was exactly as Alex had described—an aging Ford F-150 with faded blue paint and a dent in the passenger door. The keys dangled from the ignition, a testament to small-town security assumptions or simple carelessness.

Meg took the driver's seat while Alex slid in beside her, immediately pulling out a folded map.

"Head north on Highway 18," she instructed as Meg started the engine. "We'll need to turn onto Forest Service Road 42 in about fifteen minutes. From there, it gets tricky."

As they pulled out of the motel parking lot, Meg caught a final glimpse of Reid in her rearview mirror, still examining his cruiser for signs of tampering. A twinge of guilt tugged at her conscience—he'd been nothing but helpful, and she was repaying him with deception. But the image of Emily from the photograph pushed the guilt aside, replacing it with resolve.

The highway stretched before them, a ribbon of black cutting through darker forest on both sides. Meg drove carefully but quickly, maintaining a speed that wouldn't attract attention from any late-night patrol cars while still covering ground efficiently. Beside her, Alex remained silent, her focus entirely on the map and occasional glances at her watch.

Twenty minutes later, they turned onto the now-familiar gravel surface of Forest Service Road 42, the truck's headlights illuminating swirls of mist that had settled in the lower areas. The vehicle handled the rough road better than Meg's Subaru had, but she still drove with caution, mindful of the washout they'd encountered during their escape earlier.

"Turn off the headlights up ahead," Alex said as they approached a bend in the road. "We're getting close, and we don't want to announce our arrival."

Meg complied, immediately plunging them into near-total darkness. She slowed to a crawl, relying on ambient moonlight filtering through breaks in the forest canopy to navigate. The truck inched forward, gravel crunching softly beneath its tires.

"Stop here," Alex instructed after another tense mile. "We'll continue on foot. The coordinates are about half a mile east, through those trees."

They left the truck partially concealed behind a stand of Douglas firs and continued on foot, moving with the careful silence of people acutely aware they might be walking into danger. Alex led the way, seemingly able to navigate in the darkness with uncanny precision. Meg followed closely, one hand keeping contact with Alex's jacket to avoid separation.

The forest was eerily quiet at this hour—even the nocturnal wildlife seemed to be holding its breath. Only the occasional whisper of wind through the pine needles above broke the stillness. It was the kind of silence that pressed against the eardrums, that made every small sound—a twig snapping underfoot, a rustle of clothing—seem magnified to an alarming degree.

After twenty minutes of careful progress, Alex raised a hand, signaling for Meg to stop. Ahead, barely visible through the trees, was a small clearing illuminated by what appeared to be vehicle headlights.

"There," Alex whispered, pointing to a dark shape at the center of the clearing. "Someone's there."

Meg squinted, trying to make out details in the uneven light. The shape resolved into a figure seated in what looked like a simple wooden chair. Even from this distance, the long chestnut hair was a match for the photos she'd seen of Emily Reeves.

Alex's sharp intake of breath confirmed the identification. "It's her," she said, her voice tight with emotion. "It's Emily."

Meg placed a restraining hand on Alex's arm as she felt her tense to move forward. "Wait. This is too easy. Where's Blackwood? Where's anyone?"

"I don't care," Alex replied, already pulling away. "That's my sister."

"Alex, think!" Meg hissed, tightening her grip. "This is obviously a setup. We need to approach carefully, assess the situation."

But Alex wasn't listening. With a strength born of desperate hope, she wrenched free of Meg's grasp and moved toward the clearing, staying low but moving with unmistakable purpose.

"Damn it," Meg muttered, left with no choice but to follow. Every instinct screamed that this was wrong—the isolated location, the conveniently positioned hostage, the apparent absence of captors—but she couldn't let Alex face whatever waited alone.

As they neared the edge of the clearing, details became clearer. Emily sat rigid in the chair, her hands apparently bound behind her back. Her head was bowed, chin against her chest, hair obscuring her face. The vehicle providing illumination was a black SUV—possibly the same one that had followed them earlier, though Meg couldn't be certain from this angle.

Alex paused at the tree line, finally exercising some caution as she studied the scene. Meg caught up to her, breathing heavily from the rushed approach.

"Something's wrong," Alex whispered, fear edging into her voice. "She's not moving at all."

Meg scanned the clearing, looking for any sign of Blackwood or other threats. Nothing moved. The only sound was the idling engine of the SUV, its exhaust creating ghostly tendrils in the cool night air.

"Could be drugged," Meg suggested. "Or..." She couldn't bring herself to voice the darker alternative.

Alex's face hardened with determination. "I'm going to her. Cover me. If you see anything—anyone—shout."

Before Meg could protest further, Alex darted into the clearing, moving in a half-crouch toward the seated figure. Meg followed more cautiously, staying closer to the tree line where shadows offered some concealment, her eyes constantly sweeping the area for threats.

Alex reached Emily first, dropping to her knees before the chair, hands reaching up to lift her sister's face. "Em? Emily, it's me. It's Alex. I'm here to take you home."

But as Alex tilted Emily's head back, a sound escaped her that Meg would remember for the rest of her life—a raw cry of horror and disbelief that cut through the night like a physical blade.

It wasn't Emily.

It was a mannequin, dressed in Emily's clothing, a wig of chestnut hair attached to its featureless head. A piece of paper was pinned to its chest, but Meg couldn't make out the words from her position.

"Alex," she called urgently, alarm bells screaming in her mind. "We need to go. Now!"

But it was too late. Lights blazed to life around the perimeter of the clearing—powerful spotlights that instantly transformed night into harsh, shadowless day. Meg threw up an arm to shield her eyes, momentarily blinded by the sudden illumination.

When her vision cleared, the situation was starkly apparent. They were surrounded. Men in tactical gear stood at regular intervals around the clearing, weapons raised and aimed. And from behind the SUV stepped a familiar figure—Nathan Blackwood, his calm demeanor unchanged from their earlier encounter in his cabin.

"Ms. Reeves," he called, his deep voice carrying easily across the clearing. "And Ms. Sawyer. How kind of you to accept my invitation." He smiled, the expression never reaching his eyes. "I believe we have some unfinished business."

Alex hadn't moved from her kneeling position before the mannequin, her body frozen in shock or despair. Meg took an instinctive step toward her, only to halt when multiple weapon sights tracked her movement.

"I wouldn't," Blackwood advised pleasantly. "My colleagues are rather jumpy this evening."

Meg raised her hands slowly, mind racing through scenarios, searching for any path out of this trap. Each possibility seemed worse than the last. They were outnumbered, outgunned, and completely exposed.

"Where is my sister?" Alex demanded, finally finding her voice. She rose to her feet, facing Blackwood with the rigid posture of someone barely containing their rage. "Where is Emily?"

Blackwood's expression shifted to something resembling sympathy. "Ms. Reeves, I understand your concern. Truly, I do. But I'm afraid Emily's location is not something I'm prepared to share just yet." He took a step forward. "Not until we've resolved the matter of what you took from my home."

"We have it," Meg said quickly, drawing his attention away from Alex. "The driver's licenses, the personal items. We'll return everything. Just tell us where Emily is."

Blackwood's gaze shifted to her, and Meg felt the weight of his assessment—cold, calculating, like a scientist studying a particularly interesting specimen. "Ms. Sawyer. The insurance investigator turned amateur detective. You've proven quite resourceful." He sounded almost impressed. "But I'm afraid it's not that simple anymore. You've involved the authorities, created quite a mess that needs cleaning up."

"Sheriff Hanover knows everything," Meg bluffed, hoping to inject some caution into his plans. "She knows about the missing women, about your connection to them. If anything happens to us, she'll come for you with everything she has."

Blackwood seemed amused rather than concerned. "Sheriff Hanover is a dedicated public servant operating within a system that has... certain limitations. By morning, her investigation will have been redirected in more productive channels. The official record will show that Nathan Blackwood's property was searched and nothing incriminating was found." His smile widened slightly. "After all, why would there be? I'm just a freelance graphic designer who enjoys his privacy."

The confidence with which he said this sent a chill down Meg's spine. He wasn't speaking hypothetically—he was describing a set of events already in motion, a corruption of justice that reached beyond local law enforcement.

"Who are you?" she asked, the question escaping before she could stop herself.

"Someone who values privacy," he replied simply. "Someone who prefers to resolve problems efficiently and permanently." He gestured to one of his men, who approached with a small black case. "Which brings us to our current situation."

Alex had been silent, but now she moved, a sudden lunge toward Blackwood that was intercepted by two of his men before she'd covered half the distance. They restrained her with practiced ease, seemingly unsurprised by the outburst.

"Where is my sister?" Alex demanded again, struggling against the grip of her captors. "What have you done with her?"

Blackwood opened the case his associate had brought, removing what appeared to be a pre-filled syringe. "Emily is quite safe, Ms. Reeves. In fact, she's thriving in her new role. You'll understand soon enough."

He approached Alex, syringe in hand, nodding to his men to secure her more firmly. Meg watched in horrified fascination as he tapped the syringe, checked the dosage with the precision of someone with medical training.

"Don't worry," he said to Alex, his voice almost gentle. "This won't hurt. And when you wake up, everything will make so much more sense."

"No!" Meg shouted, finally spurred to action. She lunged forward, knowing it was futile but unable to simply watch. As expected, she was immediately intercepted, strong hands gripping her arms, forcing her to her knees on the damp ground.

Blackwood glanced her way, seeming mildly disappointed by the interruption. "Your turn will come, Ms. Sawyer. I suggest you save your energy."

Meg could only watch helplessly as Blackwood administered the injection to Alex, who fought desperately against her restraints until the drug took effect. Within seconds, her struggles weakened, then ceased entirely as her eyes rolled back and her body went limp in her captors' grip.

"Take her to the facility," Blackwood instructed, handing the empty syringe back to his associate with the careful attention of someone disposing of medical waste properly. "Standard intake protocol. I'll join you there shortly after I've dealt with Ms. Sawyer."

As Alex was carried to a waiting vehicle at the edge of the clearing, Blackwood turned his full attention to Meg. He studied her with the same clinical interest he might give a lab specimen, his head tilted slightly as if trying to solve a particularly interesting puzzle.

"You intrigue me, Ms. Sawyer," he said finally. "Most people, when confronted with something that doesn't concern them directly, choose to look away. Path of least resistance. Yet you've placed yourself in considerable danger for a woman you've just met and another you've never met at all." He crouched down to her level, his face inches from hers. "Why is that, I wonder?"

Despite her fear, Meg met his gaze directly. "Because some things are wrong no matter who they happen to. Because some lines shouldn't be crossed."

"Lines," Blackwood repeated thoughtfully. "An interesting concept. Arbitrary boundaries created by social consensus." He smiled, the expression making Meg's skin crawl. "But I've found that most lines people claim are uncrossable disappear quite readily under the right circumstances. The right incentives. The right... adjustments to perspective."

He stood, nodding to someone behind Meg. She felt a presence approach, heard the rustling of fabric, sensed rather than saw a hand reaching toward her.

"Don't worry, Ms. Sawyer," Blackwood said, his voice the last thing she heard clearly as a sweet-smelling cloth covered her nose and mouth. "We're not going to harm you. Quite the contrary. We're going to help you see things more clearly. The world is so much simpler when you're on the right side of the line."

Consciousness faded rapidly, her last coherent thought a desperate hope that someone would find the note she'd left, that someone would come looking for them before whatever Blackwood had planned could be completed.

Then darkness claimed her, and Meg Sawyer knew no more.

CHAPTER FOUR
TRUST ISSUES

Meg jerked awake, disoriented by the unfamiliar surroundings. For a moment, panic gripped her as the memories flooded back—Blackwood, the clearing, the sweet-smelling cloth pressed against her face. Most horrifying was the image of Alex, limp and unconscious, being carried away by Blackwood's men after being forcibly drugged. Her heart hammered against her ribs as she sat up and took in her surroundings.

She was in a small, sparse room—a motel room. Cheap floral wallpaper peeled at the corners, the carpet worn thin in high-traffic areas. A dim lamp on the nightstand cast just enough light to reveal a figure slumped in a chair near the window.

"Claire?" Meg whispered.

Claire Winters startled awake, blinking rapidly. Her normally neat ponytail had come loose, red strands framing a face drawn with exhaustion. "Meg? Thank God." She crossed the room and sat on the edge of the bed. "How are you feeling?"

"Like I got hit by a truck," Meg admitted, wincing as she touched a tender spot on the back of her head. "Where are we? How did I get here?"

Claire reached for a water bottle on the nightstand and handed it to Meg. "Sheriff's department safe house. Well, safe motel, technically. Reid found you on the side of Forest Service Road 42 around dawn. You were unconscious but otherwise unharmed."

Meg drank deeply, the cool water washing away the chemical aftertaste that lingered in her mouth. As her mind cleared, a single thought pushed forward with urgency. "Alex—they took her. We need to find her. Blackwood drugged her first, then me."

Claire nodded grimly. "We've been searching, but there's no sign of her yet. By the time Reid and Hanover's team arrived at the clearing, there was only you, left at the roadside. The rest—Blackwood, his men, Alex—were gone."

"Blackwood had a whole team waiting," Meg said, the details coming back in sharper focus now. "Professional. Military precision. They knew we were coming."

"But how?" Claire's brow furrowed. "You said in your note you were following a lead about Emily. What happened exactly?"

The weight of responsibility settled heavy on Meg's shoulders. "Alex received what looked like proof of life—a photo of Emily with yesterday's newspaper. There was a message demanding she come alone to coordinates in the forest. I insisted on going with her." Meg rubbed her temples, fighting against the lingering fog of the sedative. "It was a trap. When we got there, it wasn't Emily at all—just a mannequin dressed in her clothes. Blackwood was waiting with armed men."

Claire sat back, processing this information. "You need to get some proper rest. That drug is still in your system."

"No time," Meg protested, struggling to sit upright. "We have to find Alex before—"

"Before you pass out from exhaustion?" Claire's tone was gentle but firm. "You won't be any help to Alex if you're not thinking clearly. Sheriff Hanover has deputies searching the entire area. The best thing you can do right now is recover."

Meg wanted to argue, but the room was already starting to spin. Claire was right—whatever Blackwood had given her was still affecting her system.

"Just a few hours," she conceded reluctantly. "Then we need to regroup."

"Deal," Claire agreed. "I'll wake you if there's any news."

Meg didn't remember falling asleep, but when she next opened her eyes, sunlight was streaming through a gap in the curtains. The clock on the nightstand read 2:17 PM. She'd been out for hours.

"Claire?" she called, pushing herself up, relieved to find the dizziness had mostly subsided.

The bathroom door opened, and Claire emerged, her hair wet from a shower. "You're awake. How's the head?"

"Better," Meg admitted, experimentally touching the tender spot at the back of her skull. "Any news?"

Claire shook her head. "Nothing concrete. Reid called about an hour ago. They found the vehicle Blackwood's team used abandoned in a quarry about thirty miles from here. Wiped clean, of course."

"Professional," Meg muttered.

"Very. The FBI has officially joined the investigation. Two agents arrived at the sheriff's department this morning." Claire sat on the edge of the bed. "Reid thinks it's time to move you from here. My beach house was compromised, but we can't stay at this motel indefinitely."

"Where then?"

"My place in town. It's small, but secure. Building has decent security, and no one would connect it to you."

Meg nodded, the practicality of the suggestion overriding her instinct to keep moving, keep searching. "I could use a real shower and some clean clothes."

"My thoughts exactly," Claire said with a small smile. "And maybe some of that lasagna I've got in the freezer."

The normalcy of the suggestion—hot food, a clean bed, everyday comforts—suddenly seemed unbearably luxurious compared to whatever Alex might be experiencing right now. Meg swallowed against the tightness in her throat.

"Hey," Claire said softly, reading her expression. "We're going to find her. But you need to be at your best when we do."

Reid arrived thirty minutes later to escort them to Claire's apartment. His weathered face looked even more lined than usual, testament to the hours of searching he'd already put in.

"Sheriff Hanover sends her regards," he said as they loaded Meg's few belongings into his unmarked car. "She's coordinating with the FBI on expanding the search parameters."

"Any leads?" Meg asked, settling into the back seat as Claire took the front.

"Maybe," Reid replied, his tone cautious. "There's a former county librarian who reached out to the department this morning. Says she has information about Blackwood and Axion Enterprises that might be relevant to our investigation."

"A librarian?" Claire sounded skeptical.

"Eleanor Blackwell," Reid clarified. "Retired five years ago, but apparently still keeps tabs on local goings-on. Her nephew Thomas went missing about six months ago—another case that might be connected to Blackwood."

The name triggered a memory for Meg. "Wait—Eleanor Blackwell as in Judge William Blackwell's widow?"

Reid nodded, glancing at her in the rearview mirror. "You know of her?"

"Only by reputation," Meg admitted. "When I was researching local property records for an insurance case a few years back, every clerk in the county offices mentioned Mrs. Blackwell. Said she knew more about land ownership in this region than all the official registrars combined."

"That tracks," Reid said with a hint of respect. "Sheriff wants to speak with her tomorrow. Thought you might want to sit in, given your involvement."

"Absolutely," Meg agreed, curiosity piqued despite her exhaustion. A county librarian with detailed knowledge of local property records could be exactly what they needed to unravel Blackwood's operation.

Claire's apartment occupied the third floor of a converted Victorian near the center of Seacliff. The building's exterior maintained its historical charm, but inside, modern security features were evident—keycard entry, security cameras in the lobby, solid core doors with substantial deadbolts.

"Home sweet home," Claire said, unlocking her door. "It's not much, but it's safe."

The apartment was quintessentially Claire—organized but not sterile, comfortable but not cluttered. Law books shared shelf space with murder mysteries and travel guides. Case files were neatly stacked on a small desk in the corner, while framed photographs of Claire with friends and family dotted the walls.

"The guest room is through there," Claire pointed down a short hallway. "Bathroom's across from it. Make yourself at home while I heat up that lasagna."

The simple domesticity of the moment—a friend offering shelter, a hot meal, a safe place to regroup—brought an unexpected lump to Meg's throat. After the madness of the past days, these small kindnesses felt almost overwhelming.

She took a long, hot shower, watching as forest dirt and dried sweat swirled down the drain. If only the memories could be washed away as easily. As she toweled off, the mirror revealed a purplish bruise forming at the back of her head where she must have hit something after being drugged—a rock, perhaps, or the floor of a vehicle.

Claire had left clean clothes on the guest bed—jeans, a soft flannel shirt, even fresh underwear still with tags attached. The thoughtfulness was so characteristic of her friend that Meg had to blink back sudden tears.

By the time she emerged, the apartment was filled with the rich aroma of baking lasagna and garlic bread. Claire had set the small dining table with actual plates and glasses, a bottle of red wine open and breathing beside them.

"You didn't have to go to all this trouble," Meg said, running a hand through her damp hair.

"It's not trouble," Claire replied simply. "It's what friends do."

They ate in comfortable silence for a while, the familiar routine of sharing a meal creating a bubble of normalcy that both knew was temporary but cherished nonetheless.

"Tell me about this librarian," Meg said finally, refilling her water glass. She'd declined the wine, not wanting anything that might further fog her still-recovering brain. "Eleanor Blackwell. What exactly did she tell Reid?"

Claire swirled her wine thoughtfully. "Not much over the phone. Just that she'd been researching Nathan Blackwood since her nephew Thomas disappeared, and that she'd uncovered 'concerning connections' between Blackwood and a financial criminal named Victor Krane."

Meg's fork paused halfway to her mouth. "Krane? Why does that name sound familiar?"

"Probably because he was all over the news about fifteen years ago," Claire replied. "Massive Ponzi scheme that collapsed and took thousands of people's retirement savings with it. Judge Blackwell—Eleanor's husband—presided over the case."

"And she thinks there's a connection to Nathan Blackwood?"

"Apparently. She wouldn't elaborate over the phone, just said she wanted to speak with someone investigating the recent disappearances." Claire took a sip of her wine. "Reid says she's respected in the community, not known for wild conspiracy theories or attention-seeking."

Meg considered this as she finished her lasagna. A financial criminal, a respected judge, disappearances that might be connected... the pieces were starting to suggest a pattern, but she couldn't quite see the full picture yet.

"When are we meeting her?" she asked.

"Tomorrow morning at the sheriff's department. Nine o'clock." Claire studied her friend's face. "You're already piecing things together in that investigator brain of yours, aren't you?"

Meg smiled slightly. "Professional hazard. Fifteen years of insurance fraud investigations trains you to look for connections, patterns in seemingly unrelated events."

"Like mysterious messages on cabin roofs and missing environmental scientists?"

"Exactly." Meg leaned back in her chair, fatigue finally catching up with her despite the good meal and stimulating puzzle. "If Blackwood is connected to this Krane person somehow, it might explain the resources he has at his disposal. Financial crimes generate serious money."

Claire began clearing the dishes, waving away Meg's attempt to help. "Rest. I've got this."

Too tired to argue, Meg moved to the couch, tucking her feet under her as she watched Claire move efficiently around the small kitchen. The familiar rhythms of everyday life—dishes being washed, leftovers being stored, counters being wiped down—created a comforting soundtrack that belied the chaos of their situation.

"You know," she said after a while, "when I arrived at your beach house a week ago, all I wanted was some quiet time to recover from my divorce. Figure out what came next."

Claire glanced over with a wry smile. "And instead you stumbled onto a mystery involving masked messages, kidnappings, and possible financial crimes. Only you, Meg Sawyer."

"Not exactly the peaceful retreat you promised," Meg acknowledged with a small laugh.

"No," Claire agreed, coming to sit beside her on the couch. "But then again, you were never very good at sitting still, even when we were in college. Remember when you were supposed to be recovering from that appendectomy and I caught you investigating the TA you suspected was changing grades for certain female students?"

"I was right about him, though," Meg pointed out.

"You usually are," Claire admitted. "It's what makes you such a good investigator." She paused, then added more quietly, "And it's why I know you won't rest until you find Alex and the others."

Meg nodded, grateful for her friend's understanding. "It feels personal now. Not just because I was there when Alex was taken, but because... I don't know. Something about this whole situation feels unfinished, like I've been drawn into it for a reason."

"Just promise me you'll be careful," Claire said, her green eyes serious. "Whoever Blackwood is, whatever his connection to Krane might be, he's demonstrated he's willing to go to extreme lengths to protect his operation."

"I promise," Meg agreed, though both knew her definition of "careful" was somewhat more flexible than Claire's would prefer.

Later, lying in the unfamiliar guest bed, Meg found her thoughts circling back to the pieces of the puzzle they'd accumulated so far. Blackwood's cabin. The message on the roof. Alex's search for her sister Emily. The connection to environmental research. Axion Enterprises purchasing properties along jurisdictional boundaries. A possible link to Victor Krane, financial criminal. A missing nephew of Judge Blackwell's widow.

The pieces swirled in her mind, occasionally aligning in tantalizing patterns before dissolving again. The last thought before sleep claimed her was of Alex—where she might be, what she might be enduring, whether they would find her before whatever Blackwood had planned could be completed.

Morning arrived with the smell of coffee and the sound of Claire moving quietly around the kitchen. Meg emerged from the guest room feeling more like herself than she had since spotting that message on Blackwood's roof. The lingering effects of the drug had largely dissipated, and her thoughts were clearer, sharper.

"You look better," Claire observed, sliding a mug of coffee across the counter. "More color in your face."

"Feel better," Meg agreed, gratefully accepting the caffeine. "Ready to meet this librarian and figure out what she knows."

They arrived at the sheriff's department fifteen minutes early, escorted by Reid who had picked them up in his personal vehicle rather than a marked car—a small precaution that reminded Meg they still weren't sure who might be watching or reporting back to Blackwood.

Sheriff Abigail Hanover met them in the small conference room, her silver-streaked hair pulled into its customary tight bun, her posture ramrod straight despite what must have been minimal sleep over the past days. Her sharp eyes assessed Meg immediately.

"You're looking recovered, Ms. Sawyer," she noted. "Good. We need clear minds today."

Before Meg could respond, the door opened again to admit a woman who could only be Eleanor Blackwell. Though she must have been in her mid-seventies, she carried herself with quiet dignity, her silver hair arranged in an elegant twist, wire-rimmed glasses perched on her nose. She wore a well-tailored navy suit that spoke of quality rather than fashion, and carried an obviously expensive leather briefcase that looked decades old but meticulously maintained.

"Sheriff Hanover," she greeted in a voice that managed to be both soft and precisely articulated. "Thank you for agreeing to meet with me." Her gaze shifted to Meg, and something like approval flickered in her blue eyes. "And you must be Ms. Sawyer. The woman who found the message on Nathan Blackwood's roof."

"Yes," Meg confirmed, immediately impressed by the older woman's composure and perceptiveness. "Thank you for coming forward with information, Mrs. Blackwell."

"Eleanor, please," she corrected gently. "And I only regret not doing so sooner. Perhaps it might have prevented what happened to you and Ms. Reeves."

They settled around the conference table, Eleanor placing her briefcase precisely before her. She opened it and withdrew several file folders, each neatly labeled and color-coded.

"I understand you're investigating Nathan Blackwood in connection with the disappearance of Alexandra Reeves," she began without preamble. "As well as her sister Emily and potentially others, including my nephew Thomas."

Sheriff Hanover nodded. "That's correct. We have evidence suggesting Blackwood and his organization, Axion Enterprises, may be involved in these disappearances."

"It's more than involvement," Eleanor stated, opening the first folder. "Nathan Blackwood is Victor Krane. And this is not merely about kidnapping. It's about revenge."

The declaration landed like a stone in still water, sending ripples of tension through the room. Eleanor seemed unfazed by their reactions, methodically laying out documents from her folder—photographs, property records, financial transactions.

"Victor Krane was sentenced to twenty-five years in federal prison fifteen years ago for orchestrating one of the largest Ponzi schemes in the state's history," she explained, her librarian's precision evident in the way she organized her information. "My husband, Judge William Blackwell, presided over the case and showed no leniency despite Krane's attempts to portray himself as a victim of market forces."

She placed a photograph on the table—a court scene showing a younger man in an expensive suit standing before a judge's bench. Despite differences in hair and facial hair, the eyes were unmistakably Blackwood's.

"Seven years ago, Krane was released on compassionate grounds—terminal pancreatic cancer, supposedly. Six months later, he was reported dead. Cremated, no autopsy." Eleanor's voice held a hint of disdain at the bureaucratic failures. "The doctor who certified his condition and later his death disappeared shortly afterward, along with a substantial sum from an offshore account."

"He faked his death," Reid concluded, studying the photographs. "And created a new identity as Nathan Blackwood."

"Complete with extensive plastic surgery," Eleanor confirmed. "But while his appearance changed, his essential nature did not. The moment he was 'dead,' he began implementing a plan for both rebuilding his financial empire and exacting revenge on everyone connected to his conviction."

She opened another folder, this one containing what appeared to be a meticulously constructed organizational chart—names, companies, properties, all connected with precisely drawn lines.

"Victor Krane blames specific individuals for his downfall—my husband, who sentenced him; Robert Reeves, the FBI agent who built the case; Margaret Chen, the prosecutor who argued it; and several key witnesses whose testimony was particularly damaging." Eleanor's voice remained steady, though her fingers trembled slightly as she pointed to each name. "Since he couldn't reach them directly without revealing he was still alive, he began targeting their families."

"Emily and Alex Reeves," Meg said, the pattern becoming clear. "Daughters of the FBI agent."

"Yes. And my nephew Thomas, a promising environmental scientist whose research accidentally uncovered chemical contamination from one of Krane's properties." A flash of pain crossed Eleanor's composed features. "Thomas disappeared six months ago while collecting water samples downstream from an Axion facility."

Sheriff Hanover leaned forward, studying the documents with focused intensity. "You've been investigating this for six months? Alone?"

A small, sad smile touched Eleanor's lips. "I was county librarian for forty-three years, Sheriff. Finding information is what I do. Property records, business filings, financial reports, personnel backgrounds—the paper trail never lies if you know how to read it."

"And what does the paper trail tell you about where they might be holding the people they've taken?" Meg asked, admiration for this formidable elderly woman growing by the minute.

Eleanor withdrew another folder from her briefcase. "Axion Enterprises owns multiple properties throughout the region, but based on utility usage, security features, and proximity to jurisdictional boundaries, I believe this one is most likely." She slid a property record across the table. "New Genesis Wellness Center. Officially a private rehabilitation facility for long-term recovery from traumatic injuries and addiction."

Reid studied the document with growing excitement. "Remote location, limited visitors, medical staff on-site who wouldn't question security protocols or restricted access..."

"The perfect place to hold people against their will," Eleanor concluded. "Particularly if sedation or other medical control methods are being employed."

"But why?" Claire asked, speaking for the first time since Eleanor's arrival. "Why take these specific people? If it's about revenge, why not simply... harm them?" She paused, clearly uncomfortable with the direction of her own question.

"Because Victor Krane is, above all, practical," Eleanor replied. "Each person taken has specialized skills he needs for rebuilding his financial operation. Emily's environmental science credentials provide legitimate cover for Axion's activities. Thomas's knowledge of local geology helps identify properties for acquisition. And I suspect Ms. Reeves was taken because she was getting too close to the truth."

Meg's mind was racing, connections forming rapidly. "So they're being held at this New Genesis place while Krane forces them to assist his operation."

"That's my theory," Eleanor confirmed. "Though without access to the facility, I can't prove it."

Sheriff Hanover had been studying the property records with growing intensity. "We'll need a warrant to search the premises. Given what you've shown us, I believe we have sufficient probable cause."

"Be cautious who you trust with this information," Eleanor warned. "Krane's operation is extensive, with connections in local government, law enforcement, and the judicial system. People who either don't know they're working for a criminal enterprise or have been compromised in some way."

"That explains how he's operated undetected for so long," Reid noted grimly.

"And why traditional law enforcement approaches have failed to locate the missing persons," Eleanor added. "You need to be extremely careful about who you share this information with."

Hanover nodded, her expression grave. "Thank you, Eleanor. This is... exceptional work. The kind of case-building most professional investigators would envy."

The elderly woman inclined her head slightly, accepting the compliment with dignity. "When you've spent your life organizing information, patterns become clear. And when the stakes are personal..." She trailed off, a flash of something—grief, determination, resolve—crossing her composed features.

"We'll move on this immediately," Hanover promised. "I'll contact Judge Peterson directly for the warrant. He has no connection to this region or the original Krane case, which should minimize the risk of interference."

"What can we do to help?" Meg asked, unwilling to be sidelined now that they finally had a concrete lead.

Hanover considered her for a moment. "You have insurance fraud investigation experience—that includes surveillance, documentation, recognizing inconsistencies?"

"Fifteen years' worth," Meg confirmed.

"Then I may have an assignment for you, depending on how we approach this facility." She turned back to Eleanor. "Would you be willing to continue assisting us? Your knowledge of these records and Krane's operation is invaluable."

"Of course," Eleanor agreed without hesitation. "Whatever it takes to find Thomas and the others."

As the meeting continued, plans taking shape for how to approach New Genesis without alerting Krane, Meg found herself watching Eleanor Blackwell with growing respect. This unassuming elderly librarian had accomplished in six months what professional law enforcement hadn't managed—identified a presumably dead financial criminal operating under a new identity, tracked his operation through shell companies and property records, and located the most likely place where kidnapped victims were being held.

All while navigating her own grief for her missing nephew.

It was a powerful reminder that ordinary people could accomplish extraordinary things when motivated by justice and love. Whatever came next—surveillance operations, warrant executions, potential confrontations with Krane's security forces—Meg felt more centered, more certain of their purpose.

They weren't just solving a mystery anymore. They were fighting for Emily, for Thomas, for Alex—people whose lives had been upended by a vengeful criminal who believed himself above the law.

And with allies like Eleanor Blackwell, they might just succeed.

CHAPTER FIVE

DEEP WOODS

Meg stood at Claire's kitchen window, coffee mug in hand, watching as dawn's first light transformed the harbor from a dark void into a textured landscape of boats, docks, and rippling water. She'd been awake for hours, her mind methodically turning over the pieces of information Eleanor Blackwell had provided.

New Genesis Wellness Center. A remote "rehabilitation facility" that might be holding Alex, Emily, Thomas, and who knew how many others. Victor Krane hiding in plain sight as Nathan Blackwood, exacting revenge on those who'd brought him to justice fifteen years ago while simultaneously rebuilding his criminal empire.

The coffee had gone cold in her mug, but she hardly noticed. She was too focused on the surveillance photos Reid had sent to her secure email last night. New Genesis looked exactly as advertised in its glossy brochures – a modern facility nestled in a picturesque mountain setting, expansive grounds with walking paths through wooded areas, a helipad for "emergency medical transport."

Perfect for a wellness center. Also perfect for moving people in and out without questions.

"You're up early," Claire observed, padding into the kitchen in slippers and a faded law school sweatshirt. Her red hair was pulled back in a messy bun, and the worry lines around her eyes had deepened over the past few days.

"Couldn't sleep," Meg admitted. "Too many thoughts circling."

Claire retrieved her own mug from the cabinet, filling it from the still-warm coffee pot. "Want to share some of those thoughts? Might help to say them out loud."

Meg turned from the window, leaning against the counter. "I keep thinking about how methodical this all is. Krane didn't just fake his death and run. He created an entirely new identity, established legitimate-looking businesses, and systematically targeted the families of those who'd brought him down."

"That level of planning suggests serious resources," Claire noted.

"And patience. He spent years setting this up." Meg sipped her cold coffee, grimacing slightly. "That's what worries me about today's operation. Someone who plans that carefully will have contingencies for everything, including law enforcement interest in New Genesis."

Sheriff Hanover had spent yesterday coordinating with Judge Peterson, securing warrants not just for New Genesis but for all properties connected to Axion Enterprises. The plan was to stage simultaneous raids at dawn, catching Krane's operation before they could move their captives or destroy evidence.

Meg and Claire were meant to join Hanover at the command post at six AM, just fifteen minutes from now. Not to participate in the raid itself – Hanover had been explicit about that – but to be available for identification and advisory purposes.

"We should get ready," Claire said, glancing at the clock. "Reid will be here in ten."

They dressed quickly, opting for practical clothing – jeans, layers that could adapt to changing temperatures, sturdy boots. Meg borrowed a waterproof jacket from Claire, the forecast calling for rain later in the morning.

As promised, Reid arrived at 5:45, looking remarkably alert for someone who had probably slept as little as they had. His cruiser was the only one on the quiet street, most of Seacliff still slumbering in the pre-dawn light.

"Morning," he greeted as they slid into the back seat. "Sheriff's already at the command post with the tactical team. New Genesis is under surveillance, no unusual activity reported so far."

"That's a good sign," Claire said, buckling her seatbelt.

"Maybe," Meg replied, unable to shake her unease. "Or maybe they're just very good at appearing normal."

Reid met her eyes in the rearview mirror, a flicker of shared concern passing between them. "Eleanor had the same reaction when I updated her last night. Said Krane was always one step ahead during his original case – anticipating investigation angles, hiding evidence before warrants could be executed."

"Is she joining us at the command post?" Meg asked.

Reid nodded. "Already there. Been helping the tactical team with the building layout, security systems, possible hiding places within the facility. Her memory for detail is extraordinary."

As they drove out of town, following the coastal highway before turning inland onto narrower, less traveled roads, Meg watched the landscape transform from small-town streets to dense forest. This was the same route they'd traveled to reach Blackwood's cabin, though they turned off earlier, following a maintenance road that wound up into the foothills.

The command post had been established in a forest service station about five miles from New Genesis – close enough for quick deployment, far enough to avoid detection. When they arrived, the small clearing was filled with tactical vehicles, communications equipment, and law enforcement personnel from multiple agencies.

Sheriff Hanover stood at a folding table covered with maps and building schematics, Eleanor Blackwell beside her, pointing out details with a precision that belied her age. FBI agents in tactical gear checked weapons and communications equipment while state police officers co-ordinated with county deputies.

"Quite the operation," Claire murmured as they approached.

"Largest multi-agency raid in the county's history," Reid confirmed. "Hanover called in every favor she had."

The sheriff looked up as they approached, acknowledging them with a brief nod. "Good, you're here. We're moving in thirty minutes. Final briefing in five."

Eleanor greeted them with her characteristic composure, though the circumstances were far from normal. "Ms. Sawyer, Ms. Winters. I'm glad you're here. We may need your assistance with identification once the facility is secured."

"Have there been any developments overnight?" Meg asked, scanning the tactical preparations with a practiced eye.

"Nothing obvious," Eleanor replied. "The facility maintains its normal patterns – shift changes, supply deliveries, even patient activities in the external areas." She gestured to surveillance photos pinned to a board nearby, showing people in casual clothing walking along garden paths accompanied by staff in medical attire.

"Could those be actual patients?" Claire wondered. "Maybe it really is a rehabilitation center too, providing cover for the... other activities."

"Entirely possible," Eleanor agreed. "The best cover operations interweave legitimate activities with illegal ones. It creates plausible deniability and makes detection much more difficult."

Hanover called for attention, gathering the team leaders around the main table. Meg, Claire, and Eleanor stood slightly back, observers rather than active participants in the tactical planning.

"Our primary objective is the safe recovery of potential captives," Hanover emphasized, her voice carrying the weight of command. "We believe they may be held in the facility's lower level, which the building plans designate as 'specialized treatment rooms.'"

She indicated the area on the schematic, a section accessible only by service elevator or a secure stairwell.

"Secondary objective is securing evidence and apprehending Nathan Blackwood, aka Victor Krane," she continued. "Intelligence suggests he visits the facility twice weekly but doesn't maintain an office there. Today is not one of his usual visiting days, but be alert regardless."

The tactical team leaders nodded, already familiar with their assignments. The plan called for simultaneous entry at three points, securing the main building quadrant by quadrant while minimizing risk to any legitimate patients or staff.

"Questions?" Hanover asked, scanning the assembled faces.

A FBI agent raised his hand. "Ma'am, what's our protocol if legitimate patients or staff are present? This isn't a typical raid scenario."

"Non-threatening presence," Hanover replied firmly. "We present the warrant, explain we're conducting a search related to specific individuals, and maintain professionalism throughout. Medical staff will remain with patients to minimize disruption or distress. Agent Collins has medical credentials and will liaison with the facility's medical director."

The briefing continued, covering communications protocols, evacuation procedures, evidence handling. Throughout it all, Meg found herself watching Eleanor, noting how the elderly woman absorbed every detail with sharp attention, occasionally making notes in a small leather-bound notebook.

"You seem concerned," Meg observed quietly when there was a brief lull.

Eleanor glanced up, her blue eyes thoughtful behind wire-rimmed glasses. "Not concerned, precisely. Just... aware of patterns. Victor Krane has evaded capture for seven years by anticipating law enforcement actions. It would be uncharacteristic of him not to have contingency plans for this very scenario."

"You think he'll be warned somehow?"

"I think we should be prepared for complications," Eleanor replied diplomatically. "And I think the 'specialized treatment rooms' may not contain what we hope to find."

Before Meg could press further, Hanover concluded the briefing, and the tactical teams began moving toward their vehicles. The operation was officially underway.

"You three will remain here with Deputy Martinez," Hanover informed them, gesturing to a young female deputy who would coordinate communications. "Once the facility is secured, we'll bring you in for identification purposes."

Meg wanted to object, to insist on being closer to the action, but she recognized the sense in Hanover's decision. They weren't trained for tactical operations, and their presence could complicate an already complex situation.

"Be careful," she said instead. "Krane's been underestimated before."

Hanover's expression softened slightly. "We'll proceed with appropriate caution, Ms. Sawyer. But it's time to end this."

With that, she joined the lead tactical vehicle, and the convoy departed, leaving Meg, Claire, Eleanor, and Deputy Martinez in the suddenly quiet command post.

"Now we wait," Claire said, settling into a folding chair beside the communications setup.

"The hardest part," Eleanor agreed, her composure intact but her hands betraying a slight tremor as she opened her notebook.

Meg found herself unable to sit, moving instead to the surveillance board, studying the photos of New Genesis with renewed intensity. Something about the facility's layout tugged at her investigator's instincts – a pattern she couldn't quite articulate but sensed nonetheless.

Martinez established the communications link, and they listened as the tactical teams approached New Genesis, their voices professionally calm as they reported positions and observations. So far, everything was proceeding according to plan.

"Perimeter teams in position," came the first update. "No visible security response. Proceeding to primary entry points."

Minutes ticked by, filled with the clipped, coded language of tactical operations. Meg paced the small space, tension building with each update.

"Entry teams breaching now. Alpha team through main entrance. Bravo team accessing east wing. Charlie team securing service entrance."

More minutes passed. Claire's knuckles had gone white where she gripped the edge of her chair. Eleanor continued making notes, her pen moving in quick, precise strokes.

"First floor secured. Medical staff and patients being gathered in common areas. No resistance encountered. Proceeding to second floor."

Then: "Second floor secured. Proceeding to lower level. Service elevator locked down, using secure stairwell access."

Meg held her breath, waiting for the next update, the one that would confirm they'd found Alex and the others. But when the transmission came, it carried a different message entirely.

"Lower level secured. No captives found. Repeat, specialized treatment rooms are empty. Evidence of recent occupation but no individuals present."

The crushing disappointment in the command post was palpable. Claire closed her eyes briefly, while Eleanor's pen stilled mid-note.

"How recent?" Hanover's voice demanded over the comm.

"Very," came the reply. "Personal effects still present. Food in one area barely touched. They left in a hurry, ma'am. Within the last few hours, according to our initial assessment."

Meg slammed her palm against the table in frustration. "They were warned. Someone tipped them off."

Martinez looked troubled but maintained her professional demeanor. "We don't know that for certain."

"Don't we?" Meg challenged. "The timing is too perfect. They cleared out just hours before a meticulously planned raid that took days to organize."

"Ms. Sawyer is right," Eleanor said, her voice calm despite the set-back. "This bears all the hallmarks of Krane's operational pattern. He maintains infiltrators in key positions precisely for this purpose."

Before Martinez could respond, Hanover's voice came through again: "We've found something. Documentation, medical files, surveillance equipment. Evidence team processing now. Also, facility director Dr. Mercer is cooperating. Claims he can provide information."

A glimmer of hope in an otherwise grim outcome. Meg exchanged glances with Claire and Eleanor, seeing her own cautious optimism reflected in their expressions.

"Deputy Martinez, bring our consultants to the facility," Hanover continued. "We need Ms. Blackwell's expertise with these files, and Ms. Sawyer may recognize details relevant to Alexandra Reeves."

Twenty minutes later, they pulled up to New Genesis Wellness Center, the serene exterior now disrupted by tactical vehicles and law enforcement personnel moving purposefully in and out. The facility itself was impressive – a modern three-story building with large windows overlooking landscaped grounds, more reminiscent of an exclusive resort than a medical facility.

Martinez escorted them through the main entrance, where staff and what appeared to be legitimate patients were being interviewed by FBI agents in a spacious lobby. The atmosphere was tense but controlled, Hanover's instructions for "non-threatening presence" clearly being followed.

"This way," Martinez directed, leading them past the common areas to a secure door marked "Administrative Personnel Only." Beyond it lay a corridor that felt distinctly different from the welcoming spaces they'd just passed through – utilitarian, monitored by security cameras, leading to another set of doors requiring keycard access.

Hanover met them there, her expression revealing nothing of her thoughts on the operation's outcome. "Dr. Mercer is in the conference room," she informed them. "Claims he was coerced into allowing the lower level to be used, that he feared for his family's safety if he refused or reported it."

"Do you believe him?" Meg asked.

"Remains to be seen," Hanover replied. "He's providing details that align with what we know, but that could be calculated cooperation now that he's been caught."

The conference room looked like it belonged in any upscale medical facility – sleek furnishings, state-of-the-art presentation equipment, a wall of windows overlooking a pine forest that stretched toward distant mountains. Dr. Mercer sat at the table, a man in his fifties with silver-streaked dark hair and the composed demeanor of someone accustomed to authority, though his current circumstances had clearly shaken that composure.

Reid was already there, along with an FBI agent Meg hadn't met, both reviewing documents spread across the table.

Dr. Mercer looked up as they entered, his gaze moving over each of them before settling on Eleanor with a flash of recognition. "Mrs. Blackwell," he said, surprise evident in his voice. "I didn't expect... that is, I had no idea you were involved in this investigation."

"My nephew Thomas is among those missing, Dr. Mercer," Eleanor replied coolly. "As you're well aware, having facilitated his captivity in your facility."

A flush crept up Mercer's neck. "I had no choice. They threatened my daughter in Boston. Showed me photos of her entering her apartment, leaving her job. Said they'd make her disappear if I didn't cooperate."

"Yet you never reported this to authorities," Hanover observed.

"They have people in law enforcement," Mercer insisted. "Showed me evidence of it – confidential police reports, internal communications. I didn't know who to trust."

It was the same pattern Eleanor had described – Krane's network extending into official channels, creating fear and uncertainty that paralyzed potential whistleblowers.

"Where are they now?" Meg asked, cutting to the heart of the matter. "The people being held in your lower level. Where were they taken?"

Mercer shook his head. "I don't know exactly. The order came at 2 AM – transfer all 'special patients' to the secondary site immediately. They were loaded into medical transport vehicles and gone within the hour."

"How many people?" Claire asked.

"Five," Mercer replied. "Three women, two men."

"Alexandra Reeves?" Meg pressed. "Was she among them?"

"Blonde woman, brought in about forty-eight hours ago? Yes." Mercer seemed eager to provide details now that the dam had broken. "She'd been injured – gunshot wound to the shoulder, multiple fractures. My staff treated her under supervision."

Relief flooded through Meg – Alex was alive, at least as of a few hours ago. Injured but receiving medical treatment.

"And the others?" Eleanor asked, her voice perfectly steady despite what must have been emotional turmoil. "Thomas Blackwell? Emily Reeves?"

"Yes, both were among the five. Thomas had been here longest, almost six months. The Reeves woman about three months." Mercer hesitated, then added, "They weren't kept sedated, if that's what you're wondering. They were... managed. Allowed limited movement within the lower level, provided with work stations, treated humanely."

"While being forced to assist a criminal operation," Hanover pointed out sharply.

Mercer had the grace to look ashamed. "I told myself they weren't being harmed physically, that I was protecting my daughter... but yes. They were prisoners, used for their expertise."

"This secondary site," Reid interjected. "You must have some information about it. Transportation routes, staff who assisted with transfers, communication protocols."

"It's called Northwood Lodge," Mercer replied. "That's all I know officially – it's supposedly another wellness facility deeper in the mountains. But I overheard conversations... it's more secure than this location. More isolated. Designed specifically for their operation rather than adapted like this facility was."

"Do you have an address? Coordinates?" the FBI agent asked.

"No exact location. Just that it's accessible only by helicopter or specialized all-terrain vehicles." Mercer gestured to a stack of files. "But there are transfer records, staff rotation schedules. Those might help narrow it down."

Eleanor had already begun examining the files, her practiced librarian's eye scanning for relevant details. "These are all coded," she observed. "Patient transfers listed under procedure names rather than destinations."

"Standard practice for privacy," Mercer confirmed. "But in this case, deliberately obscured. Only the transportation team knew the actual destination."

Meg moved to the windows, studying the mountainous terrain visible in the distance. Somewhere out there, Alex and the others were being held – moved in haste to a more secure location, their captors aware that law enforcement was closing in.

"What about Blackwood – Krane?" she asked, turning back to Mercer. "Was he here during the transfer?"

"No. He was notified, but he never comes here during operations like that. Too risky. He directs everything remotely, through secure communications." Mercer hesitated, then added, "There's something else you should know. About Alexandra Reeves."

Meg felt her pulse quicken. "What about her?"

"She's not just another captive to them. When she was brought in, Krane himself called to give specific instructions for her treatment. Said she was 'high value' and needed to be 'fully functional' as quickly as possible." Mercer's expression grew troubled. "The security around her was tighter than for the others, and they were particularly concerned about what information she might share if she regained consciousness while in medical care."

"Did she say anything?" Meg asked. "While being treated?"

"Very little. She was heavily sedated for the first twenty-four hours." Mercer looked uncomfortable. "But when they were preparing to transfer her last night, I heard her talking to one of the guards. She said, 'Tell Meg Sawyer to check the fourth notebook. She'll understand.'"

Meg felt all eyes turn to her. "Fourth notebook? What does that mean?"

"I have no idea," Mercer admitted. "That's all she said before they increased her sedation for the transfer."

Eleanor had gone very still, her hand paused over the file she'd been examining. "My research notebooks," she said quietly. "Alexandra Reeves visited my home office two weeks ago, identified herself as FBI, asked to review my findings on Krane's operation."

"You never mentioned this," Hanover said sharply.

"Because I wasn't certain of her legitimacy at the time," Eleanor replied with dignity. "Many people have claimed to be investigating Thomas's disappearance, and I've learned to be cautious. She examined my research, took some notes, and said she'd be in touch. When she disappeared, I assumed she was another dead end, or possibly even working for Krane."

"But if she's referencing your notebooks now..." Reid began.

"Then she found something in my research I missed," Eleanor concluded. "Something important enough to risk sending a message about it."

"We need to see those notebooks," Hanover decided. "All of them."

Eleanor nodded, already gathering her things. "They're in my home office. Everything I've compiled on Krane's operation over the past six months."

As they prepared to leave, Meg found herself studying Dr. Mercer with the practiced eye of an investigator accustomed to detecting deception. His story was plausible – coercion through threats to family members was a known tactic in organized crime. But something about his manner suggested he wasn't sharing everything.

"Dr. Mercer," she said casually, "how did you communicate with Krane? Phone? Email? In-person meetings?"

He looked startled by the shift in questioning. "Uh, secure phone only. Burner phones, changed regularly."

"And the warning last night – how did that come? Same method?"

"No... that came through a staff member. The night supervisor received the call and woke me."

"Which staff member?" Meg pressed, sensing they were approaching something important.

"Lisa Chen, the night nursing supervisor." Mercer's expression changed almost imperceptibly – a tightening around the eyes, a tension in his jaw. "She's been with us about six months."

"Where is she now?" Hanover asked, picking up on Meg's line of questioning.

"Off duty. She completed her shift at 6 AM and left. Standard rotation."

Reid was already moving toward the door. "I'll have someone locate her."

"Don't bother," Mercer said, resignation creeping into his voice. "She won't be found. She's one of them – Krane's people. Placed here to monitor the operation and ensure my cooperation."

"And you didn't think to mention this earlier?" Hanover demanded.

"I'm mentioning it now," Mercer replied, some of his professional authority reasserting itself. "I'm cooperating fully, telling you everything I know. Lisa Chen is not her real name. She appeared after I received the first threat against my daughter, presented perfect credentials, and was installed as night supervisor despite my objections. I understood the message clearly – she was there to watch me as much as the captives."

"Description?" Hanover snapped.

"Asian-American, mid-thirties, about five-foot-six. Always professional, extremely competent. She has a small scar on her right jawline, barely noticeable unless you're looking for it."

Meg and Eleanor exchanged glances, the same thought clearly occurring to both of them.

"We need to see those notebooks now," Meg said urgently. "And we need to know everything about this Northwood Lodge. If Alex risked sending that message, it means there's something critical in Eleanor's research that could help us find them before they disappear completely."

The drive to Eleanor's home took thirty minutes, winding through Seacliff's quiet residential streets to a modest but well-maintained Craftsman house on a corner lot. The garden showed the same meticulous attention to detail that characterized Eleanor herself – neat beds of early spring flowers, precisely trimmed shrubs, a stone path that curved gracefully to the front door.

Inside, the home reflected its owner's personality – books everywhere, but organized in a system that likely made perfect sense to Eleanor, comfortable furnishings chosen for function rather than fashion, family photographs in simple frames documenting decades of life well lived.

"My office is through here," she said, leading them through the living room to what had originally been a dining room but now served as a research space. A large desk occupied the center, its surface covered with precisely arranged stacks of papers, file folders, and notebooks. Bookshelves lined the walls, while a large corkboard displayed what appeared to be a timeline of Krane's activities over the past seven years.

Eleanor went directly to a shelf containing a row of identical leather-bound notebooks, each labeled with a number and date range. She selected the fourth in the sequence and brought it to the desk.

"This covers my research from approximately two to three months ago," she explained, opening it carefully. "When I was focusing on Krane's property acquisitions and personnel movements."

They gathered around as she turned the pages, each filled with her precise handwriting, occasional photographs or documents carefully attached, margin notes creating an additional layer of analysis.

"What exactly are we looking for?" Claire asked, overwhelmed by the volume of information.

"I don't know," Eleanor admitted. "But Alexandra must have seen something significant that I missed or didn't recognize the importance of."

They worked methodically through the notebook, page by page, everyone reading in silence, occasionally pointing out items of interest. Eleanor had documented everything from property purchases to staff hiring patterns, supply deliveries to vehicle registrations. The level of detail was impressive, but nothing immediately stood out as the critical information Alex had referenced.

Until page 73.

"Wait," Meg said, pointing to a small notation in the margin beside a list of vehicle registrations. "What's this about a specialized medical transport company?"

Eleanor peered at her own writing. "Alpine Medical Transport. They appeared about four months ago, supposedly providing specialized patient transfer services for remote medical facilities. I noted it because the company registration seemed irregular – filed in Delaware but operating exclusively in this region, with no history of similar services elsewhere."

"And they handled transfers for New Genesis?" Hanover asked.

"According to my research, yes," Eleanor confirmed. "I tracked three of their vehicles making regular trips to the facility, always during night hours, always following the same route afterward – north into the mountains, but I lost their trail where the paved roads end."

Reid had been examining the corkboard timeline while they reviewed the notebook. "Eleanor, is this map marking their route?"

She turned, nodding. "Yes. The red pins show where I was able to track the vehicles. The question mark indicates where I lost visual confirmation – a point where the forest service roads branch in three directions, all becoming increasingly difficult to navigate."

"That's near Settler's Ridge," Reid observed. "Extremely remote territory, few year-round residents, limited accessibility during winter months." He turned to Hanover. "Perfect location for a secure secondary facility."

"Northwood Lodge," Meg murmured, remembering Mercer's information. "Accessible only by helicopter or specialized all-terrain vehicles."

"Did you ever try to follow them past this point?" Hanover asked Eleanor.

A flicker of something – embarrassment, perhaps – crossed the elderly woman's composed features. "I attempted to, once. My vehicle was unsuitable for the terrain, and I was concerned about drawing attention to myself. I retreated when I observed what appeared to be security measures – cameras disguised as wildlife monitoring equipment, vehicle detection sensors embedded in the roadway."

"Professional security setup," Reid noted. "Not something a legitimate medical transport company would typically employ."

Meg was still studying the notebook, something nagging at her investigator's instincts. "Eleanor, you've noted vehicle registrations, staff credentials, property records... but what about patients? Did you ever determine who was supposedly being treated at these remote facilities?"

"I attempted to," Eleanor replied, turning to another section of the notebook. "New Genesis maintains the appearance of legitimacy by treating actual patients – people recovering from traumatic injuries, addiction, psychological trauma. Their medical outcomes are excellent, which provides perfect cover for the other activities."

"But the patients transferred by Alpine Medical Transport?" Meg pressed.

"That's where the pattern breaks down," Eleanor said, her voice taking on the precise tone of a librarian presenting research findings. "I could find no medical records, insurance claims, or family connections for any of the individuals transported by those vehicles. They appear in the system as 'private patients' with numerical designations rather than names, all expenses paid through a shell company that traces back to Axion Enterprises."

Hanover leaned forward, her focus sharpening. "So the legitimate patients enter and leave through normal channels, while the captives are moved secretly using this specialized transport company."

"Exactly," Eleanor confirmed. "And based on the timing of these transports, they align perfectly with the disappearances we're investigating. Thomas vanished six months ago – the first Alpine transport to New Genesis occurred five days later. Emily Reeves disappeared three months ago – another transport three days after that."

"And Alex was just moved within the past few hours," Meg added, the pattern now clear. "Along with all the others, to this Northwood Lodge facility."

Reid was already on his phone, coordinating with the tactical teams still processing New Genesis. "We need satellite imagery of the Settler's Ridge area, focusing on potential locations for a facility matching Mercer's description of Northwood Lodge."

Claire, who had been unusually quiet throughout the examination of Eleanor's research, suddenly straightened. "The fourth notebook," she said. "It's not just about the transport company or the route. Look at the date Alexandra Reeves visited you, Eleanor."

Eleanor checked her calendar. "April 3rd. Twelve days ago."

"And what happened the next day?" Claire prompted, excitement growing in her voice.

Eleanor's eyes widened slightly as she made the connection. "Thomas's birthday. I visited his apartment, as I've done each month since his disappearance. Left fresh flowers, checked that everything was still in order."

"And?" Claire pressed.

"And... it had been searched. Subtly, professionally – nothing obviously disturbed, but I know how Thomas kept his things. Someone had been through his research materials, his computer files."

"Alexandra must have gone there after meeting with you," Meg realized. "Following up on something she found in your fourth notebook. Something about Thomas's environmental research."

"The water samples," Eleanor breathed, the final piece clicking into place. "Thomas was testing water downstream from Axion properties when he disappeared. He found chemical compounds that shouldn't have been there – industrial solvents used in document destruction, specialized cleaning agents for removing trace evidence."

"Where are his research materials now?" Hanover asked urgently.

"Here," Eleanor replied, moving to another shelf and retrieving a plastic storage container. "I brought everything home after I realized his apartment had been searched. Didn't know what might be important, so I kept it all."

Inside the container were neatly labeled sample vials, field notebooks, data printouts, and a waterproof tablet computer. Eleanor extracted the tablet, powering it on.

"Thomas documented everything meticulously," she explained. "GPS coordinates for each sample site, chemical analyses, photographic evidence."

The tablet came to life, requesting a password. Eleanor entered it without hesitation, and Thomas's research database appeared – organized by date, location, and significance of findings.

"There," Meg said, pointing to an entry dated just days before Thomas disappeared. "Sample site SR-42. Elevated levels of multiple industrial compounds, including some only used in specialized document destruction."

Reid leaned closer. "SR-42. Settler's Ridge, site 42?"

"Thomas's coding system," Eleanor confirmed. "SR for Settler's Ridge, followed by a numerical designation for the specific collection point."

"Does it have coordinates?" Hanover asked.

Eleanor tapped the entry, and a detailed record appeared, including precise GPS coordinates and several photographs of the collection site – a small stream running through dense forest, with mountains visible in the background.

"This is upstream from where Eleanor lost track of the transport vehicles," Reid observed, comparing the coordinates to the map on the corkboard. "Following the water source would lead directly to..."

"Northwood Lodge," Meg finished. "Thomas wasn't just randomly sampling water. He found contamination and was methodically tracking it to its source when he disappeared."

"And the source was Krane's secret facility," Hanover concluded grimly. "Where he's now moved all five captives, including Alexandra Reeves."

The implications were clear to everyone in the room. Thomas had stumbled onto Krane's operation while conducting legitimate environmental research, followed the evidence to Northwood Lodge, and been captured for his discoveries. Now, he and the other captives were being held at the very facility he'd been trying to locate.

"We need to move quickly," Hanover decided, already contacting the tactical teams. "If Krane realizes we've made this connection, he might relocate the captives again, or worse."

"The terrain will be challenging," Reid warned. "Standard vehicles can't access that area. We'll need helicopters, all-terrain equipment."

"Already coordinating with state police air support," Hanover replied. "And FBI has tactical teams with wilderness training. We'll establish a staging area here—" she indicated a point on the map about three miles from the suspected facility location, "—and approach on foot for final reconnaissance."

As the law enforcement personnel mobilized, Meg found herself studying Thomas's photographs more carefully, something about the terrain nagging at her memory.

"Claire," she said suddenly, "doesn't this look familiar?"

Claire examined the image, recognition dawning. "The ridge line. It's visible from the hiking trail we took last fall – the one with the waterfall overlook."

"Exactly. We've been there, or at least near there. That trail passes within a couple of miles of these coordinates." Meg turned to Reid.

"That could give us an advantage – an approach route Krane might not have secured as heavily, since it's not accessible by vehicle."

Reid considered this, then nodded. "It's worth investigating. If we can get a team in from an unexpected direction, it might give us the element of surprise."

"I should go with that team," Meg said, determination clear in her voice. "I know that trail, I can guide them to the overlook point, and from there they can approach using Thomas's coordinates."

"Absolutely not," Claire objected immediately. "You're not law enforcement. This is a tactical operation against armed suspects."

"I wouldn't participate in the actual entry," Meg clarified. "Just guide them to the overlook, then stay back at a safe position. But time is critical, and having someone who knows that trail could save hours of navigation in unfamiliar terrain."

Hanover studied her thoughtfully. "She has a point. Even with GPS, that kind of wilderness navigation is challenging. An experienced guide who knows the specific trail could be valuable."

"I'll go too," Eleanor said quietly, surprising everyone. "I've hiked that area extensively with Thomas. I know not just the main trails but the game paths and seasonal routes."

"Mrs. Blackwell," Hanover began gently, "I appreciate your offer, but—"

"My nephew is being held in that facility," Eleanor interrupted, her composed demeanor giving way to the fierce determination that had driven her six-month investigation. "I've spent half a year tracking Victor Krane's operation while everyone else dismissed Thomas's disappearance as an unfortunate accident or a mental health crisis. I will see this through."

The room fell silent, no one quite willing to challenge the elderly woman's right to participate in her nephew's rescue. Finally, Hanover nodded.

"You'll both remain with the support team at the staging area," she said, making it clear this was non-negotiable. "Provide guidance on approaching the facility, then stay back while tactical handles the entry and extraction. Understood?"

"Perfectly," Eleanor agreed, composure returning though the determination remained evident in her eyes.

"What about me?" Claire asked, crossing her arms. "If you two are joining this expedition, I'm not sitting around waiting for updates."

Hanover looked like she might object, but after a moment of consideration, she nodded. "You can assist with the command post operations, Ms. Winters. Your prosecutor's experience might be useful for documenting evidence as it's discovered."

As the plans took shape around them, Meg felt a hand on her arm. Eleanor had moved beside her, her voice lowered for privacy.

"We should prepare ourselves," the older woman said quietly. "Tactical operations are unpredictable, and we don't know what condition Thomas and the others might be in when they're found."

The simple statement, delivered with Eleanor's characteristic composure, carried the weight of six months of uncertainty and fear. Meg covered the librarian's hand with her own.

"We'll find them," she promised. "All of them."

<hr>

THE AFTERNOON SUN CAST LONG SHADOWS ACROSS CLAIRE'S apartment as Meg stuffed an extra sweater into her backpack. Despite Hanover's insistence that they wouldn't be venturing beyond the staging area, Meg's years of investigative work had taught her to prepare for the unexpected.

"You're determined to do this," Claire observed from the doorway, her expression caught between admiration and concern.

"I have to," Meg replied simply, checking the batteries in her flashlight. "If I'd never found that message on Blackwood's roof, never dragged Alex into investigating with me, she might not be in Krane's hands right now."

"Or she might have gone alone and been taken without anyone knowing what happened to her," Claire countered. "You can't blame yourself for a criminal's actions."

Meg zipped the backpack closed, then sat heavily on the edge of the bed. "I keep thinking about what Dr. Mercer said—that Alex is 'high value' to them. What does that mean? Why would Krane consider her more important than the others?"

Claire joined her on the bed, the mattress dipping slightly under their combined weight. "Maybe because she's FBI? Access to law enforcement information would be valuable to someone like Krane."

"Maybe," Meg conceded, though something about that explanation didn't quite satisfy her investigator's instincts. "Or maybe there's something we're still missing about this whole operation."

A knock at the front door interrupted their conversation. Claire went to answer it while Meg finished her preparations. When she emerged from the guest room, she found Reid in the living room, his expression grave.

"Change of plans," he announced without preamble. "The operation's been delayed."

"Why?" Meg demanded, alarm sharpening her voice. "What's happened?"

Reid hesitated, glancing at Claire before answering. "Judge Peterson was found dead an hour ago. Apparent heart attack in his chambers."

The news landed like a physical blow. Judge Peterson had signed the warrants for the New Genesis raid just yesterday, after Hanover specifically sought him out as someone with no connection to the original Krane case.

"Heart attack," Meg repeated flatly. "Just happened to occur the day after he signed warrants against Krane's operation."

"The timing is... concerning," Reid acknowledged grimly. "Medical examiner is conducting the autopsy immediately, but preliminary examination showed no obvious signs of foul play."

"Krane wouldn't need to leave obvious signs," Claire pointed out, her prosecutor's mind already working through the implications. "There are plenty of substances that can induce cardiac arrest without leaving traceable evidence."

"Sheriff Hanover shares your suspicion," Reid confirmed. "She's implemented total operational security—only she, myself, and the lead FBI agent know the revised plans. Everyone else is on a need-to-know basis."

Meg sank onto the couch, mind racing. "If Krane can reach a federal judge, if he's willing to commit murder to protect his operation..."

"Then the stakes just got higher," Reid finished for her. "And our window for finding those captives just got narrower."

Claire paced the small living room, tension radiating from her normally composed frame. "This doesn't make sense. Killing a federal judge attracts massive attention—exactly what someone trying to operate in the shadows would want to avoid."

"Unless he's accelerating his timeline," Meg suggested. "Moving to some final phase where secrecy matters less than eliminating obstacles."

Reid nodded, clearly having reached the same conclusion. "That's Hanover's assessment as well. Which is why the operation is still proceeding, just with adjusted protocols. We move at dawn tomorrow, using only personnel directly verified by Hanover or the FBI special agent in charge."

"And us?" Meg asked.

"Still part of the plan, but with additional security measures." Reid checked his watch. "Eleanor's being brought to a secure location now. We'll join her there for final briefing and rest before deploying to the staging area at 0400."

The "secure location" turned out to be an FBI safe house outside Seacliff—a nondescript ranch-style home surrounded by enough land to ensure privacy. Two agents met them at the door, conducting thorough identity verifications before allowing them entry.

Eleanor was already there, seated at the kitchen table with a cup of tea, looking remarkably composed despite the circumstances. Her only concession to the operation ahead appeared to be a change to more practical clothing—hiking pants, sturdy boots, and a fleece jacket that somehow maintained her dignified appearance.

"Ms. Sawyer, Ms. Winters," she greeted them with a small nod. "Deputy Reid. I understand the situation has become more complicated."

"That's putting it mildly," Claire replied as they joined her at the table. "A federal judge is dead."

Eleanor's expression revealed nothing beyond polite attention, but Meg noticed her hands tighten fractionally around her teacup. "Judge Peterson. Yes, I was informed. A convenient 'heart attack' just after signing warrants against Krane's operation."

"You don't seem surprised," Meg observed carefully.

"I'm not," Eleanor admitted. "In my research into Krane's original case, I found that two key witnesses died unexpectedly before they could testify. One from a stroke, another in a single-vehicle accident on a dry, straight road. The deaths were dismissed as unfortunate coincidences, but I've always had my doubts."

The FBI agents had provided sandwiches and coffee, which no one seemed particularly interested in consuming. Reid checked his phone repeatedly, awaiting updates from Hanover, while Claire reviewed maps of the Settler's Ridge area, familiarizing herself with the terrain they'd be facing tomorrow.

"Eleanor," Meg said after a period of tense silence, "tell me more about this hiking trail you and Thomas used to take. The one near where we think Northwood Lodge is located."

The question seemed to ease some of the tension in the elderly woman's posture, drawing her back to less troubling memories. "It's called Blackbird Trail—named for the blackbirds that nest in the area during spring. Thomas and I hiked it frequently when he was growing up. It follows a natural ridge line for about three miles before descending to a series of connected waterfalls."

"That's the one Claire and I hiked last fall," Meg confirmed. "We took it to the waterfall overlook but didn't continue beyond that point."

"Few people do," Eleanor noted. "The trail becomes much less maintained after the overlook. But Thomas and I always continued to what he called the 'secret pool'—a natural swimming hole at the base of the lowest falls. From there, game trails branch in several directions, including one that would lead very close to the coordinates where we believe Northwood Lodge is located."

Reid joined the conversation, professional interest overriding his preoccupation with the operational challenges. "How difficult is the terrain beyond the overlook?"

"Challenging but not technical," Eleanor replied. "The game trails are narrow and sometimes obscured by undergrowth, but the navigation is straightforward if you know the landmarks. Thomas and I could reach the area near the Lodge's suspected location in approximately ninety minutes from the overlook."

Meg felt a renewed surge of hope. This route provided a genuine tactical advantage—an approach from a direction Krane's security might not be monitoring as heavily, using trails familiar to Eleanor but not marked on standard maps.

"We should get some rest," Reid suggested, checking the time. "0400 comes early, and tomorrow will be physically demanding even if we're just guiding the team to the staging area."

The safe house had three bedrooms, allowing them each some privacy. Meg found herself in a sparse but clean room with blackout curtains drawn tightly across the windows. Despite the day's developments and the tension of the operation ahead, exhaustion pulled at her, and she was asleep almost as soon as her head hit the pillow.

Her dreams were fragmented—forests and mountain paths, Alex's face as she was dragged away by Blackwood's men, Judge Peterson clutching his chest as an unseen hand reached toward him. She woke with a start at 3:15 AM, momentarily disoriented before remembering where she was and why.

The house was already stirring, quiet voices in the kitchen, the smell of coffee providing a beacon to follow. Claire sat at the table, hair damp from a recent shower, nursing a mug that steamed in the pre-dawn chill.

"You look like I feel," Meg observed, pouring herself coffee from the pot.

"Didn't sleep much," Claire admitted. "Kept thinking about Judge Peterson. I appeared in his courtroom dozens of times over the years. He was a good man, tough but fair. Married forty years, three grandchildren he doted on."

The personal details made the judge's death more real, more tragic—not just an operational complication but a life cut short, a family devastated. It was a sobering reminder of what they were up against: not just a financial criminal hiding his activities, but a man willing to murder a federal judge to protect his operation.

Reid and Eleanor joined them shortly, everyone moving with the hushed efficiency of people focused on a difficult task ahead. They ate a simple breakfast, reviewed the operational plans one final time, and loaded their gear into the FBI transport vehicle that would take them to the initial staging area.

The drive took them north along the coastal highway before turning inland on increasingly rural roads. The pre-dawn darkness gave the journey a surreal quality, headlights illuminating brief segments of forest and occasional glimpses of rocky outcroppings. No one spoke much, each lost in their own thoughts and preparations.

They arrived at the staging area—a small clearing at the trailhead— just as the first hint of dawn lightened the eastern sky. Tactical teams were already in position, equipment laid out with military precision, communications gear being tested. Sheriff Hanover stood with the FBI special agent in charge, both studying a topographical map spread across the hood of a vehicle.

"Our guides have arrived," Hanover announced as they approached. "Ms. Sawyer, Ms. Blackwell, thank you for your assistance with this operation. Ms. Winters, you'll remain here at the command post with Agent Lopez."

Claire nodded, though Meg could see she wasn't entirely pleased with the assignment. Separation anxiety, perhaps—after the events of the past days, being apart created its own particular stress.

The FBI agent, a woman in her forties with the lean build of a distance runner, stepped forward. "Special Agent Diane Lopez. I'll be coordinating communications between the teams. Ms. Winters, I understand you have prosecutor experience that could be valuable for documenting evidence as it's discovered."

"I've handled complex criminal cases for twelve years," Claire confirmed. "Including financial crimes and abductions."

"Good. You'll work with me to ensure proper chain of custody and evidence handling protocols." Agent Lopez turned to Meg and Eleanor. "You two will guide Alpha Team to the overlook point, then remain there with a security detail while the tactical operators continue to the facility. Clear?"

"Perfectly," Eleanor replied with a composure that belied both her age and the circumstances.

Alpha Team consisted of six FBI tactical operators and Reid, all dressed in forest-appropriate camouflage and carrying compact but clearly professional gear. Their team leader, Agent Mercer, conducted a final equipment check before turning to Meg and Eleanor.

"We move at your pace," he said, his tone respectfully professional. "Your knowledge of the terrain is our advantage. If anything seems wrong or unfamiliar as we proceed, stop immediately and alert me."

The hike began in the gray half-light of early dawn, shadows still thick among the trees, dew dampening their boots and pant legs within minutes. Meg and Eleanor led the way, setting a pace that was deliberate but steady, Reid positioning himself just behind them while the tactical team spread out in a loose formation designed to minimize visual and audio detection.

The first mile passed in near silence, broken only by the natural sounds of the forest awakening—birds beginning their morning chorus, occasional rustling in the underbrush as small animals moved about their business. The trail was well-maintained at this stage, gently ascending the ridge line that would eventually lead to the waterfall overlook.

Eleanor moved with surprising agility for her age, each step placed with the confidence of someone intimately familiar with the terrain. Occasionally she would point out features not obvious to the casual hiker—a particular rock formation, a distinctive tree, subtle markers that helped confirm they were on the correct path.

"Thomas and I used to play a game when he was young," she explained quietly during a brief rest stop, her voice pitched low to avoid carrying in the morning stillness. "I would describe a specific landmark, and he would navigate to it without further guidance. It taught him to truly see the forest, not just move through it."

The simple story offered a glimpse of the relationship between Eleanor and her nephew—a bond built on shared experiences and mutual respect. It made the stakes of their mission even more tangible, more personal.

As they continued upward, the trail narrowed and became steeper, requiring more careful footing. The tactical team maintained their professional focus, moving efficiently despite the challenging terrain, communications limited to occasional hand signals and single-word confirmations.

"Almost to the overlook," Meg said as they approached a distinctive bend in the trail marked by a lightning-struck pine. "About a quarter-mile ahead."

Agent Mercer acknowledged with a nod, then signaled his team to perform another security sweep before proceeding. Two operators moved ahead, checking for any signs that the area might be monitored or compromised.

They returned ten minutes later, reporting all clear, and the group continued to the overlook—a natural rocky outcropping that provided a spectacular view of the waterfall system below and the forested valley beyond. From this vantage point, with the morning sun now fully risen, they could see for miles across the wilderness area.

"There," Eleanor said quietly, pointing to a distant ridge line partially obscured by morning mist. "That's where Thomas's water sample site SR-42 would be located. And somewhere just beyond it…"

"Northwood Lodge," Reid finished, studying the terrain through compact binoculars. "Visibility is limited by the tree cover, but there's definitely something man-made visible just below that ridge. Structures of some kind."

The tactical team set up observation equipment, including a high-powered spotting scope and thermal imaging devices. Agent Mercer spent several minutes studying the distant site before turning to Eleanor.

"Mrs. Blackwell, can you describe the game trail that would lead us from the base of the waterfalls toward that ridge? Any distinctive features we should look for?"

Eleanor nodded, her expression focused. "From the pool at the base of the falls, you'll find a narrow trail heading northeast, marked by a rock formation that resembles a turtle's back. Follow that for approximately half a mile until you reach a fallen cedar that crosses the path. The trail splits there—take the right fork, which will lead uphill through a stand of younger trees before emerging on the far side of the ridge."

The precision of her directions, delivered from memory, impressed even the tactical operators. Mercer made careful notes, then consulted with Reid and the other team members.

"We'll proceed on foot from here," he decided. "Mrs. Blackwell, Ms. Sawyer, this is where you'll remain with Agents Chen and Rodriguez for security. We'll maintain radio contact through Deputy Reid."

As the tactical team prepared to continue down the trail toward the waterfalls, Meg found herself studying the distant ridge where Northwood Lodge was presumably located. Somewhere in that facility, Alex and the other captives were being held, their specialized skills leveraged for Krane's operation, their freedom sacrificed to his revenge scheme.

"They'll find them," Eleanor said quietly, seeming to read Meg's thoughts. "Thomas has survived six months in captivity. He's strong, resourceful. And if Alexandra Reeves managed to send a message even while injured and under guard, she's equally determined."

The tactical team departed, moving with practiced stealth down the steep trail toward the waterfall system. Agents Chen and Rodriguez established a small security perimeter around the overlook, setting up communications equipment to maintain contact with both the advancing team and the command post back at the trailhead.

"Now we wait," Reid said, settling onto a rock with his binoculars trained on the distant ridge. "Tactical will maintain radio silence until they're in position near the facility. Could be two hours or more before we hear anything."

Waiting had never been Meg's strong suit. As an investigator, she preferred action—following leads, interviewing witnesses, building cases piece by methodical piece. This enforced inactivity while others took the risks and did the work chafed against her nature.

Eleanor, by contrast, seemed perfectly content to wait, her patience perhaps honed by decades as a librarian and months of meticulous research into Krane's operation. She sat with perfect posture on a fallen log, occasionally scanning the valley with a pair of borrowed binoculars, but otherwise showing no signs of anxiety or impatience.

"How did you do it?" Meg asked her after nearly an hour of silence. "Maintain the investigation for six months with no official support, no confirmation Thomas was even alive?"

Eleanor lowered the binoculars, considering the question. "When you've lived as long as I have, Ms. Sawyer, you develop a certain perspective on persistence. My husband used to say that justice isn't a sprint but a marathon—the truth emerges not through dramatic revelations but through steady, methodical pursuit."

"Your husband sounds like a wise man."

"He was," Eleanor agreed, a hint of sadness touching her composed features. "We were married forty-two years. He taught me that systems may be flawed, but they're the best mechanism we have for pursuing justice, provided people of integrity insist on their proper function."

"Is that why you became a librarian?"

Eleanor smiled slightly. "I was a librarian long before I met William. But yes, our professions complemented each other. He believed in the law as an instrument of justice. I believed in information as the foundation of informed decisions. Together, we tried to build something meaningful in this community."

The radio crackled softly, drawing their attention. Agent Chen adjusted the frequency, listening to a brief transmission before turning to them.

"Alpha Team has reached the base of the falls," she reported. "Proceeding to the game trail as directed. No signs of security measures or surveillance yet."

Reid nodded, his expression revealing little of his thoughts. "Good progress. They're moving faster than expected."

Another hour passed, the sun climbing higher, burning off the morning mist and revealing more of the valley below. The distant ridge where Northwood Lodge was located stood in sharper relief now, though the facility itself remained largely obscured by the dense forest.

The radio crackled again, Agent Rodriguez answering this time. His expression shifted as he listened, becoming more alert, more focused.

"Alpha Team has visual on the facility," he reported, turning to them. "Confirms at least five buildings in a secured compound, multiple guards visible, two vehicles in what appears to be a loading area."

"Any sign of the captives?" Meg asked immediately.

"Negative. No personnel visible outside the buildings except security. Team is continuing reconnaissance, establishing full perimeter visualization before planning entry."

It was progress, but frustratingly limited. Knowing the facility existed, that it was staffed and secured, told them nothing about whether

Alex and the others were still there, what condition they might be in, or how to extract them safely.

"Movement at the facility," Agent Chen announced suddenly, listening to another transmission. "Multiple personnel emerging from the main building. Appears to be... a medical evacuation scenario. Gurney being loaded into one of the vehicles."

Meg and Eleanor exchanged alarmed glances. A medical evacuation could indicate many things—an injured guard, a legitimate medical emergency—but given the circumstances, it more likely meant one of the captives was being moved, possibly due to injury or illness.

"Can they identify who's on the gurney?" Reid asked urgently.

Agent Chen relayed the question, listening intently to the response. "Negative. Distance too great for clear identification. But tactical team confirms it's an adult female with dark hair."

"Not Alex then," Meg said, relief mingling with continued concern. "Her hair is blonde. Could be Emily Reeves or the other woman Dr. Mercer mentioned."

"Vehicle is departing the compound," Agent Rodriguez reported. "Heading north on a service road. Tactical team requests permission to proceed with entry plan while security forces are reduced."

Reid conferred briefly with the agents, then made the call. "Permission granted. Primary objective remains locating and extracting captives. Secondary objective is securing evidence and apprehending suspects."

The radio fell silent as the tactical team prepared for entry. Minutes stretched into an eternity of waiting, the peaceful forest setting at odds with the knowledge that a high-risk operation was unfolding just a few miles away.

"Something's wrong," Eleanor said suddenly, her gaze fixed on the distant ridge.

Meg followed her line of sight, at first seeing nothing unusual. Then she noticed it—a thin column of smoke rising from where the facility should be located, barely visible against the blue sky but definitely present.

"Fire," Reid confirmed, already reaching for the radio. "Could be tactical deployment of smoke grenades for cover, or—"

The radio burst to life before he could complete the thought, Agent Mercer's voice tense but controlled. "Command, this is Alpha Team. Facility is compromised. Repeat, facility is compromised. Multiple small fires, evidence destruction in progress. Proceeding with immediate entry."

The next minutes were a blur of radio communications, tactical movements, and rising tension at the overlook. The tactical team had entered the facility, encountering sporadic resistance from the remaining security personnel. They reported systematic destruction of evidence—documents being burned, computers destroyed, any trace of the facility's true purpose being methodically erased.

"They're clearing out," Reid said grimly. "They must have been warned somehow."

"The captives," Meg pressed, anxiety tightening her chest. "Have they found any of them?"

Agent Chen shook his head. "Still clearing the buildings. No confirmation yet."

Eleanor had gone very still, her usual composure finally cracking to reveal the worry beneath. "They knew we were coming. Again. Despite all the precautions, all the security measures."

"Krane's reach is extensive," Reid acknowledged. "But this operation involved only personnel directly vetted by Sheriff Hanover and the FBI special agent in charge. The leak must have come from somewhere else."

"Or someone we all trust implicitly," Meg suggested quietly.

Before Reid could respond, the radio crackled again. This time, the transmission brought better news.

"Command, we've located two captives. Repeat, two captives secured. Adult males, one approximately 30-35 years old, one approximately 40-45. Both conscious and mobile."

"Thomas," Eleanor breathed, hope and fear warring in her voice. "It must be Thomas and the other male captive Dr. Mercer mentioned."

"What about the women?" Meg demanded. "Alex and Emily Reeves? The third woman?"

Agent Rodriguez relayed the question, then listened to the response. "Negative. No sign of female captives. Male subjects report all three women were moved approximately one hour ago. Medical evacuation we observed was Emily Reeves, reportedly experiencing complications from prolonged sedation."

The news landed like a stone in Meg's stomach. They'd found Thomas and the other man, but Alex, Emily, and the third woman were gone—moved just before their arrival, their trail already cold.

"Ask if the male captives know where the women were taken," Eleanor suggested, her composed pragmatism reasserting itself despite the emotional situation.

The question was relayed, the answer coming back moments later. "Negative. Captives were kept in separate areas, only allowed limited interaction. They were aware the women were being moved but not informed of the destination."

Reid was already coordinating with the command post, arranging medical transport for the rescued captives and deploying additional resources to search for the vehicle that had left with Emily Reeves. Agent Mercer continued to report as his team secured the facility—evidence of hasty departure, systematic destruction of documents and equipment, a facility designed for both legitimate medical treatment and something more sinister.

"We should head back to the command post," Reid decided after conferring with the agents. "The rescued captives will be brought out via helicopter to the nearest medical facility. We can meet them there and perhaps get more information about the operation and where the women might have been taken."

As they prepared to depart the overlook, Meg found herself studying Eleanor's face—the controlled hope, the lingering worry, the determination that had driven her six-month investigation. They had found Thomas—a partial victory snatched from what had nearly been a complete failure. But Alex and the other women remained in Krane's hands, their location unknown, their fate uncertain.

The hike back to the trailhead seemed both faster and more emotionally complex than the journey in. Relief at Thomas's rescue mingled with continued concern for the missing women and frustration at another near-miss with Krane's operation. The tactical team had secured the facility but missed Krane himself, who had apparently departed hours before the raid.

At the command post, they found organized chaos—FBI agents coordinating with local law enforcement, medical teams preparing to receive the rescued captives, Sheriff Hanover directing operations with calm efficiency. Claire rushed to meet them, relief evident in her expression at seeing them safe.

"They found Thomas," she told Eleanor, taking the older woman's hands in hers. " Doctor's initial assessment is dehydration and mild malnutrition, but no life-threatening injuries."

The news visibly lifted a weight from Eleanor's shoulders, though she maintained her characteristic restraint. "And the other man?"

"Jason Martinez, environmental engineer," Claire supplied. "Similar condition to Thomas. He was apparently abducted about five months ago while conducting soil samples near another Axion property."

"But no sign of Alex or the other women," Meg said, needing the confirmation despite already knowing the answer.

Claire shook her head. "They were moved shortly before the raid. Sheriff Hanover has every available unit searching for the vehicle that transported Emily Reeves, but so far no sightings."

A helicopter approached from the direction of the facility, the distinctive thump of its rotors growing louder as it prepared to land in the clearing. FBI agents created a secure perimeter as the aircraft touched down, rotors still spinning as medical personnel rushed forward with gurneys.

Meg watched as two men were carefully transferred from the helicopter—both conscious but clearly weakened, one with curly brown hair who bore a striking resemblance to Eleanor, presumably Thomas. The other man was older, his face gaunt beneath several days' growth of beard, but his eyes alert as he scanned his surroundings.

Eleanor stepped forward as Thomas was wheeled toward the waiting ambulance, maintaining her composure through what must have been an overwhelming emotional moment. Thomas reached for her hand as she approached, his fingers clasping hers with visible relief.

"Aunt Eleanor," he said, his voice hoarse but steady. "You found me."

"Of course I did," she replied simply, years of worry and investigation distilled into those four words. "I never stopped looking."

Their reunion was necessarily brief, the medical team insistent on getting both men to the hospital for proper treatment. Eleanor would travel with Thomas in the ambulance, while Sheriff Hanover wanted Meg and Claire to join her at the command center in Seacliff to process what they'd learned and plan next steps for locating the missing women.

As they prepared to depart, the older rescued captive—Jason Martinez—suddenly called out to them from his gurney.

"Wait," he said urgently. "You need to know—Krane isn't finished. This was just phase one of his operation."

Sheriff Hanover stepped forward. "What do you mean, Mr. Martinez? What operation?"

"The revenge scheme is just a cover for something bigger," Martinez replied, his voice growing weaker but his determination evident. "He's been using us—our skills, our knowledge—to build something. A financial mechanism of some kind, designed to trigger market instability when activated."

"Market instability?" Claire repeated, her prosecutor's mind immediately grasping the implications. "You mean like a market crash?"

Martinez nodded weakly. "Targeted at specific sectors, specific companies. All connected to the people who brought him down fifteen years ago. He calls it 'The Reset'—wiping the slate clean, starting over with him in control."

The medical team insisted on moving him then, his condition requiring immediate attention, but his words lingered in the clearing like a physical presence. The stakes had just escalated dramatically—not just the lives of three women, but potentially financial chaos affecting thousands or even millions of innocent people.

"He's going to crash the market as revenge?" Claire said as they drove back toward Seacliff, the morning's operation already feeling like it had happened days rather than hours ago. "That seems excessive even for someone as vindictive as Krane."

"It's not just revenge," Meg realized, the pattern finally becoming clear in her mind. "It's profit too. If he knows which market sectors will collapse and when, he can position himself to benefit enormously from the crash. He'd emerge not just with his revenge complete but potentially wealthier and more powerful than before his original conviction."

Reid nodded grimly from the driver's seat. "Classic market manipulation, just on an unprecedented scale. And with Alexandra Reeves and the other women still in his custody..."

"He has the final pieces he needs to execute the plan," Meg finished. "Whatever their specialized skills are, they must be critical to this 'Reset' he's planning."

The implications settled over them like a dark cloud. Finding Alex and the others wasn't just about rescuing kidnap victims anymore—it was about preventing what could be one of the largest financial crimes in history, a market manipulation scheme that would devastate countless innocent people while enriching the man who had orchestrated it all.

As they approached Seacliff, Meg found herself thinking of Eleanor's words from earlier: "When you've lived as long as I have, Ms. Sawyer, you develop a certain perspective on persistence." They had rescued Thomas and Jason Martinez—a significant victory by any measure. But the greater challenge still lay ahead, with the stakes higher than any of them had imagined.

The game wasn't over. It was just entering its most dangerous phase.

CHAPTER SIX

PAPER TRAILS

The morning after the raid on Northwood Lodge dawned with a biting chill that belied the calendar's insistence it was spring. Meg stood at Claire's kitchen window, hands wrapped around a mug of coffee that had long since gone cold, watching raindrops trace jagged paths down the glass. The weather matched her mood—gray, unsettled, pregnant with the promise of something worse to come.

"You should eat something," Claire said from behind her, the quiet concern in her voice cutting through Meg's dark reverie.

"Not hungry."

"Didn't ask if you were hungry," Claire countered, sliding a plate of toast onto the counter beside her. "Said you should eat."

The familiar banter—Claire's no-nonsense nurturing, Meg's stubborn self-neglect—felt surreal against the backdrop of what they'd experienced. Yesterday, they had rescued two men from captivity while failing to find three women. Yesterday, they had learned that Victor Krane, financial criminal presumed dead, was alive and operating an elaborate revenge scheme under a new identity. Yesterday, a federal judge had died under suspicious circumstances mere hours after signing warrants against Krane's operation.

And today, they were supposed to attend Judge Peterson's funeral.

"What time do we need to leave?" Meg asked, finally turning from the window.

"Service starts at eleven. Reid's picking us up at ten-thirty." Claire was already dressed in somber navy, her red hair pulled back in a neat chignon, her prosecutor's mask of composure firmly in place despite the shadows beneath her eyes.

Meg nodded, forcing herself to take a bite of toast. It tasted like cardboard, but she chewed mechanically, knowing Claire wouldn't relent until she'd eaten something. "Thomas is being discharged this morning, right?"

"Yes. Eleanor's bringing him straight to the service. Jason Martinez is still under observation—that infection from the untreated wound on his leg needs more aggressive antibiotic therapy."

The mundane details—hospital discharges, transportation arrangements, funeral schedules—created a veneer of normalcy that felt both comforting and deeply false. Nothing about their situation was normal. Three women remained captive, a judge was dead, and the man responsible remained at large, always seeming one step ahead of their efforts to stop him.

Meg forced down another bite of toast before setting the plate aside. "I'm going to shower."

Under the hot spray, she allowed herself the brief luxury of unfocused thought, letting the water sluice away the tension that had settled like concrete between her shoulder blades. She rested her forehead against the cool tile, memories of the raid on Northwood Lodge playing through her mind on an endless loop—the frantic search through emptied rooms, the moment of discovering Thomas and Jason while realizing the women had been moved just hours before their arrival, the systematic destruction of evidence that suggested someone had warned Krane they were coming.

As she dressed in the black suit she'd packed for no particular reason when fleeing to Claire's beach house after her divorce, Meg caught a glimpse of herself in the bathroom mirror. She hardly recognized the woman staring back—dark circles under hazel eyes, a new hardness to her mouth, an intensity in her expression that hadn't been there a week ago when her biggest concern was processing Daniel's betrayal.

When she emerged, Claire was in full prosecutor mode, phone pressed to her ear as she paced the small living room.

"No, I understand the concerns, but postponing the Henderson trial again is not an option," she was saying, her professional voice brooking no argument. "The defense has already received two continuances... Yes, I'm aware of the scheduling conflict... Then find someone else to cover the Mercer deposition."

Meg settled onto the couch, listening with half an ear as Claire navigated the demands of her day job—a world of trial schedules, depositions, and plea agreements that seemed impossibly distant from kidnappings and market manipulation schemes. There was something reassuring about Claire's crisp efficiency, the way she compartmentalized the chaos of their current situation to focus on the immediate professional demands.

When she ended the call, Claire sighed, dropping onto the couch beside Meg. "Sorry about that. Defense counsel in the Henderson case trying to weasel out of the trial date again."

"You're still working your regular cases?" Meg asked, surprised despite herself. "Even with all...this?"

Claire shrugged, a gesture belied by the tension evident in her shoulders. "Crime in Seacliff didn't conveniently pause because we stumbled onto a financial conspiracy. The DA's already giving me side-eye for the time I've taken to help with the Krane investigation."

"I'm sorry," Meg said, guilt threading through her voice. "I've completely disrupted your life."

"Don't be ridiculous," Claire replied, bumping Meg's shoulder with her own. "This isn't about you disrupting my carefully scheduled life.

It's about a criminal who's kidnapped people, manipulated markets, and probably murdered a federal judge."

"Still..." Meg began, but Claire cut her off with a look.

"Meg Sawyer, don't you dare apologize for dragging me into an investigation that's saved two lives already and might save three more. That's not how friendship works, and you know it."

Before Meg could respond, a knock at the door announced Reid's arrival. He stood in the hallway looking simultaneously uncomfortable in his dress uniform and weary beyond words, the lines around his eyes deeper than they had been just days ago.

"Ladies," he greeted them, his usual formality softened by shared experience. "Sheriff Hanover's meeting us at the service. She's been at the station all night coordinating with the FBI on search parameters for Eagle's Rest."

"Any progress?" Meg asked as they descended to Reid's waiting car.

"Nothing concrete. Satellite imagery confirms it's an extensive property, but the structures are largely obscured by tree cover. Thermal imaging shows heat signatures consistent with occupation, but we can't determine numbers or positions with any accuracy."

The drive to St. Michael's Episcopal Church passed in contemplative silence, each lost in their own thoughts. The rain had intensified, drumming against the car roof and blurring the coastal landscape beyond the windows. Meg watched droplets race down the glass, her mind drifting to Alex, Emily, and Valerie—where they might be, what conditions they might be enduring, whether they were even still alive.

St. Michael's was a stone edifice that had weathered a century of coastal storms, its gray walls and stained glass windows projecting permanence in a way that felt almost accusatory given the circumstances. The parking lot was filled with law enforcement vehicles from multiple jurisdictions—Judge Peterson had been respected across county lines, his death sending shockwaves through the regional judicial system.

Inside, the church was already crowded, the air heavy with the scent of flowers and rain-dampened wool. Reid led them to seats reserved for those connected to the investigation, where Sheriff Hanover waited, her silver-streaked hair pulled into its customary severe bun, her uniform immaculate despite what must have been minimal sleep.

"Ms. Sawyer, Ms. Winters," she greeted them with a nod that conveyed both acknowledgment and shared burden. "Thomas Blackwell and his aunt are seated toward the front, with Judge Peterson's family."

Meg glanced in the indicated direction, spotting Eleanor's straight-backed figure beside a young man who could only be Thomas. Even from a distance, the family resemblance was evident—the same composed posture, the same precise movements as Thomas leaned to whisper something to his aunt. He looked remarkably recovered for someone who'd spent six months in captivity, though Meg could detect a certain careful fragility in the way he held himself, a wariness in his occasional glances toward the entrance.

"Judge Peterson's widow requested their presence," Hanover explained, noting Meg's questioning look. "Apparently she and Eleanor have been friends for decades. Book club."

The simple detail—two elderly women sharing literature and friendship over years—humanized the situation in a way the investigation reports hadn't. Judge Peterson wasn't just a victim in their case; he was a man with a life, relationships, a place in the community that extended far beyond his judicial role.

As the service began, Meg found herself studying the mourners around them. Judges, attorneys, law enforcement officers—the professional circles of a man who had dedicated his life to the law. But there were others too—ordinary citizens, shopkeepers, people whose connections to Peterson might have been casual or profound, each face bearing the particular gravity of communal loss.

In the front pew, Peterson's widow sat surrounded by family—adult children and what appeared to be grandchildren, ranging from teenagers to a toddler who periodically disrupted the solemn proceedings with questions pitched too loudly in the reverential quiet. Rather than seeming inappropriate, the child's innocent interruptions provided moments of lightness in the heavy atmosphere, small reminders of the life that continued even in grief's shadow.

The eulogies painted a portrait of a man Meg wished she'd had the opportunity to know—principled but compassionate, serious about the law but with a surprising dry wit, devoted to his family while maintaining a profound commitment to public service. One speaker, a fellow judge, described Peterson as "the kind of jurist who understood that justice without mercy is merely vengeance with a gavel."

As the service concluded and the mourners moved toward the reception hall, Meg noticed a distinguished older man approach Eleanor and Thomas, his bearing suggesting authority tempered by genuine concern. He spoke briefly with them, Thomas's posture tensing visibly during the exchange, before moving on to offer condolences to Peterson's widow.

"Who's that?" Meg asked Reid quietly.

"Chief Judge Marcus Harmon," he replied, keeping his voice low. "Peterson's colleague on the federal bench. They've served together for nearly twenty years."

"Harmon," Meg repeated, the name triggering a connection in her mind. "Wasn't he the judge who kept blocking our warrants for searching Blackwood's properties?"

Reid nodded, his expression carefully neutral in the public setting. "Sheriff Hanover had to specifically seek out Peterson for the New Genesis warrants because Harmon repeatedly found reasons to delay or question the probable cause."

The coincidence prickled at Meg's investigator instincts. One judge repeatedly obstructed their investigation, while the one who finally approved their warrants died of a "heart attack" hours later.

"Do we know anything about Harmon's connection to Krane's original case?" she asked, watching as the judge moved through the reception, shaking hands and offering condolences with practiced gravity.

"Nothing specific," Reid admitted. "But Eleanor might. She's researched everyone connected to the original prosecution."

Before they could pursue that line of thinking, Sheriff Hanover approached, her expression conveying the need for discretion even before she spoke.

"We need to step outside," she said quietly. "There's been a development."

They followed her through a side door to a small garden area, partially sheltered from the rain by an ancient oak tree. Once certain they were alone, Hanover turned to them, her composed features betraying the barest hint of disturbance.

"Medical examiner just called. Judge Peterson's autopsy results came back. It wasn't a heart attack."

"Poison?" Meg guessed, remembering Claire's earlier speculation about substances that could induce cardiac symptoms.

"No," Hanover replied, her voice tight. "Someone physically stopped his heart. Precise pressure applied to specific points on the chest—expertly done to mimic a natural cardiac event. No bruising, no external indications of assault. Only detectable through microscopic examination of the tissue."

The implications settled over them like the damp chill of the rain-soaked garden. Not a poisoning that could have been administered subtly, perhaps even hours before death, but a direct physical assault requiring close contact, specific knowledge, and the opportunity to act without witnesses.

"That's... specialized knowledge," Claire said slowly. "Not something an ordinary criminal would know how to do."

"No," Hanover agreed grimly. "It's a technique taught to certain special operations units, some intelligence agencies. The kind of killing method that requires specific training."

"A professional hit," Reid concluded, his weathered face hardening. "Made to look like natural causes."

"But who would have access to Judge Peterson in his chambers?" Meg wondered. "That's a secure area of the courthouse."

"Someone with legitimate reason to be there," Hanover replied. "Another judge, court staff, attorneys with scheduled meetings."

The implication hung unspoken between them—the killer was likely someone within the judicial system itself, someone with both access to Peterson and the specialized knowledge to stop his heart in a way that initially appeared natural.

"We need to get back inside," Hanover decided after a moment. "Maintain normal appearances while we process this information. Reid, contact the FBI team and update them on the M.E.'s findings. Ms. Winters, Ms. Sawyer, stay close to Eleanor and Thomas. I want to speak with them as soon as it's appropriate to leave the reception."

The reception had the surreal quality of all such gatherings—genuine grief mingling with social obligation, quiet conversations punctuated by occasional inappropriate laughter quickly stifled, food consumed mechanically by people whose appetites had been suppressed by sorrow but who understood the rituals required of them.

Meg and Claire made their way to where Eleanor and Thomas stood near a window, slightly removed from the main flow of mourners. Up close, Thomas looked even more fragile than he had in the church, his composed demeanor clearly requiring significant effort to maintain.

"Ms. Sawyer, Ms. Winters," Eleanor greeted them, her voice pitched low. "Deputy Reid mentioned you'd be attending. This is my nephew, Thomas."

"We've met, technically," Thomas said, offering his hand. His grip was firmer than Meg had expected given his physical condition, his eyes sharper. "Though I was pretty heavily sedated at the time. Thank you both for your part in finding me and Jason."

"I'm just glad you're recovering," Meg replied, meaning it. "How are you feeling?"

A shadow crossed his face, quickly mastered. "Physically, improving. The rest... will take time."

The simple acknowledgment of trauma without minimization or overemphasis spoke to a psychological resilience that matched his aunt's.

These were people who faced reality squarely, neither denying difficulties nor allowing themselves to be defined by them.

"Judge Peterson was a good man," Eleanor said after a moment, her gaze drifting to where the widow was receiving condolences from a seemingly endless line of mourners. "Catherine and I have been friends since our husbands served on the bench together. William always said Robert Peterson was one of the few colleagues he trusted implicitly."

"Were they close professionally?" Claire asked, the casual question masking what Meg recognized as careful information gathering.

"Very. They took similar approaches to the law—principled but not rigid, focused on justice rather than mere technical application of statutes." Eleanor's eyes, sharp behind her wire-rimmed glasses, studied them with the librarian's gift for seeing beyond the surface question to the underlying purpose. "Robert was also involved in the Krane prosecution, though in a less public role than William. He was the magistrate who approved the original search warrants for Krane's properties."

This new information clicked into place like a tumbler in a lock—Peterson's connection to the original case, his willingness to sign warrants for their current investigation, his subsequent death in circumstances that increasingly appeared to be murder.

"Aunt Eleanor," Thomas said quietly, his gaze fixed on a point across the room. "Judge Harmon is coming this way again."

Something in his tone—not quite fear, but a wariness that transcended normal social discomfort—caught Meg's attention. She turned slightly, observing Chief Judge Harmon's approach with new awareness.

"Thomas, Eleanor," Harmon greeted them, his voice carrying the practiced warmth of a public figure. "I was just speaking with Catherine. She mentioned you might be joining us for dinner next week, once things have... settled."

"If Thomas is feeling up to it," Eleanor replied, her tone polite but reserved. "His recovery remains our priority."

Harmon's gaze shifted to Thomas, something assessing in his expression that raised the hair on the back of Meg's neck. "Of course. Remarkable recovery already, though. Not many would be attending public functions so soon after such an... ordeal."

"Judge Peterson was important to our family," Thomas said simply. "Some obligations transcend personal discomfort."

Harmon nodded, seeming satisfied with the response, before turning his attention to Meg and Claire. "I don't believe we've met. Marcus Harmon."

"Claire Winters, county prosecutor's office," Claire supplied, her professional mask firmly in place. "And this is Meg Sawyer, consulting with the sheriff's department on a related investigation."

"Ah, yes. The investigation Robert was so... enthusiastic about supporting." Something in Harmon's tone suggested he didn't share that enthusiasm. "Tragic timing, his passing. Just when you'd finally secured those warrants you've been pursuing."

The observation, delivered with such casual precision, sent a cold wave through Meg's chest. Was he actually acknowledging the connection between Peterson's approval of their warrants and his subsequent death? Or was she reading too much into a comment that might be innocent, if insensitive?

"Very tragic," Claire agreed, her prosecutor's instincts visibly engaged. "Judge Peterson's guidance will be deeply missed by our office."

"Indeed." Harmon's smile never reached his eyes. "Well, I should continue my rounds. Eleanor, Thomas—we'll speak again soon, I'm sure. Ms. Winters, Ms. Sawyer—a pleasure."

As he moved away, Meg noticed Thomas release a breath he'd apparently been holding, his shoulders dropping fractionally from their rigid position.

"You don't like him," she observed quietly.

Thomas exchanged a glance with Eleanor before responding. "Judge Harmon makes me... uncomfortable. There's something beneath the professional exterior that feels... wrong."

"Thomas's instincts about people are quite refined," Eleanor added, her voice barely above a whisper. "A skill that likely kept him alive during his captivity."

Before Meg could pursue this line of conversation, Sheriff Hanover approached, her expression conveying urgency beneath a veneer of social propriety.

"Ms. Blackwell, Mr. Blackwell," she greeted them formally. "If you're ready to leave, Deputy Reid is available to escort you home. I believe the doctor recommended limited public exposure for the first few days after discharge."

The pretext was transparent but effective. Within minutes, they had made their excuses to the appropriate people and were following Reid to his vehicle, the rain having mercifully subsided to a fine mist that beaded on their coats and hair.

"Not my home," Eleanor said firmly as they reached the parking area. "I've arranged temporary accommodations at a property owned by a friend—more secure than my house, and unknown to anyone who might be watching my movements."

Reid nodded, unsurprised. "Sheriff Hanover mentioned you might have alternative arrangements. She'd like to meet us there to discuss next steps in the investigation, if you're feeling up to it, Mr. Blackwell."

"Thomas, please," he corrected. "And yes, I'm up to it. More than up to it. I've spent six months as a passive participant in Krane's scheme. I'm ready to actively work against it."

The determination in his voice reminded Meg forcefully of Eleanor—the same quiet intensity, the same resolve masked by mild manners and precise speech. She found herself wondering how much of Thomas's resilience could be attributed to his aunt's influence, to growing up with such a formidable role model of composed strength.

The "temporary accommodations" proved to be a charming cottage on the outskirts of Seacliff, set back from the road and partially screened by mature pine trees. A gravel drive curved through the trees to a small clearing where a modest but well-maintained one-story home overlooked a steep drop to the ocean beyond.

"Catherine Peterson's vacation property," Eleanor explained as they parked. "She insisted we use it once she learned Thomas had been found. It's not in her name—it belonged to her brother, who left it to her when he passed last year. The property records haven't been updated yet."

The strategic advantage was immediately apparent—a location unknown to Krane or his associates, not connected to any of the principals in the investigation, but with the comforts necessary for Thomas's continued recovery.

Inside, the cottage was warm and inviting—polished wooden floors, comfortable furniture arranged to take advantage of the ocean view, a stone fireplace dominating one wall of the open-concept living area. Someone—Catherine Peterson, presumably—had stocked the kitchen with essentials, left fresh flowers on the dining table, and provided a stack of clean linens.

"Make yourselves comfortable," Eleanor instructed, moving with the easy familiarity of someone already acquainted with the space. "I'll prepare some tea while we wait for Sheriff Hanover."

As Eleanor busied herself in the kitchen, Thomas settled into an armchair near the fireplace, his movements still carrying that careful quality Meg had noticed earlier—a man reacquainting himself with the freedom to move without restraint or observation.

"This is the first time I've been in a normal house in six months," he said quietly, noticing Meg's observation. "It feels... surreal. No guards, no locked doors, no surveillance cameras. Just ordinary rooms with ordinary furniture and windows that actually open."

The simple statement, delivered without dramatic emphasis, conveyed the reality of his captivity more powerfully than any detailed account could have. Meg felt a renewed surge of determination to find Alex, Emily, and Valerie—to free them from the conditions Thomas had endured for half a year.

Sheriff Hanover arrived fifteen minutes later, accompanied by an FBI agent Meg hadn't met before—a woman in her forties with the lean build of a distance runner and the alert eyes of someone accustomed to assessing threats in ordinary situations.

"Special Agent Diana Lopez, FBI Financial Crimes Division," Hanover introduced her. "She's been coordinating with our department on tracking Krane's market manipulation scheme."

Introductions complete, they gathered around the dining table where Eleanor had laid out tea with the same precise attention to detail she brought to her research. For a moment, the scene might have been any small gathering—friends sharing afternoon refreshments—if not for the grave expressions and the files Hanover spread across the polished wood surface.

"The medical examiner's findings confirm what we suspected," she began without preamble. "Judge Peterson was murdered using a specialized technique designed to mimic natural cardiac arrest. The killer needed direct physical access, specific knowledge of pressure points, and the ability to act without witnesses."

"Someone within the courthouse," Eleanor concluded, her expression grieved but not surprised. "Someone with legitimate reason to be in Robert's chambers."

"Most likely," Agent Lopez agreed. "We're reviewing security footage, visitor logs, and staff movements, but the courthouse isn't designed for the kind of comprehensive surveillance that would capture every interaction."

Thomas was staring into his teacup as if it contained answers rather than Earl Grey. "Krane has people everywhere," he said, his voice low but steady. "At Northwood, he would sometimes mention his 'associates' in law enforcement, banking, even the judiciary. He enjoyed describing how easy it was to place people in positions of trust."

"Did he ever mention specific names?" Claire asked, her prosecutor's instincts engaged. "Particularly Judge Harmon?"

Thomas shook his head. "Never specific names. He was careful about that, compartmentalizing information so none of us knew more than was necessary for our assigned tasks." He hesitated, then added, "But there was something about Judge Harmon at the reception today—the way he looked at me, like he was checking for... damage. Not out of concern, but like someone inspecting merchandise they've mishandled."

The description sent a chill through Meg. She'd sensed something off about Harmon during their brief interaction, but Thomas's impression was both more specific and more disturbing.

"Harmon was the judge who repeatedly blocked our warrant requests," Reid reminded them. "Always finding technical reasons, jurisdictional issues, probable cause concerns."

"And he served alongside both Judge Blackwell and Judge Peterson during Krane's original prosecution," Eleanor added, opening one of her ubiquitous notebooks. "Though his role was peripheral—he handled some preliminary motions but wasn't involved in the trial itself or the sentencing."

Agent Lopez made a note in her own file. "We'll add him to the list of judicial personnel requiring deeper background investigation. But our immediate concern remains locating the missing women and identifying the mechanism Krane intends to use for his market manipulation scheme."

Thomas straightened, a new focus entering his expression. "I can help with that. During my captivity, I was forced to analyze geological surveys of properties Krane was acquiring—supposedly for environmental research, but actually to identify locations with specific characteristics for his operation."

"What kind of characteristics?" Meg asked.

"Remote locations with access to underground water sources, proximity to fiber optic trunk lines, and geological formations that could shield electromagnetic signatures." Thomas's explanation was precise, professional, his expertise evident despite his ordeal. "I believe he was establishing a network of server farms—distributed computing centers that could execute coordinated financial transactions without being easily traced or disrupted."

Agent Lopez leaned forward, her interest visibly sharpened. "Server farms capable of injecting malicious algorithms into trading systems?"

"Precisely," Thomas confirmed. "From what I could gather—and we were kept deliberately isolated from the full picture—each location houses servers programmed with specialized algorithms designed to exploit vulnerabilities in specific market sectors. When activated simultaneously, they could create the appearance of a market-wide panic, triggering automatic sell-offs from institutional investors' algorithmic trading systems."

"A cascade effect," Claire murmured, remembering their earlier conversations. "One failure triggering another until the entire system destabilizes."

"And Krane positioned to profit from the collapse," Agent Lopez added grimly. "Classic market manipulation, just on an unprecedented scale."

Sheriff Hanover, who had been studying the map included in her files, looked up with renewed focus. "Do you have any idea where these server farms are located? Or which one might be serving as this 'Nexus' you mentioned at the hospital?"

Thomas closed his eyes briefly, his face tight with concentration. "I was shown maps with approximately seven locations throughout the region, but never given exact coordinates. The Nexus, though... Emily mentioned something about it being 'where it all began' for Krane. Something symbolic."

"His father's hunting lodge," Eleanor said suddenly, setting down her teacup with uncharacteristic abruptness. "Eagle's Rest. It's where Victor Krane first developed his investment scheme, where he recruited his initial partners."

The connection seemed to energize everyone around the table. Hanover immediately began making notes while Agent Lopez pulled out her phone to coordinate with her team. Reid studied the map with renewed intensity, trying to identify the likely location based on Eleanor's information.

"Do you know where this Eagle's Rest is located?" Meg asked Eleanor.

"In the Pine Ridge National Forest," Eleanor replied, flipping through her notebook to a precisely tabbed section. "My husband and I attended a fundraiser there years ago, before Krane's crimes came to light. It's situated on a bluff overlooking the valley, perhaps fifteen miles north of where Northwood Lodge was located."

"Property records?" Hanover asked, already anticipating the next step in the investigation.

"The property was seized as part of the asset forfeiture in Krane's original case, then sold at auction to a private buyer named Gerard Mitchell." Eleanor's recall was impressive even by professional standards. "I suspect Mitchell is one of Krane's aliases or proxies, used to reacquire properties connected to his original operation."

"Mitchell," Meg repeated, something clicking in her mind. "As in Mitchell hunting lodge, which became Northwood?"

"Precisely," Eleanor confirmed, satisfaction evident in her voice despite her composed demeanor. "I believe Gerard Mitchell is the identity Krane has used to rebuild his network of properties while maintaining the Nathan Blackwood persona for direct interactions."

This was the breakthrough they needed—a specific location where Krane might be operating his control center, where the missing women might be held, where the heart of "The Reset" scheme might be accessible.

"We need to move on this immediately," Hanover decided, already reaching for her phone. "Lopez, coordinate with your tactical teams. Reid, contact our department's special operations unit. We'll need detailed satellite imagery, approach routes, perimeter assessment."

As the law enforcement professionals launched into operational planning, Meg found herself watching Thomas, who had grown increasingly pale during the discussion. Despite his evident desire to contribute, the strain of the day—his first out of the hospital, the funeral, the intense debriefing—was clearly taking its toll.

Eleanor had noticed as well, her sharp eyes missing nothing. "Thomas needs to rest," she said, her tone making it clear this wasn't a suggestion. "He's provided valuable information, but he's still recovering."

"Of course," Hanover acknowledged, her professional focus softening with genuine concern. "We've imposed on you both enough for one day. Agent Lopez and I will continue our planning at the station and keep you updated on developments."

As they prepared to leave, Thomas roused himself from what appeared to be growing exhaustion. "There's something else you should know about Krane," he said, his voice quieter but insistent. "Something important about his psychology."

Everyone paused, attention refocusing on Thomas, who seemed to be drawing on his last reserves of energy to share this final insight.

"The calm, methodical exterior is a mask," he said, his expression haunted by what was clearly a disturbing memory. "Underneath, he's... volatile. Especially when things don't go according to his plan."

"Volatile how?" Meg asked, sensing they were approaching something important.

"The night Emily was caught trying to escape, he seemed perfectly composed when they brought her back—asked questions in his usual measured way, gave orders without raising his voice." Thomas swallowed hard. "Then everyone left except his personal security detail. The mask slipped. He... came apart. Screaming, threatening, completely different from his public persona. When he finished, he straightened his tie, adjusted his cuffs, and walked out as if nothing had happened."

The detail was chilling in its implication—a man who maintained rigid control most of the time but harbored explosive rage beneath the surface. A man whose carefully constructed operation had been disrupted repeatedly in recent days, whose captives had been partially rescued, whose schemes were in danger of unraveling.

"He called it his 'private time,'" Thomas added quietly. "Said it was necessary for his mental hygiene. His security people acted like it was routine—something they'd seen many times before."

The insight cast Krane in an even more disturbing light—not just a calculating financial criminal with a sophisticated revenge scheme, but a man with profound psychological instability masked by a carefully maintained façade of control. The combination of methodical intelligence and volatile rage made him more unpredictable, more dangerous than they had initially understood.

"Thank you for sharing that, Thomas," Hanover said quietly. "It's valuable context for our approach."

After the law enforcement team departed, Meg and Claire lingered briefly to help Eleanor settle Thomas in the cottage's second bedroom. Despite his protests that he could manage himself, the young man was clearly at the limits of his endurance, his hands trembling slightly as he attempted to unpack the small bag of necessities Eleanor had brought from her home.

"Let me," Meg offered gently, taking the bag from his unresisting hands. "You've done more than enough for one day."

As she placed his few possessions in the dresser drawers—clothing, toiletries, a well-worn paperback of poetry—Meg was struck by the poignant scarcity of his belongings. Six months of captivity had reduced his life to these few items, these small comforts that Eleanor had preserved in his absence.

"Thank you," he said simply as she finished. "For everything—finding me, helping Aunt Eleanor, continuing to look for the others."

"Try to rest," Meg replied, recognizing in his exhausted features the same determination that had driven her through her own moments of fatigue and doubt. "We'll find them. I promise."

Outside, as they walked to Claire's car, the afternoon light had taken on the golden quality unique to coastal settings, the air carrying the mingled scents of pine and salt. After the emotional intensity of the day— the funeral, the revelations about Judge Peterson's murder, Thomas's disturbing insights into Krane's psychology—the simple beauty of the moment felt almost disorienting.

"What now?" Claire asked as they reached her Subaru.

"Now," Meg said, decision forming as she spoke, "we go back to your place, change into something that isn't funeral attire, and go for a run on the beach."

Claire's eyebrows rose in surprise. "A run? In the middle of all this?"

"Precisely because of all this," Meg replied. "We've been operating in crisis mode for days. Our brains need space, movement, something that isn't funeral services or tactical planning or debriefing traumatized captives."

For a moment, Claire looked like she might argue, but then her expression shifted toward understanding. "The beach at Lighthouse Point should be nearly empty this time of day. Three miles round trip."

"Perfect."

Forty minutes later, they were jogging along the packed sand at the water's edge, the rhythmic crash of waves on their right, the towering bluffs on their left. The rain had cleared completely, leaving behind the kind of crystalline clarity that made the horizon seem impossibly distant, the boundary between sea and sky a precise line drawn across the universe.

They ran in companionable silence, their footfalls creating twin patterns in the damp sand that lasted only moments before being erased by the tide's persistent advance and retreat. The simple physical exertion—lungs working, muscles burning pleasantly, heart pumping—created space in Meg's mind where thoughts could flow more freely, connections forming without the pressure of immediate decision-making.

When they reached the lighthouse and turned back, Claire finally broke the silence. "This was a good idea," she admitted, her breathing controlled but audible. "I needed this without realizing it."

"Sometimes the brain works better when we stop consciously pushing it," Meg replied. "My father used to say his best insurance fraud insights came during his evening walks with our dog."

The casual mention of her father—something she rarely did since his death five years ago—felt natural in this moment of shared exertion and mental clearing. Claire glanced at her but didn't comment, understanding the significance of the reference without needing to mark it explicitly.

They continued along the shore, finding a rhythm that allowed them to run side by side despite the uneven terrain. The physical activity had done exactly what Meg had hoped—created mental space where connections could form more organically, where the various pieces of the case could rearrange themselves without the pressure of immediate crisis response.

"Harmon," she said suddenly, the name emerging from the background processing her mind had been doing. "There's something about his connection to all this that keeps nagging at me."

Claire nodded, not breaking stride. "The timing of Peterson's murder immediately after he signed our warrants is too convenient to be coincidence."

"And Thomas's reaction to him at the reception—that observation about being inspected like 'damaged merchandise.'"

"Plus the fact that he consistently blocked our warrant requests while Peterson approved them immediately."

They continued a few more paces in silence, the implications building between them.

"He was on the bench during Krane's original trial," Meg said finally. "Not directly involved, according to Eleanor, but present in the system. What if he's been Krane's inside man from the beginning? His eyes and ears in the judicial system?"

The possibility seemed to gather substance as they ran, their footfalls marking a steady rhythm against which they could organize their thoughts.

"It would explain a lot," Claire agreed, pushing a strand of red hair from her face as they rounded a curve in the shoreline. "The blocked warrants, his appearance at the funeral, the way he specifically mentioned Peterson signing your warrants right before his death."

"Almost like he was... bragging," Meg said, the realization sending a chill through her despite the exertion of their run. "Like he wanted someone to make the connection but knew no one could prove anything."

They slowed as they approached the path leading up from the beach to the parking area, both reluctant to end the clarity that physical activity had brought. The late afternoon sun cast long shadows across the sand, the day's warmth beginning to fade as evening approached.

"We need to look deeper into Harmon's background," Claire said as they climbed the wooden steps carved into the bluff. "Financial records, case history, personal connections."

"Eleanor might already have that research," Meg suggested. "She seems to have investigated everyone connected to the original case."

At the top of the stairs, they paused to catch their breath, looking out over the ocean one last time before heading to the car. The horizon was beginning to blur, the clear line of earlier now softening as day moved toward dusk.

"I keep thinking about what Thomas said," Meg said after a moment. "About Krane's 'private time' when the mask slips. The contrast between his public persona and that hidden rage."

"The most dangerous predators," Claire replied grimly.

"Exactly. And if he's as volatile as Thomas described, with his operation under increasing pressure from our investigation..."

She didn't need to finish the thought. They both understood the implication—a man with both methodical intelligence and uncontrolled rage, feeling his carefully constructed schemes beginning to unravel, might become increasingly unpredictable, increasingly dangerous.

Back at Claire's apartment, they showered and changed, the simple routines of everyday life creating a temporary bubble of normalcy. Claire prepared a quick dinner—pasta with a sauce she pulled from the freezer, garlic bread, a simple salad—while Meg called Sheriff Hanover to share their thoughts about Judge Harmon.

"Already on it," Hanover informed her, the background noise suggesting she was still at the station. "Agent Lopez has requested Harmon's financial records for the past decade, and we're reviewing every case where he intersected with Krane's interests."

"Any progress on locating Eagle's Rest?" Meg asked, settling onto a bar stool at Claire's kitchen counter.

"Satellite imagery confirms a large structure at the coordinates Eleanor provided, but tree cover obscures most details. We're assembling tactical plans based on the limited intelligence available, with approaches from multiple directions to minimize the risk of detection."

"When do you plan to move?"

A slight hesitation on the line told Meg that Hanover was weighing how much to share with a civilian consultant. "Within the next forty-eight hours," she said finally. "We need additional equipment for the terrain, and FBI is bringing in specialized tactical teams familiar with wilderness operations."

After ending the call, Meg joined Claire at the small dining table, the events of the day settling around them like a heavy blanket. The normalcy they'd briefly recaptured during their run and dinner preparations was fading, reality reasserting itself with uncomfortable persistence.

"Forty-eight hours," Meg repeated, pushing pasta around her plate without much appetite. "That feels like an eternity when three women are being held captive."

"Tactical operations require proper planning," Claire reminded her. "Especially in remote terrain against an adversary with resources and preparation. Going in half-cocked would just endanger Alex and the others more."

Meg knew she was right, but the knowledge did little to ease the restless energy coursing through her. After six months of captivity, Thomas had provided the key information they needed to locate Krane's control center. Now they had to wait while law enforcement assembled the resources necessary to act on that intelligence.

"I just keep thinking about what they might be enduring while we wait," she admitted, finally setting down her fork. "Especially Alex. Thomas said she'd been shot, had broken bones. Medical care in captivity isn't exactly going to be optimal."

Claire reached across the table, covering Meg's hand with her own. "I know. But rushing in without proper preparation could get them killed. We have to trust the professionals to do this right."

The simple touch, the understanding in Claire's green eyes, reminded Meg that she wasn't carrying this burden alone. Whatever came next—the raid on Eagle's Rest, the confrontation with Krane, the effort to dismantle his financial scheme—she had allies in this fight.

After dinner, they settled in the living room with case files Hanover had permitted them to review—sanitized versions of the evidence gathered so far, organized into a timeline of Krane's activities since his supposed death seven years ago. The work was detailed, methodical, requiring focus that helped distract from the anxious waiting.

"Look at this," Claire said after nearly an hour of silent review. "Six months before Thomas disappeared, Axion Enterprises made a substantial donation to Judge Harmon's judicial scholarship fund. Two million dollars to support 'future guardians of the legal system.'"

Meg leaned over to study the document—a press release from Harmon's office announcing the donation, complete with a photo of the judge shaking hands with a man identified as "Gerard Mitchell, CEO of Axion Enterprises."

"Gerard Mitchell," she repeated, remembering Eleanor's research. "The same name used to purchase properties connected to Krane's original operation."

"Including Eagle's Rest," Claire confirmed, pulling another file from the stack. "And look at the timing—this donation came just as Harmon was assigned to oversee the judicial district that includes Pine Ridge National Forest, where most of Axion's properties are located."

The pattern was becoming clearer with each document they reviewed—Krane systematically positioning his assets under the judicial oversight of a man who had received millions in "donations" from Axion. Whether Harmon was actively complicit or merely compromised, the effect was the same—protection for Krane's operation from legal scrutiny.

As the evening deepened into night, fatigue began to cloud Meg's thinking. She had slept poorly since her drugging and abduction, her dreams filled with fragmented images—Alex being carried away unconscious, Thomas describing Krane's explosive rage, Judge Peterson's widow surrounded by family at the funeral.

"We should get some rest," Claire suggested, noting Meg's increasingly unfocused gaze. "Pick this up fresh in the morning."

"You're right," Meg agreed reluctantly. "My brain's starting to go in circles anyway."

They organized the files for the next day's review, setting aside the most promising leads for immediate attention when they resumed. The simple routine—stacking papers, marking pages for later reference, returning materials to their folders—had a grounding effect, bringing Meg back to the present moment from the anxious future scenarios her mind had been constructing.

Later, lying in the guest room bed, Meg found herself staring at the ceiling, sleep elusive despite her exhaustion. Through the wall, she could hear Claire's quiet movements as she prepared for bed, the familiar sounds a reminder of college days when they'd shared adjacent dorm rooms.

Her phone buzzed on the nightstand—a text from Reid with an update on the tactical planning. She read it quickly, noting the progress without retaining many details, her mind too tired to process new information effectively.

Just as she was finally drifting toward sleep, another text arrived. This one from an unknown number. Her first instinct was to ignore it until morning, but something—investigator's curiosity, perhaps, or the heightened alertness that had become her constant companion since stumbling onto Krane's operation—prompted her to check the message.

The text contained no words, only an image. A photograph that sent adrenaline surging through her system, instantly banishing all trace of fatigue.

The image showed a man lying face-up on what appeared to be an expensive rug, his unseeing eyes fixed on the ceiling, a small, precise wound visible at his temple. Even without the caption that followed in a second text, Meg would have recognized Judge Marcus Harmon.

"The price of betrayal," the second text read. "Choose your allies more carefully, Ms. Sawyer."

A third text arrived as she stared in horror at her screen: "The clock is ticking. Eagle's Rest. Midnight tomorrow. Come alone or they all die."

Attached was another image—Alex, Emily, and Valerie seated side by side, restrained but conscious, a digital clock visible on the wall behind them showing the current time. Proof of life, delivered with chilling precision.

Meg's hand shook as she called out to Claire, her voice cracking with the strain of maintaining control in the face of this new horror. The message was clear—Krane had eliminated Harmon, either because the judge had outlived his usefulness or because their investigation had made him a liability. And now Krane was issuing a direct challenge to Meg herself, bypassing law enforcement entirely to establish a personal connection between them.

As Claire appeared in the doorway, alarm evident in her expression, Meg held up the phone so she could see the images.

"He's killed Harmon," she said, the words feeling unreal even as she spoke them. "And now he wants me to come to Eagle's Rest. Alone."

Claire crossed the room quickly, taking the phone to examine the messages more closely. Her face paled as she absorbed the implications.

"We need to call Hanover. Now."

The next hours passed in a blur of urgent activity—Sheriff Hanover and Reid arriving at Claire's apartment, FBI agents securing the building perimeter, technical specialists attempting to trace the untraceable texts. Meg repeated everything exactly as it had happened, handed over her phone for evidence processing, answered the same questions multiple times as different agencies became involved in the response.

Through it all, the images remained burned in her mind—Harmon's lifeless body arranged like a discarded doll, the three women alive but captive, the clinical precision with which Krane had delivered his message and demand.

"He's escalating," Agent Lopez observed as they gathered in Claire's living room, converted now into an impromptu command center. "First Peterson, now Harmon. The pattern suggests increasing instability, willingness to take greater risks."

"Thomas warned us," Meg reminded them. "He said beneath the controlled exterior, Krane is volatile, especially when his plans are disrupted."

"And we've certainly disrupted his plans," Reid agreed grimly. "Rescued two of his captives, identified his control center, begun dismantling his financial operation."

"But why target me specifically?" Meg asked, the question that had been haunting her since she received the first message. "I'm not law enforcement, not connected to his original case. I stumbled onto this by accident."

"Perhaps that's precisely why," Eleanor suggested, having been brought to Claire's apartment for security reasons after Harmon's body was discovered. "You were the random factor, the unpredictable element that set this chain of events in motion. For someone like Krane, who controls every aspect of his operation, such unpredictability would be... intolerable."

The assessment made a disturbing kind of sense. From the moment Meg had spotted that message on Blackwood's roof, she had been the variable Krane couldn't account for—the civilian who kept appearing at critical junctures, the amateur who somehow managed to unravel threads of his carefully constructed scheme.

"Regardless of his motivation," Hanover said firmly, "there is absolutely no scenario in which you actually go to Eagle's Rest alone, Ms. Sawyer."

"Of course not," Meg agreed, though a part of her mind was already considering what might happen if she did—if she could somehow use Krane's fixation to create an opportunity for the captives to be rescued.

"His demand gives us one advantage," Agent Lopez noted, studying the tactical maps spread across Claire's coffee table. "We now know exactly when to stage our operation—just before midnight tomorrow. And his expectation that Ms. Sawyer might appear alone could mean reduced security at certain approach points."

The planning continued through the night, tactical teams assembling equipment, approach routes being finalized, contingencies established for various scenarios. Meg participated where she could, offering insights based on her unexpected connection to Krane, but increasingly found herself functioning on autopilot as exhaustion clouded her thinking.

Around 4 AM, Claire firmly intervened, insisting that Meg get at least a few hours of sleep before the final operational briefing scheduled for 9 AM. Too tired to argue, Meg retreated to the guest room, FBI agents now stationed throughout the apartment building ensuring their security.

Sleep, when it finally came, was fitful and filled with fragmented dreams—Judge Harmon's lifeless eyes, Thomas describing Krane's explosive rage, Alex's bruised face in the proof-of-life photograph. She woke shortly after 7 AM feeling scarcely more rested than when she'd lain down, but with a clarity that had been absent during the night's chaotic response.

In the kitchen, she found Claire already dressed and making coffee, dark circles beneath her eyes suggesting she'd slept little better than Meg had.

"Morning," Claire greeted her, pushing a mug across the counter. "Briefing's been moved up to 8:30. Hanover called about fifteen minutes ago."

"Any updates on Harmon?"

"Medical examiner confirmed he was killed with a single shot to the head, close range, precision placement suggesting professional execution. Time of death estimated between 6 and 8 PM last night."

The clinical details somehow made the horror more real, more immediate. Judge Harmon—a man they had spoken with at Peterson's funeral just hours before his death—had been executed with cold efficiency, his body photographed and used as a warning to Meg.

"They've confirmed the location of Eagle's Rest," Claire continued, her prosecutor's voice providing facts with admirable steadiness. "Satellite imagery shows increased activity over the past twelve hours—more vehicles arriving, personnel movement consistent with security preparations."

"He's expecting us," Meg concluded grimly. "Or rather, he's expecting me."

"Which we can use to our advantage," Claire reminded her. "If he's focused on your potential arrival, other approach vectors may be less heavily secured."

The briefing, when it began, had the tense focus of an operation moving from planning to execution phase. Sheriff Hanover and Agent Lopez led, outlining the final tactical approach with the precision of seasoned professionals. Three teams would approach Eagle's Rest from different directions, using the natural terrain for cover, timing their movements to coincide with the midnight deadline Krane had specified.

"Ms. Sawyer will remain at the command post with Ms. Winters and Ms. Blackwell," Hanover emphasized, her tone making it clear this was non-negotiable. "Deputy Reid will coordinate communications between the teams and the command post."

As the briefing continued, covering extraction protocols, evidence preservation, and contingency plans, Meg found her mind returning to the images Krane had sent—the three women restrained but alive, the clock on the wall behind them, the implicit threat in his message.

The timing bothered her. Why midnight? Why give them nearly twenty-four hours to prepare a response? A man as methodical as Krane, as careful in his planning, must have a reason for selecting that specific deadline.

"The timing feels wrong," she said suddenly, interrupting a discussion of helicopter support options. "Why midnight? Why give us so much advance notice?"

The room fell silent, everyone turning to look at her.

"Explain," Hanover prompted, her expression suggesting she'd already had similar concerns.

"Krane is methodical, strategic. He plans everything in advance and anticipates countermoves. By giving us almost a full day between his message and the deadline, he's practically inviting a tactical response." Meg's mind was racing ahead as she spoke, connections forming. "Unless that's exactly what he wants—to draw law enforcement resources to Eagle's Rest at a specific time while something else happens elsewhere."

Agent Lopez straightened, her attention sharpening. "The market manipulation scheme. You think the midnight deadline coincides with the activation of 'The Reset'?"

"It would make strategic sense," Reid observed. "Financial markets in Asia would be opening around that time. If his system is designed to create cascading failures across global markets, starting when U.S. markets are closed but Asian markets are opening would maximize the impact."

"A diversion," Eleanor said quietly, her composed features showing the first signs of genuine alarm. "Eagle's Rest is a diversion to occupy law enforcement resources while the true operation activates elsewhere."

The realization sent a ripple of reassessment through the room, tactical plans being mentally recalibrated to account for this new possibility. The stakes had just risen dramatically—not just the lives of three captive women, but potentially global financial stability hanging in the balance.

"We need to locate the server farms Thomas mentioned," Agent Lopez said, turning to her team. "If Eagle's Rest is the control center but the actual market manipulation algorithms are housed elsewhere, we need to neutralize those locations simultaneously."

Hanover nodded her agreement. "We'll proceed with the Eagle's Rest operation as planned, but allocate resources to identifying and securing these server locations as well. Ms. Blackwell, did Thomas provide any details that might help us locate them?"

Eleanor shook her head regretfully. "Only general characteristics—remote locations with access to underground water sources, proximity to fiber optic trunk lines, and geological formations that could shield electromagnetic signatures. Without specific coordinates, the search area remains extensive."

"Wait," Meg said, something clicking in her mind. "Thomas mentioned he was forced to analyze geological surveys for Krane, identifying locations with those specific characteristics. Would those surveys still exist somewhere? Some record of the properties he evaluated?"

Eleanor's eyes lit with understanding. "His research materials. When his apartment was searched after his disappearance, I brought everything home—his laptop, field notebooks, data files. They're in storage at my house."

"Which we can access now that the immediate threat to you and Thomas has been addressed," Hanover concluded, already reaching for her phone. "Reid, take Ms. Blackwell to her home with a security detail. Retrieve those materials and bring them directly to the technical analysis team at the station."

As the operation regained momentum, adapting to this new understanding of Krane's potential strategy, Meg found herself studying the tactical maps with renewed intensity. Eagle's Rest remained their primary target—the location where Alex, Emily, and Valerie were being held, the control center from which Krane directed his operation. But the possibility that it might be a carefully planned diversion added a new layer of complexity to their approach.

Through it all, one question continued to nag at her—why had Krane specifically demanded her presence? What purpose did it serve in his broader scheme? Was it merely the vindictive targeting of the random factor who had disrupted his plans, or was there a deeper strategic purpose to drawing her personally into the confrontation?

The answer, she suspected, would only become clear when they finally came face to face with Victor Krane—the financial criminal who had cheated death, changed his identity, and embarked on a years-long scheme of revenge and market manipulation. A man whose calm exterior masked volcanic rage, whose methodical planning concealed increasingly dangerous instability.

The clock was indeed ticking—not just for the midnight deadline, but for Krane's elaborate scheme, for the captive women, for the global financial system itself. And somewhere in this complex web of revenge and manipulation, Meg Sawyer had become not just an investigator but a target, a variable Krane could no longer ignore or control.

The final phase was about to begin, and whatever happened at Eagle's Rest tonight would determine whether Krane's years of planning culminated in triumphant revenge or spectacular failure. For Meg and her allies, failure wasn't an option—not with lives and livelihoods hanging in the balance, not with the shadow of Krane's volatility looming over every calculation and countermove.

The endgame had begun.

CHAPTER SEVEN
DEADLINES

The command post had been established in an old forest service station about five miles from Eagle's Rest—close enough for quick response, far enough to remain undetected by Krane's security perimeter. As evening descended over the Pine Ridge National Forest, the small clearing buzzed with the controlled tension of professionals preparing for a high-risk operation.

Meg watched from the station's covered porch as tactical teams conducted final equipment checks, communications specialists tested secure channels, medical personnel prepared for potential casualties. The organized chaos had a surreal quality after the emotional intensity of the past days—Judge Peterson's funeral, Harmon's murder, Thomas's disturbing revelations about Krane's psychology.

"They know what they're doing," Claire said quietly, joining her at the porch railing. "These people are the best at what they do."

Meg nodded, knowing it was true but finding little comfort in the knowledge. "I just keep thinking about Alex and the others. What they must be going through while we prepare."

The proof-of-life photograph Krane had sent with his demand haunted her—Alex's bruised face, Emily's hollow-eyed exhaustion, Valerie's rigid posture suggesting pain or fear or both. All three alive but clearly suffering, their fates now tied to the success or failure of tonight's operation.

Inside the station, Eleanor sat with Thomas, who had insisted on being present despite his still-precarious health. His research materials—retrieved from Eleanor's home earlier that day—had proven invaluable, containing detailed geological analyses of potential server farm locations. FBI technical teams were currently moving to secure those sites, coordinating their approach with the Eagle's Rest operation to ensure simultaneous neutralization of Krane's entire network.

"Ms. Sawyer." Sheriff Hanover's voice drew Meg's attention back to the present moment. "A moment of your time, please."

She followed Hanover to a quiet corner of the station, away from the main tactical planning area. The sheriff's expression was grave, her silver-streaked hair pulled back in its customary severe bun, her uniform immaculate despite the day's activities.

"I need to be absolutely clear about something," Hanover said without preamble. "Under no circumstances are you to attempt any form of contact with Krane or approach to Eagle's Rest. Regardless of any developments, regardless of any messages he might send, you remain at this command post until the operation is complete. Is that understood?"

The directness of the instruction suggested Hanover suspected exactly what had been flickering through Meg's mind since receiving Krane's demand—the possibility of using his fixation on her as a distraction, a way to draw attention from the tactical teams' approach.

"Understood," Meg replied, meeting Hanover's gaze directly. "I'll stay put."

Hanover studied her for a moment longer, clearly assessing the sincerity of her agreement. "Good. Because I've instructed Deputy Mills to physically restrain you if necessary. This isn't personal, Ms. Sawyer. It's operational security."

The bluntness was actually refreshing—no sugar-coating, no gentle persuasion, just the clear statement of parameters and consequences. Meg found herself respecting Hanover's approach even as she chafed at the restrictions.

"For what it's worth," she offered, "I have no desire to become another hostage for Krane to leverage. I'll stay here and help however I can from the command post."

Something in Hanover's expression softened fractionally. "You've already helped more than most civilians would or could. Without your initial investigation at Blackwood's cabin, without your partnership with Ms. Reeves, we might never have connected these disappearances or identified Krane's operation."

The acknowledgment was unexpected, especially from someone as professionally reserved as Sheriff Hanover. Before Meg could respond, Reid approached, his weathered face set in lines of focused determination.

"Final communications check complete," he reported. "Tactical teams are in position for initial approach. Timeline remains on schedule for midnight convergence."

Hanover nodded, immediately shifting back to operational mode. "Keep me updated on their progress. Any movement detected at the target site?"

"Minimal external activity. Satellite thermal imaging shows heat signatures consistent with approximately fifteen to twenty personnel distributed throughout the main structure and perimeter positions."

"And the server farm locations?"

"FBI teams report approach phase complete at five of the seven identified sites. Waiting for confirmation on the remaining two." Reid glanced at his watch. "All teams should be in position for synchronized action at midnight."

The precision of the operation was impressive—multiple tactical teams approaching different targets across a wide geographic area, all coordinated to act at the same moment. It spoke to the seriousness with which law enforcement was treating Krane's threat, the resources being deployed to counter his scheme.

As full darkness settled over the forest, the command post transitioned to night operations—exterior lights minimized, tactical communications conducted in hushed tones, movement restricted to essential personnel only. Through it all, Meg remained on the porch, watching the forest shadows deepen, listening to the natural sounds of the wilderness gradually yielding to the artificial quiet of human presence.

"You should try to rest," Claire suggested around 10 PM, bringing a cup of coffee that Meg accepted gratefully. "It's going to be a long night."

"Couldn't sleep if I tried," Meg admitted, sipping the bitter brew. "Too wired."

Claire settled beside her on the wooden bench that ran along the porch railing, their shoulders touching in a gesture of solidarity that required no words. They had known each other long enough that silence between them was comfortable, each understanding the other's thoughts without needing to articulate them.

"Remember that cabin trip senior year?" Claire asked after several minutes of companionable quiet. "When we got lost hiking and ended up at that creepy abandoned ranger station?"

The memory surfaced unexpectedly—the two of them, much younger, hiking in unfamiliar woods after taking a wrong turn, the relief of finding shelter as darkness fell, the subsequent discovery that the "abandoned" station was actually the weekend project of a local artist who returned to find two college students had broken into his studio.

"He was so mad," Meg recalled, a small smile breaking through her tension. "Until you went full pre-law on him about proper signage and the attractive nuisance doctrine."

"Ended up giving us dinner and driving us back to our cabin," Claire finished, her own smile visible in the dim light from the station's windows. "Said we were the most entertaining trespassers he'd ever had."

The shared memory, seemingly random, served its purpose—breaking the building tension, providing a moment of connection outside the immediate crisis. Claire had always known how to ground Meg when her focus became too intense, too all-consuming.

"We're going to get through this too," Claire said quietly, returning to the present. "And afterward, we're taking that coastal road trip we talked about. Convertible, too much wine, seafood at every meal."

"Deal." Meg's simple response carried the weight of promise—a future beyond tonight's operation, beyond Krane's scheme, beyond the danger and uncertainty that had dominated their lives since she'd spotted that message on Blackwood's roof.

Inside the station, the rhythm of the operation continued—status updates from tactical teams marked in precise increments, satellite imagery refreshed to track any changes at Eagle's Rest, communication with FBI teams at the server farm locations maintained on separate secure channels.

At 11:15 PM, the atmosphere in the command post shifted subtly—the approaching deadline creating a heightened focus, conversations reduced to essential communication only, movements becoming more deliberate as the operation entered its critical phase.

"All tactical teams report ready positions," Reid announced, his voice pitched low but carrying clearly in the focused quiet. "Awaiting final authorization for approach."

Hanover, who had been reviewing the latest satellite imagery with Agent Lopez, straightened and addressed the assembled personnel. "Operational parameters remain unchanged. Primary objective is the safe recovery of the hostages. Secondary objectives are apprehension of Victor Krane and securing of evidence related to the financial scheme. Authorization for approach is granted."

A ripple of acknowledgments moved through the command post as team leaders confirmed receipt of the authorization and relayed it to their personnel in the field. On the tactical map displayed on the main table, small indicators began moving toward Eagle's Rest from three different directions—specialized teams navigating the dark forest with night vision equipment and precise GPS guidance.

Meg returned to the porch, finding it impossible to remain inside watching the slow progress of markers on a map. The night air carried a chill that penetrated her borrowed jacket, but she welcomed the discomfort as a counterpoint to the nervous energy coursing through her system.

The forest around them had gone unnaturally quiet, as if the wildlife sensed the human tension radiating from the command post. No owl calls, no rustling underbrush, just the occasional soft creak of trees swaying in the gentle breeze.

At 11:30, Reid stepped onto the porch, his expression unreadable in the dim light. "Teams report approach phase complete. All units in final position awaiting synchronized breach signal."

"And the server farm locations?" Meg asked, unable to contain her need for information.

"All teams in position. Technical specialists standing by to neutralize the systems once physical access is secured." Reid checked his watch. "Thirty minutes to execution phase."

The time seemed to stretch endlessly, each minute passing with excruciating slowness. Inside the command post, the tension had reached near-palpable levels—every person acutely aware of the stakes, the risks, the potential consequences of success or failure.

At 11:45, Meg's phone vibrated in her pocket. She withdrew it with a sense of foreboding, already anticipating what she might find.

A text from an unknown number—the same number that had sent the images of Harmon's body and the captive women. This time, the message contained no photographs, just text that sent ice through her veins:

"I know they're coming, Ms. Sawyer. Did you think I wouldn't anticipate this response? The game changes now. The women die at midnight unless you personally approach the main gate within the next ten minutes. Come alone or don't bother coming at all."

Meg stared at the screen, her heart hammering against her ribs. The timing was calculated for maximum effect—too late to adjust the operational plan, too close to the deadline to develop an alternative approach, just enough time for her to potentially reach Eagle's Rest if she left immediately.

She looked up to find Claire watching her, concern evident in her expression. "What is it?"

"Krane," Meg replied, her voice steadier than she felt as she handed over the phone. "He knows about the operation."

Claire read the message, her face paling in the dim light. "Meg, you can't—"

"I know," Meg cut her off. "But we need to tell Hanover immediately."

They hurried inside, finding the sheriff deep in conversation with Agent Lopez and the tactical team commanders. Hanover's expression darkened as she read the message, her eyes flicking to the operational timeline displayed on the main screen—eleven minutes until the synchronized breach.

"He's bluffing," Agent Lopez stated firmly. "Trying to disrupt our approach by drawing attention to the main gate. Classic diversionary tactic."

"Or he genuinely knows we're coming and is changing the parameters," Reid countered. "We've seen throughout this investigation that he has sources within law enforcement, access to information that should be secure."

"Either way, Ms. Sawyer is absolutely not approaching that gate," Hanover said with finality. "We proceed as planned. If Krane detected our approach, it only increases the urgency of the operation."

Meg wanted to argue, to suggest that she could create a distraction while the tactical teams completed their approach, but she recognized the tactical logic behind Hanover's decision. More importantly, she recognized that her impulse to act was being driven by exactly what Krane intended—emotional reaction rather than strategic assessment.

"Understood," she said simply. "I'll stay here."

Hanover studied her for a moment, then nodded, apparently satisfied with her compliance. "Maintain communications blackout except for essential operational traffic. All teams hold position and prepare for synchronized breach on my mark."

The final minutes ticked by with excruciating slowness, each second feeling weighed with potential consequences. Meg found herself holding her breath as the digital display approached midnight, her mind filled with images of Alex, Emily, and Valerie—captive, vulnerable, their lives hanging on the success or failure of this operation.

At exactly midnight, Hanover gave the command: "Execute breach. All teams go."

The tactical communications erupted with coordinated status reports as teams at Eagle's Rest and the server farm locations simultaneously began their approach. In the command post, everyone's attention was fixed on the communications feed, each terse update building a fragmented picture of the operation in progress.

"Alpha team breaching east entrance." "Charlie team encountering resistance at perimeter checkpoint." "Server Farm Delta secure, technical team accessing systems." "Bravo team proceeding to main structure, no contact yet."

Meg stood motionless beside Claire, every sense attuned to the flow of information, searching for any indication of the captives' status. The tactical language was precise but limited, conveying operational progress without revealing the human dynamics unfolding at the target locations.

"Alpha team entering main structure, first floor secure." "Charlie team has neutralized resistance, proceeding to objective." "Server Farm Echo secure, systems being isolated from network." "Bravo team encountering locked doors, deploying breaching equipment."

The operation appeared to be proceeding according to plan—tactical teams making steady progress through Eagle's Rest, server farm locations being secured, resistance encountered but managed with professional efficiency. Meg allowed herself the first flicker of hope that they might succeed—that Alex, Emily, and Valerie might be rescued, that Krane's scheme might be neutralized before it could activate.

Then everything changed.

"Command, this is Alpha leader," a tense voice reported through the tactical channel. "We've reached the room from the proof-of-life photo. It's empty. Repeat, no sign of the hostages."

Meg's heart seemed to stutter in her chest, hope giving way to cold dread. Empty. The room where the women had been photographed just hours earlier was empty.

"Check adjacent spaces," Hanover ordered, her voice remaining steady despite the setback. "Expand search pattern to all floors."

The tactical teams responded with professional efficiency, adapting their search parameters, reporting as each section of the structure was cleared. But the updates carried the same message with increasing finality:

"Second floor clear, no hostages." "Basement level clear, no hostages." "Outbuildings secured, no personnel located." "Vehicle garage empty, no transport present."

Eagle's Rest—the fortified compound they had approached with such careful planning, such synchronized precision—was empty. No Krane, no captives, no security personnel. Just an abandoned structure with evidence of recent occupation but no trace of the people they had come to find and arrest.

"Server farms reporting similar status," Agent Lopez informed them, her professional mask slipping to reveal genuine concern. "Security systems active but no personnel present. Systems appear to have been wiped clean—no data, no operational algorithms, just empty hardware."

The reality settled over the command post like a physical weight—they had been outmaneuvered, led to commit their resources to locations Krane had already abandoned. But where had he gone? Where had he taken Alex, Emily, and Valerie?

"Command, this is Bravo leader," a new voice reported through the tactical channel. "We've found something in what appears to be the main office. A message addressed to Sheriff Hanover. Handwritten."

Hanover exchanged a glance with Reid, tension radiating between them like heat from asphalt on a summer day.

"Secure and photograph it," she instructed, her voice betraying nothing of the turmoil Meg could see in her eyes. "Then bring it in."

While they waited, Meg paced the command center, every muscle in her body coiled tight. Claire watched her from the corner, nursing a cup of coffee that had gone cold hours ago.

"Meg," Claire said gently. "You should sit down."

"I can't," Meg replied, running a hand through her tangled hair. The fluorescent lights overhead buzzed with a persistent hum that seemed to vibrate through her skull. "Every minute we waste is another minute they—"

The door swung open, admitting a tactical officer in full gear. His face was slick with sweat, eyes sharp with adrenaline. He carried a clear evidence bag containing a single folded piece of paper.

"We verified it's clean, ma'am," he reported, handing the bag to Hanover. "No chemical agents, no biologicals, no triggering mechanisms."

Hanover accepted the bag with latex-gloved hands, carefully extracting the note. The paper was heavy, expensive—the kind used for formal correspondence. The handwriting was elegant, measured, each letter formed with meticulous precision.

"'Sheriff Hanover,'" she read aloud, "'I commend your efficiency. Unfortunately, it was anticipated. By now you've discovered our facilities empty, our personnel gone. This was never about resisting law enforcement—merely delaying it. We have what we need, and those who serve our purpose. The three women you seek are with us. One by coercion. One by deception. One by choice. Can you determine which is which? It's a shame we couldn't meet under different circumstances. I believe we might have understood each other. Regards, Krane.'"

The room fell silent, the only sound the steady hum of electronics and the distant chatter of radios.

"Typical Krane," Reid muttered, his jaw tight. "Even now, he's playing games."

"It's not just a game," Claire said, setting down her mug. "It's psychological warfare. He's trying to make us doubt ourselves, doubt each other."

Meg stared at the note, the words burning into her consciousness. *One by coercion. One by deception. One by choice.* Emily. Valerie. Alex. But which was which?

"There's something else," she said, the realization crystallizing. "He's not just taunting us. There's information here. Specific information he wants us to have."

Hanover raised an eyebrow. "Go on."

"He's telling us about the three women differently," Meg continued, her investigator's instincts firing rapidly now. "It's a deliberate clue about their situations. Why would he do that unless he wanted to sow discord in our ranks?"

"Especially given what Thomas and Jason told us about Krane's operation," Claire added, referencing their recent debriefing with the rescued men. "Each captive had a specific role, a particular skill set Krane needed."

The command center erupted into renewed activity, the lethargy of defeat replaced by focused determination.

Meg moved to the evidence board, studying the timeline they'd constructed. Something nagged at her—a connection just beyond her grasp. *One by coercion. One by deception. One by choice.* Why tell them this? What purpose did it serve?

The answer hit her with such force that she physically recoiled.

"He's trying to make us doubt each other," she said, her voice cutting through the bustle. "That's what this is about. Sowing distrust."

Reid approached, his weathered face grave. "What do you mean?"

"Think about it," Meg insisted. "From the beginning, we've never been sure who to trust. The deputy who was feeding information to Blackwood. The federal agents who weren't actually federal. The local judge blocking warrants." She tapped the note. "This is more of the same. Make us question who's really a victim and who's complicit."

Hanover studied her thoughtfully. "You sound like you have a theory about which is which."

Meg hesitated. Did she? The evidence was circumstantial at best, but her gut was screaming.

"Emily was described as being in recovery from addiction," she said carefully. "Vulnerable. Easy to control through medication or threat of withdrawal. That's coercion."

"Valerie had no known vulnerabilities," Reid added, following her logic. "Young professional, no history of trauma or addiction."

"Deception," Meg nodded. "She could have been recruited under false pretenses. A job offer, a research project—something that appealed to her professionally."

The unspoken conclusion hung in the air between them. If Emily was coerced and Valerie deceived, that left only one possibility for Alex.

"By choice," Claire murmured, the implications settling over the room like a shadow.

The unspoken conclusion hung in the air between them. If Emily was coerced and Valerie deceived, that left only one possibility for Alex.

"By choice," Claire murmured, the implications settling over the room like a shadow.

No one spoke for several long moments. Meg felt a hollowness opening inside her chest. Alex had saved her life. They'd searched Blackwood's cabin together, fled from him together. She'd trusted Alex completely.

"We don't know that," Meg said finally, her voice sounding distant even to her own ears. "It's what Krane wants us to think. That's the point of the note—to make us doubt each other."

Hanover tapped her pen against the desk. "We need to consider all possibilities. For now, let's focus on what we know for certain."

"Which isn't much," Reid said, rubbing his eyes. He looked exhausted, the day's failures weighing on him.

"We should call it a night," Hanover decided, glancing at her watch. "It's late, and we've been at this for hours. My team needs to review what we found at Eagle's Rest, compare notes, see if anything points us to Krane's next location."

"So we're just going home?" Meg asked, not hiding her frustration.

"We're resting," Hanover corrected. "There's a difference. I have analysts reviewing data overnight, but the rest of us need clear heads."

Claire placed a hand on Meg's arm. "She's right. We won't help anyone if we're dead on our feet."

The rational part of Meg's brain knew they were right, but the thought of returning to Claire's apartment, trying to sleep while Alex remained in Krane's hands—whether victim or collaborator—seemed impossible.

"We'll meet again at nine tomorrow morning," Hanover said, closing her folder. "Thomas mentioned he might have additional information about the storage facility listed in the Axion files. I've asked Eleanor to bring him in."

The small group dispersed without much ceremony. No dramatic speeches, no grand promises—just tired people gathering their things, checking their phones, heading home to grab what sleep they could.

The drive back to Claire's apartment passed in weary silence. The adrenaline that had sustained Meg was ebbing, leaving a bone-deep exhaustion that made even keeping her eyes open a struggle.

"You know," Claire said as they waited at a red light, "you never did eat anything."

"Not hungry," Meg replied automatically.

"Liar." Claire turned onto her street. "I've got leftover lasagna. You're having at least three bites before you collapse."

The normality of the exchange—Claire's no-nonsense nurturing, Meg's stubborn self-neglect—felt strangely comforting amid the chaos of the day.

Claire's apartment welcomed them with familiar scents and sounds. Meg sank onto a kitchen stool while Claire reheated food, the microwave's hum filling the silence.

"Eat," Claire commanded, sliding a plate in front of Meg. "Then shower. Then bed."

Meg obediently took a bite, surprised to find herself suddenly ravenous. They ate without much conversation, the day's events too heavy for casual discussion, the uncertainty about Alex's true role hanging between them unspoken.

Later, lying in the guest bed, Meg stared at the ceiling, sleep frustratingly elusive despite her exhaustion. Krane's note kept repeating in her mind. *One by coercion. One by deception. One by choice.*

Had Alex chosen to betray her? Or was this part of some strategy Meg couldn't yet see?

Her phone glowed briefly—a text from Reid saying Thomas had called with some recollections about the storage facility he wanted to share in the morning. She silenced the phone, knowing morning would arrive soon enough.

Sleep finally came in fitful bursts, dreams tangling with half-formed theories. Somewhere in the early morning hours, she dreamed of Alex trying to explain something important, but no sound emerged from her moving lips.

She woke to the smell of coffee and the sound of Claire's shower running. Sunlight filtered through the blinds, a clock on the nightstand showing 7:42 AM. She dragged herself up, pulled on jeans and a sweater, and made her way to the kitchen.

A pot of coffee waited, still warm. Meg poured herself a mug and leaned against the counter, rubbing sleep from her eyes. Claire emerged a few minutes later, dressed for the day, hair still damp.

"You look awful," she said bluntly, reaching for her own coffee.

"Thanks. You always know just what to say," Meg replied with a half-smile.

"Thomas called Eleanor this morning," Claire said, opening her refrigerator. "Said he remembered something about the storage facility. He's meeting us at the department."

Thomas. Meg felt a flicker of hope. Their conversation at Judge Peterson's funeral had been brief, but she'd sensed his sharp intelligence beneath the fatigue of recent captivity. If anyone might have insights into Krane's operation, it would be someone who'd been inside it for months.

The sheriff's department was surprisingly quiet when they arrived—a few officers at their desks, phones ringing occasionally, the coffee pot in the break room brewing a fresh batch. No dramatic command center, no bustling tactical teams—just the normal morning routine of a small-town law enforcement office.

Thomas and Eleanor were already there, sitting in Hanover's office. Thomas looked better than he had at the funeral—some color had returned to his face, though he still moved with the careful precision of someone recovering from extended captivity.

"Morning," he greeted them as they entered. "Thanks for coming."

"Eleanor mentioned you remembered something about the storage facility," Meg said, taking a seat across from him.

Thomas nodded, reaching for a notepad where he'd sketched something. "I've been trying to recall everything from when I was cataloging properties for Krane. The storage facility wasn't just storage—it was designed as a backup command center."

He spread the sketch on Hanover's desk—a rough layout showing three buildings, access roads, and what appeared to be security checkpoints.

"I never visited it personally," he continued, "but I saw the plans. There's something unusual about its design. The main warehouse has a subterranean level that doesn't appear in the county records."

Sheriff Hanover entered the office, coffee in hand, Reid following behind her. No dramatic entrance, no entourage—just two law enforcement officers starting their day.

"Good morning," she said, setting her coffee down and taking her seat. "Thomas, appreciate you coming in."

For the next thirty minutes, Thomas explained what he remembered about the facility—security systems, access points, the underground level's purpose. The conversation was focused, practical, occasionally interrupted by a question or clarification.

"So you believe this is where Krane would relocate?" Hanover asked, studying the sketch.

"It's designed for exactly this scenario," Thomas confirmed. "A fallback position if primary locations were compromised. Low profile, looks ordinary from the outside, but with everything needed to continue operations."

Reid made a call to request satellite imagery of the location, while Hanover pulled up property records on her computer.

"The deed shows it's owned by a company called Meridian Storage Solutions," she reported. "Incorporated in Delaware three years ago."

"That's one of Krane's shell companies," Eleanor confirmed, referencing her ever-present notebook. "The same structure he used for acquiring the Northwood property."

The evidence was circumstantial but compelling. No dramatic revelations, just methodical investigation building a case piece by piece.

"We'll need to verify current activity before taking any action," Hanover decided. "Satellite imagery, utility usage, ground surveillance—all done quietly."

Meg felt a renewed sense of purpose. Not the breathless excitement of imminent action, but the steady determination of professionals following a lead.

"What about Alex?" she asked, the question that had been haunting her since reading Krane's note.

Hanover's expression remained neutral. "Right now, we treat all three women as potential victims until we have evidence suggesting otherwise. If Ms. Reeves has chosen to align with Krane, we'll deal with that when the time comes."

It wasn't the definitive answer Meg wanted, but it was the right approach. Assumptions and emotions couldn't drive their actions—only evidence and careful planning would lead to a successful resolution.

"I'd like to help with the surveillance," Meg offered. "I've done it before in insurance fraud cases."

Hanover considered this. "We'll see. For now, I need you to work with Thomas and Eleanor, review everything we know about the facility and Krane's operation. Your outside perspective has been valuable—you see connections others might miss."

As the meeting concluded and they prepared to move to a conference room to continue their analysis, Meg found herself walking beside Thomas.

"How are you holding up?" she asked quietly.

"Better than yesterday," he replied with a small smile. "At the funeral, I was barely functional. But being able to help, to do something tangible toward finding the others... it helps."

The simple honesty of his response reminded Meg of what was really at stake—not just solving a case or catching Krane, but bringing Emily, Valerie, and yes, Alex, home safely. Whatever complications lay ahead, whatever revelations about Alex's true role might emerge, that core purpose remained unchanged.

As they settled in the conference room, spreading out files and notes, the work of the day began in earnest. No dramatic speeches, no oversized tactical maps—just focused professionals methodically building a case, following the evidence, and preparing for whatever came next.

One step at a time.

CHAPTER EIGHT
FALSE FRONTS

Four days had passed since Eagle's Rest. Four days of dead ends, false leads, and diminishing hope. The storage facility Thomas had identified showed no signs of activity—satellite imagery revealed an abandoned property with no heat signatures, no vehicle movement, nothing to suggest it served as Krane's backup command center.

Meg stood at the kitchen window in Claire's apartment, watching an early spring rain transform the world into watercolor smudges of gray and green. The temperature had dropped overnight, bringing a bone-deep chill that seemed to match her mood—a persistent cold that no amount of coffee or hot showers could dispel.

Her reflection stared back at her from the rain-streaked glass—shadows beneath her eyes, hair pulled back in a careless ponytail, a furrow between her brows that hadn't been there two weeks ago. The woman who had arrived at Claire's beach house seeking refuge from a broken marriage seemed like a stranger now, a naive version of herself who believed the worst thing that could happen was discovering her husband's betrayal.

"Anything interesting out there?" Claire asked, entering the kitchen in her bathrobe, red hair tousled from sleep.

"Just rain," Meg replied, turning away from the window. "And more rain."

Claire yawned, moving to the coffee maker with the practiced efficiency of morning ritual. "Court starts at ten. I should be finished by three, unless Henderson's attorney tries another delay tactic."

The mundane details of Claire's workday—her returning to the prosecutor's office after a week of leave—felt surreal against the backdrop of their ongoing search for Alex, Emily, and Valerie. Life continued, ordinary and relentless, even with three women still missing, even with Krane still at large.

"What's your plan for today?" Claire asked, measuring coffee with precise scoops.

Meg shrugged, lifting her own half-empty mug. "Thomas is sending over some property records he and Eleanor have been reviewing. Thought I might look them over, see if anything stands out."

The trail had gone cold. Sheriff Hanover's team had exhausted their immediate leads, the FBI had scaled back their presence as other cases demanded attention, and the initial urgency had given way to the grinding reality of a complex investigation with no clear path forward.

"You should get out of the apartment," Claire suggested, the coffee maker gurgling to life behind her. "Maybe walk down to the pier. It's supposed to clear up this afternoon."

Meg knew what Claire was really saying: *You need to do something besides obsess over this case. You need to breathe.* And she wasn't wrong. Meg had spent the past four days poring over files, analyzing satellite imagery, constructing elaborate theories about Krane's next move—and achieving nothing but increasing frustration.

"Maybe," she conceded, though they both knew it was unlikely.

Claire studied her over the rim of her coffee mug, concern evident in her green eyes. "Henderson's case should wrap by the end of the week. Chief Prosecutor Grant mentioned a complex insurance fraud case coming up that might interest you. Something about medical billing across state lines."

"You're trying to distract me," Meg observed.

"Is it working?" Claire asked with a small smile.

Despite herself, Meg felt an answering smile tug at her lips. "Maybe a little."

Claire disappeared to prepare for court, leaving Meg alone with her thoughts and the steady percussion of rain against the windows. The apartment felt too small suddenly, too confined. Maybe Claire was right about getting some air, even in the rain.

She pulled on a jacket and boots, tucking her phone into her pocket in case Thomas called with updates. Outside, the rain had softened to a fine mist that clung to her skin and hair, not quite wet enough to soak but persistent enough to gradually dampen everything it touched.

The streets of Seacliff were quietly bustling with mid-morning activity—locals running errands, shop owners sweeping water from storefronts, tourists huddled under colorful umbrellas despite the inclement weather. Normal life, untouched by the shadow that had fallen over her world.

Meg walked without conscious destination, letting her feet carry her while her mind turned over the same questions that had occupied her for days. Where had Krane taken the women? What was his ultimate goal? And the question that haunted her most persistently—had Alex really chosen to join him?

She found herself at the harbor, drawn to the rhythmic movement of boats bobbing at their moorings. The rain had intensified again, driving most pedestrians to seek shelter, leaving the waterfront nearly deserted. She pulled her jacket tighter against the chill and continued along the weathered boardwalk.

A fishing boat was docking, crew members tossing lines with practiced efficiency despite the weather. The vessel looked worn but well-maintained, its blue paint faded in places, its name—*Second*

Chance—barely visible on the stern. The irony wasn't lost on Meg. Second chances seemed in short supply these days.

"Nasty weather for a walk," a voice observed from behind her.

Meg turned to find Thomas Blackwell standing a few feet away, a black umbrella sheltering him from the rain. He looked markedly better than when she'd last seen him—color in his cheeks, less hesitation in his movements, though still thin from his captivity.

"Thomas," she said, surprised. "What are you doing here?"

He moved closer, extending the umbrella to cover her as well. "Aunt Eleanor had a dental appointment. I decided to walk rather than wait in the reception area. Saw you standing here looking like a drowned cat."

The blunt assessment, delivered with a hint of amusement rather than mockery, startled a laugh from Meg. "That bad, huh?"

"Worse," he confirmed with a small smile. "There's a café just up the street. Decent coffee, better pastries. Join me?"

The invitation was unexpected but welcome. Thomas had a perspective on Krane that none of them shared—months of captivity, observing the man's operation from the inside. They'd had debriefings, formal interviews, but never a casual conversation about his experience.

The café was warm and dimly lit, smelling of cinnamon and coffee—a cozy refuge from the rain. They found a corner table, ordered, and sat in companionable silence for a moment, both watching raindrops race down the steamed windows.

"So," Thomas said finally, "you haven't given up."

It wasn't a question, but Meg answered anyway. "No."

"Good." He cupped his hands around his coffee mug, as if absorbing its warmth. "Neither have I."

Something in his tone—a quiet determination that matched her own—broke through the isolation Meg had been feeling. Here was someone who understood, not just intellectually but viscerally, what was at stake.

"The trail's gone cold," she admitted. "Every lead we thought we had has dried up."

Thomas nodded, unsurprised. "Krane is methodical. He plans for contingencies, anticipates opposition. When we were at Northwood, he would sometimes speak about 'variables' and 'control factors.' People were just elements in his equations."

"What was he like?" Meg asked, the question she'd been wanting to ask since Thomas's rescue. "Really like, when no one was watching?"

A shadow crossed Thomas's face, his fingers tightening almost imperceptibly around his mug. "On the surface, he's everything he appears to be—controlled, articulate, almost pleasant. It's underneath where the rot lives."

Thomas paused, gathering his thoughts, or perhaps his courage. "I saw his mask slip once. About two months into my captivity. One of his security personnel made a mistake—left a door unsecured, allowing me access to a computer terminal briefly. I didn't even have time to do anything with it before they caught me, but when Krane found out..."

He stared into his coffee, as if seeing the scene replayed on its dark surface. "He came to the containment area where they were holding me. Perfectly calm, asking questions in that measured voice of his. The guard was there too, standing at attention, clearly terrified but trying not to show it."

Thomas took a sip of coffee, his hand not quite steady. "Krane dismissed everyone else. Just him, me, and the guard who'd made the mistake. The moment the door closed, he...changed. It was like watching a human mask slide off to reveal something else entirely."

"What happened?" Meg asked quietly.

"He beat the man unconscious," Thomas said flatly. "Used a paperweight from his pocket. Bronze, I think. Heavy. The whole time, his face was...wrong. Twisted. He never raised his voice, never shouted, just kept up this quiet monologue about disappointment and consequences while he methodically destroyed the man's face."

Meg felt cold despite the café's warmth. "And afterward?"

"He straightened his tie, used a handkerchief to wipe the blood from his hands, and called for someone to 'clean up the mess.' His voice was exactly the same as when he orders coffee. When he left, he thanked me for my patience during the 'interruption.'"

The matter-of-fact recounting, delivered without dramatic emphasis, somehow made the story more chilling. Thomas wasn't trying to shock her—he was simply reporting what he'd witnessed.

"Did you ever see the guard again?" Meg asked, though she suspected the answer.

Thomas shook his head. "No. And no one ever mentioned him. It was as if he'd never existed."

They sat in silence for a moment, the rain's gentle patter against the windows a stark contrast to the violence Thomas had described.

"That's what makes him truly dangerous," Thomas continued eventually. "Not just the capacity for violence—many people have that. It's the absolute control he maintains, the way he compartmentalizes. One moment he's calmly destroying a man's life, the next he's discussing market fluctuations or architectural plans as if nothing happened."

"A sociopath," Meg suggested.

"Something more complex, I think," Thomas replied thoughtfully. "He's capable of genuine emotion—I've seen it. But it's as if he's built internal walls, separate rooms in his mind that never connect. The civilized financier never has to acknowledge what the vengeful destroyer does. They exist in parallel, never conflicting because they never truly meet."

The insight aligned with what Meg had observed in her brief encounter with Krane as Nathan Blackwood—that eerie calm, the sense of a performance so practiced it had become second nature. Not the absence of emotion, but the perfect control of it.

"That's why he's been so hard to track," she realized. "He doesn't make emotional mistakes. Everything is calculated, even his rage."

Thomas nodded. "Exactly. And his patience is...remarkable. The operation at Northwood had been in development for years. Every detail planned, every contingency accounted for."

"Except us," Meg pointed out. "He didn't plan for me finding that message on his roof, or for you and Jason being rescued."

"No," Thomas agreed, a hint of satisfaction in his voice. "Those were variables he couldn't control. And now he's had to accelerate his timeline, adapt his plans. That creates opportunities for more mistakes."

Their conversation shifted to more practical matters—properties Thomas remembered from his forced work for Krane, security protocols at Northwood, the rhythms and patterns of the operation. Nothing that immediately solved the puzzle of where Krane might have relocated, but pieces that might eventually connect to form a clearer picture.

As they prepared to leave, the rain having finally subsided to reveal patches of blue sky, Thomas hesitated. "There's something else you should know about Krane. Something I didn't include in my official statements because it seemed…too personal to share with a room full of federal agents."

Meg waited, sensing the importance of whatever he was about to reveal.

"He talked about you," Thomas said quietly. "After you and Alex discovered his cabin, after you escaped. He was fascinated by you—specifically you, not Alex. He called you 'the random factor,' the element he hadn't accounted for."

A chill ran through Meg despite the café's warmth. "Why me and not Alex?"

"I think because Alex made sense to him—a woman searching for her missing sister, following a logical investigative path. But you…" Thomas shook his head slightly. "You were the civilian who spotted a message on Google Maps and drove into the wilderness alone to investigate. The insurance investigator playing detective without backup or authority. You didn't fit his models of predictable behavior."

The assessment was uncomfortably accurate. Meg had acted on impulse, following an investigative instinct that had led her far beyond her usual boundaries. It had been reckless, unplanned—exactly the kind of variable someone like Krane would find disruptive.

"Be careful, Meg," Thomas added, his expression serious. "He's not just trying to evade capture or complete his market scheme. He's developed a specific interest in you. That makes you both valuable and vulnerable."

The warning stayed with Meg as she walked back to Claire's apartment, the afternoon sun now breaking through the clouds, transforming puddles into mirrors that fragmented and reconstituted her reflection with each step. Krane was interested in her. Had been watching her, thinking about her, while she searched for him.

The knowledge should have been terrifying—and part of it was—but it also offered something she'd been lacking for days: a potential avenue of approach. If she was a variable in Krane's equation, perhaps she could use that to disrupt his calculations further.

***

"Absolutely not," Claire declared that evening, her fork clattering against her plate as she set it down with more force than necessary. "You are not going to use yourself as bait for a murderous sociopath with a personal fixation on you."

They sat at Claire's small dining table, the remains of takeout Thai food spread between them, case files temporarily pushed aside for the basic human necessity of dinner. Outside, darkness had fallen early, a spring storm rolling in from the coast with distant thunder punctuating their conversation.

"I'm not suggesting anything reckless," Meg argued, though they both knew that wasn't entirely true. "But we're at a standstill. Every conventional approach has failed. We need to try something different."

Lightning flashed, illuminating Claire's skeptical expression in stark white light. Thunder followed almost immediately, close enough to rattle the windows.

"Different doesn't have to mean suicidal," Claire pointed out. "Hanover would never approve this."

"Which is why I'm not planning to ask her," Meg admitted.

Claire closed her eyes briefly, the gesture of someone praying for patience. "Meg. Think about what you're saying. This man—who Thomas witnessed beating someone to death with a paperweight—has a specific interest in you. And your plan is to deliberately attract his attention?"

Put that way, it did sound insane. But the alternatives—continuing to wait for leads that weren't materializing, watching the investigation gradually lose momentum as other cases demanded resources—seemed worse.

"I'm not suggesting I walk into his operation alone," Meg clarified. "Just that we consider using his interest in me as part of our strategy. Make him think I'm working independently from law enforcement, following my own leads. See if that draws him out or at least gets him to communicate."

Claire still looked unconvinced, but something in her expression had shifted from outright rejection to reluctant consideration. "And how exactly would you signal this independent investigation to someone who's gone completely underground?"

"That's what I haven't figured out yet," Meg admitted. "But if Krane is watching—and Thomas seems to think he is—then the right kind of visible activity might catch his attention."

The conversation was interrupted by Meg's phone ringing—a number she didn't recognize. She hesitated before answering, putting it on speaker out of caution.

"Meg Sawyer."

"Ms. Sawyer." The voice was female, unfamiliar, with a slight accent Meg couldn't immediately place. "You don't know me, but I have information about Victor Krane. Information you'll want to hear."

Claire was instantly alert, reaching for her own phone, likely to text Hanover or Reid about the call.

"Who is this?" Meg asked, keeping her voice neutral despite the surge of adrenaline.

"Someone with a mutual interest in finding him," the woman replied. "I can't speak more on the phone. Meet me at Lighthouse Point in one hour. Come alone."

"That's not going to happen," Meg said firmly. "I don't meet anonymous callers in isolated locations after dark."

A soft laugh, without humor. "Sensible. The café at Harbor View Hotel, then. Public, well-lit, plenty of witnesses. Still in one hour. Ask for a reservation under Campbell."

The call ended before Meg could respond. She stared at her phone, uncertainty warring with the desperate need for any lead, any new information.

"Obvious trap is obvious," Claire said, already texting rapidly. "Hanover can have undercover officers at the hotel before you arrive."

"And if the caller spots them and disappears?" Meg countered. "This is the first potential lead we've had in days."

Claire set her phone down, fixing Meg with a stern look. "This is exactly the kind of reckless behavior we were just discussing. An anonymous call, a cryptic meeting, the insistence on your coming alone—it practically screams 'ambush.'"

She wasn't wrong. Every investigative instinct Meg possessed recognized the red flags. But desperation had a way of overriding caution.

"What if we compromise?" Meg suggested. "You come with me, but stay at the bar, not at my table. Hanover can have officers nearby but not obviously positioned. If anything seems off, I walk away immediately."

Claire's expression suggested she was weighing the risks against the potential benefits. "And if this mysterious Campbell tells you to go somewhere else, or asks you to leave with them?"

"I refuse," Meg promised. "The conversation happens there, in public, or not at all."

After further negotiation—and several texts between Claire and Sheriff Hanover—a plan took shape. Meg would meet the mysterious caller, with Claire and two undercover deputies positioned to intervene if necessary. The risk wasn't eliminated, but it was managed as much as possible given the circumstances.

The Harbor View Hotel stood on a bluff overlooking the ocean, its Victorian architecture a testament to Seacliff's history as a prestigious resort town. The lobby gleamed with polished wood and brass, soft lighting creating an atmosphere of refined comfort despite the storm raging outside.

The café occupied a corner of the ground floor, windows on two sides offering views of the garden and, beyond it, the churning sea barely visible in flashes of lightning. At this hour, only a handful of tables were occupied—hotel guests seeking late dinners or nightcaps, a couple engaged in quiet conversation by the fireplace, a solitary business traveler working on a laptop.

"Reservation for Campbell," Meg told the host, scanning the room for anyone who might be watching for her arrival.

"Yes, Ms. Sawyer," the host replied, surprising her by using her name. "Your party is already seated. This way, please."

He led her to a corner table partially screened by an ornamental palm, where a woman sat with her back to the wall, a position that afforded a clear view of both the café entrance and the garden beyond the windows. She was perhaps fifty, with steel-gray hair cut in a severe bob, sharp features, and the kind of watchful eyes that missed nothing. She wore a simple black blazer over a white blouse, professional but unremarkable, the kind of outfit designed to blend rather than stand out.

"Ms. Sawyer," she greeted, her voice confirming she was the caller. "Thank you for coming. Please, sit."

Meg took the chair opposite, positioning herself where Claire—seated at the bar with a clear line of sight—could observe their interaction. "You have me at a disadvantage. You know my name, but you haven't shared yours."

The woman smiled slightly, the expression not reaching her eyes. "Campbell will do for now. I'm sure you understand the need for discretion."

"What I understand," Meg replied, keeping her tone even, "is that anonymous individuals claiming to have information about active investigations tend to be either unreliable or dangerous. Sometimes both."

Campbell inclined her head, acknowledging the point. "Fair enough. Let me establish some credibility." She pushed a manila envelope across the table. "Take a look."

Meg opened it cautiously, half-expecting some kind of trap despite the public setting. Inside were photographs—surveillance images showing Nathan Blackwood, or rather Victor Krane, entering what appeared to be an office building. The timestamp showed a date three days ago.

"Where were these taken?" Meg asked, carefully controlling her reaction.

"Portland. He maintains an office there under the name Gerard Mitchell. Very exclusive, very private, accessible only by appointment." Campbell sipped from a glass of water, watching Meg's response. "This is his tertiary identity, used primarily for business transactions that require a physical presence."

Meg studied the woman across from her with renewed wariness. This wasn't some random informant with vague information—this was someone with detailed knowledge of Krane's operation and resources sophisticated enough to conduct surveillance on him.

"Who are you?" she asked directly. "Law enforcement would have shared this with Sheriff Hanover. Private investigator?"

Campbell smiled again, this time with genuine, if restrained, amusement. "Let's just say I represent interests that have been adversely affected by Mr. Krane's activities and would prefer to see those activities permanently discontinued."

The careful phrasing, the deliberate ambiguity—Meg had encountered it before in her insurance work. This woman was almost certainly connected to private security or intelligence, possibly corporate, possibly something less official.

"Why come to me instead of law enforcement?" Meg asked, the question that had been foremost in her mind since receiving the call.

"Because law enforcement has constraints—jurisdictional boundaries, warrant requirements, chains of evidence," Campbell replied matter-of-factly. "And because Krane has penetrated those organizations at multiple levels. The judge who died of a 'heart attack'? Not his first such intervention."

She retrieved another photograph from the envelope, this one showing Krane with a man Meg recognized with a jolt—Judge Harmon, who had consistently blocked their warrant requests.

"Harmon was found murdered," Meg noted, keeping her voice low.

"Yes," Campbell agreed. "Once his usefulness ended, so did his life. Krane tolerates no loose ends, no potential liabilities. Judge Peterson made the mistake of signing your warrants. Harmon made the mistake of failing to prevent it."

The casual assessment of calculated murder sent a chill through Meg despite the café's warmth. "And the women? Alex Reeves, Emily Reeves, Valerie Cortez?"

Something flickered in Campbell's eyes—a hesitation, perhaps, or a calculation being adjusted. "They remain with Krane's operation. Their status is... complex."

"Meaning what, exactly?"

"Meaning," Campbell said carefully, "that the situation is not as straightforward as your law enforcement colleagues believe. 'One by coercion, one by deception, one by choice'—Krane's note wasn't merely psychological warfare. It was the literal truth."

Before Meg could press further, Campbell slid another photograph across the table. This one showed Alex—alive, apparently uninjured, dressed in business attire—walking into the same Portland building where Krane had been photographed. The timestamp showed it was taken just yesterday.

"Alexandra Reeves has been working with Krane for nearly a year," Campbell stated, watching Meg closely. "Her presence in Seacliff, her supposed search for her sister—all carefully orchestrated aspects of Krane's operation."

The confirmation of what they had feared, what Krane's note had implied, landed like a physical blow. Meg stared at the photograph, searching for any sign that Alex was under duress, any indication that this was staged or manipulated. There was none. She moved with the confident purpose of someone exactly where they intended to be.

"Why?" Meg asked, the single word encompassing a multitude of questions. "Why would she—"

"Money, primarily," Campbell interrupted, her tone clinical, detached. "Alexandra Reeves isn't FBI, as she claimed to Eleanor Blackwell. She's a former military intelligence officer who transitioned to private security work after discharge. Krane recruited her specifically because of her background—she has the skills needed to manage certain aspects of his operation while maintaining a convincing cover identity."

Meg thought back to their interactions—Alex's tactical awareness, her comfort with surveillance equipment, her ability to navigate the forest with military precision. All consistent with the background Campbell described, yet all would have seemed equally consistent with Alex's cover story of being a photojournalist who had worked in conflict zones.

"And Emily? Is she actually Alex's sister?"

"Yes, though their relationship is more complicated than presented," Campbell replied. "Emily Reeves was genuinely abducted by Krane's operation due to her environmental research uncovering evidence of Axion's activities. Alexandra's initial involvement was indeed motivated by finding her sister, but somewhere along the way, priorities... shifted."

The careful phrasing suggested there was more to the story than Campbell was sharing, but before Meg could probe further, the woman continued.

"Valerie Cortez remains a legitimate hostage, controlled through threat of harm to her family. Emily's status has evolved—she's now essentially a cooperative prisoner, working on Krane's environmental projects to protect both herself and her sister."

Meg struggled to reconcile this new information with everything she thought she knew about the case. "Why are you telling me this? What do you want from me?"

Campbell leaned forward slightly, her voice dropping lower. "Because Victor Krane's operation has expanded beyond financial crimes and personal revenge. He's developing something that could destabilize global markets on an unprecedented scale. My employers want it stopped—preferably with Krane alive to assist in dismantling it, but stopped regardless."

"And I fit into this how, exactly?"

"You've become an unexpected factor in Krane's calculations," Campbell explained, echoing what Thomas had told her earlier. "He's developed a specific interest in you—your tenacity, your refusal to follow expected patterns. That makes you uniquely positioned to approach him in ways law enforcement cannot."

The parallels to Meg's earlier conversation with Claire were unsettling. "You want to use me as bait."

"I want to give you the opportunity to resolve this situation before more people die," Campbell corrected smoothly. "Including Alexandra, Emily, and Valerie. Because that is the inevitable conclusion if Krane believes they've become liabilities."

Lightning flashed again, closer now, illuminating Campbell's face in stark relief—the lines around her eyes more pronounced, the set of her mouth revealing a determination that matched or exceeded Meg's own.

"I'm offering you information, resources, and support that law enforcement cannot provide. In return, I ask only that you consider approaches they would never approve." Campbell slid a small business card across the table, blank except for a phone number. "Think about it. Call that number when you're ready to discuss specifics."

She stood, gathering her belongings with efficient movements. "The photographs are yours to keep. Share them with Sheriff Hanover if you wish, though I suggest discretion regarding our conversation. Krane's reach within local law enforcement remains uncertain."

With that, she departed, moving through the café with the confident stride of someone who belonged everywhere and was noticed nowhere. Meg remained seated, staring at the photographs spread before her, feeling as if the ground had shifted beneath her feet yet again.

Claire appeared at her side moments later, sliding into the chair Campbell had vacated. "Well? What did our mysterious informant have to say?"

Meg hesitated, Campbell's warning about discretion echoing in her mind. But this was Claire—her oldest friend, the person she trusted most in the world. "She says Alex has been working with Krane all along. And she has proof."

She pushed the photograph across the table, watching as Claire studied it with the careful assessment of a prosecutor evaluating evidence. "This could be manipulated," Claire suggested, though her tone lacked conviction. "Or taken out of context."

"Or it could be exactly what it appears to be," Meg countered. "Alex entering Krane's Portland office voluntarily, no signs of duress, dressed like she works there."

Claire set the photograph down, her expression troubled. "If that's true, then everything—from the moment you met her at Blackwood's cabin—was an act. She used you, used all of us, to gather intelligence on the investigation."

The realization settled in Meg's stomach like a stone. All those moments she'd interpreted as genuine connection, as shared purpose—the discussions in the hunting blind, their escape from Blackwood's cabin, their late-night strategy sessions at the diner—all potentially calculated performances designed to infiltrate the investigation.

"Campbell says Emily and Valerie are still alive," Meg continued, sorting through the new information. "Emily apparently working with Krane to protect herself and her sister, Valerie under more direct coercion."

"And who exactly is this Campbell person? FBI? Some other agency?"

"Private sector, I think. Corporate security, maybe, though she was deliberately vague. She says Krane is developing something that could destabilize global markets, and her employers want it stopped."

Claire's expression grew more concerned. "So an anonymous operative for unnamed corporate interests wants your help pursuing their agenda against Krane. That doesn't raise any red flags for you?"

It did, of course. Everything about the encounter screamed caution. But the photographs were real—or at least appeared to be—and the information aligned with what they already suspected about Alex's true role.

"She gave me her number," Meg said, fingering the blank business card. "Said to call when I'm ready to discuss specifics."

"You're not actually considering this," Claire stated, though her tone suggested she already knew the answer.

Meg gathered the photographs, sliding them back into the envelope. "I'm considering all options that might lead to finding Krane and rescuing Emily and Valerie. Campbell has resources and information we don't. That doesn't mean I trust her, but it means I'd be foolish to dismiss what she's offering without hearing more."

Thunder crashed directly overhead, rattling the windows and causing several patrons to glance up in alarm. The storm had arrived in full force, matching the turbulence Meg felt as she weighed impossible choices with inadequate information.

"Let's get home," Claire suggested, eyeing the worsening weather. "We can talk more there, decide how much of this to share with Hanover."

The drive back to Claire's apartment was tense, both from the storm's intensity and the weight of their discoveries. Rain lashed the windshield faster than the wipers could clear it, turning the world beyond into a smeared impressionist painting of streetlights and shadows.

As Claire navigated the increasingly treacherous roads, Meg found her thoughts returning to her first encounter with Alex—the hunting knife held with casual competence, the assessing gaze that had cataloged everything about Meg in an instant, the deliberate approach that had intercepted her before she could reach Blackwood's cabin.

Had it all been calculated? Had Alex been watching, waiting for someone to spot the message, ready to insert herself into any investigation that might threaten Krane's operation? The possibility made Meg revisit every interaction, every conversation, questioning what had been genuine and what had been manipulation.

By the time they reached Claire's apartment, the storm had reached its peak—wind howling around the building's corners, rain hammering the roof and windows with percussive intensity. They hurried inside, shedding wet jackets and shoes in the entryway.

"Power might go out," Claire warned, moving to gather candles and matches from a kitchen drawer. "This storm's worse than they forecast."

Meg stood at the living room window, watching the rain transform the street below into a shallow river, debris carried along by the current. Her reflection stared back at her, superimposed on the storm's chaos—a woman caught between forces she only partially understood, trying to navigate by instinct when facts proved unreliable.

"What are you thinking?" Claire asked, setting candles on the coffee table.

"That I've been played," Meg admitted, turning from the window. "By Alex, maybe by Campbell too. That I'm out of my depth."

Claire's expression softened. "Or maybe you're exactly where you need to be. Think about it—if Campbell is right about Krane being fixated on you, that gives you leverage he didn't anticipate."

"Leverage I have no idea how to use," Meg pointed out. "I'm an insurance investigator, not a spy or a hostage negotiator."

"But you're also the woman who spotted a cry for help on Google Maps and drove into the wilderness alone to investigate," Claire countered. "The 'random factor' that disrupted Krane's careful plans. Don't underestimate that."

Before Meg could respond, the apartment plunged into darkness as the power failed. For a moment, they stood in perfect blackness, the storm's fury the only sound. Then Claire struck a match, its tiny flame growing as she lit the candles one by one, golden light pushing back the shadows, creating a small circle of warmth and visibility in the surrounding darkness.

"We should call Hanover," Claire said, reaching for her phone. "Let her know about the photographs, at least."

Meg nodded, though something held her back from immediately agreeing to share everything Campbell had told her. The warning about Krane's reach within law enforcement, the implication that there were aspects to this case that extended beyond what the sheriff's department could address—it all suggested caution.

As Claire made the call, Meg returned to the window, watching lightning illuminate the storm-lashed street in staccato bursts. Somewhere out there, Krane was executing his plan, whatever it was. Alex was working with him, for reasons Meg still didn't fully understand. Emily and Valerie remained captives, their fates tied to decisions being made beyond their control.

And here she stood, caught in the middle, uncertain which path to take, which story to believe, which version of Alex was real—the determined sister searching for Emily, or the calculating operative who had used Meg to monitor the investigation.

Perhaps both were true, in their way. Perhaps Alex had begun with genuine concern for her sister and been drawn into Krane's operation through a combination of necessity and opportunity. The line between victim and accomplice could blur under the right pressure, the right incentives.

Lightning flashed again, closer this time, briefly transforming the window into a mirror that reflected Meg's troubled expression back at her. The storm seemed a fitting backdrop to her thoughts—chaotic, unpredictable, powerful.

But storms eventually passed. And when this one did, Meg intended to be ready for whatever came next—whether that meant working with Hanover and traditional law enforcement, exploring what Campbell was offering, or charting her own course through the contradictions and complexities that had engulfed her life since spotting that message on Blackwood's roof.

CHAPTER NINE
SHELL GAME

The storm that had battered Seacliff through the night left behind a transformed world. Morning light revealed branches strewn across rain-slicked streets, small lakes where parking lots had been, a delicate lacework of leaves and debris plastered against chainlink fences. The air felt scrubbed clean, carrying the sharp scent of wet earth and salt from the churning ocean beyond.

Meg stood on Claire's balcony, hands wrapped around a steaming mug of coffee, watching gulls wheel and dive in the wake of the tempest. Power had been restored around dawn, but cell service remained spotty—towers down somewhere between Seacliff and the county seat. The enforced disconnection felt fitting somehow, a physical manifestation of her growing isolation from the certainties she'd once taken for granted.

Behind her, through the sliding glass door, she could see Claire moving around the kitchen, preparing for her day at the courthouse. Claire's world retained a structure that Meg's had lost—depositions scheduled, motions to be filed, arguments to be presented. The mundane machinery of justice grinding forward regardless of storms, physical or metaphorical.

"You're brooding again," Claire observed, stepping onto the balcony with her own coffee. She'd dressed for court—charcoal pantsuit, crisp white blouse, hair pulled back in a professional twist—but hadn't yet applied makeup, the lingering shadows beneath her eyes testament to their late night.

"Not brooding," Meg corrected. "Thinking."

"Same difference." Claire leaned against the railing, her shoulder brushing Meg's. "Hanover wants to meet at eleven to discuss the photographs. But I need to be in court from nine to at least ten-thirty."

Meg nodded, unsurprised. They'd forwarded the images Campbell had provided to Sheriff Hanover late last night, after debating how much of their meeting to share. In the end, they'd been selective—mentioning an anonymous contact with access to surveillance resources, but omitting Campbell's corporate connections and her warnings about Krane's reach within law enforcement.

"I'll go alone," Meg decided. "You focus on your case."

Claire studied her over the rim of her coffee mug, the morning sunlight catching auburn highlights in her hair. "Are you going to tell her about the phone number? About Campbell's offer?"

The question had kept Meg awake long after the storm had passed, weighing loyalties against practicalities, trust against evidence.

"Not yet," she replied finally. "Not until I understand more about what Campbell's really offering. And who she's working for."

Claire didn't look surprised. "Just be careful. People with resources like that rarely share them out of altruism."

"Says the woman who let me move into her beach house rent-free," Meg pointed out with a small smile.

"That's different. I had ulterior motives—keeping my best friend from sliding into a post-divorce depression spiral." Claire checked her watch and sighed. "I need to go. Breakfast prep is all yours. I might have time between court and the meeting with Hanover to grab something."

"I'll make extra," Meg promised. "Take the umbrella—they're saying more showers later."

After Claire left, the apartment felt suddenly larger, emptier. Meg had grown accustomed to their shared routine over the past weeks—Claire's morning efficiency, her running commentary on upcoming cases, the comfortable silence that fell between them as they prepared for their respective days.

She moved to the kitchen, pulling ingredients for omelets from the refrigerator. The simple ritual of cooking—whisking eggs, dicing vegetables, grating cheese—provided a temporary anchor, something tangible to focus on while her thoughts circled back to Campbell's revelations and the photographs that confirmed Alex's betrayal.

Or did they? As she poured the egg mixture into a heated pan, Meg found herself questioning the evidence yet again. A photograph showed a moment, not a context. Alex entering Krane's Portland office voluntarily didn't necessarily prove willing collaboration. It might indicate coercion, manipulation, or even a deeper game than Campbell had revealed.

The smell of butter and herbs filled the kitchen as the omelet cooked, a homey counterpoint to the dangerous puzzle she was trying to solve. She flipped the eggs with practiced ease, muscle memory taking over while her mind continued working through possibilities and contingencies.

By the time she'd eaten, cleaned up, and prepared for her meeting with Hanover, Meg had reached a decision. She would continue compartmentalizing, maintaining separate channels of investigation—the official path with Hanover and the sheriff's department, and a parallel exploration of what Campbell was offering. Not out of disloyalty to Hanover, but from a growing conviction that the full picture remained obscured, visible only from multiple angles of approach.

The sheriff's department occupied a two-story brick building near the center of town, its architecture suggesting solidity and permanence. Storm damage was evident even here—a large branch resting against the front steps, maintenance workers clearing debris from the parking lot, a temporary sign directing visitors to the side entrance where flooding had been minimal.

Inside, the usual bustle of a small-town law enforcement office had taken on an added dimension, deputies fielding calls about downed power lines and flooded basements alongside their regular duties. Meg made her way through the controlled chaos to Sheriff Hanover's office, where Reid was already waiting, a stack of papers spread across the desk between them.

"Ms. Sawyer," Hanover greeted her, gesturing to an empty chair. "Thank you for coming. I understand Ms. Winters will join us later."

"Court obligations," Meg explained, settling into the offered seat. "The Henderson case."

Hanover nodded, her expression revealing nothing beyond professional focus. She wore her uniform as always—crisp, immaculate, a symbol of authority that seemed both reassuring and slightly intimidating. Reid looked more casual but no less professional, his weathered face bearing the signs of a man who'd spent the early morning hours dealing with storm-related emergencies.

"These photographs," Hanover began without preamble, tapping the prints they'd forwarded last night. "Your source. How reliable are they?"

Direct question, requiring a direct answer. Meg chose her words carefully. "I believe the photographs themselves are genuine. As for the source... I have no reason to doubt their accuracy, but limited information about their motivations."

"Anonymous tip?" Reid asked, his tone neutral but his eyes sharp with assessment.

"Initially," Meg confirmed. "Then a face-to-face meeting arranged at Harbor View Hotel. My contact identified herself only as Campbell—no first name, no credentials. Professional, mid-fifties, extensive knowledge of Krane's operation."

"And this meeting was her initiative?" Hanover pressed.

"Yes. She contacted me, not the other way around."

Hanover exchanged a glance with Reid, some unspoken communication passing between them. "And she provided no explanation for why she approached you specifically, rather than law enforcement?"

Here Meg had to tread carefully. "She indicated that Krane has compromised some law enforcement channels. And that he's developed a specific interest in my involvement in the case."

"That aligns with what Thomas Blackwell reported," Reid noted, making a notation in his file. "Krane's fascination with Ms. Sawyer as the 'random factor' in his calculations."

Hanover studied the photograph showing Alex entering the Portland office building, her expression unreadable. "If Alexandra Reeves has indeed been working with Krane all along, it reconfigures our entire understanding of this case."

"It would explain her ability to anticipate our moves," Reid added. "Her knowledge of operational details that seemed too precise for someone outside law enforcement."

Meg felt a tightness in her chest that had nothing to do with the morning's rich omelet. Hearing her own suspicions voiced by others made Alex's betrayal seem more real, more devastating. "Have you been able to verify the location? The Portland office?"

"The building exists," Hanover confirmed. "Twenty-fourth floor houses several private offices, including one registered to Mitchell Consulting Group—likely one of Krane's shell companies. Portland PD is conducting discreet surveillance, but so far no sign of Krane or Alexandra Reeves returning to the location."

A thought occurred to Meg. "The timestamps on these photos—this was three days ago for Krane, yesterday for Alex. After Eagle's Rest was raided, after Krane knew we were closing in. Why maintain an office that could be traced? Why risk physical presence at all?"

Reid leaned forward, interest sharpening his gaze. "Valid question. If Krane is as cautious as we believe, why not operate completely remotely? Why maintain physical locations that could be discovered?"

"Because some things require physical presence," Hanover suggested. "Meetings that can't be conducted virtually. Access to systems that aren't connected to external networks."

"Or signatures," Meg added, a connection forming. "Financial transactions that require in-person verification. Banking protocols, property transfers..."

Hanover nodded thoughtfully. "The scale of Krane's operation would necessitate significant financial movement. Even with digital systems, certain thresholds trigger physical verification requirements."

The conversation continued, exploring the implications of Campbell's photographs, the potential purposes of Krane's Portland office, strategies for expanding surveillance without alerting him to their knowledge. Throughout, Meg maintained the careful balance she'd decided on earlier—sharing information relevant to tracking Krane and the missing women, but holding back Campbell's direct offer of assistance and the business card now tucked into her wallet.

By the time Claire arrived, fresh from court with the harried look of someone who'd been forced to compress complex legal arguments into an artificially constricted timeframe, they had developed the outline of a revised approach—focusing on financial tracking rather than physical surveillance, looking for patterns in property acquisitions and banking activity that might reveal Krane's movements.

"Henderson's attorney tried another delay tactic," Claire explained, dropping into the chair beside Meg. "Judge wasn't having it. Trial starts Monday, ready or not."

"You look ready to me," Reid observed with a small smile.

Claire shrugged, though Meg could see she appreciated the vote of confidence. "Six months of prep, three continuances. I'd better be ready." She scanned the notes and photographs spread across Hanover's desk. "Catch me up?"

As Hanover summarized their discussion, Meg found herself watching Claire—the professional mask she presented in these settings, the slight tension in her shoulders that only someone who knew her well would notice, the way she occasionally twisted her class ring when confronted with particularly troubling information. Twelve years of friendship had taught Meg to read these subtle signals, to understand the emotional currents beneath Claire's composed exterior.

"So we pivot to financial tracking," Claire concluded when Hanover finished. "Looking for Krane's money rather than Krane himself."

"Exactly," Hanover confirmed. "Agent Lopez is coordinating with FBI financial crimes specialists. We're reaching out to contacts at major banks, focusing on transactions matching known patterns from Krane's previous operations."

The meeting continued for another hour, details hammered out, assignments distributed, a methodical approach taking shape from the chaos of possibilities. Throughout, Meg contributed where her insurance investigation experience offered relevant insight, but found herself increasingly detached from the process, a part of her mind circling back to Campbell's offer, to the blank business card, to the question of what might be happening to Emily and Valerie while they pursued paper trails and financial transactions.

"You're quiet," Claire observed as they walked back to her car afterward, the promised afternoon showers having materialized as a fine mist that beaded on their jackets and hair. "Second thoughts about our approach?"

Meg shook her head, raindrops scattering from her ponytail with the movement. "Not second thoughts exactly. Just... awareness of the time factor. Financial investigations move slowly. Emily and Valerie don't have that luxury."

Claire unlocked her car, both of them sliding into the shelter it provided from the increasing rain. "What are you not saying, Meg? I know that look."

The interior of the car felt suddenly intimate, a confined space where truths might be spoken that wouldn't survive in the open air. Meg stared through the windshield, watching raindrops trace patterns on the glass, each following its own inevitable path to join others in larger streams.

"I'm thinking about calling Campbell," she admitted finally. "Hearing what she's really offering."

Claire didn't respond immediately, her fingers tapping a thoughtful rhythm on the steering wheel. "I figured you might. That's why I didn't push when you omitted her offer from your report to Hanover."

"You're not going to tell me it's a terrible idea? Lecture me on the dangers of working with unknown operatives with unclear agendas?"

"Would it make any difference if I did?" Claire asked, a hint of resignation in her voice.

"Probably not," Meg conceded.

"Then I'll save my breath." Claire started the car, the engine's purr providing background to their conversation. "But I reserve the right to say 'I told you so' if this goes sideways."

"That's fair," Meg agreed, feeling a rush of gratitude for her friend's understanding, even when that understanding came with reservations. "For what it's worth, I'm not planning to go rogue or do anything reckless. Just... explore an additional avenue while the financial investigation proceeds."

Claire pulled out of the parking lot, navigating carefully through puddles that concealed the true depth of storm-related flooding. "Speaking of additional avenues, I nearly forgot—Henderson case prep all afternoon, then I'm meeting Thomas and Eleanor for dinner at Harborside Grill at seven. Eleanor insisted. Said she has new information she doesn't want to discuss over the phone."

"New information about what?"

"Wouldn't say. Just that it relates to Krane's early years in Seacliff, before the original financial crimes case." Claire navigated around a fallen branch, her movements precise, controlled. "You're welcome to join us. Might be a good distraction from... other pursuits."

The offer was genuine, Meg knew, but also strategic—an attempt to keep her connected to their established investigative circle rather than drifting toward Campbell's murky alternatives.

"I'll try," she said, noncommittal. "Depends on what the afternoon brings."

Claire accepted this with a nod, apparently deciding not to press further. They drove in comfortable silence for several minutes, the rhythm of windshield wipers marking time, the rain intensifying then easing in unpredictable patterns.

"You know what's strange?" Meg said eventually. "I keep thinking about Alex. Not with anger, but with... curiosity. If she's been working with Krane all along, why bother with the elaborate performance? Why involve me at all?"

"The obvious answer would be to monitor the investigation," Claire suggested, turning onto her street. "Keep tabs on law enforcement's progress."

"Maybe," Meg acknowledged. "But there are simpler ways to do that. Informants within the department, digital surveillance, conventional intelligence gathering. Why the personal approach? Why spend hours in a hunting blind watching Blackwood's cabin, risk breaking in with me, maintain the pretense of searching for her sister?"

Claire pulled into her assigned parking space, turning off the engine but making no move to exit the car. "I don't know," she admitted. "Unless..."

"Unless what?"

"Unless she needed something specific from you. Something beyond just information about the investigation." Claire turned to face Meg directly. "What if you weren't just a convenient monitor, but a specific target? What if Krane's interest in you isn't recent, but was part of the plan from the beginning?"

The suggestion landed like a stone in still water, ripples of implication spreading outward. "But that would mean they knew about me before I ever spotted that message on the roof. Before I had any connection to the case at all."

"Exactly," Claire said quietly. "And that raises a much more disturbing question: what made you a target in the first place?"

The question hung between them, unanswerable with their current information yet impossible to dismiss now that it had been voiced. What if Meg hadn't stumbled onto Krane's operation by chance? What if she had been drawn in deliberately, for reasons still obscured?

"I need to make that call," Meg decided, reaching a conclusion that had been forming since her conversation with Campbell. "Not because I trust her, but because we need more information than we currently have. About everything."

Claire nodded, resigned but understanding. "Just promise me one thing? No meeting with her alone again. I'm there, or Reid, or someone we trust."

"Promise," Meg agreed readily. That much caution, at least, seemed obvious given the multiplying complexities of the situation.

They made their way to Claire's apartment, the afternoon stretched before them with their separate tasks—Claire preparing for the Henderson trial, Meg contemplating a call that might change the trajectory of their investigation entirely.

Inside, the apartment felt different somehow, as if the previous night's storm had subtly rearranged things beyond the physical debris visible through the windows. Sunlight broke intermittently through scudding clouds, creating shifting patterns on the walls and floors, shadows advancing and retreating in a silent dance.

"I'll be in my office if you need me," Claire said, already pulling files from her briefcase, her mind visibly transitioning to the case that would consume her professional focus for the coming week. "If you're going to call Campbell, use the burner phone in the kitchen drawer. The one I keep for confidential informants."

Meg raised an eyebrow, surprised. "You have a burner phone for CIs?"

"Prosecution isn't always as straightforward as they teach in law school," Claire replied with a faint smile. "Sometimes you need communications that won't appear in discovery."

This glimpse of Claire's professional world—the gray areas she navigated, the pragmatic compromises between ideal justice and achievable results—reminded Meg that her friend understood complexity far better than she sometimes acknowledged.

"Thanks," she said simply.

Claire disappeared into her home office, leaving Meg alone with her thoughts and the decision before her. She found the burner phone where Claire had indicated—a basic model with prepaid service, its simplicity a stark contrast to their usual technology. The blank business card felt strangely heavy as she removed it from her wallet, the single phone number representing a choice with unknowable consequences.

She moved to the balcony, wanting space and air for this conversation, needing to see the broader world beyond their immediate crisis. The rain had stopped for the moment, leaving behind a freshly washed quality to the light, colors more vibrant against the backdrop of pewter clouds still lingering on the horizon.

The number connected after just two rings, Campbell's voice emerging from the speaker with the same controlled precision Meg remembered from their meeting.

"Ms. Sawyer. I was beginning to think you'd decided against further communication."

"I needed time to consider my options," Meg replied, keeping her tone neutral. "And to verify certain aspects of what you shared."

"Understandable caution," Campbell acknowledged. "Have you reached a decision?"

"That depends on what exactly you're offering. And what you expect in return."

A slight pause, the sound of a door closing on Campbell's end. "What I'm offering is information, resources, and operational support outside official channels. What I expect is your assistance in approaching Krane in ways that might neutralize his market manipulation scheme before it activates."

"Neutralize how, exactly?" Meg pressed. "Are we talking about arrest and prosecution, or something more... permanent?"

"My employers prefer Krane alive and cooperative," Campbell replied carefully. "His expertise would be invaluable in dismantling what he's built. But prevention of the scheme's activation takes priority over all other considerations."

Translation: they'd prefer not to kill him, but would if necessary. The cold calculation behind the statement reminded Meg that whatever Campbell's resources and information might offer, they came with moral ambiguities she wasn't sure she was prepared to navigate.

"And your employers are...?" Meg tried, expecting evasion.

She wasn't disappointed. "Financial institutions with significant exposure to the markets Krane intends to destabilize. Beyond that, discretion serves both our interests at this stage."

Meg leaned against the balcony railing, watching a solitary gull ride air currents above the harbor, effortlessly adjusting to shifting winds. "You said Alex—Alexandra Reeves—has been working with Krane for nearly a year. How do you know that? What proof do you have beyond the photographs?"

"Financial transfers to offshore accounts in her name. Communications intercepted between her and Krane's operation. Witness testimony from former Axion personnel who observed her role." Campbell's voice remained even, factual. "She was recruited initially as security, leveraging her military background. Over time, she became more integral to the operation."

"And Emily? Her sister? Was that relationship fabricated as well?"

"No. Their familial relationship is genuine. Emily Reeves was indeed abducted by Krane's operation last year after her environmental research threatened to expose certain Axion activities." A slight hesitation, then: "Alexandra's search for her sister was initially legitimate. She approached Krane's organization demanding Emily's release. Instead, she was offered a proposition—work for the operation, ensure Emily's continued safety and eventual freedom."

The picture taking shape was more complex than Meg had imagined, layers of coercion and choice intertwined in ways that defied simple categorization. "So Alex chose to work with Krane to protect her sister. But where do I fit in? Why involve me at all?"

"That," Campbell said with what sounded like genuine regret, "remains unclear even to our intelligence. Alexandra's decision to intercept you at Blackwood's cabin, to form an alliance, appears to have been improvisation rather than planned strategy. Once established, however, Krane recognized the value of having direct access to the investigation through your connection."

Meg absorbed this, trying to reconcile it with her experiences, with the moments that had felt genuine despite the deception underlying them. "And now? Where are they? What is Krane planning?"

"That's where we need your help, Ms. Sawyer." Campbell's voice took on added intensity. "We believe Krane is accelerating his timeline. The market manipulation algorithm is complete, the server infrastructure in place. What remains is final positioning of key assets and the triggering sequence."

"Assets meaning what? Or who?"

"Both. Financial instruments positioned to capitalize on the market collapse, and personnel placed to ensure the sequence executes without intervention." Campbell paused, then added: "Including Alexandra Reeves, who we believe has been tasked with eliminating potential witnesses and loose ends."

The implication sent a chill through Meg despite the afternoon warmth. "You're saying Alex is not just working with Krane, but actively eliminating people for him? That she's become his... what, assassin?"

"Her military background included specialized training," Campbell replied, neither confirming nor denying directly. "Her skills make her valuable for operations requiring... precision."

Meg thought of Judge Peterson's death, the medical examiner's conclusion that his "heart attack" had been induced through precise application of pressure to specific points. The kind of technique that would require specialized knowledge, the kind Alex might possess given the background Campbell described.

"Why are you telling me this?" Meg demanded, a surge of anger cutting through her analytical detachment. "If you have all this intelligence, all these resources, why not stop them yourself? Why involve me at all?"

"Because Krane has gone completely dark," Campbell admitted, a hint of frustration coloring her usually controlled tone. "After Eagle's Rest, after the Portland office, he's implemented extreme operational security protocols. Our surveillance assets have lost him completely. But you—" She paused significantly. "You represent an avenue of approach he might still respond to."

"You want to use me as bait," Meg concluded, echoing her assessment from their first meeting. "Dangle me in front of Krane and hope he bites."

"I want to give you the opportunity to resolve this situation before more people die," Campbell corrected, using the same phrasing as before. "Including, potentially, yourself. Because make no mistake, Ms. Sawyer—as Krane's operation enters its final phase, everyone connected to the investigation becomes a liability he cannot afford."

The warning wasn't subtle, nor did it seem intended to be. Campbell was laying out the stakes as she saw them—Krane eliminating loose ends, the window for intervention narrowing, Meg herself potentially on a list of liabilities to be addressed.

"What exactly would working with you entail?" Meg asked, decision still suspended, gathering information before committing.

"Initially, information sharing," Campbell replied promptly. "What you know, what we know, creating a more complete picture than either of us currently possesses. Then, a carefully managed approach to Krane through channels he monitors, presenting you as having broken from the official investigation, seeking answers independently."

"And then?"

"Then we improvise based on his response. But the goal remains constant—locate Krane, neutralize the market scheme, secure the safety of Emily Reeves and Valerie Cortez." Campbell paused, then added: "And determine Alexandra Reeves' true position and culpability."

The last addition caught Meg's attention. "You're not certain about Alex? Despite everything you've told me?"

A slight hesitation. "The intelligence is clear regarding her employment with Krane's operation. Less clear is the degree of coercion involved, the extent of her willing participation versus forced compliance. People in her position... sometimes the lines blur. Survival requires adaptation."

It was the first hint of nuance in Campbell's assessment, the first suggestion that the situation might not be as black and white as initially presented. It resonated with Meg's own uncertainty, her reluctance to completely condemn Alex despite the mounting evidence.

"I need time to think," she said finally. "And to discuss this with someone I trust."

"Ms. Winters, I presume," Campbell replied, unsurprised. "Understandable. But do not delay too long. Our intelligence suggests Krane's timeline has advanced significantly. Days matter now, perhaps even hours."

"I'll call you tomorrow," Meg promised. "After I've had time to process everything you've shared."

"Very well." Campbell's tone suggested neither approval nor disappointment, merely acknowledgment. "One final piece of information, Ms. Sawyer, which may influence your decision. Yesterday afternoon, a financial analyst at Meridian Bank was found dead in his home. Carbon monoxide poisoning, apparently from a malfunctioning water heater. Except our sources indicate the water heater was deliberately tampered with, and the analyst in question had recently flagged suspicious transactions matching patterns associated with Krane's previous operations."

The implication was clear—another death, another loose end eliminated, the circle of danger tightening around anyone who might threaten Krane's plans.

"Tomorrow," Meg repeated, unwilling to be rushed despite the pressure Campbell was applying. "I'll call this same number."

"Until then," Campbell agreed, ending the call.

Meg remained on the balcony afterward, phone clutched in her hand, mind racing through implications and possibilities. The new information about Alex—that her initial search for Emily had been genuine, that her involvement with Krane might have begun as an attempt to protect her sister—complicated an already complex situation. It suggested a narrative less about betrayal and more about impossible choices made under duress.

And yet, if Campbell's intelligence was accurate, Alex had moved far beyond reluctant cooperation. She had become an active participant, perhaps even an enforcer eliminating threats to the operation. The suggestion that she might be responsible for Judge Peterson's death, and now possibly this financial analyst, added a dimension of horror to the betrayal Meg had been struggling to process.

Lost in these thoughts, she didn't hear Claire approach until she spoke from the doorway.

"So you called her."

Meg turned, finding Claire leaning against the door frame, expression carefully neutral. "Yes. I needed to understand what she's really offering. What she really knows."

"And?"

"It's complicated." Meg summarized the conversation, watching Claire's face as she processed the new information about Alex, about the financial analyst's death, about Campbell's proposed approach to Krane.

"She's manipulating you," Claire observed when Meg finished. "Feeding you just enough information to draw you in, applying just enough pressure to create urgency."

"Probably," Meg agreed. "But that doesn't mean the information is false, or that the urgency isn't real."

Claire moved to join her at the railing, both of them looking out over the harbor where afternoon light turned the water to hammered gold between cloud shadows. "What are you going to do?"

"I don't know yet," Meg admitted. "Working outside official channels, potentially putting myself in Krane's sights deliberately... it's not exactly a safe approach."

"No," Claire agreed quietly. "It's not. But neither is waiting for financial tracking to reveal something while Krane continues eliminating people who might expose him."

They stood in silence for a moment, each following her own thoughts, the weight of decisions and consequences settling between them. Finally, Claire straightened, decision made.

"Let's table this for now," she suggested. "We both need time to think, and I have Henderson prep that can't wait. Plus dinner with Thomas and Eleanor at seven. Whatever you decide about Campbell, that's still happening, and Eleanor might have information that changes our calculations."

The practical approach, the focus on immediate tasks rather than nebulous future decisions, felt like a lifeline Meg hadn't realized she needed. "You're right. One step at a time."

"Exactly." Claire squeezed her shoulder briefly. "And Meg? Whatever you decide about Campbell's offer... I've got your back. Even if I think it's a terrible idea."

The simple statement, delivered without drama but with absolute conviction, reminded Meg why their friendship had endured through years and challenges. Claire might disagree, might worry, might eventually say "I told you so" if things went sideways—but she would be there regardless, a constant in an increasingly uncertain world.

"I know," Meg said simply. "Thank you."

Claire disappeared back into her office, leaving Meg alone with her thoughts and the gradually shifting light as afternoon began transitioning toward evening. She remained on the balcony for a while longer, watching seabirds wheel above the harbor, fishing boats returning with their day's catch, ordinary life continuing despite the shadow Krane cast over her corner of the world.

Eventually, she moved inside, restless energy demanding outlet. With no case files to review until after Claire's dinner with Thomas and Eleanor, no immediate decisions required about Campbell's offer, she found herself gravitating toward the one activity that had always provided both escape and clarity—photography.

Her camera had remained largely untouched since the day she'd discovered the message on Blackwood's cabin, used only for documenting evidence rather than capturing beauty or meaning. Now she retrieved it from its case, checking settings, battery level, available memory. The familiar weight in her hands felt both strange and comforting, a connection to the self she had been before all this began.

Outside, the storm's aftermath provided endless subjects—raindrops suspended from unfurling leaves, puddles reflecting fractured skies, branches arranged in abstract patterns by wind and water. Meg lost herself in the viewfinder, in the meditative process of seeing, framing, capturing. Each image existed in isolation, complete unto itself, requiring no context beyond what was visible in that single frozen moment.

She walked without conscious destination, letting intuition guide her eye and feet, gradually working her way toward the harbor where the storm's impact was most dramatic. Waves still crashed against the breakwater with unusual force, spray leaping higher than the lighthouse at the harbor entrance, fishing boats secured with extra lines against the lingering swells.

Through her lens, she captured a commercial vessel returning to port, crewmen visible on deck securing equipment, their yellow slickers bright against the gray-green sea. The zoom brought their faces into focus—weathered, tired, satisfied with the day's work. Ordinary people doing ordinary jobs, untouched by kidnappings or financial schemes or the machinations of people like Krane and Campbell.

As she adjusted her position for a better angle, something caught her peripheral vision—a figure walking along the pier, moving with a distinctive confidence that triggered immediate recognition despite the distance. Meg lowered her camera, heart suddenly pounding, unable to trust what she thought she'd seen.

She raised the camera again, using the zoom to bring the distant figure into sharper focus. The image stabilized, clarity replacing uncertainty.

It was Alex.

Here in Seacliff, walking calmly along the harbor pier as if she belonged, as if she hadn't disappeared days ago, as if she weren't potentially working for the man they were all hunting.

Meg's first instinct was to call out, to run toward her—but caution overrode impulse. If Campbell's intelligence was accurate, if Alex was truly working for Krane, if she had been responsible for Peterson's death and now possibly the financial analyst's... approaching her directly could be more than merely unwise. It could be fatal.

Instead, Meg raised her camera again, documenting, gathering evidence, mind racing through possibilities. Alex was alone, dressed casually in jeans and a navy peacoat against the lingering chill, nothing in her appearance suggesting operational status rather than a simple walk along the harbor. But her presence in Seacliff, after days of absence, after Eagle's Rest, after everything... it couldn't be coincidence.

CHAPTER TEN
THE BREAKWATER

Through the viewfinder, Meg watched as Alex paused at the end of the pier, looking out over the churning water, apparently lost in thought. For a brief moment, the composed operator slipped, revealing a woman who looked... troubled. Conflicted. The expression lasted only seconds before the mask returned, but Meg had captured it, preserved it as evidence that whatever Alex had become, whatever choices she had made, some part of her remained capable of doubt.

Alex turned then, her gaze sweeping the area around her with the practiced awareness of someone accustomed to surveillance—both conducting it and detecting it. Meg lowered her camera, stepping into the shadow of a nearby building, heart pounding as she waited to see if she'd been spotted.

Apparently satisfied with her survey, Alex continued along the pier, moving toward the harbor master's office with purposeful strides. Meg raised her camera again, capturing the sequence—Alex entering the small building, emerging minutes later with what appeared to be a set of keys, then proceeding to a row of rental boats secured at the neighboring dock.

What was she doing? Where was she going? Meg's mind raced through possibilities as she watched Alex approach a small motorboat, unlock its security chain, and begin preparing it for launch. The obvious conclusion—that she was establishing transportation for Krane, or for captives, or for some aspect of the operation—warred with the uncertainty Meg still felt about Alex's true role and motivations.

She needed to alert someone. Reid, Hanover, Claire—someone with the authority and resources to intercept Alex, to question her, to determine once and for all whose side she was truly on. But as she reached for her phone, Meg hesitated. The department's approach to date had yielded few results. By the time Hanover mobilized resources, coordinated an intercept, navigated the bureaucracy of approved operations, Alex would be long gone.

And there was something else, something Meg couldn't quite articulate even to herself—a need to understand, to confront, to hear directly from Alex rather than through Campbell's intelligence or law enforcement analysis.

Decision crystallizing, Meg tucked her camera into its case and moved toward the harbor master's office, maintaining a careful distance from the dock where Alex was preparing the boat. Through the office window, she could see an elderly man with sun-weathered skin bent over paperwork, no other staff visible.

The bell above the door jangled discordantly as she entered, drawing a distracted glance from the man at the desk.

"Help you?" he asked, voice graveled by decades of salt air and cigarettes.

"I need to rent a boat," Meg said, forcing confidence into her tone. "Something small, easy to handle. Just for a few hours."

The harbor master—Stan, according to the nameplate on his desk—assessed her with the skepticism of someone who'd seen too many inexperienced boaters create problems on his watch.

"Experienced?" he asked, cutting directly to the point.

"Yes," Meg replied, the lie coming easily. She'd been on boats, certainly, but piloting one herself would be a first. "Just want to get out on the water for a bit. Clear my head after the storm."

Stan grunted, apparently accepting this. "Got a seventeen-footer available. Two-stroke engine, simple controls. Fifty for two hours, plus fuel. Need to see ID and a credit card."

Meg complied, hyperaware that Alex could depart at any moment while she completed paperwork and received basic instructions. Through the office's salt-streaked windows, she could see the boat Alex had claimed—a similar model to the one she was renting, already fueled and nearly ready to launch.

"Weather's still unsettled," Stan warned as he handed over keys and a life vest. "Stay within the harbor markers. Radio channel 16 if you get in trouble. Boat's at slip fourteen."

"Thanks," Meg said, already turning toward the door, mentally calculating how to follow Alex without being immediately obvious.

The air outside tasted of salt and diesel, the harbor's distinctive perfume intensified by the storm's aftermath. Alex's boat was pulling away from the dock as Meg hurried toward her own rental, forcing herself to maintain a casual pace despite the urgency pulsing through her veins. Too fast, too direct, and she'd draw attention. Too slow, and Alex would disappear across the harbor before she could even start her engine.

Slip fourteen contained a white fiberglass boat with faded blue trim, rocking gently against its bumpers. Meg stepped aboard carefully, the vessel shifting beneath her weight in a way that momentarily disrupted her balance. She settled into the pilot's seat, inserted the key, and mentally reviewed Stan's abbreviated instructions.

The engine coughed into life on the third attempt, its vibration transmitting through the hull and into Meg's bones. She eased away from the slip with more caution than skill, acutely aware of her inexperience, of the gulf between knowing theoretically how to operate a boat and actually navigating one through a busy harbor.

Ahead, perhaps two hundred yards and increasing the distance with each passing second, Alex's boat cut a white path across waters still churning from the storm's passage. She appeared to be heading toward the harbor entrance, where the protected waters gave way to the open ocean beyond the breakwater.

Meg opened the throttle slightly, her boat responding with an increased growl from the engine and a surge of speed that pushed her back against the seat. The wind caught her hair, whipping loose strands across her face as she navigated around moored vessels, trying to maintain visual contact with Alex without closing the distance too obviously.

The late afternoon sun broke through cloud cover intermittently, casting the harbor in alternating patterns of brilliant light and shadow, the water's surface transforming from slate to silver and back again with each passing cloud. In this shifting illumination, Alex's boat appeared and disappeared from view, a visual metaphor for the woman herself—present then absent, revealed then concealed, a figure moving between worlds.

As they approached the harbor entrance, Meg felt the first serious swells from the open ocean, her small craft rising and falling with greater amplitude than before. The motion sent her stomach lurching uncomfortably, a reminder that whatever her determination, she remained at the mercy of natural forces far beyond her control.

Ahead, Alex passed the navigation markers indicating the harbor's outer boundary, her boat now fully exposed to the ocean's power. Meg followed, gripping the wheel tightly as her vessel crested a swell and plunged down its far side, spray flying as the bow impacted the next wave.

The radio crackled to life, Stan's voice emerging from the speaker. "Rental fourteen, this is harbor master. You're exceeding harbor limits. Weather advisory still in effect for coastal waters. Return to protected waters immediately."

Meg ignored the call, focus locked on Alex's boat now heading parallel to the shore rather than directly out to sea. The coastline here was rugged, rocky protrusions alternating with small, isolated coves inaccessible by land. An ideal location for clandestine meetings or exchanges, for activities that required privacy from prying eyes.

The pursuit continued for perhaps fifteen minutes, Meg maintaining distance while trying to anticipate Alex's destination. Controlling the boat demanded more attention than she'd expected, each wave requiring adjustment, each gust of wind threatening to push her off course. Her hands ached from gripping the wheel, shoulders tight with tension, every sense heightened by the combination of physical challenge and investigative urgency.

Finally, Alex's boat slowed, turning toward what appeared to be a narrow inlet cut into the rocky coastline. Meg reduced power, allowing the distance between them to increase, calculating that following too closely into such a confined space would make her presence obvious.

She watched as Alex navigated the narrow passage with practiced precision, her boat disappearing behind rocky outcroppings that obscured whatever lay beyond. Meg waited several minutes before approaching, engine at its lowest setting, moving as quietly as possible through waters that had calmed somewhat in the lee of the land.

The inlet proved to be the entrance to a small, sheltered cove, rocky walls rising steeply on three sides, a narrow strip of pebbled beach at its innermost point. Alex's boat was secured to a weather-beaten dock extending from the beach, but Alex herself was nowhere visible.

Meg cut her engine entirely, allowing momentum to carry her vessel closer, the sudden silence accentuating natural sounds—waves lapping against rock, seabirds calling from nests in the cliff face, wind sighing through crevices in the stone. She drifted toward the inside edge of the inlet, using an oar to guide her boat alongside a rocky projection that provided both concealment and a secure point to tie off.

The position offered a clear view of the dock and beach while keeping her presence hidden from anyone returning to the cove. From here, she could see what appeared to be a narrow path leading up from the beach, cutting switchbacks into the cliff face before disappearing over the top.

Alex had gone inland, then. But to where? And to meet whom?

Meg considered her options. Following up that path meant abandoning her boat, potentially stranding herself if Alex returned and departed by water. Not following meant losing whatever opportunity this unexpected encounter might provide.

The decision made itself when a figure appeared at the top of the cliff path—not Alex, but a man Meg had never seen before. Tall, lean, dressed in dark clothing that suggested functionality rather than fashion, moving with the same controlled awareness she'd observed in Alex.

Another operative? Someone from Krane's security team?

The man descended the path with practiced ease, showing none of the caution such steep terrain would normally require. At the bottom, he strode directly to the dock where Alex's boat was secured, examined it briefly, then took up a position that suggested he was serving as lookout or sentry.

Whatever was happening here, it involved more than just Alex.

Meg eased her phone from her pocket, activating the camera function, zooming in on the man's face to document his presence. Not ideal photographic quality, but sufficient for identification purposes if needed later.

As she watched, a second figure appeared at the cliff top—Alex, returning along the same path the man had descended. She moved more cautiously than he had, one hand trailing along the cliff face for stability, the other holding what appeared to be a small package or envelope.

The two spoke briefly when Alex reached the beach, a short exchange that involved Alex handing over the package and receiving something in return—money, Meg guessed, though the distance made details difficult to discern. The transaction complete, Alex returned to her boat while the man began climbing back up the path, both moving with the efficiency of people following established protocols.

Meg ducked lower behind her rocky cover as Alex's boat engine roared to life, the sound amplified by the cove's natural acoustics. She watched through a narrow gap as Alex navigated back through the inlet, heading roughly in the direction of Seacliff harbor, apparently considering her business here concluded.

Once Alex's boat had disappeared from view, Meg faced a crucial decision—follow her back to harbor, potentially discovering where she was staying or who she was meeting next, or investigate the cliff path, trying to determine what lay at its top and why Alex had gone there.

The choice became academic when the man who had met Alex reappeared at the cliff top, this time accompanied by a second individual. Both stood looking down into the cove, their stances suggesting they were scanning for something—or someone. Meg pressed herself against the rock face, heart pounding, suddenly acutely aware of her vulnerability, of the risk she'd taken pursuing Alex without backup or even telling anyone where she was going.

The men remained visible for perhaps two minutes before withdrawing from the cliff edge, disappearing from Meg's line of sight. Had they spotted her boat? Were they coming back down? Or continuing to whatever destination had brought them to this isolated location?

She couldn't risk finding out. Starting her engine would announce her presence if they were still within earshot. Instead, she used the oar to push away from the rock face, allowing the natural current flowing out of the cove to carry her vessel gradually toward the inlet.

The process was agonizingly slow, each foot of progress measured in patience rather than power. As she drifted, Meg studied the cliff path and surrounding terrain, committing details to memory—the distinctive shape of a lightning-struck tree near the cliff top, the pattern of rock strata visible in the cliff face, the specific curve of the coastline visible through the inlet. Details that might help identify this location on maps or satellite imagery, that might lead back to whatever Alex had visited.

Finally reaching the inlet, Meg allowed herself to drift through it into more open water before risking the engine. The starter caught on the first attempt, the sudden noise seeming obscenely loud after the tense silence of her drift, but no shouts of discovery followed, no figures appeared at the cliff top to investigate.

She opened the throttle carefully, building speed gradually, heading back toward Seacliff harbor with mind racing through implications and possibilities. Alex was clearly operational, conducting what appeared to be a dead drop or information exchange. But was it for Krane? Was it related to the market manipulation scheme Campbell had described? Or was it something else entirely?

The return journey passed in a blur of competing hypotheses and physical discomfort as the sea conditions deteriorated with approaching evening. By the time Meg navigated back into the harbor's protected waters, her clothes were damp with spray, hands cramped from gripping the wheel, body aching from tension maintained too long.

Stan emerged from his office as she approached slip fourteen, his expression communicating displeasure before he spoke a word.

"Ignored my radio call," he said flatly as she cut the engine. "Went outside harbor limits during advisory conditions. Not exactly building trust with the rental agreement, are you?"

"Sorry," Meg offered, genuine despite her distraction. "Got caught up in the moment, misjudged the distance."

He harrumphed, clearly unconvinced but apparently deciding further lecture would be wasted effort. "Boat looks intact, at least. That's something."

She completed the return paperwork mechanically, mind still processing what she'd witnessed, calculating next steps. Alex had returned to harbor before her, but a quick scan of the docks showed no sign of her or the boat she'd rented. Already gone, then. But to where?

The harbor master's office had windows overlooking most of the docks. If Stan had been at his desk, he might have seen Alex's return, might have noticed which direction she went afterward.

"The woman who rented a boat earlier," Meg ventured, keeping her tone casual. "Blonde, about my age, navy peacoat. Did she return already?"

Stan's weathered face registered mild surprise at the question. "Short while ago, yeah. Friend of yours?"

"Sort of," Meg hedged. "Thought I recognized her from college, but wasn't sure. Hoped to catch her before she left."

"Missed her by maybe twenty minutes," Stan said, apparently seeing no reason to withhold the information. "Returned the boat, paid in cash, left in a hurry. Headed toward town, I think."

It wasn't much, but it was something—confirmation that Alex had returned to Seacliff rather than departing by water, that she might still be in the area, potentially trackable.

Meg thanked him and left the office, phone already in hand to call Claire. Outside, the light had shifted toward evening, the water reflecting deep oranges and purples from the sunset beginning to unfold behind scattered clouds to the west. The air temperature had dropped with approaching night, her damp clothes suddenly inadequate against the chill, sending a shiver through her body that had nothing to do with fear or excitement.

Claire answered on the second ring, her voice tight with what sounded like carefully controlled alarm. "Where are you? I've been trying to reach you for an hour."

"Harbor," Meg replied, momentarily confused by Claire's tone. "Sorry, I was on the water, didn't hear the phone. What's wrong?"

A pause, then: "Thomas is dead."

The words landed like physical blows, incomprehensible in their suddenness, impossible in their finality. Thomas—alive just yesterday, recovering, helping them understand Krane's operation, planning to meet Claire and Eleanor for dinner just hours from now.

"How?" Meg managed, voice sounding distant to her own ears.

"Car accident, apparently. Driving Eleanor's car, went off the coastal road near Lighthouse Point. They're still recovering the vehicle."

The location registered alongside the timing—Thomas dead, Alex in Seacliff conducting some kind of exchange, the two events separated by mere hours. Coincidence seemed not merely unlikely but impossible.

"It wasn't an accident," Meg said, certainty crystallizing from fragments of information and intuition. "Alex is here, in Seacliff. I just followed her to some kind of dead drop or meeting along the coast. This is connected, Claire. It has to be."

Silence stretched between them, Claire presumably processing this new information against the backdrop of Thomas's death. When she spoke again, her voice had shifted from shock to focused urgency.

"Where exactly are you? I'm coming to get you."

"Harbor master's office. But Claire, we need to tell Hanover, get people looking for Alex—"

"Already on it," Claire interrupted. "Called her as soon as I heard about Thomas. She's with Eleanor now. I'll explain everything when I get there. Stay put. Don't approach anyone, don't trust anyone you don't know personally. Fifteen minutes."

The call ended, leaving Meg standing alone in the gathering dusk, the harbor's evening activities continuing around her—boats securing for the night, fishermen unloading late catches, tourists taking sunset photographs—all oblivious to the horror unfolding in parallel to their ordinary lives.

Thomas was dead. Alex was operational in Seacliff. These facts connected to form a picture too terrible to fully comprehend but impossible to ignore. If Campbell's intelligence was accurate, if Alex had truly become Krane's enforcer, if she was eliminating loose ends and potential witnesses... then Thomas had been killed not for what he knew, but for what he might reveal at tonight's dinner with Claire and Eleanor.

Information that Eleanor had specifically said she didn't want to discuss over the phone. Information about Krane's early years in Seacliff, before the original financial crimes case.

Information that someone didn't want shared.

Meg paced outside the harbor master's office, physically unable to remain still under the weight of these realizations, mind racing through scenarios and contingencies. If Thomas had been targeted, Eleanor might be next. Or Claire. Or Meg herself. Anyone who might threaten Krane's operation, anyone who might expose whatever secret Eleanor had discovered.

Claire's car appeared at the harbor entrance exactly fourteen minutes after their call, pulling in at a speed that suggested urgency without drawing undue attention. Meg slid into the passenger seat, registering Claire's tension in the tightness of her jaw, the precision of her movements, the carefully controlled expressions cycling across her face.

"Tell me everything," Claire said as she pulled away from the harbor, heading not toward her apartment but in the direction of the sheriff's department. "From the beginning. Every detail."

Meg complied, describing her chance sighting of Alex, the decision to follow, the boat pursuit, the cove, the exchange with the unknown man, the second figure at the cliff top, her careful exit and return to harbor. Throughout, Claire listened without interrupting, her focus divided between Meg's account and the road ahead, occasionally checking the rearview mirror with the alertness of someone who understood they might be followed.

"And you're certain it was Alex?" she asked when Meg finished. "Not someone who resembled her?"

"Positive," Meg confirmed. "I had my camera with zoom lens. It was her, Claire. No question."

Claire nodded, accepting this without further challenge. "Hanover's meeting us at the department. Eleanor's there too—they moved her to a secure room as soon as the call came in about Thomas. Initial report says mechanical failure caused the crash—brake lines cut, according to first responders on scene."

The confirmation of sabotage rather than accident was expected but still chilling. "Do they have any witnesses? Anyone who saw who did it?"

"Not yet. Eleanor's car was parked at her house until this afternoon. Thomas took it to run errands while she prepared for dinner. Security cameras at the pharmacy where he stopped caught him leaving around 3:30 PM. Accident was reported at 4:12 PM."

The timeline aligned with Meg's sighting of Alex at the harbor—after Thomas's death, not before. Not direct verification of her involvement, but certainly not excluding the possibility.

"What was Eleanor going to tell you tonight?" Meg asked, the question that had been forming since learning of Thomas's death. "About Krane's early years here?"

Claire's fingers tightened on the steering wheel, knuckles whitening momentarily before she consciously relaxed her grip. "She wouldn't say, even over a secure line at the department. Just that she'd been reviewing old records, connections between Krane and certain local figures before his financial crimes case. Something that might explain his fixation on this area, on specific individuals."

The vagueness was frustrating but understandable given the circumstances. Whatever Eleanor had discovered, she clearly believed it sensitive enough to discuss only in person, important enough to risk meeting despite the escalating danger surrounding the investigation.

"If Alex is targeting people connected to the case," Meg said, thinking aloud, "then Eleanor is at serious risk. And you. And me."

"Hence meeting at the department rather than my apartment," Claire confirmed. "And the secure room for Eleanor. Hanover's implementing protection protocols for everyone involved in the investigation."

The sheriff's department appeared ahead, its windows illuminated against the deepening dusk, patrol cars and unmarked vehicles filling the parking area. Claire pulled into a space near the side entrance, cutting the engine but making no immediate move to exit the car.

"Meg," she said, voice suddenly quieter, more personal than professional. "I need to know where your head is with all this. With Alex. With Campbell's offer. With everything."

The question caught Meg slightly off-guard, forcing her to articulate thoughts she'd been processing internally without fully confronting.

"Honestly? I'm angry. And confused. And scared." She stared through the windshield at the department building, symbol of order and protection that suddenly seemed inadequate against the forces arrayed against them. "If Alex is really working for Krane, if she's really killing people to protect his operation... then everything I thought I knew about her was a lie. And I fell for it completely."

Claire's expression clearly showed support rather than pity. "We all did. She was convincing because she had to be. That's what professional operators do—they make you believe whatever serves their purpose."

The reassurance helped, but didn't entirely dissolve the sense of betrayal, of being manipulated by someone she'd trusted with her life. Someone who, despite everything, she still couldn't bring herself to fully condemn without hearing directly from her.

"As for Campbell," Meg continued, "I'm still not sure. Her information about Alex seems accurate based on what I saw today. But her motivations, her employers, what she really wants... that remains unclear."

"And Krane? The investigation?"

"I want it to end," Meg said simply. "I want Emily and Valerie found and rescued if they're still alive. I want Krane stopped before he can hurt anyone else. And I want answers—from Alex, from Krane, from everyone involved. Real answers, not just theories or intelligence reports."

Claire nodded, apparently finding what she needed in Meg's response. "Then let's go see what Eleanor can tell us. Because I think she might have some of those answers you're looking for."

They exited the car together, moving toward the side entrance with the shared purpose of people who had faced danger together and emerged more determined rather than intimidated. Whatever came next—protection protocols, Campbell's offer, the continuing search for Krane—they would approach it as a team, complementing each other's strengths, supporting each other's vulnerabilities.

CHAPTER ELEVEN

ENDINGS

The department door opened before they reached it, Reid emerging to escort them inside. His face told a story his professional demeanor couldn't entirely mask—skin pale beneath his weathered tan, eyes rimmed with red, jaw clenched against emotions threatening to break through. This wasn't just an officer dealing with a case development; this was a man who had come to care about Thomas during his recovery, who had spent hours debriefing him, who had witnessed his remarkable resilience.

"Hanover's with Eleanor in the secure conference room," he informed them, voice rougher than usual. As he led them through corridors unusually crowded for early evening, Meg noticed officers speaking in hushed tones, some openly wiping away tears. Thomas had touched more lives than she'd realized during his brief freedom.

Reid paused before the conference room door, swallowing hard. "Eleanor... she's not..." He struggled for words, composure cracking. "Damn it. She just got him back. After six months of searching, of never giving up when everyone told her he was probably dead. She just got him back."

The raw emotion in his voice—from a man who typically maintained such careful professional distance—made the tragedy viscerally real in a way the clinical report of "car accident" hadn't managed to convey.

"Is she alone with Hanover?" Claire asked softly.

Reid shook his head. "Department chaplain was with them earlier. Eleanor asked him to leave. Said she needed to focus on the investigation, on what Thomas had discovered." His face darkened. "That's Eleanor—using work to hold herself together. But she's... fragile. I've never seen her like this."

"How bad?" Claire asked quietly.

Reid's eyes met hers, haunted. "When they pulled Thomas's body from the car, Eleanor was already there. Someone called her before notifying the department officially. She insisted on seeing him, wouldn't be kept behind the police line." His voice dropped almost to a whisper. "She held his hand. Kept telling him she was sorry she couldn't protect him. That she'd failed him again."

The image struck Meg like a physical blow—proud, composed Eleanor Blackwell, kneeling beside wreckage, clutching her nephew's lifeless hand, apologizing for a failure that was never hers.

"The car..." Meg began, needing details beyond "accident" and "brake lines cut."

"Over the cliffs near Lighthouse Point," Reid supplied, understanding her need for specifics. "Witnesses say the vehicle accelerated suddenly while navigating a curve, crashed through the guardrail. No skid marks. No attempt to brake." His professional mask reasserted itself slightly, focusing on investigative facts rather than emotional impact. "First responders initially assumed mechanical failure. It was Eleanor who demanded they check the brake lines specifically. She knew immediately this wasn't random."

"And it wasn't," Claire concluded.

"No." Reid's jaw tightened. "Clean cut. Professional job. Would have allowed Thomas to drive some distance before the fluid drained enough to cause complete failure." He rubbed a hand across his face. "We're pulling security camera footage from every business along his route, checking the pharmacy parking lot where he stopped last. So far, nothing useful."

He squared his shoulders visibly, preparing himself to re-enter the conference room. "Eleanor's discovered something significant about Krane. Something that might explain why Thomas was targeted now, why the timing was so precise. But..." He hesitated.

"What is it?" Meg prompted.

"She's holding herself together with nothing but will and fury," Reid said quietly. "Focusing on the investigation like it's the only thing keeping her from falling apart completely. Which it probably is. Just... be prepared. This isn't the Eleanor you've dealt with before."

With that warning, he opened the conference room door.

The scene inside struck Meg immediately as wrong—jarringly, fundamentally wrong. Sheriff Hanover stood at the head of a table covered with files, photographs, and what appeared to be old newspaper clippings. But it was Eleanor who commanded attention, who transformed the environment from merely somber to actively disturbing.

She sat ramrod straight beside Hanover, back rigid despite visible exhaustion, eyes red-rimmed and swollen in a face drained of all color. Her hands, usually so steady, trembled visibly as she sorted through documents with mechanical precision. Most shocking was her appearance—immaculately dressed as always, but wearing the same clothes as yesterday, now creased and stained with what looked horribly like dried blood along one sleeve.

She looked up as they entered, and Meg nearly stepped back at the expression in her eyes—grief so profound it had transcended into something else entirely, a burning intensity that seemed to consume her from within.

"Ms. Sawyer. Claire." Her voice emerged as a raw whisper, damaged from what must have been hours of weeping. "Claire said you saw Alexandra Reeves today. That she's operational in Seacliff."

The directness was startling—no social niceties, no acknowledgment of condolences, just immediate focus on the investigation. Meg understood instantly what Reid had meant about Eleanor using work to hold herself together. The investigation wasn't just professional obligation now; it was a psychological lifeline.

"Yes," Meg confirmed, matching Eleanor's directness out of respect for her evident need. "At the harbor, then at a cove along the coast east of town. She met someone, exchanged what looked like information or documents."

Eleanor nodded once, a jerky movement suggesting muscles held too tight for too long. Her hand moved automatically to arrange a file, and Meg noticed with a shock that her perfectly manicured nails were broken, several torn to the quick. The image of her clawing at wreckage, trying to reach Thomas, flashed unbidden through Meg's mind.

"Then what I've discovered is even more relevant than I realized," Eleanor said, voice strengthening slightly through force of will. "Please, sit. There are things you need to understand about Victor Krane. About his connection to Seacliff."

As she spoke, Eleanor reached for a tissue, dabbing at eyes that had begun leaking tears again despite her evident determination to maintain control. The gesture—so ordinary, so human—contrasted painfully with her otherwise rigidly controlled demeanor.

"I'm sorry," she said, anger flashing briefly across her features. "I can't seem to—" She broke off, pressing the tissue hard against her eyes, drawing a deep breath that shuddered visibly through her slender frame. When she lowered her hand, her expression had hardened into something closer to her usual composure, though the effort required was painfully apparent.

"Thomas was murdered because of what we discovered," she continued, voice steadier now. "Because he asked questions about a girl named Caroline Whittaker, and a secret that's been buried in this town for nearly forty years."

Eleanor reached for one of the older photographs—a group shot of what appeared to be a high school graduating class, dated nearly forty years earlier. Her hand trembled so violently that she dropped it twice before managing to slide it across the table. The third time, Sheriff Hanover gently took it from her and passed it to Meg, a silent compassion in the gesture that spoke volumes about what Eleanor had endured since Thomas's death.

"This is where it begins," Eleanor said, visibly fighting for the focus and precision that had always characterized her investigations. "Not with financial crimes or market manipulation. But with a boy named Victor Kranepool, his stepfather Judge William Blackwell, and a—" Her voice broke, emotion overwhelming control despite visible resistance. "A secret that killed my Thomas."

The raw grief in those final words shattered the fragile composure she'd been maintaining. Eleanor covered her face with shaking hands, shoulders heaving with silent sobs she couldn't suppress any longer. Sheriff Hanover moved immediately to her side, placing a gentle hand on her back, murmuring something too quiet for Meg to hear.

The moment stretched, painful in its intimacy, a private breakdown occurring in what should have been a professional setting. None of them looked away, none pretended not to notice—this wasn't embarrassment to be politely ignored, but human suffering demanding witness and respect.

After several minutes, Eleanor straightened, wiping her face with a fresh tissue Hanover had silently provided. "Forgive me," she said, the formal phrase incongruous with raw eyes and trembling hands. "William was Victor's stepfather. My husband."

The revelation landed with seismic force—Victor Krane connected to Eleanor's husband, to the very judge who had later sentenced him for financial crimes. Not just a criminal returning to take revenge on those who prosecuted him, but a man with deeper, more personal motivations driving his elaborate schemes.

"William was Victor's stepfather?" Meg asked, trying to process this unexpected connection. "He never mentioned this during the trial? During sentencing?"

"He recused himself initially," Eleanor explained, voice steadier now, as if the release of emotion had granted her temporary stability. "But Victor's attorneys requested him specifically, waiving any conflict of interest concerns. William should have declined regardless, but..." She paused, gaze dropping to her damaged hands. "There were complexities in their relationship that clouded his judgment, that made him believe he could remain impartial despite their history."

Eleanor continued, outlining the dark relationship between her husband and his stepson—the abuse, the escalating troubling behaviors, the path that led from disturbed teenager to murderer to financial criminal. Throughout her recitation, the professional researcher would briefly emerge, only to crumble again when emotion overwhelmed her carefully constructed narrative.

Most devastating was her account of Caroline Whittaker's death—the local girl found in the woods, the hidden evidence William discovered, his certainty of Victor's guilt contrasted with his inability to prove it.

"Caroline had been dating Victor," Eleanor explained, voice hollow with exhaustion and grief. "Her parents were prominent in the community, friends with the medical examiner, the sheriff at that time. No one wanted to believe a seventeen-year-old honors student from a good family could be capable of such violence."

She reached for a photograph—the teenage girl with a bright smile, school portrait style—and her composure fractured again. "She was seventeen. The same age Thomas was when I took him in after his parents died." Her fingers traced the edge of the photograph with terrible gentleness. "William couldn't save her. I couldn't save Thomas. We failed them both."

The equation of these losses—one from decades past, one brutally immediate—revealed the weight Eleanor was carrying, the double burden of historical grief resurrected alongside fresh, bleeding trauma.

"This explains the targeting pattern," Reid observed carefully, giving Eleanor a moment to collect herself. "Judge Peterson had been a junior attorney in the prosecutor's office during Caroline's case, signed off on the accidental death classification. Judge Harmon was William's colleague on the bench, supported his decision to remain on Victor's financial crimes case despite the conflict of interest concerns."

"And Thomas?" Meg asked, the question gentle but necessary.

Eleanor's composure wavered briefly, then held. "Thomas discovered the connection while researching Axion's property acquisitions. One of the properties Krane purchased through shell companies was the Whittaker family home—Caroline's childhood house, abandoned for years after her parents moved away following her death."

She drew a shuddering breath. "When Thomas realized the connection, he began looking deeper into Victor's past in Seacliff, into his relationship with William, into Caroline's death. We didn't realize how dangerous those questions would be."

Her voice broke on the last word, grief once again threatening to overwhelm her carefully maintained control. She pressed a hand hard against her mouth, struggling visibly, before continuing in a voice barely above a whisper.

"Last night, I told Thomas I'd found Caroline's diary hidden among William's effects after his death. A diary that contains explicit descriptions of Victor's escalating control and threats in the weeks before her death." Her damaged hands clenched into fists atop the table. "If I had said nothing... if I hadn't told him..."

"This is not your fault, Eleanor," Hanover said firmly, the first time she'd spoken directly since Meg and Claire arrived. "Thomas was killed because Krane is eliminating anyone who threatens to expose his past. That responsibility lies with Krane and his organization, not with you."

Eleanor nodded mechanically, but the gesture held no conviction. "I anticipated that Thomas might be at risk once he started asking questions about Caroline Whittaker." Her voice caught slightly, the first audible evidence of her grief. "I didn't anticipate they would move so quickly, so decisively. I thought we had more time."

The admission carried no self-recrimination, no suggestion that she had failed Thomas by underestimating the threat. Just the clear-eyed assessment of someone who understood the strategic landscape but had miscalculated the timing of enemy movement.

As the meeting continued, Eleanor's emotional state fluctuated visibly—moments of almost unnatural clarity and focus punctuated by periods where grief resurfaced with such raw intensity that she seemed physically unable to speak. Throughout, Hanover remained close, offering silent support that Eleanor seemed simultaneously to lean on and resist, as if divided between needing help and resenting its necessity.

When discussion turned to retrieving Caroline's diary, Eleanor's demeanor shifted yet again—a hardness entering her expression that had not been present before, something beyond determination or resolve. Something closer to vengeance.

"I'll take you to it," she said, voice steadier than it had been all evening. "But not tonight, not while they're watching, expecting exactly that move. Tomorrow, after we've established proper security protocols, after they believe the immediate threat has passed."

As arrangements were made for Eleanor's protection overnight, Meg observed the subtle changes in her demeanor—the grief never abating but becoming channeled, directed, weaponized. This wasn't just a researcher seeking truth anymore, or even a woman mourning her nephew. This was someone who had crossed into a different territory entirely, for whom the investigation had become intensely, lethally personal.

When Meg and Claire prepared to leave, Eleanor approached Meg privately, her voice pitched for her ears alone. The formal "Ms. Sawyer" was gone, an intimacy born of shared purpose replacing professional distance.

"Meg," she said, the use of her first name jarring after so many formal exchanges. "There's something else you should know about Alexandra Reeves."

The unexpected address, the shift to personal rather than professional interaction, caught Meg's attention immediately. "What about her?"

Eleanor hesitated, exhaustion momentarily overwhelming even her iron will. She pressed fingers to her temples, as if physically holding thoughts in place. When she looked up again, her eyes held a clarity that seemed almost feverish against her pallid complexion.

"Two weeks before you discovered the message on Blackwood's cabin roof, Alexandra Reeves contacted me directly," she continued, words precise despite visible effort. "She knew about Thomas's disappearance, knew about my research into Krane's operation. She presented herself as FBI, interested in the same connections I was tracking."

Eleanor's gaze held Meg's with an intensity that transcended her physical fragility. "She was very specific in her questions about certain properties, certain dates. Looking back now, it's clear she was assessing how much I knew, how close I was to connecting Thomas's environmental research to the Whittaker property, to Krane's past."

This revelation shifted Meg's understanding yet again—Alex actively investigating Eleanor weeks before Meg's involvement, specifically probing connections to the Whittaker property, to the secrets that might be buried there.

"Did she mention Emily during these conversations?" Meg asked, searching for any thread that might connect the Alex who approached Eleanor with the Alex who had intercepted Meg at Blackwood's cabin.

"Briefly," Eleanor confirmed, a flicker of something like sympathy crossing her exhausted features. "She described her as a missing sister, environmental researcher who had disappeared while working on a wetlands project. The details matched what you later told us about Emily's background."

"So that part wasn't fabricated," Meg murmured, more to herself than Eleanor. "Emily is real, is actually missing..."

"Or was, at that time," Eleanor amended gently. She paused, swaying slightly where she stood, fatigue momentarily overwhelming even her formidable will. Meg reached out instinctively to steady her, shocked at how fragile she felt beneath her perfectly tailored blazer—bird bones and grief held together by nothing but determination.

Eleanor straightened with visible effort. "There was something else, something I only recognized in retrospect, after learning more about Krane's operation from Thomas. The questions Alexandra asked, the specific properties and transactions she focused on... they weren't random. They were precisely the areas where my research was getting closest to uncovering connections between Krane and his father."

The conversation continued, Eleanor revealing crucial information about Krane's connection to the cove where Meg had followed Alex, about the cabin at the cliff top, about the potential significance of the property once belonging to Krane's biological father.

Throughout, Eleanor's physical state deteriorated visibly—words sometimes slurring with exhaustion, hands trembling more violently, periods where she seemed to lose her train of thought mid-sentence before forcing herself back to coherence through sheer will. Yet she persisted, determined to convey every detail that might help them understand what they faced, what had cost Thomas his life.

As they concluded their discussion, Eleanor gripped Meg's arm with surprising strength, her broken nails digging into the fabric of Meg's sleeve. "Find them," she said, voice suddenly clear and hard as diamond. "Find Emily and Valerie. Bring them home. Don't let Thomas's death be for nothing."

The raw plea, coming from a woman who had maintained such dignity throughout unimaginable pain, struck Meg to her core. This wasn't just professional commitment to solving a case or academic dedication to uncovering truth. This was the desperate need to give meaning to senseless loss, to extract purpose from unbearable tragedy.

"I promise," Meg replied, the words emerging before she could consider their weight, their implications. But once spoken, she knew she meant them with absolute conviction. "Whatever it takes."

Eleanor nodded once, releasing Meg's arm. She straightened her jacket with automatic precision, the gesture pathetically incongruous with her disheveled appearance and damaged hands. "Good. Because I intend to destroy Victor Krane for what he's done. Not just arrest or prosecution. Destruction. Complete and irreversible."

The cold certainty in her voice, the implacable resolve beneath her shattered exterior, made Meg understand something fundamental about grief's transformative power. Eleanor Blackwell—who had spent decades in service to order, procedure, and legal principle—had been remade in the crucible of Thomas's murder. What emerged was something new and dangerous: a woman with nothing left to lose, for whom conventional boundaries no longer applied.

CHAPTER TWELVE
OPPOSING DANGERS

As they left the department, Meg carried the weight of that interaction—Eleanor's raw grief, her steely resolve, her transformation from researcher to avenger. It colored everything that followed, every calculation and consideration, every step toward whatever awaited them in the hours and days ahead.

Outside, the world had fully transitioned to night, stars emerging between drifting clouds, temperature dropping enough to make their breath visible in brief, ghostly clouds. Two deputies waited beside an unmarked department SUV, their postures conveying professional alertness without obvious tension—the balanced awareness of experienced officers who understood both the reality of threats and the importance of not appearing unnecessarily alarmed.

The drive to Claire's apartment passed in attentive silence, all involved scanning for any sign of surveillance or pursuit, none observed. Security protocols were established upon arrival—deputies checking the apartment's interior before allowing entry, establishing observation positions with clear sightlines to all approaches, confirming communication channels with dispatch and patrol units assigned to the area.

Inside, with the door locked behind them and deputies stationed outside, Claire finally broke the silence that had extended from the department through the security check.

"I've never seen grief like that," she said quietly, moving to the kitchen on autopilot, filling the kettle for tea despite the late hour, the action suggesting a need for routine amid chaos rather than actual thirst. "So raw, so... transformative."

Meg settled at the counter, watching her friend's precise movements as she selected mugs, tea bags, spoons—small certainties in a world increasingly defined by the unknown.

"She's not just grieving," Meg observed. "She's weaponizing her grief, channeling it into something purposeful. Something dangerous."

Claire set the kettle on the stove, turning to face Meg with renewed focus. "Can you blame her? She spent six months searching for Thomas when everyone told her he was probably dead. Then she found him, got him back for less than a week, only to lose him permanently. And knowing it was directly connected to their investigation, to questions they were asking..."

She didn't finish the thought, didn't need to. The horror of Eleanor's position was clear—the particular cruelty of having hope restored only to be violently, permanently extinguished.

"The accident itself," Meg said after a moment. "Reid mentioned brake lines cut, no skid marks. Professional job. But who had access to Eleanor's car? When?"

The kettle began to whistle, a domestic counterpoint to their decidedly non-domestic conversation. Claire silenced it, pouring water into waiting mugs, the fragrant steam carrying bergamot and citrus notes that briefly softened the apartment's atmosphere.

"According to Reid, the car was parked at Eleanor's house until yesterday afternoon," Claire said, setting a mug before Meg. "Thomas took it to run errands while she prepared for dinner with us. Last confirmed sighting was security footage from the pharmacy where he stopped around 3:30 PM. Accident reported at 4:12 PM."

Meg wrapped her hands around the warm ceramic, grateful for its tangible comfort. "So whoever tampered with the brake lines either did it while the car was parked at Eleanor's house, or during the brief time it was parked at the pharmacy."

"The pharmacy seems more likely," Claire observed. "Less secure, public parking lot, Thomas inside for approximately fifteen minutes according to the timestamp on his receipt. Plenty of time for someone with the right skills to access the undercarriage, cut the lines, and disappear before he returned."

"And the timing aligns with when I saw Alex at the harbor—after Thomas's death, not before," Meg noted, the chronology clicking into place. "Not direct verification of her involvement, but definitely not excluding the possibility."

Claire leaned against the counter, considering. "If Alex was responsible—or someone in Krane's organization acting on similar orders—the precision is chilling. Thomas visits the pharmacy, someone follows, executes the sabotage, ensures he makes it back onto the road before the brake fluid drains enough to cause catastrophic failure at exactly the worst possible location—the curve near Lighthouse Point, with its cliff drop on one side."

The clinical analysis, delivered in Claire's prosecutor's voice, somehow made the horror more immediate rather than more abstract. This wasn't random violence or opportunistic crime, but calculated murder executed with professional efficiency—the kind of precision that suggested extensive planning, resources, and a complete disregard for human life.

"The cove where Alex went today," Meg said, shifting focus slightly. "Eleanor said it's on property that belonged to Krane's biological father. Land Krane repurchased through one of his shell companies."

Claire straightened, tea momentarily forgotten. "That's significant. Not just a random meeting place but a location with personal meaning to Krane."

"Exactly. And Alex specifically asked Eleanor about that property weeks before I ever got involved in this. Before I found the message on Blackwood's roof."

The kettle began to whistle, a domestic counterpoint to their decidedly non-domestic conversation. Claire silenced it, pouring water into waiting mugs, the fragrant steam carrying bergamot and citrus notes that briefly softened the apartment's atmosphere.

"So Alex was operational in Seacliff before you ever arrived," Claire concluded, setting a mug before Meg. "Specifically investigating connections between Krane and properties linked to his family history."

"Which means what, exactly?" Meg wrapped her hands around the warm ceramic, grateful for its tangible comfort. "That finding the message on the roof, meeting Alex at the cabin—none of it was coincidence?"

Claire leaned against the counter, considering. "Unclear. Alex was clearly targeting Eleanor's research, trying to determine how close she was to uncovering certain connections. But you spotting that message, deciding to investigate... that appears to have been genuine chance. Unless..."

"Unless what?"

"Unless someone wanted you to find it," Claire suggested carefully. "Unless the message itself was bait, designed to draw someone in, to create a distraction or gather intelligence about who might be watching Blackwood's cabin."

The possibility hadn't occurred to Meg—that the "HELP ME" message itself might have been strategic rather than desperate, might have been placed specifically to be discovered rather than as a genuine cry for assistance.

"But that would mean they anticipated someone checking Google Maps satellite imagery of that specific location," Meg objected. "The odds against that are astronomical."

"Not necessarily," Claire countered. "If they knew Eleanor was researching property connections, knew she was using online resources including mapping services, knew others might be conducting similar research... placing a visible message that would only be detected through satellite imagery creates a filter. Only someone looking closely, paying specific attention to that location, would notice it."

The reasoning was sound, but felt incomplete. "But why? What's the strategic value in having someone like me discover the message, investigate the cabin?"

Claire sipped her tea, thinking. "Confirmation of who's watching. Intelligence gathering about law enforcement interest or approaches. Even simply creating a diversion, pulling attention toward Blackwood's cabin and away from other operational areas."

All plausible, all suggesting a level of strategic calculation that made Meg increasingly uncomfortable with her own role in events unfolding around her. Had she been manipulated from the beginning? Had her every action since discovering that message been anticipated, perhaps even directed along channels Krane had prepared?

"I don't like being a pawn in someone else's game," she said finally, frustration evident.

"Then don't be," Claire replied simply. "Pawns move in predictable patterns, follow expected paths. If someone has been manipulating events, anticipating your responses, then the most disruptive thing you can do is make moves they haven't calculated."

The advice crystallized something that had been forming in Meg's mind since her conversation with Campbell, since witnessing Alex's clandestine meeting, since learning about Thomas's death and Eleanor's discoveries about Krane's past.

"I'm going to call Campbell," she decided, reaching for the burner phone still in her jacket pocket. "But not to accept her offer of support. To negotiate terms, to establish a parallel channel of investigation while maintaining our connection to Hanover and official resources."

Claire studied her over the rim of her mug, expression indicating neither approval nor disapproval, merely careful assessment. "You think that's the unexpected move? Working both sides against the middle?"

"I think it's the move that maintains maximum flexibility while committing to neither approach exclusively," Meg clarified. "We keep working with Hanover, with Eleanor, through official channels. But we also explore what Campbell's offering, what her resources might provide that traditional law enforcement can't access."

"Walking a tightrope between competing interests," Claire observed, not disagreeing but ensuring Meg understood the complexities involved. "With the constant risk of falling toward one side or the other."

"More like sailing between Scylla and Charybdis," Meg countered, the classical reference emerging from college literature courses long dormant in her memory. "Navigating between opposing dangers, trying to find the narrow channel that leads to our actual goal—finding Emily and Valerie, stopping Krane, ending this before anyone else dies."

Claire nodded, appreciation for the analogy evident in her slight smile. "Just remember that in the original story, Odysseus lost crew members to both monsters. No path through such narrow straits comes without sacrifice."

The warning was gentle but clear—pursuing both official and unofficial approaches simultaneously carried inherent risks, potential costs that couldn't be fully anticipated or controlled. Meg acknowledged this with a nod of her own, accepting the caution without abandoning the strategy.

"I'll make the call tomorrow," she decided. "After we've had time to process everything Eleanor shared, after we've updated Hanover on the cove's connection to Krane's father, after we've gotten some rest and can approach this with clear heads."

"Good call," Claire agreed, draining the last of her tea. "Thomas's death changes everything—the timeline, the stakes, the assessment of how far Krane will go to protect his secrets. We need to be at our best for whatever comes next."

The reminder of Thomas—his life cut short by calculated violence, his connection to them severed permanently—sobered both women, returning them from strategic planning to the human reality underlying their investigation. A good man was dead, others remained in danger, and the individual responsible continued to operate from shadows they had yet to fully penetrate.

They prepared for sleep with the subdued efficiency of people who understood that rest was strategic rather than indulgent, necessary maintenance rather than luxury. The apartment felt different with deputies stationed outside, with the knowledge that they were being protected from threats that had moved from theoretical to lethally real within the past twelve hours.

In the guest bedroom that had become familiar territory over recent weeks, Meg found sleep elusive despite physical and emotional exhaustion. Her mind continued processing, connecting, questioning—analyzing Alex's appearance in Seacliff against the backdrop of Thomas's death, Eleanor's revelations about Krane's past, the cove's connection to his father's property.

What was in the package Alex had exchanged at the cove? Who was the man she'd met there? What lay in the cabin at the cliff top, and how did it connect to Krane's early life, to his father's disappearance, to the path that had led him from troubled teenager to murderer to financial criminal to the architect of elaborate revenge decades later?

Questions without answers, mysteries without resolution, cycling through her consciousness as she stared at the ceiling, seeking patterns in the subtle texture of paint illuminated by streetlights filtering through partially closed blinds.

Sleep came eventually, fragmentary and disturbed, dreams blending reality and imagination—Alex in the boat, Thomas's car plunging from coastal cliffs, Eleanor clutching an old diary while blood stained her immaculate sleeve, Caroline Whittaker's school portrait smile transforming into an accusation that spanned decades.

And beneath it all, a question that had no answer yet: what move would disrupt Krane's calculations, what approach could untangle this web of revenge and manipulation, what path might lead to salvation for those still caught in his elaborate game?

CHAPTER THIRTEEN
THE BOATHOUSE

Morning arrived with the insistent buzz of Claire's alarm, pulling Meg from fitful sleep. For a moment, disorientation clouded her thoughts—the unfamiliar angle of sunlight through the guest room blinds, the distant sounds of movement in the kitchen, the weight of security protocols that had transformed Claire's apartment into something between safe house and command center.

She dressed quickly, choosing practical clothing—jeans, layered tops that could adapt to changing conditions, boots that could handle varied terrain. Whatever the day brought, comfort and mobility would matter more than style.

The kitchen smelled of coffee and toast, Claire already dressed for court in a charcoal suit that emphasized her professional competence. A deputy—Rodriguez, according to her nameplate—sat at the small table, radio positioned beside her coffee mug, alert despite what must have been a long night of guard duty.

"Morning," Claire greeted, sliding a mug toward Meg. "Sleep at all?"

"Some," Meg hedged, not wanting to admit how her dreams had been populated by fragments of yesterday's revelations—Thomas's death, Eleanor's grief, Caroline Whittaker's diary, Alex's betrayal. "Any updates?"

Claire glanced at Rodriguez, who shook her head slightly. "Quiet night. No sign of surveillance or approach to the building."

"Hanover called about twenty minutes ago," Claire added, buttering toast with efficient movements. "Eleanor's secure at the safe house. They're retrieving Caroline's diary this morning—unmarked vehicle, alternate routes, full tactical support."

The diary—the evidence that connected Victor Krane to a decades-old murder, that explained his fixation on Seacliff, on the families who had known him in his previous life. Evidence that might finally provide leverage against a man who had evaded justice for too long.

"I need to be there," Meg said, the decision crystallizing as she spoke. "When they recover the diary, when they start piecing together what it means for the investigation."

Claire studied her over the rim of her coffee mug, something cautious in her expression. "Hanover didn't invite you, Meg."

"I know. But this connects to everything—to Alex, to Emily and Valerie, to what happened to Thomas." Meg gripped her mug tighter, warmth seeping into her palms. "And I promised Eleanor I'd help find them, bring them home."

Rodriguez shifted uncomfortably, clearly recognizing this conversation had moved beyond professional coordination into personal territory.

"I need to check in with the unit outside," she said, standing with the practiced smoothness of someone accustomed to providing privacy when needed. "Back in five."

When the door closed behind her, Claire's professional mask slipped, revealing the concerned friend beneath.

"You promised a grieving woman you'd solve an impossible case," she said gently. "In the immediate aftermath of her nephew's murder. No one expects you to personally rescue these women, Meg."

"I do," Meg replied, the simple statement carrying the weight of conviction that had been building since her first glimpse of that message on Blackwood's cabin roof. "Not alone, not without help, but I need to see this through. For Thomas. For Eleanor. For myself."

Claire sighed, recognizing the determination in Meg's voice. "And for Alex? Even knowing what she's done, what she might be?"

The question struck at the heart of the ambivalence Meg had been struggling with since Campbell's revelations, since witnessing Alex's clandestine exchange at the cove. What did she owe someone who had used her, manipulated her, potentially participated in murder? And yet, what if there was more to the story than they currently understood?

"For the Alex I thought I knew," Meg said finally. "The one who might still exist somewhere beneath whatever Krane's made her become."

Claire didn't argue further, recognizing the futility. Instead, she reached for her phone. "I'll call Hanover, see if she'll agree to your joining. But Meg—" Her expression turned serious. "Professional boundaries. This is her operation, her jurisdiction. You're there as a consultant at best, an observer at worst."

"Understood," Meg agreed readily, knowing Claire was right, that she needed to temper her growing personal investment with respect for proper procedure.

While Claire made the call, Meg forced herself to eat, knowing the day ahead would demand energy she couldn't spare. The toast tasted like cardboard, the coffee too bitter despite the cream she'd added, but she consumed them mechanically, body accepting what her mind barely registered.

"She's agreed," Claire reported, ending her call with an expression suggesting surprise at her own persuasive success. "They'll pick you up in twenty minutes. I'd go with you, but the Henderson trial—"

"Starts today. I know." Meg said. "You have responsibilities too. I'll keep you updated as much as possible."

"Just—" Claire hesitated, choosing her words carefully. "Remember what we talked about last night. If you're going to contact Campbell, if you're going to explore that avenue of approach, be explicit about your boundaries. These people aren't governed by the same rules as law enforcement."

"I will," Meg promised, the burner phone heavy in her pocket where she'd placed it earlier, already anticipating making that call once she understood what Caroline's diary revealed.

Rodriguez returned, professional mask firmly in place, pretending she hadn't been giving them privacy for a difficult conversation. "Vehicle approaching, matches the description Sheriff Hanover provided. One occupant, Deputy Reid."

The confirmation of friendly arrival released tension Meg hadn't realized she'd been holding. Whatever came next, she was moving forward, taking action rather than waiting passively for developments beyond her control.

She gathered her things quickly—phone, wallet, jacket against the morning chill. At the door, Claire caught her arm, holding her gaze with uncommon intensity.

"Be careful," she said simply, the phrase encompassing all they'd discussed and more. "I've got court until at least four. After that, I'm available for whatever you need."

The unspoken support, the implicit understanding that Claire would drop everything if necessary, warmed something cold that had settled in Meg's chest since Thomas's death. Whatever happened, she wasn't alone in this.

"I will," she replied, meaning it. "Good luck with Henderson."

Outside, Reid waited in an unmarked department SUV, his weathered face betraying little beyond professional attention as Meg approached. She'd come to appreciate his stoic competence, his ability to navigate complex situations without drama or excessive conversation. As she settled into the passenger seat, she wondered briefly about Jason Martinez, the environmental engineer who had been rescued alongside Thomas. His debriefing had provided valuable information about

Krane's operation, but with Thomas's murder, the focus had naturally shifted to more immediate concerns.

"Morning," he greeted as she slid into the passenger seat. "Hanover's meeting us at the rendezvous point. Eleanor's already there with the tactical team."

"Good morning. Before we get into that," Meg said, "what happened with Jason Martinez? Is he still under protection?"

Reid nodded, his expression grim. "FBI took him into protective custody yesterday after Thomas's death. They moved him to a secure location out of state. His information about Krane's environmental operations is proving valuable for tracking the offshore financial network."

"Good," Meg said, relieved to hear Martinez was safe. "That was my next question—where exactly are we going?"

"Catherine Peterson's vacation property," Reid replied, navigating morning traffic with practiced ease. "Eleanor's been staying there since Thomas's death. The diary is hidden in a sealed container in the boathouse."

"Seems risky, retrieving it from a known location," Meg observed, scanning the side mirror for any sign of pursuit or surveillance. "If Krane has been watching Eleanor..."

"We're counting on him focusing on her home address and Catherine's primary residence," Reid explained. "The vacation property belongs to a trust established by Catherine's brother. Property records haven't been updated since his death last year."

The strategy made sense, creating a window of opportunity while Krane's operation scrambled to respond to Thomas's murder, to adjust their surveillance and intelligence gathering. A small advantage, perhaps, but in this deadly game of move and countermove, even minor edges mattered.

They drove in silence for several miles, the landscape gradually transforming from suburban development to coastal countryside, occasional glimpses of ocean visible through breaks in the rolling terrain. Reid maintained a careful adherence to speed limits, nothing in his driving suggesting urgency or official business, just another local making a morning trip along familiar roads.

"How's Eleanor?" Meg asked finally, needing to know the human reality behind tactical considerations and security protocols.

Reid's expression softened slightly, the professional mask slipping to reveal genuine concern. "Holding together through sheer will. Using this investigation as a lifeline." He shook his head slightly, hands tightening on the steering wheel. "I've seen grief do strange things to people, Ms. Sawyer. Transform them in ways you wouldn't expect."

"She blames herself," Meg said quietly, remembering Eleanor's broken nails, the blood on her sleeve, the desperate apology to Thomas at the crash site.

"Yes." A single syllable carrying volumes of understanding. "Though from everything we know, there's nothing she could have done differently. Krane's organization is sophisticated, professional. They would have found a way to reach Thomas regardless of precautions."

The cold calculation behind that reality—a targeted assassination executed with precision by people who viewed human life as merely an obstacle to their objectives—chilled Meg despite the morning sun now streaming through the windshield.

"And the diary?" she prompted. "Eleanor said it contains evidence connecting Krane to Caroline Whittaker's death?"

Reid nodded, turning onto a narrow road that wound closer to the coastline. "According to Eleanor, Caroline documented Krane's escalating behavior in the weeks before her death—controlling patterns, specific threats, detailed accounts that paint a clear picture of someone capable of violence. Evidence that would have been compelling if properly investigated at the time."

"But it wasn't," Meg concluded, the familiar pattern of justice delayed, of powerful connections protecting the guilty, evident even in this decades-old case.

"No." Reid's tone carried professional frustration, the recognition of a system that sometimes failed those it was designed to protect. "Caroline's parents were friends with the medical examiner, the sheriff at that time. The official report listed her death as accidental—a fall during a solo hike in an area known for unstable terrain."

"And Judge Blackwell?" Meg asked, curious about Eleanor's late husband's role in this tragic history. "He knew the truth but couldn't prove it?"

"He suspected," Reid corrected carefully. "Had concerns about his stepson's behavior, about inconsistencies in Victor's account of his whereabouts when Caroline disappeared. But without physical evidence, without witnesses, there wasn't enough for criminal charges."

The conversation paused as Reid slowed the vehicle, turning onto an even narrower track that disappeared into a stand of pine trees, the ocean now audible beyond though not visible through the dense vegetation.

"We're approaching the rendezvous," he said, voice shifting back to professional focus. "From here on, we maintain operational security protocols. No names over radio, no discussion of specific evidence outside secure areas."

Meg nodded, understanding the precaution. If Krane truly had infiltrated local law enforcement, as both Campbell and Eleanor suggested, then even routine communications could be compromised.

The track emerged from the trees onto a bluff overlooking a small, sheltered cove. A modest cottage stood back from the edge, weathered shingles and blue trim suggesting decades of peaceful summer retreats, family gatherings untouched by the darkness that now brought armed deputies to its doorstep.

Below, a winding path led down to a small dock where a boathouse perched at the water's edge, its weathered structure seeming to grow from the rocky shoreline as if it had always been there, a natural extension of the landscape.

Reid parked beside two unmarked vehicles, cutting the engine. "Ready?"

The simple question encompassed far more than their immediate task. Was she ready to see Eleanor again, raw with grief yet somehow functioning? Ready to encounter evidence connecting a teenage Victor Krane to violence that foreshadowed his current operation? Ready to potentially learn more about Alex's role, about Emily and Valerie's situation?

"Yes," Meg said, the answer equally simple but carrying similar weight.

Together, they walked toward the cottage, where Sheriff Hanover stood on the porch, engaged in low conversation with a deputy Meg didn't recognize. Eleanor was visible through the front window, seated at a small table, focused on what appeared to be old photographs spread before her.

"Ms. Sawyer," Hanover greeted as they approached, her crisp uniform contrasting with the rustic setting. "Thank you for respecting operational protocols. Ms. Winters was quite insistent about your involvement."

"Claire can be persuasive," Meg acknowledged with a small smile. "Especially when she believes she's right."

"A useful quality in a prosecutor," Hanover observed, something like approval briefly visible in her otherwise professional expression. "Eleanor is reviewing materials that may provide context for the diary. She asked specifically to speak with you before we proceed to the boathouse."

The request surprised Meg slightly, though perhaps it shouldn't have given Eleanor's direct appeal to her the previous night. She nodded, following Hanover into the cottage, its interior carrying the distinctive scent of a place opened after winter closure—slight mustiness overlaid with pine-scented cleaner, a hint of salt air through partially opened windows.

Eleanor looked up as they entered, her appearance marginally improved from the previous evening—fresh clothing, hair neatly arranged, the bloodstained jacket replaced. But her eyes remained haunted, skin pale against silver hair, hands still showing evidence of her desperate attempts to reach Thomas at the crash site.

"Meg," she greeted, the same direct address, the same absence of formality that had marked their interaction at the department. "Thank you for coming. I wanted to show you something before we retrieve the diary."

She gestured to the photographs spread before her—school portraits, family gatherings, casual snapshots from what appeared to be the 1980s, judging by the clothing styles and photographic quality.

"Caroline," she said, indicating a smiling teenage girl with feathered brown hair and bright eyes that seemed to look directly into the camera, into the future she would never experience. "And this—" Her finger moved to another photograph, this one showing a young couple at what appeared to be a school dance. "Caroline with Victor, at junior prom."

Meg studied the image, trying to see in the teenage boy any trace of the man who would become Nathan Blackwood, who would orchestrate complex financial schemes and targeted revenge decades later. He was handsome in a conventional way—dark hair carefully styled, confident smile, arm draped possessively around Caroline's waist. Nothing in the photograph hinted at darkness beneath, at capacity for the violence that would apparently claim Caroline's life weeks later.

"They look... normal," Meg observed, the banality of the observation failing to capture the cognitive dissonance of seeing Krane as an ordinary teenager, engaged in ordinary activities.

"That was his gift, even then," Eleanor said quietly. "Appearing entirely conventional while concealing what lay beneath. William—my husband—was the only one who saw it, who recognized the patterns. The sudden mood shifts, the obsessive control, the careful performance for adults while behaving very differently with peers."

She selected another photograph from the array—an older man with kind eyes and a serious expression, dressed in judge's robes for what appeared to be an official portrait.

"William believed in rehabilitation, in the possibility of change," Eleanor continued, voice steady despite the emotion clearly lurking beneath her composure. "It's why he agreed to hear Victor's financial crimes case years later, why he believed he could remain impartial despite their history. He thought perhaps adult consequences, structured incarceration, might accomplish what teenage interventions had failed to do."

"But it didn't," Meg said gently, understanding where this narrative led.

Eleanor shook her head, a single tear escaping despite her evident determination to maintain control. "No. It made everything worse. Made Victor's need for revenge more focused, more sophisticated. And now here we are, decades later, still dealing with the consequences of decisions made when Caroline was alive, when Victor was just beginning to reveal what he would become."

She arranged the photographs with careful precision, the librarian's instinct for order asserting itself even in grief. "The diary is in a waterproof container beneath the floorboards of the boathouse. William hid it there after Caroline's parents gave it to him—they couldn't bear to read it, to know the details of their daughter's final weeks, but they couldn't bring themselves to destroy it either."

"And you've read it?" Meg asked, sensing there was more to this story, more that Eleanor wanted to share before they retrieved the physical evidence.

"Yes." Eleanor's hands stilled on the photographs, her gaze distant with memory. "After William died, after Victor was supposedly released on compassionate grounds then reported dead. I needed to understand what had happened, why William remained so troubled by the case even decades later."

She focused on Meg again, something intense in her expression. "It's not just about Caroline's death, though that's tragic enough. It's about what came after—the systematic destruction of evidence, the coercion of witnesses, the corruption of local officials to ensure the case remained classified as accidental."

"A pattern he's repeated," Meg observed, "with compromised law enforcement, judges like Harmon protecting his interests, targeted elimination of threats."

"Exactly." Eleanor selected one final photograph—a family portrait showing a younger version of herself, William in casual clothing rather than judicial robes, and a teenage boy who bore a striking resemblance to Thomas. "This was taken the summer before Victor killed Caroline. Thomas's father—William's son from his first marriage—brought the family to visit. Thomas would have been about four."

The connection crystallized, the familial relationships suddenly clear. "Thomas was William's grandson."

"Yes. After his parents died, I became his guardian. Raised him from age seventeen." Eleanor's voice caught, emotion finally breaking through her careful control. "He never knew the full story of Caroline, of Victor. I thought I was protecting him. Instead, I failed to prepare him for the danger his research might uncover."

Meg reached across the table, covering Eleanor's damaged hand with her own—a gesture of human connection transcending professional boundaries or investigative roles.

"You didn't fail him," she said firmly. "You gave him a home, stability, your own passion for seeking truth. He became an environmental scientist, dedicated to protecting natural resources, directly because of your influence."

Eleanor looked down at their joined hands, seeming to draw strength from the contact. "Perhaps. But now we must ensure his death serves purpose—that the evidence he helped uncover, combined with Caroline's diary, finally brings Victor Krane to justice. Not just for financial crimes, not just for revenge schemes, but for murder spanning decades."

She straightened, composure returning through visible effort. "Sheriff Hanover is waiting. We should proceed to the boathouse."

Outside, tactical preparations had advanced—deputies in position around the property perimeter, communications equipment established on the cottage porch, Hanover conferring with what appeared to be the team leader for the retrieval operation.

"Ready?" Hanover asked as they emerged, addressing Eleanor directly but with a glance that included Meg in the question.

"Yes," Eleanor replied, the single syllable carrying determination that transcended her evident physical and emotional exhaustion.

Together, they made their way down the winding path to the boathouse, Eleanor setting a deliberate pace that suggested both age-related caution on the steep slope and psychological preparation for what awaited. Reid walked beside her, occasionally offering a steadying arm at particularly tricky sections, his support matter-of-fact rather than patronizing.

The boathouse stood partially over water, its weathered structure smelling of salt, marine growth, and ancient creosote from the pilings supporting it. Inside, filtered light created dappled patterns on worn floorboards, small waves lapping gently beneath the structure, the rhythmic sound a counterpoint to their careful movements.

"There," Eleanor said, indicating a section of flooring near the back wall, away from the boat slip that occupied most of the structure. "William installed a hidden compartment when he rebuilt the floor after a storm twenty-five years ago. I helped him then, never realizing it would one day house such important evidence."

Two deputies carefully removed the indicated floorboards, revealing a space beneath. One reached down, withdrawing a metal ammunition box, sealed with heavy waterproof tape and showing no signs of moisture damage despite decades in the damp environment.

"Combination lock," he reported, studying the container. "Three digits."

Eleanor stepped forward. "Caroline's birthday. May 12th. Five-one-two."

The deputy entered the combination, the lock releasing with an audible click that seemed unnaturally loud in the hushed atmosphere. Inside, wrapped in plastic and further protected by a sealed plastic bag, lay a small book with a floral cover—the diary of a teenage girl, preserved as evidence of a crime decades old yet newly relevant.

Hanover supervised as the deputy carefully documented the retrieval—photographs of the container in situ, the process of opening it, the condition of the diary before it was handled. Standard evidence protocols applied with meticulous attention to detail, ensuring chain of custody that would withstand later legal scrutiny.

"We'll need to review this in a secure location," Hanover said once the diary had been properly handled and placed in an evidence bag. "Not here, not at the department. Somewhere Krane wouldn't anticipate."

"The federal building in Portland," Reid suggested. "I can coordinate with Agent Lopez, arrange secure space in their evidence review facility."

"Perfect." Hanover nodded approval. "Ms. Blackwell, you'll need to come with us to authenticate the diary, confirm it's the document you've previously read. Ms. Sawyer—" She turned to Meg, her expression professionally neutral. "Your continued participation is valuable but optional. This next phase involves significant security protocols and potential exposure to danger if Krane's operation realizes what we've recovered."

The statement was neither encouragement nor discouragement, simply a clear outlining of reality, letting Meg make an informed decision about her continued involvement. She appreciated the approach— being treated as a capable adult who understood risks rather than a civilian to be protected or directed.

"I'd like to remain involved," Meg said, the decision requiring no deliberation. "I've come this far. I want to see it through."

Hanover nodded once, accepting her choice without further discussion. "We leave in twenty minutes. Two-vehicle convoy, alternate routes to Portland. Cell phones powered off, communication restricted to secure channels."

As preparations for departure began, Meg found herself standing at the boathouse entrance, looking out over the small cove where wavelets caught morning sunlight, transforming water into scattered diamonds. The peaceful scene contrasted sharply with the tension surrounding them, with the knowledge that Caroline's diary might finally provide leverage against a man who had evaded justice for too long.

Reid appeared beside her, his presence unobtrusive but somehow comforting in its professional solidity.

"You're thinking about Alex," he observed quietly. "About what this diary might reveal about her role in all this."

Meg nodded, surprised but not entirely shocked by his perceptiveness. "And about Emily and Valerie. If what Eleanor says is true—that Krane's been systematically eliminating anyone who threatens to expose his past—then they're in more danger than ever."

"We'll find them," Reid assured her, the promise delivered without dramatic emphasis but with absolute conviction. "This evidence, combined with what Thomas discovered, what Eleanor already knows—it gives us leverage we didn't have before."

"I hope you're right," Meg said, watching a seabird dive into the clear water, emerging moments later with a small fish gleaming in its beak.

She didn't voice her deeper concern—that leverage might come too late for those already in Krane's grasp, that Emily and Valerie might become collateral damage in his increasingly desperate efforts to maintain control of his operation, his narrative, his carefully constructed vengeance.

And Alex? What would Caroline's diary mean for her, for whatever complex role she played in this web of deception and manipulation?

The questions remained unanswered as they prepared to depart, the diary secured in an evidence container, Eleanor seated in the lead vehicle with Hanover, deputies establishing the convoy formation that would take them to Portland and whatever revelations awaited in the pages of a teenage girl's final testimony.

Whatever came next, Meg was committed now—to finding the truth, to helping Eleanor achieve justice for both Caroline and Thomas, to determining once and for all Alex's true role and motivations. Most importantly, to ensuring that no one else fell victim to Krane's decades-long campaign of revenge and control.

She took one last look at the peaceful cove before joining Reid in the second vehicle, struck by the realization that there were truly no safe havens in this conflict, nowhere to hide from the consequences of challenging someone as ruthless and resourceful as Victor Krane.

CHAPTER FOURTEEN
FLASHPOINT

Rain fell in sheets as they lowered Thomas Blackwell's casket into the sodden earth. The downpour seemed fitting—nature's own rebellion against the injustice of a life cut short. Meg stood slightly apart from the small gathering of mourners, rain plastering her hair to her skull, soaking through her black coat despite the umbrella Claire held over them both. She welcomed the discomfort. It gave her something to focus on besides the raw devastation on Eleanor's face.

The elderly woman stood closest to the grave, her silver hair pulled back severely, her posture defying both grief and weather through sheer force of will. Sheriff Hanover remained at her side, one hand discreetly supporting Eleanor's elbow—not for balance, Meg thought, but as an anchor to reality when everything else had been ripped away.

"He shouldn't have ended this way," Claire whispered, her voice barely audible above the drumming rain. "Twenty-six hours. That's all he had after six months of captivity."

Meg didn't respond. There was nothing to say that wouldn't sound hollow against the finality of that dark rectangle cut into the earth, the polished wood of the casket already beaded with raindrops like tears.

At the edge of the cemetery, three black SUVs with tinted windows were parked in a formation that spoke of security rather than mourning. FBI agents in rain gear maintained a subtle perimeter, their eyes scanning constantly, hands never far from concealed weapons. Thomas's funeral had been arranged in haste, with minimal public notice, but no one doubted Krane might make it a target.

The service ended with brutal efficiency, the small group dispersing toward waiting vehicles. Eleanor paused at the graveside, her damaged hand trailing over the casket in farewell. Meg caught the movement of her lips—final words for her nephew that would remain private, locked in this moment of rain and grief.

"We should go," Claire said softly. "Reid's arranged a safe house for Eleanor. She needs rest after... all this."

Meg nodded, but her attention was drawn to a solitary figure standing beneath a distant oak tree, partially obscured by its massive trunk. The watcher made no attempt to join the mourners, maintained a careful distance from the FBI security perimeter.

"Hold on," Meg said, handing her portion of the umbrella to Claire. "I'll meet you at the car."

"Meg—" Claire started, but Meg was already moving, cutting across the rain-slicked grass between elaborate headstones and simple markers.

The watcher didn't flee, didn't change position even as Meg approached. Only when she was twenty feet away did Campbell step fully into view, her steel-gray hair darkened by rain, her black coat indistinguishable from those worn by the legitimate mourners.

"I wondered if you'd notice me," she said by way of greeting.

"You wanted to be noticed," Meg countered, stopping at a distance that allowed conversation without intimacy. "Otherwise you wouldn't have come."

Campbell's mouth tightened briefly—not quite a smile, but acknowledgment of a point scored. "Thomas Blackwell deserved more respect than he received in life. Someone should witness his passing who understands the true significance of what he uncovered."

"And what exactly was that?" Meg asked, rainwater tracing cold paths down her neck, beneath her collar. "You've shared fragments of intelligence, hints about Krane's operation, but always with an agenda. What did Thomas find that was worth killing him for?"

For a moment, Campbell seemed to consider her options, weighing disclosure against strategic advantage. Then she reached into her coat, producing a waterproof envelope that she extended toward Meg.

"You didn't return my call," she said, not answering the question directly. "I decided a more tangible approach might be necessary."

Meg made no move to take the envelope. "What is this?"

"The location of Emily Reeves and Valerie Cortez," Campbell replied, her voice matter-of-fact despite the bombshell she'd just dropped. "Plus documentation of Krane's market manipulation algorithm—the technical architecture, the trigger mechanisms, the scheduled execution."

Meg's heart rate doubled instantly, but she kept her expression neutral with effort. "Why give this to me? Why not Hanover or the FBI?"

"Because they're compromised." Campbell's certainty was chilling. "Not all of them, not even most, but enough that any information passing through official channels reaches Krane within hours. That's how he's stayed ahead of you at every turn."

"And I'm supposed to take your word for this?" Meg didn't bother hiding her skepticism. "Trust that this information is accurate, that your motives are pure?"

"My motives aren't remotely pure, Ms. Sawyer." Campbell's honesty was almost refreshing. "I represent interests that will lose billions if Krane's algorithm executes. But right now, our interests align perfectly with yours—stopping Krane, rescuing his captives, preventing market destabilization."

The rain intensified, wind driving it sideways in stinging sheets. In the parking area beyond, Meg could see Claire watching their exchange with visible concern, Reid beside her with one hand inside his jacket, clearly accessing a weapon.

"Why me?" Meg asked the question that had haunted her since Campbell's first contact. "Of all the people involved in this investigation, why focus on me?"

"Because you're the random factor Krane couldn't calculate for," Campbell said, using the same phrase Thomas had. "The civilian who spotted a message on a roof, who pursued it without authority or back-up, who kept pushing when professionals retreated. And because—" She hesitated, something almost like compassion crossing her features. "Because Alexandra Reeves trusts you."

The statement hit Meg like a physical blow. "Alex? She betrayed me, betrayed everyone. She's working for Krane."

"It's considerably more complicated than that." Campbell pushed the envelope toward her again, more insistently. "Read this. Then decide whether to share it with your official channels. You have approximately six hours before Krane's operation moves to its final phase."

Meg took the envelope, the weight of it suddenly disproportionate to its physical mass. "What happens at the end of those six hours?"

"Either you use this information to stop him, or the largest coordinated market manipulation in history begins." Campbell glanced toward the parking area, where Reid was now moving in their direction, hand still inside his jacket. "Your law enforcement colleague is getting nervous. You should go. And Meg?"

The shift to her first name caught Meg's attention more effectively than any dramatic emphasis could have.

"Trust Alexandra's original intentions, not her current actions," Campbell said, already turning to leave. "There's more at stake than any of you realize."

Before Meg could respond, Campbell was moving away through the cemetery, her path taking her behind a large mausoleum that blocked Reid's view. By the time he reached Meg's position, Campbell had vanished entirely, leaving only the envelope and her cryptic warning.

"Who was that?" Reid asked, his professional alertness tempered with genuine concern. "Claire said you just took off toward someone watching from the trees."

The rain had soaked through Meg's clothing now, her hair plastered to her scalp, water running in rivulets down her neck and beneath her collar. But she barely felt the discomfort, her attention fixed on the envelope in her hand and the implications of Campbell's warning.

"A contact," she said finally, choosing her words carefully. "Someone with information about Krane's operation."

Reid's expression darkened. "The same source who provided those surveillance photographs of Alexandra Reeves?"

"Yes." Meg held his gaze, searching for any hint that Campbell's warnings about compromised officials might apply to him. She'd come to trust Reid, to respect his steady professionalism, but Campbell's certainty had planted seeds of doubt that couldn't be easily dismissed.

"What did they give you?" he asked, glancing at the envelope.

Meg hesitated, rain dripping from her nose and chin, indecision warring with the urgency Campbell had impressed upon her. Six hours before Krane's operation reached its final phase. Six hours to stop what might be the largest market manipulation in history.

"Information about Krane's next move," she said, revealing only part of the truth. "I need to verify it before sharing details."

Reid studied her for a long moment, water beading on his weathered face, his eyes reflecting both understanding and concern. "You're worried about who you can trust."

It wasn't a question, and Meg appreciated that he didn't take offense at her caution. "After what happened to Thomas, to Judge Peterson, to Harmon... yes."

He nodded once, decision made. "Let's get you somewhere dry and secure. Eleanor's going to the safe house—she needs rest. We can look at whatever you've got tomorrow, after everyone's had a chance to process today."

The response confirmed Meg's instinctive trust in Reid, whatever Campbell's warnings might suggest. He was putting her judgment ahead of protocol, recognizing the complexity of their situation and the potential dangers of standard procedures.

Together they walked back toward the parking area, where Claire waited beneath her umbrella, concern evident in the tightness around her eyes.

"Everything okay?" she asked as they approached.

"Fine," Meg replied, not quite meeting her eyes. The half-truth felt uncomfortable between them, but she needed time to process Campbell's information, to understand its implications before involving others—even Claire.

As they reached the car, Eleanor was being helped into Sheriff Hanover's vehicle, her stoic dignity intact despite the visible toll grief had taken. The funeral director watched from the shelter of the cemetery office, his professional composure unable to completely hide his curiosity about the security presence and hushed consultations among law enforcement personnel.

The weight of the envelope seemed to increase with each passing minute, its contents potentially changing everything they thought they knew about Krane's operation, about Alex's role, about the true nature of the threat they faced.

Six hours. A deadline that transformed theoretical danger into immediate crisis. Six hours to stop Krane, to find Emily and Valerie, to unravel whatever complex game Alexandra Reeves was playing.

And it all began with the decision of who Meg could trust with the contents of a waterproof envelope, handed to her in a rain-soaked cemetery by a woman whose motives remained as murky as the clouds overhead.

CHAPTER FIFTEEN

PATTERNS

Meg woke to the sound of Claire moving around the kitchen, the familiar rhythm of mugs against countertop and water filling the kettle as much a part of morning as sunlight filtering through the blinds. For a moment, that normalcy created the illusion that the world hadn't shifted beneath her feet—that Thomas wasn't dead, that Alex wasn't somehow complicit, that they weren't all in the crosshairs of a man capable of calculated murder and elaborate revenge.

Then reality reasserted itself, heavy and inescapable.

She got up, pulled on a sweatshirt against the morning chill, and padded to the kitchen where Claire was measuring coffee with the precision of someone clinging to routine as an anchor in chaos.

"You look like you actually slept," Claire observed, glancing up from her task.

"Briefly," Meg admitted. "You?"

"Enough to function." Claire gestured to a folder on the counter. "Hanover sent this over with the deputy shift change at six. Analysis of the cove location you tracked Alex to. Turns out the cabin at the top

"

of the cliff is owned by a shell company linked to the same network as Krane's other properties."

Meg pulled the folder toward her, scanning its contents while Claire prepared breakfast neither of them particularly wanted but both knew they needed. The analysis was thorough—satellite imagery showing the cabin's isolation, property records tracing ownership through three layers of shell companies, utility usage suggesting occasional rather than constant occupation.

"It's not a residence," Meg noted. "More like a… meeting point. Somewhere secure for exchanges or conversations that can't happen electronically."

"That fits with what you saw," Claire agreed, sliding a plate of toast and eggs in front of Meg. "Alex delivering something physical, receiving something in return. Classic dead drop behavior."

Meg's gaze lingered on a detail in the report—an observation almost buried in technical language. The cabin's location wasn't just isolated; it offered direct line-of-sight to three cellular towers while remaining virtually invisible from standard surveillance routes. Perfect for someone who needed secure communications but was wary of electronic monitoring.

"We need to go there," she said, decision crystallizing. "Not the cove—too obvious, too easily watched. But somewhere with a view of the cabin. We need to see who's using it, what they're exchanging."

Claire's expression shifted from surprise to reluctant consideration. "Hanover would never approve a civilian operation like that."

"That's why we don't ask for approval," Meg replied, pushing aside her barely-touched breakfast. "We gather information, then bring it to her when it's actionable." She hesitated, then added: "And we need to call Campbell."

"You've decided to work with her," Claire observed, not quite a question.

"I've decided to use whatever resources might help us find Emily and Valerie before anyone else dies," Meg corrected. "Campbell has information and capabilities we don't. That doesn't mean I trust her."

Claire nodded slowly. "I'll call in to the courthouse, tell them I need another day. Family emergency."

"You don't have to—"

"Yes, I do," Claire interrupted firmly. "Nobody goes into field operations alone. Not even stubborn insurance investigators playing detective."

The simple assertion of partnership, of loyalty despite the risks, eased something tight in Meg's chest. "Thanks."

While Claire made her calls, Meg stepped onto the balcony to use the burner phone, the morning air carrying a salt tang from the harbor where just yesterday she'd spotted Alex. The encounter felt both immediate and distant, as if the events of the past twenty-four hours had somehow stretched time into new configurations.

Campbell answered on the first ring. "Ms. Sawyer. I was beginning to think you'd decided against further contact."

"I'm considering your offer," Meg replied, keeping her voice even. "But I need more specifics—both about what you're proposing and what you know about Krane's current operation."

"Understandable caution," Campbell acknowledged. "Perhaps we should meet to discuss details. Somewhere more private than our last conversation."

"Not happening," Meg said firmly. "We meet in public or not at all."

A pause, then: "Very well. The lighthouse visitor center at eleven. It's off-season, minimal staff, but public enough for your comfort."

"I'll be there," Meg confirmed. "With a colleague."

"Ms. Winters, I presume. Fine. Eleven o'clock."

The call ended with Campbell's customary abruptness, leaving Meg staring out at the harbor where boats moved through morning light, their crews focused on the practicalities of nets and engines and catch quotas. Lives untouched by the shadow that had fallen across her own.

Claire emerged onto the balcony, phone in hand. "Judge granted a continuance. Defense claimed it was prejudicial but got overruled." She studied Meg's expression. "Campbell?"

"Meeting us at the lighthouse visitor center at eleven." Meg turned away from the harbor view. "We've got two hours to prepare."

They spent those hours reviewing everything they knew about Krane's operation, Campbell's assertions, and the cove location where Alex had conducted her exchange. Claire approached it like preparing for court—organizing facts, identifying gaps, anticipating counter-moves. Meg applied her insurance investigator's perspective—looking for patterns, inconsistencies, the places where surfaces gave way to reveal underlying truths.

At 10:30, they left the apartment, taking Claire's Subaru rather than Meg's more recognizable vehicle. The deputy assigned to their protection followed at a discreet distance—Hanover's insistence on security protocols impossible to refuse completely, though they'd said nothing about their planned meeting with Campbell.

"Something's bothering me about yesterday," Meg said as they drove toward the lighthouse. "Why was Alex so visible? If she's working for Krane, if she's responsible for eliminating threats like Thomas... why operate openly in Seacliff, where she could be recognized?"

Claire considered this, eyes on the road. "Overconfidence, maybe. Or necessity—whatever exchange she conducted required personal presence, couldn't be delegated."

"Or she wanted to be seen," Meg suggested, the possibility forming as she spoke. "Specifically by me."

Claire glanced at her sharply. "Explain."

"Think about it. She's in Seacliff, walking openly along the harbor in daylight, then takes a boat to a location that requires following to discover. Almost like..." Meg's voice trailed off as connections formed. "Almost like she was creating a trail. Leading me somewhere."

"To what end?" Claire's skepticism was evident but not dismissive.

"I don't know," Meg admitted. "But it's the only explanation that addresses both her visibility and Krane's supposed interest in me. What if this isn't about eliminating witnesses but about directing attention?

Using me as a conduit to feed specific information into the investigation?"

The lighthouse came into view, its white tower stark against the blue morning sky, the visitor center a modest stone building at its base. Claire pulled into the nearly empty parking lot, cutting the engine but making no move to exit the car.

"If you're right, that makes this meeting with Campbell even more suspicious," she pointed out. "What if she's part of the same operation? Using a different approach but with the same objective—manipulating what we know, what we do, where we look?"

The possibility had occurred to Meg as well, but something about Campbell's clinical precision, her corporate backing, felt distinct from Krane's more personal vendetta. Different agendas, different methods, even if both were ultimately trying to use her for their own ends.

"We proceed carefully," Meg decided. "Listen more than we talk. Cross-reference everything she tells us against what we already know to be true."

The visitor center was as quiet as Campbell had predicted—a single elderly volunteer manning the admission desk, a middle-aged couple examining navigational exhibits, no one else visible in the main hall. Meg and Claire paid the nominal entrance fee and moved toward the circular room with panoramic windows facing the ocean.

Campbell stood at the far window, her back to them, gray hair catching sunlight, posture suggesting someone accustomed to waiting without impatience. She turned as they approached, her assessing gaze taking in their expressions, their stances, the careful distance they maintained.

"Ms. Sawyer. Ms. Winters." Her greeting acknowledged them equally, a subtle shift from their previous interaction. "Thank you for coming."

"You said you had specific information about Krane's operation," Meg replied, bypassing pleasantries. "We're here to evaluate it."

Campbell's mouth curved in what might have been appreciation for the direct approach. "Indeed." She gestured to a circular bench in the center of the room, positioned to allow visitors to rest while taking in the 360-degree views. "Shall we?"

They sat, the arrangement allowing all three to see the room's entrances while maintaining conversational privacy. Campbell withdrew a slim tablet from her bag, activated it with a complex passcode, and placed it on the bench between them.

"Victor Krane's operation has evolved beyond the financial manipulation scheme we initially detected," she began, her voice pitched for their ears only. "Recent intelligence suggests he's using that scheme as cover for something more personal, more dangerous."

"The revenge element," Claire supplied. "Eliminating everyone connected to his original case."

"That was our assessment until yesterday," Campbell confirmed. "But Thomas Blackwell's murder suggests a pattern shift. He wasn't directly connected to the original prosecution—he was targeted because of what he discovered about Krane's past in Seacliff. Specifically, about Caroline Whittaker."

Meg exchanged a glance with Claire. Campbell knowing about Caroline wasn't necessarily suspicious—that information could have been obtained through conventional intelligence gathering—but the timing of her knowledge, coinciding precisely with Eleanor's revelations, raised questions.

"What's your interest in Caroline Whittaker?" Meg asked, watching Campbell's reaction carefully.

"Caroline Whittaker's death was officially ruled accidental," Campbell replied, tapping her tablet to bring up an image—a scanned newspaper clipping yellowed with age, showing a school photograph of a smiling teenage girl alongside a report of her tragic hiking accident. "But there were inconsistencies in the investigation, irregularities in how evidence was handled. My employers believe those irregularities point to something significant about Krane, something that explains his current fixation on Seacliff and on specific individuals connected to that case."

"Including me?" Meg pressed. "Because I still don't understand why Krane would have any interest in an insurance investigator who stumbled onto his operation by chance."

Campbell's expression shifted subtly, something like genuine uncertainty crossing her features before her professional mask reasserted itself. "That remains unclear. Our intelligence suggests Krane's interest in you began after you discovered the message on Blackwood's cabin roof, after you connected with Alexandra Reeves. But the intensity of that interest seems disproportionate to your actual threat level."

"Almost like you represent something beyond yourself," Claire suggested thoughtfully. "A symbol or connection he recognizes but we don't."

The observation hung between them, unanswerable with current information yet impossible to dismiss. Meg found herself thinking of Eleanor's research, of the connections the librarian had traced through decades of Seacliff history, of patterns invisible until viewed from sufficient distance.

"What can you tell us about Alex?" she asked, changing directions. "I saw her yesterday, conducting some kind of exchange at a cove east of here. A location connected to Krane's biological father, according to Eleanor Blackwell."

Something flickered in Campbell's eyes—surprise, perhaps, or recalculation. "You followed Alexandra Reeves? Alone?"

"Answer the question," Claire interjected, her prosecutor's tone making it clear they weren't there for Campbell to interrogate them.

Campbell studied them both for a moment, then nodded slightly, acknowledging the correction. "Alexandra Reeves has been working with Krane's operation for approximately thirteen months. Initially recruited to help locate her sister Emily, she was gradually integrated into security operations, leveraging her military background. Over time, her role evolved into something more central."

"Enforcer," Meg supplied, the word bitter on her tongue.

"Among other functions," Campbell confirmed. "Her presence in Seacliff yesterday suggests the operation has entered its final phase. The cove exchange was likely part of their exit strategy—securing transportation, documentation, or resources needed for rapid departure once objectives are complete."

"Objectives including eliminating anyone who might expose Krane's past," Claire noted. "Like Thomas Blackwell."

"Yes." Campbell's expression remained professionally neutral, but something in her tone conveyed genuine concern. "Which puts everyone connected to this investigation at significant risk, including both of you. My employers have resources that could help mitigate that risk while simultaneously advancing our shared goal of stopping Krane."

"And these resources would be...?" Meg prompted.

"Intelligence, surveillance capabilities, operational support if necessary. Access to information channels outside conventional law enforcement. And protection, if you choose to accept it."

"In exchange for what?" Claire asked, the lawyer in her immediately identifying the unstated quid pro quo.

"Your cooperation in approaching Krane through channels he might respond to. Your insights into the investigation that might help us locate him before his scheme activates." Campbell paused, then added: "And your assistance in recovering certain documents we believe he possesses—records detailing financial operations that extend beyond his personal vendetta."

There it was—the corporate agenda underlying Campbell's offers of assistance. Not altruism but self-interest, protecting whatever financial entities she represented from exposure or losses connected to Krane's larger operation.

Before Meg could respond, movement near the entrance caught her attention—a man entering the visitor center, his casual demeanor at odds with the alertness in his eyes as they swept the space in a practiced security scan. He wore the anonymous outfit of a tourist—jeans, windbreaker, baseball cap—but his movements betrayed professional training, the same controlled awareness she'd observed in Alex.

"Don't react," she murmured, keeping her expression neutral while watching the man in her peripheral vision. "But I think we have company."

Campbell didn't turn, didn't change posture, but Meg saw her tapping something on her tablet—an alert or message sent without looking at the screen, muscle memory guiding her fingers.

"Describe," Campbell instructed quietly.

"Male, early thirties, dark hair, approximately six feet, baseball cap, blue windbreaker. Moving like security or military, scanning exit points and sight lines."

Campbell nodded almost imperceptibly. "One of mine, positioned as precaution. But the fact that you identified him suggests your observational skills are sharper than most civilians." She tapped her tablet again, and the man moved toward the navigational exhibit, apparently receiving new instructions.

"You brought backup to our meeting," Claire noted, disapproval evident in her tone. "After agreeing to come alone."

"I never agreed to come alone," Campbell corrected mildly. "Merely to meet in public. Given the stakes, certain precautions seemed prudent."

The exchange illustrated exactly why maintaining independence from both Campbell and official channels was essential—each operated according to their own rules, their own agendas, withholding information they deemed unnecessary to share.

"Let's get back to the question of Krane's interest in me," Meg said, redirecting the conversation. "You said it seems disproportionate to my actual threat level. What exactly does that mean?"

Campbell considered her words carefully. "It means that surveillance resources dedicated to tracking your movements, analyzing your background, and monitoring your communications far exceed what would be typical for a civilian investigator tangentially connected to a case. Our intelligence indicates your name appears in high-priority directives within Krane's operation—not just as a potential witness to be eliminated, but as someone to be specifically watched, tracked, and potentially... acquired."

The clinical term couldn't mask the disturbing implication—not just surveillance or intimidation, but potential abduction. Meg felt Claire tense beside her, though nothing in her friend's expression betrayed the reaction.

"Why?" Meg pressed. "What possible value could I have to Krane's operation?"

"That," Campbell admitted, "remains unclear. But there is one pattern worth noting. Krane's interest in you intensified significantly after you connected with Eleanor Blackwell and began reviewing her research into his past. Particularly her materials related to Caroline Whittaker."

The connection crystallized something that had been forming in Meg's mind since Eleanor's revelations about Krane's past, about Caroline's death, about the diary that documented their relationship before her "accident."

"He thinks I know something," she realized aloud. "Something from Eleanor's research or from Caroline's diary. Something he believes threatens him not just legally but personally."

"That aligns with our assessment," Campbell confirmed. "The question becomes: what information could be so damaging that it warrants this level of attention? What secret from forty years ago still carries such weight?"

Before Meg could respond, her phone vibrated with an incoming text. She checked it, expecting a message from Hanover or Reid about Eleanor's protection status. Instead, she found an unknown number and a message that stopped her breath mid-inhale:

Look outside. Silver sedan, north parking lot. I counted three surveillance teams watching you enter. One Campbell's, two Krane's. Get out NOW.

Attached was a photo taken from an elevated position—likely the lighthouse itself—showing the visitor center's parking lot with three vehicles circled: a silver sedan, a blue SUV, and a maintenance van. Each positioned with sightlines to different exits.

Meg showed the screen to Claire without comment, watched her friend's expression shift from confusion to sharp alertness.

"Problem?" Campbell inquired, her tone suggesting she'd registered their nonverbal exchange.

"We need to leave," Meg said, standing in a movement that brooked no argument. "Now."

Campbell's eyes narrowed slightly. "What's happened?"

"Someone just informed us we're being watched," Claire replied, already gathering her bag. "By multiple teams, including yours."

Campbell didn't deny it, didn't attempt explanation, merely nodded once as if confirming a suspicion. "Use the service corridor behind the gift shop. My associate will create a distraction to cover your exit."

The instructions came with practiced efficiency—clearly not the first time Campbell had managed an extraction under observation. Meg found herself simultaneously grateful for the tactical support and disturbed by how easily it was offered, how clearly it revealed Campbell's true operational capacity.

"Who sent the warning?" Campbell asked as they moved toward the gift shop with careful casualness, nothing in their posture suggesting urgency or alarm.

"Unknown," Meg replied, keeping her response deliberately minimal. Trust had become a resource too valuable to squander on someone who'd already demonstrated selective transparency.

The gift shop was empty save for a bored cashier scrolling through her phone, oblivious to the tensions radiating from the three women passing through. A door marked "STAFF ONLY" stood partially ajar at the back, revealing a dim corridor beyond.

"Go," Campbell instructed. "I'll remain visible to maintain the illusion you're still in the building."

Claire's expression made it clear she found this suspiciously convenient, but practicality overrode caution. They slipped through the door into a utilitarian hallway lined with cleaning supplies and promotional materials, emergency exit signs indicating an outlet at the far end.

"This feels like walking into another trap," Claire murmured as they moved quickly down the corridor.

"Maybe," Meg acknowledged. "But staying put definitely was one."

They reached the emergency exit just as a commotion erupted in the main hall—raised voices, something heavy falling, the perfect cacophony of distraction. Campbell's associate creating the promised diversion.

Meg pushed the door open carefully, triggering no alarm thanks to maintenance neglect or deliberate disabling. Outside, a narrow path led around the building to a service area where dumpsters provided cover from the main parking lot.

"Your car or mine?" came a voice from behind the nearest dumpster, causing both women to freeze.

Alex stepped into view, hands carefully visible at her sides, expression unreadable. She wore dark clothes, a baseball cap pulled low over her distinctive blonde hair, nothing like the confident woman who'd walked the harbor yesterday.

"What are you doing here?" Meg demanded, instinctively positioning herself slightly in front of Claire, though what protection she could offer against a trained operative was questionable at best.

"Saving your lives, apparently," Alex replied, voice flat. "Krane has three teams in the area. They're not here for surveillance, Meg. They're here for acquisition."

The confirmation of Campbell's clinical assessment—that Meg wasn't just being watched but targeted for abduction—landed with physical force.

"Why would you warn us?" Claire challenged, skepticism evident in her stance. "You work for Krane."

"It's complicated," Alex said, the simple phrase inadequate to the betrayals between them yet somehow perfectly suited to the impossible position she appeared to occupy.

"Uncomplicate it," Meg insisted.

Alex's gaze flicked to the corner of the building, checking sightlines before returning to Meg. "Not here. If you want answers—real answers—come with me now. Or stay and find out firsthand what Krane wants from you."

The ultimatum hung between them, seconds stretching as Meg weighed impossible options with inadequate information. Trust someone who had already betrayed her once, or risk whatever operation had brought three surveillance teams to a lighthouse visitor center on a weekday morning.

"Meg, we can't—" Claire began.

"We need answers," Meg cut her off, decision crystallizing. "And she's offering them."

"Along with potential abduction or worse," Claire countered, voice low but intense.

"If I wanted to take you to Krane, you'd already be unconscious," Alex interjected flatly. "The fact that we're having this conversation is proof I'm operating independently right now."

The brutal practicality of this assessment was hard to refute. Meg studied Alex's face, searching for deception, for the calculation she'd observed at the harbor. Instead, she found something closer to desperation—controlled but unmistakable.

"How do we get out without being seen?" Meg asked, the question itself committing her to at least the next step of whatever Alex was proposing.

"Service road behind the maintenance building," Alex replied immediately. "My car's there. Dark blue Accord, looks unremarkable enough to avoid immediate attention if we move now."

Claire's expression made her objections clear, but she voiced no further protest, accepting Meg's decision while clearly reserving judgment on its wisdom.

"Lead the way," Meg instructed, maintaining distance between them—not enough to appear suspicious to watchers but enough to react if necessary.

Alex nodded once, then moved with practiced efficiency toward the maintenance building, keeping to cover where available, her movements fluid and purposeful without conveying undue haste. Meg and Claire followed, the latter maintaining a position that would allow intervention if Alex suddenly changed tactics.

The service road curved around the lighthouse property before connecting to a maintenance access point rarely used by visitors. There, as promised, sat an unremarkable dark blue Accord, the kind of vehicle that appeared in every parking lot, on every street, forgettable by design.

"I'll drive," Alex said, approaching the driver's side. "You can have the keys once we're clear."

Another calculated concession—offering control while practical necessity required her to navigate them out of immediate danger. Meg opened the rear passenger door, allowing Claire the front seat position. Better visibility, easier intervention if needed.

Inside, the car smelled of nothing at all—no air freshener, no personal scent, no food or coffee spills. A vehicle maintained for function rather than comfort, wiped clean of identifying characteristics.

Alex started the engine and pulled away smoothly, checking mirrors with professional thoroughness but never turning her head fully—minimizing exposure of her face to potential observers.

"Where are we going?" Meg asked as they turned onto the coast road, heading south toward Seacliff but taking the first turnoff onto a less traveled route running parallel to the shore.

"Somewhere we can talk without surveillance," Alex replied, attention divided between the road ahead and the mirrors tracking potential pursuit. "A place Krane doesn't know about. One of mine, not his."

"And we're supposed to trust that this place exists?" Claire challenged from the front seat. "That this isn't an elaborate ruse to deliver Meg directly to Krane?"

Alex's mouth tightened almost imperceptibly, the only visible reaction to Claire's skepticism. "You have no reason to trust me," she acknowledged. "But consider this: if Krane had already connected you to

Campbell, had surveillance teams positioned before your meeting even began, what does that tell you about your other allies?"

The implication landed precisely as intended—a challenge to assumptions about who could be trusted, who might be compromised, who might be feeding information to Krane's operation.

"It means there's a leak," Meg supplied, the conclusion inescapable. "Someone knew about our meeting with Campbell. Someone with access to our movements, our plans."

"But not necessarily someone close to us," Claire countered immediately. "Our protective detail, someone at the department who knew our location—there are multiple potential sources."

"True," Alex conceded, taking another turn that carried them further from main thoroughfares. "But consider the timing. Thomas Blackwell is killed hours after discovering something significant about Krane's past. Campbell contacts you offering resources to track Krane. I appear in Seacliff conducting what looks like an operational exchange. All within a 48-hour window." She checked the mirrors again, her movements so practiced they appeared almost unconscious. "Patterns like that aren't coincidental. They're orchestrated."

The assessment aligned uncomfortably with Meg's earlier thoughts about being manipulated, directed, positioned according to someone else's calculation. But the someone might not be just Krane—it could be Campbell, could be Alex herself, could be some interplay of agendas she hadn't yet identified.

"Why does Krane want me?" Meg asked, cutting through layers of implication to the central question. "What does he think I know that makes me valuable enough to mount an abduction operation in broad daylight?"

Alex was silent for several moments, guiding the car onto an unmarked dirt road that wound upward through coastal forest, dense enough to obscure their passage from aerial observation.

"He believes you've seen Caroline Whittaker's diary," she said finally, the words precise as if extracted through careful internal editing. "He believes Eleanor Blackwell shared it with you, and that you've made connections that threaten not just his current operation but his freedom, his very identity."

"But I haven't seen the diary," Meg objected. "Eleanor mentioned it last night, said she'd take us to it today, but Thomas was killed before that could happen."

Alex's hands tightened fractionally on the steering wheel. "Krane doesn't know that. He thinks you've already seen it, already know what it contains."

"What *does* it contain?" Claire pressed, her prosecutor's instinct zeroing in on the information being withheld.

The car slowed as they approached what appeared to be an abandoned ranger station—a small wooden structure nearly reclaimed by surrounding forest, visible only because someone had recently cleared minimal access to its door.

"Evidence," Alex said simply, putting the car in park and cutting the engine. "Evidence that Victor Krane murdered Caroline Whittaker forty years ago. And evidence that he didn't act alone."

CHAPTER SIXTEEN

WITNESS

The abandoned ranger station smelled of damp wood and forest decay, morning light filtering through grimy windows in dusty columns. The interior was spartan—a metal desk pushed against one wall, two folding chairs, a propane lantern sitting cold and dark on a shelf. No personal touches, no indication that anyone occupied the space regularly, yet the absence of more extensive deterioration suggested periodic maintenance.

"No one knows about this place?" Meg asked, remaining near the door while Alex moved to check the small building's perimeter windows.

"It's not on any current Forest Service maps," Alex replied, her movements efficient, practiced. "Decommissioned fifteen years ago during budget cuts, then forgotten. I found it while tracking one of Krane's couriers and... repurposed it."

Claire stood with arms crossed, skepticism evident in every line of her posture. "Repurposed it for what?"

Alex completed her security check before answering, seeming to weigh precisely how much to reveal. "For creating distance between myself and Krane's operation. For storing information he doesn't know I have." She paused, then added with reluctant honesty: "For planning an exit strategy if things went wrong."

"Things like Thomas Blackwell's murder?" Meg challenged, the betrayal she'd been processing since learning of Alex's connection to Krane finding voice.

Alex's face tightened almost imperceptibly—not quite a flinch, but close. "I didn't kill Thomas."

"But you knew it was going to happen," Claire pressed, prosecutor's instinct identifying the careful phrasing. "You were part of the operation that targeted him."

"I knew Thomas was in danger after he started investigating Caroline Whittaker's death." Alex's gaze moved between them, assessing their reactions. "I tried to warn Eleanor through back channels, suggested increased security measures. Obviously, it wasn't enough."

The partial admission hung in the air, neither absolution nor full confession, another piece in the increasingly complex puzzle of Alex's true position within Krane's organization.

"You said Krane thinks we've seen Caroline's diary," Meg said, refocusing on the immediate threat. "That I've made connections based on what it contains."

Alex moved to the metal desk, running her hand beneath its edge until something clicked. A concealed compartment sprung open, revealing a slim laptop and several manila folders secured with rubber bands.

"Eleanor showed you pages from the diary yesterday, didn't she?" Alex asked, withdrawing one of the folders. "After Thomas died. When she explained about Caroline Whittaker and Krane's connection to her death."

Meg exchanged a glance with Claire, both recognizing the careful verification technique—asking for confirmation of information Alex already knew to test their truthfulness.

"Yes," Meg confirmed, seeing no reason to lie about this. "She had photocopies of several entries describing Krane's increasingly controlling behavior before Caroline's death. Her fear that he was becoming dangerous."

Alex nodded, apparently satisfied. "What Eleanor didn't show you—couldn't show you because she doesn't have it—is the final entry Caroline wrote. The one that details not just Krane's behavior but the involvement of someone else. Someone who helped cover up what really happened the day she died."

She opened the folder, extracting a clear plastic sleeve containing what appeared to be a photocopy of a diary page. The handwriting matched what they'd seen in Eleanor's materials—a teenage girl's neat script, the words themselves chilling in their prescience:

April 14 - Victor was different today. Cold in a way I've never seen. Said he knew about Matt, that I'd regret trying to leave him. Said his father's friend would make sure no one believed me if I told anyone what he's done. I'm scared now. Really scared. Meeting Matt tomorrow to figure out a plan to get away from Seacliff completely. Pray this works.

The date caught Meg's attention immediately. "This is dated the day before Caroline died."

"Yes," Alex confirmed. "Her 'hiking accident' occurred on April 15th. The investigation was led by Sheriff Davis—close friend of Judge Raymond Mitchell, who was Victor Krane's biological father's business partner and confidant. The same Mitchell who later helped Krane establish his financial operation."

The connection crystallized with disturbing clarity. "Mitchell ensured Caroline's death was ruled accidental," Claire concluded. "Used his influence with the sheriff to suppress evidence, steer the investigation away from Krane."

"And forty years later, Krane is still protecting that secret," Meg added, the pieces aligning with terrible precision. "That's why Thomas was killed—not just because he discovered Caroline's connection to Krane, but because he was close to identifying Mitchell's role in covering up her murder."

Alex returned the diary page to its protective sleeve with careful precision. "Mitchell died fifteen years ago, but his family remains prominent in regional politics and finance. His son sits on the state banking commission, his daughter is married to a federal prosecutor. Exposure of his role in covering up Caroline's murder would destroy legacies, careers, reputations—and potentially reveal financial connections that Krane has leveraged throughout his operation."

"But why target me specifically?" Meg pressed, returning to the question that had haunted her since Campbell's revelation about Krane's disproportionate interest. "I had no connection to this case until I stumbled onto that message on Blackwood's cabin roof."

Something shifted in Alex's expression—a hesitation, a recalculation, a decision being weighed and made.

"Because you remind him of her," she said finally, withdrawing another document from the folder. "Of Caroline."

She handed over a photograph—not a photocopy this time but an actual print, its colors faded with age. It showed a young woman with hazel eyes, dark hair pulled back in a casual ponytail, standing at what appeared to be a coastal overlook, laughing at something beyond the camera's frame.

The resemblance wasn't identical—Caroline's features were more angular, her build slightly different—but the similarities were undeniable. Enough to trigger recognition, to activate forty-year-old memories, to blur the lines between past and present in the mind of someone fixated on both.

"Jesus," Claire breathed, looking between the photograph and Meg. "It's like seeing cousins."

Meg stared at the image, a chill working through her that had nothing to do with the ranger station's dampness. "This is why he's been watching me? Because I look like a girl he murdered forty years ago?"

"It's more complicated than that," Alex said, her tone suggesting layers she was still deciding whether to reveal. "Krane doesn't just see Caroline when he looks at you—he sees a threat. After Thomas started investigating Caroline's death, after Eleanor connected with you, Krane became convinced you'd found evidence he thought was destroyed decades ago. Evidence that could destroy everything he's built."

"The diary entries," Claire suggested.

"Not just the diary," Alex corrected, retrieving another document from the folder. "This."

She handed over what appeared to be a police evidence log, dated April 1982. Most items were routine for a hiking accident investigation—clothing descriptions, personal effects found with the body, preliminary scene analysis. But one entry was highlighted:

Item #17: Minolta camera with exposed film (24 exp). Recovered from victim's backpack. Film developed, see supplementary evidence file SR-442-B.

"Caroline was a photography student," Alex explained. "Always had her camera with her, according to contemporaries interviewed during the original investigation. But the photographs from that final roll of film were never included in the official case file. Sheriff Davis claimed they showed nothing relevant—just landscape shots from Caroline's hike."

"But they showed something else," Meg guessed, the pieces connecting with horrible clarity.

Alex nodded. "According to a note in Judge Blackwell's personal files—which Eleanor discovered after his death but didn't fully understand the significance of until recently—Davis gave the photographs to Mitchell, who supposedly destroyed them. But one of Mitchell's assistants made copies first. Insurance against future problems."

"And Krane thinks we have these photographs," Claire concluded. "That's what this is about—not just the diary entries describing his behavior, but actual photographic evidence of Caroline's murder."

"But we don't have them," Meg pointed out, frustration edging her voice. "None of us do. This is all based on a misunderstanding—Krane's paranoia about evidence that might not even exist anymore."

Alex's expression remained carefully neutral, but something in her eyes suggested Meg had missed a crucial detail.

"The photographs exist," she said quietly. "I have them."

The admission landed like a stone in still water, ripples of implication expanding outward. Not just Alex's knowledge of the forty-year-old case, not just her understanding of Krane's fixation on Meg, but her possession of evidence that could destroy him completely.

"How?" Claire demanded. "How does a military officer turned private security contractor get her hands on evidence from a forty-year-old murder case?"

Alex met her gaze without flinching. "The same way I got Caroline's final diary entry—through Emily. My sister wasn't just an environmental scientist stumbling onto Axion's operations by accident. She was deliberately investigating connections between water contamination and properties owned by Mitchell's former business entities. Properties that included the area where Caroline died."

The revelation shifted everything yet again—Emily's role transforming from random victim to purposeful investigator, her connection to Caroline's case predating her disappearance.

"Why?" Meg asked, the question encompassing more than she could articulate. Why was Emily investigating? Why did Alex have the evidence? Why was any of this happening now, forty years after Caroline's death?

"Because Emily found something while testing soil samples near the old Mitchell hunting lodge," Alex replied, each word precise as if extracted through careful internal editing. "A buried camera case containing film negatives, preserved inside a waterproof container. She recognized their potential significance and began researching Caroline's death. That research is what led Krane to target her."

"And when she disappeared, you started looking for her," Meg continued, filling in the timeline. "Presented yourself as her concerned sister searching for a missing relative."

"Everything I told you about searching for Emily was true," Alex insisted, a flash of genuine emotion breaking through her controlled façade. "I've spent the past year trying to find her, to get her safely away from Krane. What I didn't tell you was that I understood exactly why she'd been taken—not just because of her environmental research, but because of what she'd discovered about Caroline Whittaker."

"So you infiltrated Krane's operation," Claire surmised, her tone suggesting professional assessment rather than moral judgment. "Used your military background to position yourself as an asset he could use, all while searching for Emily from the inside."

"Yes," Alex confirmed. "I approached as private security looking for work, let them discover my military record, my specialized training. Presented myself as someone disillusioned, financially motivated. Someone willing to compartmentalize ethics for the right price." Her mouth tightened slightly. "Krane's organization is always looking for people with certain skill sets who don't ask too many questions."

"And it worked," Meg observed, recalling Campbell's intelligence about Alex's role evolving from security to something more central.

"Too well," Alex admitted. "I found Emily—alive but essentially a hostage, her environmental expertise being used for Krane's legitimate business fronts. But extracting her proved more complicated than I anticipated. Krane's security protocols are layered, his trust limited. By the time I'd gained enough access to potentially reach Emily, I was so deeply embedded that leaving would have immediately triggered suspicion."

"So you played both sides," Claire concluded, her tone sharpening slightly. "Fed Krane enough information to maintain your cover while working toward your own agenda."

"While trying to keep people alive," Alex corrected, a hint of defensiveness breaking through her professional demeanor. "Do you have any idea how many potential witnesses, how many loose ends Krane wanted eliminated? I've spent months finding alternatives—suggesting surveillance instead of elimination, incapacitation instead of assassination, managing to delay or redirect when direct opposition would have blown my cover completely."

The claim was impossible to verify yet rang with a conviction that felt genuine. Meg found herself weighing plausibilities, examining the evidence of Alex's actions rather than just her assertions.

"The message on Blackwood's roof," she said, a new possibility forming. "Was that you?"

Alex's expression shifted subtly—relief at the question, perhaps, or appreciation for Meg's willingness to consider alternative interpretations of past events.

"No," she answered. "That was Thomas. He painted it after discovering some of Krane's operational files, before being captured. I was assigned to investigate when satellite monitoring flagged it, to determine who might have seen it and what response was needed."

"So meeting me at the cabin wasn't planned," Meg pressed, needing to understand which parts of their shared experience had been genuine, which manipulated.

"Not initially," Alex confirmed. "I was conducting standard containment assessment when I spotted you approaching through the forest. Intercepting you seemed the safest option—both for operational security and for your personal safety, given what you'd stumbled into."

"And afterward? Working with me to investigate, fleeing from Blackwood, all of it—was that just maintaining your cover?"

The question carried more weight than Meg had intended, more personal investment in the answer than professional detachment would allow. Alex seemed to recognize this, her response coming after careful consideration.

"It started as operational necessity," she admitted. "But it became... complicated. Your persistence, your commitment to finding the truth— it reminded me why I started this in the first place. Before the layers of deception, before the compromises required to maintain my position." She paused, something like genuine regret crossing her features. "I never intended for you to become a target. When Krane fixated on you, when he connected you to Caroline through Eleanor's research, I tried to redirect his attention without revealing my knowledge of the photographs."

"Which is why you were conducting that exchange yesterday," Meg concluded, connecting another piece. "Setting up some kind of extraction plan for Emily, now that your cover is at risk."

Alex nodded. "The man I met is one of the few people I trust—former military, someone who owes me from a situation in Damascus years ago. He's helping position resources for extracting Emily from Krane's primary holding facility."

"Where is she?" Claire asked, the simple question carrying the weight of all that had led them to this point.

"A private medical research center near the state line," Alex replied. "Officially developing treatments for trauma recovery. Unofficially, a secure facility where Krane keeps valuable assets under medical supervision—controlled through carefully managed medications, monitored constantly, allowed just enough autonomy to perform required tasks without presenting security risks."

The clinical description couldn't mask the horror of what Emily had endured—captivity disguised as medical care, expertise extracted through coercion, a prison with white walls and professional staff instead of bars and guards.

"And Valerie?" Meg asked, remembering the third woman whose driver's license they'd found in Blackwood's cabin.

Something like genuine grief flickered across Alex's face. "Dead. Three months ago. She attempted escape, was recaptured, and died during what they termed 'enhanced security protocols.' I couldn't prevent it without compromising my position completely." The admission carried the weight of a failure still being processed, still being balanced against whatever greater good Alex believed her deception served.

The revelation landed heavily, a reminder that despite Alex's claimed efforts to mitigate harm, real people had died, real suffering had occurred while she maintained her cover. Whatever her intentions, her hands weren't clean.

"So what now?" Claire asked, the practical question cutting through layers of revelation and recrimination. "Krane thinks Meg has evidence that could destroy him. He's actively trying to abduct her. His operation is clearly accelerating its timeline, eliminating loose ends. Where does that leave us?"

"With limited options and significant risk," Alex replied, her tactician's assessment emerging without softening. "Krane has resources positioned throughout the region, surveillance on key locations, operatives prepared for multiple contingencies. Your protective detail is insufficient against the level of threat he's mobilized."

"We need to get to Eleanor," Meg said, the realization cutting through tactical considerations to the human core of their situation. "If Krane killed Thomas to prevent him sharing information about Caroline, Eleanor remains at extreme risk—especially now that she's the only one who knows where the original diary is hidden."

"I thought she'd shown you photocopies," Alex said, her brow furrowing slightly.

"Just selected pages," Claire clarified. "Eleanor told us she discovered Caroline's diary among William's personal effects, but she kept it in a separate secure location. She was planning to take us to retrieve the original today, after Thomas's funeral. Said it was too dangerous to keep at her house."

Alex was already nodding. "Agreed. But approaching her directly is problematic—her protection detail will have standard security protocols that Krane's operation can anticipate and counter. We need an alternative approach."

"Through Reid," Claire suggested. "He's coordinating Eleanor's security, has direct access without raising alarms."

"We can't just call him," Meg pointed out. "If Krane has surveillance on our phones, on the department's communications—"

"We don't call," Alex interrupted, decision made. "We go directly to the secure location where they've moved her. Not through main approaches, not through official channels, but through back access points only local law enforcement would know."

"And you know these access points how, exactly?" Claire challenged, skepticism evident in her tone.

"Part of my infiltration prep," Alex replied without defensiveness. "Understanding local law enforcement protocols, facility layouts, security procedures—essential for any deep cover operation. Additionally, several of the safe houses Hanover uses are listed in databases Krane's operation has access to. Process of elimination narrows the possibilities considerably."

Meg found herself weighing not just Alex's words but her underlying motivations, the complex interplay of deception and apparent honesty that had characterized their entire relationship. Trust remained in short supply, yet practical necessity demanded some degree of cooperation.

"If we do this," she said carefully, "if we work with you to reach Eleanor, to secure the diary and the photographs you claim to have—what then? What's your endgame, Alex?"

The question cut through tactical considerations to the core of their dilemma—not just how to proceed immediately, but toward what ultimate purpose, what resolution that might justify the risks involved.

Alex's expression shifted subtly, professional detachment giving way to something more genuine, more personal. "Emily's safety. Her freedom. Resolution of Caroline's case in a way that honors what really happened to her." She paused, seeming to weigh whether to continue, then added: "And accountability for Krane—not just for financial crimes or current operations, but for Caroline's murder, for the decades of manipulation and violence that followed."

"That's a prosecutor's list, not an operative's," Claire observed, her legal mind identifying the distinction. "Law enforcement objectives, not extraction goals."

"Maybe I've been undercover long enough to recalibrate certain priorities," Alex replied, a hint of weariness breaking through her composure. "Or maybe I was never quite the person Krane thought I was when he brought me into his operation."

The admission, if genuine, suggested complexities to Alex's character and motivations that transcended simple categorization as ally or adversary. Meg found herself remembering their initial meeting at Blackwood's cabin, the uncertain trust that had formed during their shared investigation, the sense of betrayal when Alex's connection to Krane was revealed. None of it easily dismissed, none of it fully reconciled.

"We need to move quickly," Alex continued, checking her watch with the habitual precision of someone accustomed to operational timelines. "Krane will have identified your absence from the visitor center by now, will be reallocating resources to likely destinations. Our window for reaching Eleanor with minimal risk is narrowing."

"I need to make one call first," Meg decided. "To Campbell."

"Absolutely not," Alex responded immediately, alarm evident in her expression. "Any communication creates a digital trail Krane's people can track. And Campbell's operation has its own agenda, its own security vulnerabilities."

"I'm not planning to tell her where we're going or what we're doing," Meg clarified. "But we need to understand exactly what she knows, what her real interest is in this case. The coincidence of her appearance immediately after Thomas's death, with specific knowledge of Krane's interest in me—that timing isn't random."

Claire nodded slowly, following Meg's reasoning. "A counterintelligence play. Feed her limited information, analyze her response, potentially identify whether she's connected to Krane's operation or genuinely represents separate interests."

"And potentially create confusion about our actual movements," Meg added. "If she is reporting to Krane, directly or indirectly, feeding her misleading information about our plans could divide his surveillance resources."

Alex studied them both, tactical assessment visibly recalculating based on their proposal. "Use the burner phone," she conceded finally. "Keep it under two minutes. No specific locations, no direct questions about her knowledge of Caroline's case that might reveal what we know or don't know."

The parameters were reasonable—basic counterintelligence protocols that balanced the value of potential information against the risk of exposure. Meg retrieved the burner phone from her pocket, dialed the number Campbell had provided during their first meeting.

Campbell answered on the second ring, her voice carrying the controlled professional tone Meg had come to associate with her, though with an underlying tension not present in previous conversations.

"Ms. Sawyer. I presume you're calling about your abrupt departure from our meeting."

"I'm calling to understand exactly what you know about Caroline Whittaker," Meg replied, bypassing pleasantries to maximize the limited time available. "And why your employers are so interested in forty-year-old evidence of her murder."

A slight pause—barely perceptible but meaningful given Campbell's usual immediate responses. "That's a very specific question. One that suggests you've acquired new information since our meeting."

"Let's say certain connections have become clearer," Meg replied, deliberately vague. "Including the timing of your appearance immediately after Thomas Blackwell's murder, with specific knowledge of Krane's interest in me."

"My employers' interest in Caroline Whittaker's case is financial, not personal," Campbell responded, her tone maintaining professional detachment. "Raymond Mitchell's involvement in covering up her murder created liabilities within certain banking structures that persist to this day. Liabilities Krane has leveraged for decades to facilitate his operations."

The explanation was plausible—financial institutions concerned about exposure if Mitchell's criminal involvement came to light, protective of their reputations and legal standing. Yet something in Campbell's phrasing suggested selective disclosure, portions of truth surrounded by careful omission.

"And your interest in me specifically?" Meg pressed.

"As I explained during our meeting, Krane's fixation on you exceeded normal operational parameters. Understanding that fixation became relevant to our assessment of his priorities, his vulnerabilities." Campbell paused briefly, then added: "I should note that your current location is compromised. Krane's people identified your vehicle leaving the visitor center, tracked it to the ranger station access road. I would suggest immediate relocation."

The warning surprised Meg—either genuine concern for their safety or an attempt to manipulate their movements based on false intelligence. She glanced at Alex, who was already checking sightlines through the ranger station's grimy windows, body language shifting toward heightened alert status.

"Why are you telling me this?" Meg asked, the question encompassing more than just the immediate warning.

"Because despite your understandable reservations about my motives, Ms. Sawyer, our immediate objectives align—preventing Krane from eliminating witnesses, securing evidence of his crimes, ensuring accountability for actions past and present." Campbell's voice remained measured, professional, yet carried an underlying intensity that felt genuine. "Whether you choose to trust that alignment is, of course, entirely your decision."

The call had reached its time limit, revealed what it could about Campbell's knowledge and potential motivations without exposing their own plans. Meg ended it without confirming or denying Campbell's warning, without indicating their next moves.

"Opinions?" she asked, looking between Alex and Claire.

"She knows more than she's sharing," Claire observed. "The financial motivation is plausible, but incomplete. There's something personal driving her involvement."

"Agreed," Alex confirmed, still scanning exterior sightlines. "But her warning about this location may be accurate. Krane's surveillance resources include satellite access, drone capacity, and local operatives. If they tracked our vehicle, we need to move. Now."

The ranger station's isolation, initially an advantage for secure conversation, suddenly felt like vulnerability—limited escape routes, minimal cover, distance from potential assistance. Meg found herself reflexively checking exits, calculating approach vectors, thinking in tactical terms that would have been foreign to her just weeks ago.

"Eleanor remains the priority," she decided, focusing on the original objective rather than the expanding complications. "Securing the diary, understanding exactly what she knows about Caroline's case that made Thomas a target. Alex, you said you know where they've taken her?"

"Three possible locations based on department protocols," Alex confirmed. "The most likely is a lake house owned by retired Sheriff Davis's nephew—off official records but used by the department for protected witnesses in sensitive cases."

"Davis," Claire repeated, recognition sharpening her gaze. "The same Sheriff Davis who helped Mitchell cover up Caroline's murder forty years ago?"

"The same," Alex confirmed grimly. "He retired fifteen years ago, died three years later. His nephew inherited the property, has no connection to the original case, probably no knowledge of his uncle's involvement. The department uses it precisely because it doesn't appear in any official asset inventory."

The connection was disturbing—Eleanor potentially being protected at a property owned by the family of the man who had helped cover up the very murder she was investigating. Coincidence, perhaps, or the kind of small-town interweaving of interests and properties that transcended decades.

"We need to get there before Krane's people identify the connection," Meg said, decision solidifying. "If they haven't already."

Alex nodded, moving toward the door with renewed urgency. "We take back roads, approach through the forest line behind the property.

Vehicle stays at least a mile out to avoid triggering any perimeter surveillance."

"And if it is a trap?" Claire asked, the question pragmatic rather than pessimistic. "If this has been orchestrated to draw us exactly where Krane wants us?"

"Then we'll deal with that when we have to," Meg replied, resolute despite the uncertainty still clouding their path forward. "But Eleanor—and that diary—represents our best chance of ending this. Of finding Emily, of stopping Krane, of resolving all of it."

Alex checked sightlines once more before easing the door open, her movements fluid, controlled, watchful. Outside, the forest remained still except for natural movement—wind through branches, birds startling at their emergence, no indication of human surveillance or approach.

As they moved toward the car, maintaining cover where possible, Meg found herself scanning the surrounding forest with new awareness—not just for immediate threats, but for the patterns of surveillance and counter-surveillance that had come to define her existence since discovering that message on Blackwood's cabin roof. Conscious that each step, each decision, might be observed not just by Krane's operatives but by Campbell's people, by unknown forces with unclear agendas, by systems of observation and control extending far beyond what she had imagined possible mere weeks ago.

Somewhere in this web of watching and being watched, of truth and manipulation, of personal vendettas disguised as financial schemes, lay the answers they sought. Answers about Caroline Whittaker's murder forty years ago. About Thomas's death days earlier. About Alex's true loyalties and Campbell's real motivations.

About who Meg herself had become in the crucible of this investigation—no longer just an insurance claims adjuster nursing the wounds of a failed marriage, but something more complex, more capable, more determined than she had known herself to be.

If they reached Eleanor in time, if they secured the diary before Krane's people could intercept them, those answers might finally begin to emerge from shadows forty years in the making.

CHAPTER SEVENTEEN
CONVERGENCE

Lake water lapped rhythmically against the shore, a sound that should have been soothing but instead felt like a countdown—each gentle wave marking seconds passing, time running out. Meg crouched behind a cluster of young birch trees, their slender trunks offering minimal concealment as she studied the lake house through binoculars.

The structure was understated—weathered cedar siding, tin roof greened with age, a wraparound deck extending over the water on steel pilings. Nothing to suggest its unofficial role in law enforcement operations, nothing to mark it as the potential focal point for converging agendas decades in the making.

"Two deputies visible on the dock," she reported quietly, shifting the binoculars to scan other approaches. "One at the front entrance. No sign of additional security personnel, but the southern exposure is obscured from this position."

Alex nodded, her own assessment focused on tactical implications rather than just observational details. "Standard protection protocol for a witness not considered high-risk. Three officers, rotating positions, minimal perimeter surveillance." She lowered her own binoculars, movements precise, efficient. "They're not expecting a coordinated assault, just maintaining basic security procedures."

Claire, positioned slightly behind them, kept watch on their rear approach—ensuring no one followed the barely visible game trail they'd used to reach this observation point after leaving Alex's car hidden on a service road half a mile back.

"So what's the plan?" she asked, voice low but steady. "We can't just walk up to a secured location with armed deputies and ask to speak with Eleanor."

"We don't approach directly," Alex replied, slipping the binoculars into a pocket of her tactical vest—gear retrieved from a compartment in her car, suggesting preparation for exactly this type of operation. "We establish communication first, verify Eleanor's status and security condition before making physical contact."

"How?" Meg asked, practical challenges overriding theoretical approaches. "We can't just call the lake house—if Krane has communications surveillance—"

"Reid," Alex interrupted, already retrieving a secured phone unlike the burner they'd used earlier. "Direct contact, encrypted channel, verification protocols to ensure it's actually him responding. Standard counterintelligence measures."

The casual reference to "standard counterintelligence measures" reinforced the gulf between Alex's world of operational security and their civilian perspectives—a reminder of the professional deception that had defined their relationship from the beginning.

Alex punched in a number from memory, then entered what appeared to be an extensive passcode before raising the device to her ear. Moments passed in tense silence before her posture shifted subtly—recognition, confirmation, operational mode engaging.

"Cypress checking maple," she said into the phone, voice neutral but precise. "Verify juniper status."

The response must have satisfied whatever verification protocol she'd initiated, because she continued without hesitation. "Reid, it's Alex Reeves. I'm with Meg Sawyer and Claire Winters. We have critical information about Eleanor Blackwell's safety and need secure contact." She paused, listening, then added: "Verification: you gave me a maple donut during my debrief after Eagle's Rest. You mentioned your daughter's softball tournament was rained out that weekend."

Another pause, longer this time, tension radiating from Alex's controlled stillness.

"Understood," she said finally. "Twenty minutes at the north dock access. Minimal visibility, verification required." She ended the call, tucking the device away with the same efficiency that characterized all her movements.

"Reid's bringing Eleanor to meet us," she explained, already adjusting her position to begin moving toward the designated rendezvous. "North dock is a maintenance access point partially screened by overhanging willows. Low visibility from main approach routes, multiple exit paths if needed."

"He agreed remarkably easily," Claire observed, skepticism evident in her tone. "Considering we disappeared from protective custody, have been unreachable for hours, and are now requesting direct access to a protected witness."

"He didn't agree easily," Alex corrected. "He agreed cautiously, with verification requirements and security protocols. Standard procedure when balancing operational security against potential critical intelligence."

Meg found herself caught between Claire's warranted skepticism and the practical necessity of moving forward with the only viable approach to Eleanor. "Let's go," she decided. "But maintain awareness of all approaches, all potential surveillance points. If this is compromised—"

"Then we've lost our best chance of securing the diary and finding Emily," Alex finished for her, acknowledging the stakes without minimizing the risks. "But standing here discussing probabilities doesn't improve our position."

They moved through the forest in careful silence, Alex leading with the practiced stealth of someone trained for exactly this type of approach, Meg and Claire following her example as best they could. The path was barely discernible—more animal trail than human route, winding between trees and rocky outcroppings in an indirect approach to the lake's northern shore.

The north dock emerged gradually from forest shadow—a small wooden structure distinctly more utilitarian than the main dock they'd observed earlier. Weathered planks showed signs of regular repair rather than aesthetic maintenance, cleats for securing small craft positioned at practical intervals, a single bench providing the only concession to human comfort.

No one was visible yet, the meeting time still minutes away according to Alex's precise internal clock. They positioned themselves at the forest edge, maintaining cover while establishing clear sightlines to all approach vectors—water, dock, forest trails.

"What if Eleanor doesn't have the diary with her?" Claire asked quietly, voicing the practical concern that had been forming since they'd committed to this approach. "If it's secured elsewhere, this meeting only increases her risk without achieving our primary objective."

"She'll have it," Alex replied with surprising certainty. "After Thomas's death, after recognizing the direct threat to anyone connected to Caroline's case, she would have secured the diary immediately—relocated it from whatever separate location she'd been using to keep it protected."

"How can you be so sure?" Meg pressed, noting the specificity of Alex's assessment.

"Because it's what I would do," Alex answered simply. "And Eleanor operates with the same meticulous contingency planning I've observed in professionals with decades of intelligence experience. She may present as an academic researcher, but her instincts for operational security are remarkably sophisticated."

Before Meg could pursue this observation further, movement at the opposite end of the dock caught her attention—two figures emerging from a narrow path different from any they'd observed during their initial reconnaissance. Reid's tall form was immediately recognizable, his alert posture and hand position suggesting readiness for his sidearm if needed. Beside him walked Eleanor, her back straight despite the visible weight of grief she carried, a canvas messenger bag slung across her body held close with one hand—protective, proprietary.

Alex stepped from forest cover first, hands carefully visible at her sides, movements deliberate to avoid triggering defensive reactions. Meg and Claire followed, maintaining similar non-threatening postures while remaining alert to any sign that the meeting might be compromised.

Reid saw them immediately, posture shifting to calculated readiness rather than alarm, recognition tempering vigilance without eliminating it entirely. His gaze fixed on Alex with particular intensity—not hostility but professional assessment, reevaluation of someone whose role had been unclear until this moment.

"Alexandra Reeves," he acknowledged, voice pitched to carry no further than their small group. "You've been remarkably difficult to locate since Eagle's Rest."

"Operational necessity," Alex replied without apology or elaboration.

Reid's attention shifted to Meg and Claire, relief briefly visible beneath his professional composure. "Hanover's been worried. Your protective detail reported losing contact at the lighthouse visitor center. Campbell claimed you left voluntarily but provided no details about your destination or companions."

"Campbell was less than forthcoming about her own agenda," Claire replied, prosecutor's skepticism evident in her tone. "We needed to pursue independent verification of certain claims she made."

Eleanor had remained silent during this exchange, her focus fixed on Meg with an intensity that transcended casual assessment. "You found

Alexandra," she said finally, the simple observation carrying layers of meaning Meg couldn't fully interpret. "Or perhaps she found you."

"It's complicated," Meg admitted, honesty seeming the only viable approach with a woman who had endured so much deception. "But we have information about Caroline's case, about why Thomas was targeted, about why you remain at risk."

Eleanor nodded once, the gesture suggesting neither surprise nor dismissal—merely confirmation of something already suspected. "The diary," she said, hand tightening almost imperceptibly on the messenger bag. "And the photographs Caroline took the day she died."

Alex's control slipped momentarily, genuine surprise flashing across her features before professional composure reasserted itself. "You know about the photographs?"

"I've known about them for forty years," Eleanor replied, her voice steady despite the weight such knowledge must have carried. "William told me everything after Victor's financial crimes case concluded. His certainty about what really happened to Caroline, his suspicions about Sheriff Davis's involvement in suppressing evidence, his helplessness to prove what he knew to be true without the photographs that had supposedly been destroyed."

The revelation shifted the landscape of understanding yet again— Eleanor's knowledge more extensive than any of them had realized, her research into Krane's operations informed by decades of awareness rather than recent discoveries.

"If you've known all this time," Claire began carefully, "why only act now? Why wait until Thomas began investigating Caroline's death to pursue this?"

"Because Thomas found what William and I never could," Eleanor answered, her composure slipping just enough to reveal the grief and determination beneath. "Proof. The photographs Caroline took that day, preserved despite Davis's claims they had been destroyed." Her gaze shifted to Alex. "The same photographs you recovered from Emily after she found them near the old Mitchell property."

The precision of this knowledge—connecting Emily's discovery to Alex's possession of the photographs—created another moment of genuine surprise from the usually unflappable operative.

"How did you—" Alex began.

"Thomas told me," Eleanor interrupted. "The night before he died. He'd made the connection through property records, realized Emily's environmental research had led her to the same location where Caroline died forty years ago. He suspected you had retrieved whatever she'd found before Krane's people could secure it completely."

Reid had been monitoring the surrounding area throughout this exchange, professional vigilance never wavering despite the revelations unfolding before him. Now he stepped closer, voice lowered to minimize potential interception.

"We need to move this conversation indoors," he advised. "Maintaining perimeter security in an open area becomes increasingly problematic the longer we remain exposed."

"Agreed," Alex confirmed immediately, operational assessment aligning with professional security protocols. "But not to the lake house. If Krane has identified Eleanor's location—which seems increasingly likely given the convergence of interests—that property is potentially compromised."

"I have an alternative," Eleanor offered, surprising them with her immediate readiness with contingency plans. "A property not connected to me officially, not known to the department or any digital records. Somewhere William and I used to discuss sensitive cases decades ago, before electronic surveillance became so pervasive."

Reid studied her with new appreciation, professional respect evident in his expression. "You've maintained operational security protocols all this time? Even without official resources or training?"

A hint of something like grim amusement crossed Eleanor's face. "Deputy Reid, I was married to a federal judge who received death threats on a regular basis. William insisted I understand certain security measures, certain approaches to managing information and movement that might seem paranoid to civilians but proved essential when threats materialized." She adjusted the messenger bag against her side. "The property is thirty minutes from here, accessible only by a service road not marked on current maps. I can direct us there if you believe we can move without surveillance."

The practical question returned focus to immediate tactical considerations—how to relocate their group without being tracked, how to ensure whatever location Eleanor offered hadn't been compromised through means even she couldn't anticipate.

"We take separate vehicles, different routes," Alex decided, operational planning emerging without hesitation. "Reid with Eleanor in a department vehicle—legitimate movement that won't trigger immediate suspicion. Meg, Claire and I will take my car, approach from the opposite direction using forest service roads. Staggered departure times, communications blackout during transit, verification protocols at arrival."

Reid nodded, professional assessment accepting the tactical soundness of this approach despite any reservations he might have about Alex's trustworthiness. "I'll need to notify Hanover," he said, already anticipating the next operational concern. "Without providing specific locations or movements, but enough to prevent resources being diverted to searching for us when they could be monitoring Krane's operation."

"Secure channel only," Alex stipulated. "Verbal communication, no digital trail, minimum necessary information."

The caution might have seemed excessive from anyone else, but recent events had demonstrated all too clearly the reach of Krane's surveillance capabilities, the vulnerability of even supposedly secure communications channels.

"I'll handle it," Reid assured her, his tone suggesting professional recognition of operational parameters rather than bristling at instruction from someone with unclear allegiances.

They settled final logistics with efficient precision—rendezvous coordinates provided verbally rather than digitally, verification protocols established, contingency plans for various scenarios including surveillance detection, pursuit, or arrived to find the location compromised. Throughout, Eleanor maintained the same composed focus that had characterized her throughout their investigation, grief visible beneath her control but never overwhelming her practical engagement with necessary security measures.

As they prepared to separate for their divided approach to Eleanor's secure location, Meg found herself studying the older woman with renewed appreciation—not just for her resilience after Thomas's death, not just for her decades of careful research, but for the operational sophistication that belied her librarian's appearance and academic demeanor.

"Eleanor," she said quietly as Reid moved away to make his secure call to Hanover, "you've been preparing for this moment for forty years, haven't you? Since William first told you about Caroline's case."

Eleanor met her gaze directly, something like recognition passing between them—a shared understanding that transcended their different generations, different experiences, different paths to this moment of convergence.

"I've been preparing for justice," Eleanor corrected gently. "For truth to finally emerge from shadows where powerful men thought they had buried it permanently." She adjusted the messenger bag once more, the gesture protective rather than nervous. "I couldn't save Caroline. I couldn't save Thomas. But I can ensure their deaths weren't meaningless, that the truth they died for finally comes to light."

The simple declaration, delivered without drama but with absolute conviction, crystallized everything that had brought them to this moment—not just the immediate threats from Krane's operation, not just the tactical challenges of securing evidence and witnesses, but the fundamental human drive for justice that transcended decades, that sustained Eleanor through grief and uncertainty, that had drawn Meg into this investigation far beyond her original discovery of that message on Blackwood's cabin roof.

CHAPTER EIGHTEEN
THE FINAL APPROACH

"We should move," Alex interrupted, her tone gentle despite the operational necessity behind her words. "Maintaining position increases exposure risk with each passing minute."

They separated according to plan—Reid escorting Eleanor to his department vehicle parked at the lake house's main approach, Alex leading Meg and Claire back along the forest trail toward their more distant parking location. The divergent paths felt symbolic somehow, different approaches converging toward a shared destination, separate tactics serving a common purpose.

As they moved through dappled forest light, Meg found herself watching Alex with the same analytical attention she had once applied to suspected insurance fraudsters. The way she moved—fluid, economical, constantly scanning their surroundings. The way she positioned herself—always slightly ahead and to the side, maintaining both protective positioning and clear fields of vision. The occasional hand signals that communicated more efficiently than whispered words could.

Claire caught Meg's scrutiny, raising an eyebrow in silent question. Meg gave a small shrug in response. Whatever Alex's true allegiances, whatever her role in Krane's operation had been, she was committed to their safety now. That much seemed beyond doubt.

"Hold," Alex said suddenly, raising a fist in the universal signal to stop. She dropped to a crouch, head tilted slightly, listening with an intensity that transformed her entire body into a sensory instrument.

Meg and Claire froze, the forest around them suddenly alive with potential threat. Wind sighed through pine needles overhead, a squirrel chattered indignantly from a nearby branch, the distant call of a hawk punctuated the ambient sounds. Nothing obviously alarming, yet Alex remained motionless, focused on something beyond their perception.

"Two o'clock, approximately seventy meters," she finally whispered, pointing toward a dense stand of younger trees. "Someone moving parallel to our route. Deliberate, not random forest movement."

Meg strained her eyes and ears, detecting nothing unusual in that direction. Yet she didn't doubt Alex's assessment. The same training that had allowed her to operate within Krane's organization for months now served their collective protection.

"Options?" Claire asked, voice barely audible, prosecutor's mind immediately seeking contingencies.

"Alternate route," Alex replied, gesturing toward a slight depression to their left. "Natural drainage creates a hollow we can follow. More difficult terrain but better concealment." Her green eyes met Meg's directly. "Your call."

The deference surprised Meg—Alex acknowledging her position not just as team member but as decision-maker. She considered briefly, weighing risks against their objective. Confrontation against evasion. Direct versus indirect approach.

"The hollow," she decided. "We're still twenty minutes from the car. Better to avoid engaging if possible."

Alex nodded, seemingly approving the choice. "I'll take point. Claire between us, Meg in rear position. Maintain three-meter spacing, move only when the person ahead of you moves, freeze when they freeze."

The hollow proved challenging terrain—uneven ground concealed by layers of pine needles and fallen leaves, exposed roots creating treacherous footing, the slope itself steep enough to require occasional handholds for stability. Yet they made steady progress, moving with the measured deliberation of people who understood that speed mattered less than stealth, that detection could prove fatal.

Ten minutes into their altered route, a sound from their original path confirmed Alex's warning—the distinctive crack of a branch under deliberate weight, too heavy, too sustained to be wildlife. Someone was indeed moving through the forest, searching for something. Or someone.

Alex halted at a bend in the hollow, where an uprooted tree created both obstacle and vantage point. She gestured for Claire and Meg to hold position, then climbed with silent efficiency onto the elevated root system, using its height to scan their back trail.

"Single tracker, male, tactical gear," she reported when she rejoined them, voice clinical, professional. "Krane's security detail, not law enforcement. Moving methodically but without clear direction. Likely responding to perimeter alert rather than specific location data."

"Can we reach the car before he finds our trail?" Claire asked, practical as always.

"Possibly," Alex allowed. "But we should assume the vehicle is compromised. Standard protocol would place watchers at all potential exfiltration points."

The assessment aligned with what they'd come to understand about Krane's operation—the thoroughness, the anticipation of counter-moves, the layered security that made him so difficult to approach.

"Then we need alternative transportation," Meg concluded. "And quickly."

Alex nodded, producing a phone from an inner pocket—not her regular device, Meg noted, but something sleeker, more specialized. She typed rapidly, finger movements concealed from view, then returned it to its hiding place.

"Asset approaching alternative extraction point half a kilometer east," she informed them, confidence suggesting this contingency had been pre-arranged. "Fifteen minutes maximum."

"Asset?" Claire repeated, suspicion evident in her tone.

"Campbell's team," Alex clarified, addressing the concern directly. "Positioned as backup since we entered the forest. Part of the parallel approach strategy."

Meg exchanged glances with Claire, both recognizing the implications. Alex had maintained connection with Campbell throughout, had arranged secondary extraction options without explicitly informing them. Necessary operational security, perhaps, but an uncomfortable reminder of the compartmentalization that had defined their relationship from the beginning.

They continued through the hollow, progress slowed by increasingly challenging terrain. The drainage path narrowed, sides steepening until they were moving through what amounted to a natural trench, protection and trap simultaneously. If discovered here, they would have limited escape options, limited defensive positioning.

Alex sensed their discomfort without needing verbal expression. "Two hundred meters to extraction," she assured them. "Terrain improves ahead."

As if contradicting her assessment, the hollow abruptly terminated in a near-vertical rise—an erosion cut that would require climbing rather than walking to surmount. Alex studied it with professional assessment, already mapping potential handholds, already calculating risk versus reward.

"I'll secure the top, create anchor points for you both," she decided, shrugging off her small backpack and removing a compact coil of thin, strong rope. "Four minutes to establish, two minutes each for your climbs if we maintain efficiency."

"Eight minutes total exposure," Claire calculated. "In a location where we'd be maximally vulnerable."

"Correct," Alex acknowledged, preparation continuing despite the concern. "Alternative is backtracking twenty minutes through terrain where we know hostiles are operating."

The analysis was sound, the decision matrix limited. They would climb.

Alex moved up the erosion face with the fluid grace of someone for whom such challenges were routine training exercise rather than emergency necessity. Hand over hand, testing each hold before committing weight, never rushing despite the time pressure, understanding that a fall now would endanger not just herself but their collective mission.

Watching her ascent, Meg was struck again by the physical incarnation of Alex's contradictions—the precision that made her valuable to Krane's operation now deployed in their defense, the skills honed in deception now ensuring their safety. Like Eleanor's grief being weaponized against its cause, Alex's operational expertise had been turned against her former employer.

Eight minutes later, they crested the rise together, Alex assisting Claire over the final handhold, then turning to provide the same support to Meg. Their hands clasped briefly—warm skin, firm grip, a small moment of human connection amid tactical necessity.

At the top, the forest opened into a small clearing dominated by a massive lightning-struck pine, its upper trunk shattered and blackened but its base still living, green needles sprouting defiantly from lower branches. Alex moved directly to this landmark, confirming position with quick glances at surrounding features.

"Extraction point?" Meg guessed, recognizing the tactical value of the location—multiple approach routes visible, elevated ground providing defensive advantage, distinctive feature serving as unmistakable navigational marker.

Alex nodded, already establishing perimeter awareness, calculating fields of fire, identifying potential cover positions. "Clearing large enough for helicopter landing if necessary, though vehicle extraction more likely given noise considerations."

"You've used this before," Claire observed, not a question but an assessment.

"Twice," Alex confirmed, volunteering information with unusual openness. "Once during initial research into Krane's operation, once after making contact with Campbell's team." She gestured toward the lightning-struck tree. "Natural landmarks are preferable to manufactured ones. Less detectable, less vulnerable to tampering."

They took positions at the clearing's edge, using tree trunks as cover while maintaining clear sightlines to all potential approach routes. The waiting carried its own particular tension—the knowledge that they were committed to this extraction, that alternative options narrowed with each passing minute, that any approaching vehicle might be either salvation or threat.

"They should have found our car by now," Claire said after several minutes of silence. "Started searching outward from that position."

"Agreed," Alex replied, focus never wavering from her assigned sector. "Standard search pattern would have them approaching this location within twenty minutes, assuming they correctly identify the drainage hollow as our exit route."

"And if they don't?" Meg asked.

"Then we face different problems," Alex answered candidly. "They'll establish broader containment, call in additional resources, transition from directed search to area denial."

The technical terminology, the calm tactical assessment, reminded Meg forcefully of their dinner at the roadside diner when Alex had first told her about her background in conflict zones. Genuine information revealed within carefully constructed falsehood. Truth as camouflage rather than illumination.

A sound from the western edge of the clearing drew their collective attention—the distinctive crunch of tires on forest underbrush, the low rumble of an engine throttled down for stealth rather than speed. Alex tensed, hand moving to where Meg suspected a weapon was concealed, eyes narrowing with tactical assessment.

The vehicle that emerged from between the trees was innocuous to the point of invisibility—a Forestry Service maintenance truck, mud-spattered and weathered, the kind of official presence that generated almost no attention in these woods. It rolled to a stop at the clearing's center, engine idling but not shutting down.

"Wait," Alex instructed, hand extended to prevent movement. She studied the truck, the surrounding forest, the driver visible through the windshield—a woman in her fifties with steel-gray hair cut in a severe bob. Campbell.

Only when she'd completed her assessment, only when she'd confirmed no additional threats lurked at the periphery, did Alex signal them forward. "Quickly, directly, no hesitation," she advised. "Maintain awareness of your surroundings throughout approach."

They crossed the clearing at a controlled jog, moving as a cohesive unit rather than individuals, each positioning themselves to cover the others' vulnerabilities. The truck's rear door swung open as they approached, revealing an interior modified for tactical operations—communications equipment secured to custom mounts, weapons locked in specialized racks, medical supplies organized for immediate access.

"Your timing is impeccable as always, Alexandra," Campbell observed as they climbed in, her clipped accent more pronounced than Meg remembered from their meeting at the Harbor View Hotel. "Though your choice of extraction route left something to be desired."

"Improvisation required when baseline assumptions are invalidated," Alex replied, professional rather than defensive. "Perimeter detection occurred seventeen minutes before projected timeline."

"Indeed." Campbell put the truck in gear, executing a precise three-point turn that minimized their time in the clearing. "And the package?"

"Secured with allied asset," Alex confirmed, the formal terminology clarifying that she meant Eleanor and the diary, now safely with Reid. "Separate extraction route, separate destination, as planned."

Campbell nodded, apparently satisfied with this outcome. She navigated the forest track with the confidence of someone familiar with both vehicle and terrain, maintaining speed that balanced urgency against the risk of attention-drawing noise or movement.

Meg studied her with renewed assessment, noting details missed in their first meeting—the precision in every movement suggesting military or intelligence background, the watchful eyes that constantly scanned their surroundings, the hands on the steering wheel positioned for both control and immediate defensive response if required.

"You've been monitoring us throughout," Meg said, not accusation but acknowledgment.

"Of course," Campbell confirmed without apology. "The operation involved high-value assets and critical intelligence. Contingency support was essential to mission success."

"And if we'd been captured?" Claire asked, prosecutor's instincts probing for the limits of this woman's commitment. "What would your response have been then?"

Campbell's eyes met Claire's briefly in the rearview mirror, something like respect visible in her expression. "Extraction if possible, intelligence containment if not. But you need not concern yourselves with hypotheticals. The mission achieved its primary objective—confirmation of the link between Caroline Whittaker's murder and Krane's current operation."

"With Thomas's life as collateral damage," Meg noted sharply.

Campbell's expression tightened almost imperceptibly. "An outcome neither anticipated nor desired, Ms. Sawyer. Whatever you may think of my methods or motivations, I assure you that Thomas Blackwell's death serves no one's interests—least of all those I represent."

The forest around them gradually thinned, the maintenance track widening into something more navigable, though still remote from major roadways. Campbell drove with focused efficiency, occasionally checking what appeared to be a specialized GPS unit mounted below the dashboard, confirming their route without relying on cellular networks or standard navigation systems.

"Where are we going?" Meg asked as minutes passed without further explanation.

"Secure facility approximately forty minutes from our current position," Campbell replied. "Sheriff Hanover is meeting us there with Eleanor Blackwell. Your colleague Jason Martinez has already been relocated to the same location as a precautionary measure."

"Jason?" The name caught Meg by surprise—Thomas's fellow captive, rescued during the raid on Northwood Lodge, had maintained a lower profile during subsequent investigation. "Why would he be targeted?"

"Because he possesses detailed knowledge of Krane's server infrastructure," Alex explained. "Including potential vulnerabilities in the market manipulation algorithm. His testimony would be particularly damaging if the case reaches prosecution."

"When, not if," Claire corrected, prosecutor's confidence evident despite the circumstances.

Campbell's mouth quirked in what might have been amusement. "Your optimism is admirable, Ms. Winters. Let us hope events justify it."

They drove in silence for several minutes, each processing the implications of what had transpired at the lake house, what awaited them at the secure facility, what might unfold in the hours and days ahead. The forest around them gradually gave way to more agricultural terrain—scattered farms, fenced pastures, the occasional rural residence set back from the winding road.

"Thomas's research," Meg said suddenly, a connection forming. "He was tracking property acquisitions, focusing on places with specific geological characteristics. Including water access."

Alex nodded, encouraging her to continue.

"The lake house fits that profile," Meg continued, pieces clicking together. "It's not just historically significant to Krane because of Caroline—it's operationally valuable because of its physical characteristics."

"Correct," Campbell confirmed. "The property provides ideal conditions for server operation—natural cooling from the lake water, isolated position minimizing electronic detection, geological features that mask heat signatures from satellite surveillance."

"And Eleanor discovered this connection through Thomas's research," Claire added. "Realized that Krane wasn't just collecting properties tied to his past, but specifically those that could serve his future operations."

"The Whittaker property was unique in serving both purposes," Alex elaborated. "Emotionally significant because of Caroline, tactically significant because of its physical characteristics. A convergence that made it particularly valuable to Krane's operation."

And particularly devastating to lose, Meg thought but didn't say. The lake house represented not just operational capacity but psychological investment—Krane reclaiming the site of his first violence, transforming it into a monument to his evolved methodology. Its compromise would affect him not just strategically but emotionally, might push him beyond his usual calculated response patterns.

"He'll react to this," she said aloud, voicing the concern taking shape in her mind. "Not just tactically but personally. The lake house meant something to him beyond operational value."

"Indeed," Campbell agreed, her tone suggesting she'd reached the same conclusion. "Which is why we've implemented the current security protocols. Krane's response to personal affronts has historically been disproportionate to the tactical situation."

"Disproportionate how?" Claire asked, legal precision seeking specific examples rather than generalized assessment.

"The judge who initially sentenced him," Campbell supplied. "Found dead of apparent suicide six months after Krane's release from prison, despite no history of depression or suicidal ideation. The prosecutor who led the case against him—Margaret Chen—lost her entire investment portfolio in a series of 'accounting errors' that reduced her to financial ruin. And of course, there's Valerie's murder when she attempted to escape from Northwood."

The examples landed with the weight of implicit warning—Krane's vengeance extending beyond direct targets to their connections, their families, their futures. Not just elimination but systematic destruction.

"And now he still has Emily," Meg said, returning to the human core of their investigation, thinking of the woman still held captive while they pursued evidence and intelligence. After Valerie's murder, the stakes felt even higher.

"Yes," Alex acknowledged, something like guilt flickering across her features.

CHAPTER NINETEEN

NOWHERE TO HIDE

Shadows stretched long across the manicured grounds of Campbell's secure facility as dusk surrendered to evening. Windows glowed from within the sprawling estate house, light spilling onto stone pathways that wound through precisely maintained gardens. Inside, the atmosphere thrummed with the controlled tension of professionals tracking a dangerous quarry—Hanover's tactical team coordinating with federal agencies, Campbell's operatives processing intelligence, analysts building profiles and tracking financial movements with methodical precision.

Six hours had passed since their arrival. Six hours of debriefings, information exchanges, evidence assessment, and tactical planning. Six hours during which Meg had contributed what she could, provided insights from her unique perspective, answered the same questions in slightly different ways for slightly different agencies.

Now, standing at a floor-to-ceiling window in the facility's eastern wing, she watched darkness claim the landscape, fatigue weighing on her like a physical presence. The room behind her hummed with activity she no longer had the energy to process—Claire conferring with federal prosecutors about evidence chains, Eleanor reviewing psychological profiles with behavioral analysts, Reid coordinating local department resources with larger agencies.

All necessary. All important. All increasingly distant from her immediate capacity to engage. She slipped out quietly, no dramatic exit or announced departure, just the subtle movement of someone stepping away momentarily to clear her head. The hallway beyond offered relative quiet—reduced voices, dampened activity, space to breathe without constant input demanding response. A side door led to a stone terrace, the night air carrying autumn's distinctive blend of decay and preservation, the scent sharpening her senses even as it soothed her overloaded mind.

Meg drew in a deep breath, feeling the crisp air fill her lungs—a welcome relief after hours in climate-controlled rooms that had grown increasingly claustrophobic. Her shoulders ached from tension held too long, her temples throbbed with the dull beginnings of a headache, and her mind felt like an overworked engine, hot and dangerously close to seizing. The gardens beckoned—paths visible in subtle landscape lighting, benches positioned for contemplative solitude, the promise of momentary escape from the intensity inside. Not far, she told herself. Not long. Just enough distance to restore equilibrium, to process what they'd learned, to prepare for what came next.

Gravel crunched softly beneath her feet as she followed the winding path deeper into the manicured grounds. The sound seemed overly loud in the night's stillness, each step announcing her presence to the darkness. Moonlight bathed the scene in silver-blue illumination, transforming familiar objects into ghostly versions of themselves—benches becoming crouched figures, decorative shrubs morphing into lurking sentinels, tree branches reaching like grasping fingers against the star-scattered sky.

Security measures were evident throughout the grounds—cameras disguised within architectural features, motion sensors integrated into garden elements, personnel positioned discreetly at key junctures. The knowledge should have provided reassurance, yet something in the darkness beyond the maintained gardens tugged at Meg's awareness. Some subtle wrongness her conscious mind couldn't immediately identify but her subconscious recognized as potential threat.

The fine hairs at the nape of her neck stood on end, a primitive warning system triggered by something just beyond rational perception. Her breath caught in her throat, held there by an instinct older than thought. That sense—the one she'd developed over years of confronting liars and fraudsters—prickled along her skin like static electricity, whispering that something wasn't right.

She paused at the garden's edge, where maintained landscape yielded to more natural growth, where visibility reduced despite ambient lighting, where instinct suggested she should proceed no further. Turn back now, seek the safety of numbers, return to the protection of professionals whose entire focus was neutralizing the threat Krane represented.

Her heartbeat accelerated, a drummer picking up tempo without permission. Sweat beaded along her hairline despite the autumn chill. Logic battled against instinct—one insisting she was perfectly safe within Campbell's fortress, the other screaming that danger lurked just beyond the light's reach.

But the thought of returning to that room—to questions and strategies and coordination efforts that seemed increasingly circular—felt momentarily unbearable. Just five more minutes, she promised herself. Five minutes of quiet, of personal space, of distance from the case that had consumed her life since spotting that message on Blackwood's roof.

The path continued into a small copse of trees—decorative rather than natural forest, arranged for aesthetic effect rather than random growth. Moonlight filtered through branches that had shed most of their leaves, creating dappled patterns on the ground, shadows that shifted with subtle breezes. Beautiful in its composed desolation, peaceful in its structured wildness. She settled on a stone bench positioned to overlook a small, ornamental pond. The water reflected moonlight in rippled patterns, a family of ducks nestled against the far bank, sleeping forms huddled together against night's chill. Something in their vulnerability, their trust that morning would arrive as it always had before, struck Meg with unexpected poignancy.

The sense of being watched intensified.

Not the abstract awareness of security cameras monitoring the grounds, not the general knowledge that Campbell's personnel maintained surveillance throughout the property. Something more immediate, more targeted, more specific to her position in this moment, in this place.

It crawled across her skin like invisible insects, raising goosebumps in its wake. The sensation lodged in her chest, a cold, hard knot spreading icy tendrils through her ribcage. Her mouth went desert-dry, tongue suddenly too large, throat constricting around each breath.

She stood, pulse accelerating, eyes scanning the trees surrounding the small clearing. Nothing immediately visible, no obvious threat presented itself, yet every instinct screamed danger with increasing urgency. The peaceful garden had transformed into hostile territory in the span of heartbeats, secure grounds becoming a trap with unseen jaws ready to snap shut.

Training and experience battled against impulse—remain still and assess, or move quickly toward known safety? Her muscles twitched with conflicting commands, adrenaline flooding her system in a dizzying rush that made her fingertips tingle and her vision sharpen to painful clarity.

Movement caught her peripheral vision—not dramatic action but subtle shift, the kind professional operators executed when transitioning between covered positions. There, then gone, location already changed before she could fully register direction or distance. Not Campbell's security, whose positions she had noted during her walk. Something—someone—else.

Calm analysis yielded to raw instinct. Meg moved, abandoning the bench for the deeper shadows near the tree line, seeking concealment while establishing better position to observe potential threat. Tactical understanding absorbed from Alex during their time together, investigative assessment developed through years of fraud cases, basic survival instinct hardwired into human consciousness—all converging to guide her actions now.

From her new position, partially concealed by an ornamental pine, she studied the area around the bench she had just vacated. Silence extended, broken only by night insects and distant, muffled sounds from the main house. Had she overreacted? Imagined threat where none existed? Allowed hours of tension and fatigue to manifest as baseless anxiety?

The figure materialized like conjured nightmare—emerging from shadows where no concealment should have been possible, moving with deliberate purpose toward the bench, pausing when discovering its emptiness. Not Campbell's security personnel, not Hanover's tactical team, not any authorized presence within the facility's protected perimeter.

Victor Krane.

Not the composed, controlled financial criminal from their investigation files. Not the calculated, methodical architect of elaborate revenge schemes. This version of Krane showed physical manifestation of psychological deterioration—clothing disheveled, movements reflecting tension rather than precision, demeanor suggesting desperate calculation rather than measured strategy.

Even from a distance, she could see madness etched into the twisted lines of his face. His eyes glittered with feverish intensity as they scanned the garden. Once-immaculate hair stood in wild disarray, darkened with sweat despite the cool night. The hand that brushed impatiently at his face trembled, fingers curling and uncurling in staccato rhythm. This was Krane unraveled, the carefully maintained public persona stripped away to reveal the broken machinery beneath.

Meg remained motionless, hardly daring to breathe, mind racing through implications and options. Her lungs burned with the effort of silent, shallow breaths. Blood roared in her ears, a thunderous cascade that surely he must hear. Her body seemed to vibrate with the strain of perfect stillness, muscles rigid with the contradictory impulse to both freeze and flee. How had he penetrated Campbell's security? Where were the protective measures that should have detected unauthorized presence? What resources did he have that allowed him to locate this facility, bypass its defenses, approach with such chilling determination?

Most immediately pressing—what was his target? What had drawn him to this specific location at this specific moment?

The answer crystallized with nauseating clarity as Krane's attention shifted from the empty bench to the surrounding area, his gaze moving with predatory assessment, his posture suggesting clear purpose rather than random intrusion. He wasn't here for documents or intelligence, wasn't seeking leverage against operational planning or tactical deployment.

He was here for her.

The realization should have triggered panic, should have sent her sprinting toward the main house, toward safety in numbers and professional protection. Instead, it produced strange clarity—awareness sharpening, options presenting themselves with unusual distinctness, time seeming to expand rather than contract under pressure.

Direct retreat would expose her to immediate detection. Remaining in place risked eventual discovery as Krane methodically searched the area. Calling for help might bring response but would certainly reveal her location. Each option carried specific risks, none offered certain safety, all required immediate decision.

A bead of cold sweat traced a glacial path down her spine, the sensation heightening her awareness of how utterly alone she was. Her fingers had gone numb, extremities already suffering from the body's ruthless reprioritization of resources toward vital organs. The taste of copper flooded her mouth—she'd bitten the inside of her cheek without realizing it.

Meg chose oblique movement—not directly toward the main house but parallel to it, using available cover, minimizing exposure, prioritizing stealth over speed. The strategy might extend distance between herself and Krane without immediately triggering pursuit, might allow her to circle back toward safety without creating direct confrontation.

She moved carefully, placing each foot with deliberate precision, using shadows for concealment, maintaining awareness of both target destination and immediate threat. Her knees threatened to buckle with each step, muscles weakened by adrenaline's double-edged boost. Breath rushed in and out through flared nostrils, mouth clamped shut against the treacherous sound of panting. The watch on her wrist ticked with merciless precision, each second stretching impossibly while simultaneously rushing past too quickly to grasp. The main house remained visible through gaps in vegetation, its windows glowing with warm light, people moving within its protective walls, safety tantalizingly visible yet frustratingly distant.

Behind her, sounds suggested Krane had abandoned the bench area, was now moving through the small grove with increasing urgency, his search pattern expanding in widening circles. Not random movement but methodical hunt, the precision that had characterized his financial schemes now applied to tracking human prey.

The distance between them narrowed despite Meg's careful progress—Krane moving faster with less concern for concealment, his determination apparently outweighing caution, his focus entirely on locating specific target rather than maintaining broader situational awareness.

Time compressed, options narrowed, critical decision point approached with inexorable momentum. Continue current strategy with diminishing effectiveness, or attempt something more dramatic with higher risk but potential higher reward?

The choice dissolved as her foot connected with fallen branch, the crack impossibly loud in night's relative silence, the sound triggering immediate reaction from her pursuer. Krane's movement shifted—no longer search pattern but direct approach, no longer methodical assessment but targeted pursuit.

The sound might as well have been a gunshot for how it shattered the night. Meg's heart lurched painfully against her ribs, a physical jolt of terror that stole her breath. Time compressed to a single, horrifying moment of recognition—he'd heard her. He knew where she was. The predator had located its prey.

Concealment abandoned, Meg ran—pure survival instinct overriding tactical consideration, desperate need for distance overwhelming preference for stealth. Through decorative hedges, across landscaped pathways, toward the main house that represented safety through numbers and professional protection. Her feet pounded against the earth, each impact jarring her skeleton. Lungs heaved, straining for oxygen that never seemed sufficient. Muscles burned with sudden exertion, lactic acid accumulating with poisonous swiftness.

Behind her, Krane matched her pace—not sprinting with abandon but maintaining controlled pursuit, his movement suggesting confidant hunter rather than desperate chaser. She could hear his footfalls—measured, purposeful, the cadence of someone who didn't need to hurry because capture was inevitable. The sound penetrated her consciousness like a nail being driven into wood, each impact driving deeper terror. The distance between them remained relatively constant despite her best efforts, her lead neither increasing nor decreasing significantly regardless of route adjustments or brief acceleration.

Playing with her, she realized with cold clarity. Maintaining deliberate distance, extending pursuit intentionally, drawing out process that could have concluded more quickly had he chosen different approach. The psychological aspect more important to him than efficient resolution, the prolonged fear more satisfying than immediate conclusion.

Understanding provided neither comfort nor advantage, just additional confirmation of what she already knew—Victor Krane demonstrated sociopathic tendencies beneath his controlled exterior, his apparent rationality masking profound dysfunction, his methodical approach concealing disturbed motivations.

The main house seemed simultaneously closer and more distant with each passing moment—physically nearer yet practically unreachable as Krane steadily closed distance through superior conditioning and tactical positioning. Moonlight and garden illumination provided enough visibility to navigate but insufficient clarity to support complex evasion, each twist and turn in her path met with corresponding adjustment in his pursuit.

Think, she commanded herself. Not just reaction but considered response, not just desperate flight but strategic adjustment. What would Alex do in this situation? What would Claire suggest? What would her own insurance fraud experience recommend when evasion proved increasingly unlikely to succeed?

A new element entered the equation—soft metallic click from behind, distinct despite labored breathing and pounding footsteps. The unmistakable sound of weapon being prepared for use, hammer cocked or safety disengaged, lethal intent made mechanical reality.

Options narrowed dramatically—weapon changed calculations from potential capture to immediate danger, from possible engagement to likely fatality if current dynamic continued. No cover sufficient to stop bullets presented itself along her current path, no tactical position offered advantage against armed pursuer, no immediate assistance appeared from security personnel who should have detected unauthorized presence on the property.

A flash of inspiration—not direct path to main house but lateral movement toward small groundskeeper's shed visible at garden's edge. Not perfect protection but solid structure, potential temporary barrier, possible defensive position while summoning help or awaiting security response.

She changed direction sharply, hoping sudden adjustment might momentarily disorient pursuit, might create brief advantage in increasingly desperate situation. The gamble seemed initially successful— Krane's footsteps faltering briefly, his trajectory requiring correction, distance between them expanding slightly during adjustment period.

The shed grew closer, details emerging from darkness—weathered wood construction, single window beside sturdy door, tool rack visible through partially open entrance. Not ideal shelter but vastly preferable to open ground, especially against armed pursuer with apparent lethal intent.

Ten meters remaining. Eight. Six. Salvation through temporary shelter increasingly tangible, increasingly possible despite overwhelming disadvantage. Krane's footsteps accelerated behind her, his pace suggesting recognition of her destination, his determination intensifying as opportunity to conclude hunt potentially diminished.

Five meters. Four. Almost within—

"Stop."

The command cut through night air with chilling authority, the single word invested with absolute certainty that compliance would follow. Not shouted in desperation but delivered with controlled precision, confidence born from decades of expectation that orders would be obeyed without question.

Meg didn't stop—survival instinct overriding automatic response to authoritative directive, immediate danger outweighing socialized tendency toward compliance. Three meters remained, then two, the shed entrance tantalizingly close, potential safety nearly attainable despite armed pursuer and deteriorating situation.

The shot cracked through night's relative quiet—impossibly loud despite expectation, impossibly real despite contextual surreality. No Hollywood special effect but genuine weapon discharge, the sound containing violence and finality in equal measure.

The report shattered the night, a physical force that seemed to compress the air around her. Meg's eardrums protested with sharp pain, the sound so close it momentarily disoriented her. Her body reacted before her mind processed—muscles locking, spine rigid, an instinctive bracing against expected impact.

Meg froze, awaiting impact, awaiting pain that would indicate successful targeting, awaiting physical manifestation of what auditory evidence suggested had already occurred. Her body tensed for the burning entry of a bullet, for the blossoming agony that would follow, for the collapse of systems damaged beyond repair. Each millisecond stretched to eternity as her consciousness prepared for extinction.

Nothing came—no burning entry wound, no blossoming agony, no collapse indicating damaged bodily systems. Only the ringing echo of the shot bouncing between garden walls and the thunderous pounding of her own heart filling her ears.

Behind her, thud of something heavy hitting ground, followed by grotesque gurgling sound unlike anything she'd experienced in previous encounters with violence. The noise was primal, unsettling—air forcing its way through fluid, life escaping unwilling flesh, the soundtrack of mortality laid bare. She turned—slow movement born from shock rather than tactical consideration, response more automatic than calculated.

Victor Krane lay crumpled on the garden path, weapon fallen from nerveless fingers, blood spreading with alarming speed across expensive shirt, eyes reflecting confusion rare in someone accustomed to controlling every variable in his carefully constructed world. Behind him, another figure emerged from shadows—steady weapon still trained on fallen target, approach methodical rather than rushed, professional response rather than emotional reaction.

Crimson bloomed across Krane's chest like a grotesque flower opening in fast-motion, the pool beneath him expanding with each weakening heartbeat. His mouth worked soundlessly, lips forming words that never materialized, the eternal frustration of a man with final thoughts no one would ever hear. His eyes—those calculating eyes that had assessed variables and manipulated outcomes for decades—now held only bewilderment, the ultimate confusion of the control-obsessed confronting the one thing they could never master.

"Meg." Reid's voice, calm despite circumstances, controlled despite evident tension in stance and expression. "Are you hit? Are you injured?"

His words seemed to reach her through layers of cotton, muffled and distant despite his physical proximity. The world had taken on a strange, disconnected quality—colors too bright, sounds either too loud or impossibly faint, time moving in unpredictable lurches rather than steady progression. Some detached part of her mind recognized the symptoms of shock setting in, the body's natural response to trauma even when physical injury hadn't occurred.

The question seemed strangely disconnected from immediate reality—concern for her welfare when another human lay bleeding mere meters away, focus on her condition when circumstances suggested attention should be directed elsewhere. Yet she understood the priority structure that guided Reid's response—civilian safety before suspect neutralization, confirmation of protected status before addressing threat already contained.

"I'm okay," she managed, voice sounding distant even to her own ears. "Not hit. Just... surprised."

The words felt absurdly inadequate, a laughable understatement that failed to capture the kaleidoscope of emotions cascading through her system. Her tongue felt swollen, clumsy in a mouth suddenly parched beyond desert dryness. The ground beneath her seemed to shift subtly, as if the earth itself had become unstable in the aftermath of violence.

Reid nodded once, acknowledgment without elaboration, then stepped closer, his weapon now lowered but still ready. In the distance, they could hear shouts, the sound of running footsteps—security personnel responding to the gunshot, law enforcement converging on their position.

They stood in silence for a moment, the reality of what had just happened settling around them like the evening mist. Victor Krane—financial criminal, kidnapper, murderer—lay motionless on the garden path, his elaborate schemes and careful calculations rendered meaningless in an instant of violence.

"I followed you outside," Reid said eventually, explanation offered without prompting, details provided without defensive qualification. "Saw you leave, recognized need for space but maintained awareness of potential vulnerability. Established parallel route, maintained visual contact without direct intervention. Standard protective protocol for high-value witness in active threat environment."

The professional explanation, delivered without dramatic emphasis or emotional undertone, somehow made the reality more meaningful rather than less—not heroic last-minute rescue but methodical protective function, not cinematic coincidence but deliberate security measure. Real protection rather than fictional salvation, genuine safety rather than narrative convenience.

"Thank you," Meg replied, simple acknowledgment of both specific action and broader commitment that had guided his response throughout their investigation. "For being there. For seeing what needed to be done. For doing it without hesitation when moment required decisive action."

Reid nodded, a slight dip of his chin that communicated understanding without requiring further elaboration. Across the garden, flashlight beams cut through the darkness, voices calling out commands and confirmations as Campbell's security team and Hanover's officers converged on the scene.

They stepped aside as the first responders arrived, Reid moving forward to identify himself, to explain what had transpired, to begin the process of documentation that would follow any officer-involved shooting. Meg watched as medical personnel hurried to Krane's side, their movements efficient but unhurried, suggesting assessment rather than urgency.

Claire appeared from the direction of the main house, relief evident in her expression when she spotted Meg standing unharmed at the edge of the chaotic scene. She rushed forward, stopping just short of physical contact, her eyes scanning for any sign of injury before speaking.

"You're okay?" she asked, the simple question containing layers of concern and care.

"Yes," Meg confirmed, finding her voice steadier now. "Reid was watching over me. He—" She gestured toward Krane's fallen form, now surrounded by medical personnel and law enforcement officers, unable to fully articulate what had happened but knowing Claire would understand.

"It's over," Claire said quietly, the words both statement and question, seeking confirmation that this chapter had indeed concluded, that the threat which had pursued them for weeks had finally been neutralized.

Meg looked toward where Victor Krane lay motionless on the garden path, the man who had orchestrated elaborate revenge schemes, who had kidnapped and manipulated, who had destroyed lives with the same methodical precision he applied to financial algorithms. The man who had been watching her since she discovered that message on his roof, studying her, calculating her movements, planning her elimination with the cold detachment that characterized all his operations.

"Yes," she said finally, certainty settling within her despite the chaos surrounding them. "It's over."

The night air carried the scent of autumn—decaying leaves, damp earth, the promise of frost by morning. Meg drew it deep into her lungs, each breath marking distance from the moment of terror that had preceded Reid's intervention, each exhalation carrying away fragments of fear that had accumulated during their pursuit of Krane and his operation.

No more hiding—from painful truths, from difficult challenges, from authentic connections with others who saw her clearly and valued her genuinely. The message on Blackwood's cabin roof had initiated a journey that concluded not just with Krane's death but with Meg's re-emergence into full engagement with life's complexities, its dangers, its possibilities.

Nowhere left to hide. And finally, no desire to do so.

EPILOGUE

Three months later, Meg stood on the deck of Claire's beach house in Seacliff, the ocean breeze carrying away the last remnants of autumn. The house had been restored to normality, but Meg saw it differently now—not as a retreat from her past, but as the place where she found her future.

Inside, Claire arranged photos on a new corkboard—evidence from the trial of Krane's associates. The federal case was proceeding methodically, with prosecutors confident of securing convictions on all counts. Emily Reeves had provided crucial testimony about the operation's internal workings, her perspective as an unwilling participant adding compelling dimension to the government's case.

"Are you sure you're ready for this?" Claire asked, joining Meg on the deck with two steaming mugs of coffee. The concern in her voice was tempered by the knowledge that her friend had changed profoundly since that night in Campbell's garden. The hospital check had found no physical injuries, but both women understood that some wounds left no visible scars.

"More than ready," Meg replied, accepting the offered mug gratefully. "I need a vacation as much as you do. Two weeks of nothing but beaches, books, and drinks with little umbrellas sounds like exactly what the doctor ordered."

Claire laughed, the sound lighter than it had been in months. "Doctor Reid, you mean. I still can't believe he prescribed 'excessive relaxation' as part of your recovery regimen."

"He takes his role as my personal physician very seriously," Meg smiled, thinking of the deputy—now detective—who had saved her life that night. Their friendship had deepened in the aftermath, professional respect evolving into genuine connection as they navigated the complex emotions that followed taking a human life, even when absolutely necessary.

Sheriff Hanover arrived as they were finishing their coffee, bringing a bottle of champagne and the final paperwork confirming Meg's consultant position with the department. Her knack for spotting deception and untangling complex fraud had proven invaluable in processing the financial aspects of Krane's operation, transforming her insurance claims experience into a new career.

"The federal team sends their regards," Hanover informed them, setting the bottle on the deck railing. "The algorithm has been completely dismantled, all server locations neutralized. Whatever market manipulation Krane planned won't ever happen now."

The confirmation provided quiet satisfaction, not triumphant celebration but acknowledgment that specific threat had been fully contained, that concrete harm had been prevented through their collective efforts.

Eleanor Blackwell joined them soon after, her composed demeanor restored through healing rather than sheer force of will. The justice she had sought for Thomas had come at terrible cost, yet brought with it a measure of peace that allowed her to move forward rather than remain trapped in grief's paralysis.

"I've established the scholarship fund," she announced as they settled in the living room. "The Thomas Blackwell Environmental Research Grant. The first recipient will be announced next month." Her eyes reflected both lingering sadness and renewed purpose, the balance shifting gradually toward the latter with each passing week.

The doorbell rang, announcing the final guests for their impromptu gathering. Alex entered first, followed by Emily, both sisters showing signs of recovery that transcended physical healing. Alex had completed her debriefing with federal agencies, her cooperation against Krane's organization earning her immunity from prosecution for actions taken under duress. The weight of her choices remained, but no longer crushed her beneath unbearable burden.

Emily moved with increasing confidence despite the psychological impact of extended captivity. Her expertise, perverted for Krane's schemes, had proven crucial in dismantling the algorithms she'd been forced to help construct. The act of undoing harm she'd unwillingly facilitated provided therapeutic value no clinical intervention could have replicated.

"Sorry we're late," Alex apologized, setting a dish on the counter. "Emily insisted on making her grandmother's casserole recipe from scratch."

"Worth the wait," Sheriff Hanover assured her, already investigating the contents with professional thoroughness.

As they gathered around Claire's dining table, as conversation flowed from case details to personal updates to future plans, Meg found herself observing the unlikely community formed through extraordinary circumstances—law enforcement and civilian, professional and personal, those who had begun as strangers now connected through shared experience that defied simple categorization.

Later, as evening approached and guests began departing—Eleanor to her volunteer work at the county archives, Hanover to her evening shift oversight, Alex and Emily to their temporary apartment while Emily's treatment continued—Claire and Meg returned to the deck, watching sunset transform the ocean into burnished gold beneath crimson sky.

"We leave tomorrow," Claire observed, the anticipation in her voice reflecting weeks of careful planning. "Two weeks of absolutely nothing important or urgent or necessary."

"Exactly what we both need," Meg agreed, grateful for her friend's insistence on proper vacation despite case-related responsibilities that might have provided excuses for delay. "Time to process everything that's happened since I spotted that message on Blackwood's roof."

The reference came easily now, without emotional weight that might once have accompanied it. The event that had initiated their journey had been integrated into personal narrative rather than remaining defining moment that overshadowed everything that followed.

As darkness settled over the beach, as stars emerged in clear autumn sky, Meg reflected on distance traveled since arriving at this house months earlier, seeking refuge from personal upheaval, finding instead purpose that transcended individual concerns without diminishing their legitimacy.

She understood now what she hadn't then—that hiding offered temporary protection but prevented genuine healing, that safety emerged not from isolation but from connection, that strength developed through engagement rather than avoidance. The very things Victor Krane had rejected throughout his life had proven essential to surviving what he had set in motion.

Tomorrow they would leave for their well-earned vacation. In two weeks, they would return to responsibilities that awaited their attention. Life would continue its complex progression, with ordinary challenges alongside extraordinary memories, with mundane tasks interspersed among meaningful contributions.

But tonight, looking out over endless horizon where sky met ocean, Meg Sawyer knew that for the first time since her father's death and her marriage's end, she wasn't hiding from anything anymore. Not from painful truths or difficult challenges, not from authentic connections or genuine purpose, not from life's complexities or its possibilities.

No more hiding at all.